Party Crashers

BLUE IVY PREP
BOOK THREE

HEATHER LONG

For the family we make.
Blood and Found.

Series so Far

Problem Child
Mad Boys
Party Crashers
Money Shot

Foreword

Dear Reader,

Thank you for picking up this book, and for taking a chance on a new series. If I'm a new author to you, welcome. If you've read my previous works, hello there, it's good to see you. Party Crashers is book 3 of Blue Ivy Prep, so if you haven't read Problem Child and Mad Boys, I would recommend pausing to grab those first as this series needs to be read in order.

I would also like to add one correction for a mistake in Mad Boys. There is a mention that Pen's eyes are exactly like KC's. They are, but another point says that Pen's eyes are brown. They are not supposed to be brown, they are supposed to be the same blue as KC's. While I have submitted the corrections, they do not always reflect in previously sold material, so I wanted to own up to that oops here.

Previously at Blue Ivy Prep, KC, Aubrey, and Yvette spent their summer break together in California. KC played host to friends Ian and Frankie who were in the process of recording their first album. KC also snuck out regularly with Dix as her driver to hit the club circuit and dance. She needed to burn off her excess energy. Lachlan tracked her down at one such club, pulled off her wig and kissed her. Fleeing him and the risk of exposure, she ended up in a small car accident and then had to rely on Lachlan to get her home.

Not her favorite thing.

Summer ended all too soon, with KC and Aubrey returning to campus for their senior year. Lachlan *also* returned to campus, unbeknownst to KC, at least initially. Instead of attending Stanford, he came back to go to college at Blue Ivy and moved into Ramsey's spare room. In the meanwhile, Jonas was freezing out his brothers.

Disaster struck soon after classes resumed with a fire burning down the girls' dorm. A lot of people were hurt, and KC suffered from smoke inhalation. Ramsey, however, was able to get her and others out despite a jammed door. He also rescued her guitars that she was so determined to save.

The change in living situations found Aubrey and KC paired with Payton for a dorm room in Ramsey's dorm building. Jonas volunteered the extra room in his suite so KC didn't have to live with Payton. The separation from Aubrey sucked, but she was right across the hall. Dix helped finalize the move, separating out all the stuff and making sure they had new items to replace everything destroyed in the fire.

Amidst her focus on senior year, KC is juggling worries about her younger sister Pen's health issues even as the doctors work out a treatment approach for her cancer. She and Jonas are also slowly adapting to living together, getting to know each other better, and even getting friendlier.

In the meanwhile, Lachlan is still her ninja kisser, stealthing after her. RJ reappears on campus when the campus secret society begins tagging students for recruitment. KC is one of them. Lachlan sets out to make sure that relationship goes nowhere, including setting her up to hear an assault that RJ facilitated years before. RJ gets arrested.

KC also interrupts someone breaking into her suite with Jonas. She is knocked out but her part of the suite is trashed and the guitar she got from her father is missing. The assault triggers Lachlan and Ramsey to be even more protective. Aubrey too.

Separately, Ramsey and Jonas conclude that Pen is likely KC's "secret" love child. Though neither directly ask her about it. Throughout the semester, KC is getting to know her "stepbrothers" better but she is also forming a steady friendship with Jonas. The exchange of music and lyrics continues. They even manage a first kiss following a fun night that is then ruined with the news alert of Gibs performing one of the songs that Jonas wrote and she put lyrics too.

The sting of betrayal pushes KC away from all of them. She is just determined to finish the year out, but news about her mother going back to rehab and being unreachable, her missing guitar that she adored, and the struggle with her feelings where the guys are concerned collides headlong into the worse news about Pen not responding to treatment. It is the final straw, and despite everything she has fought to contain, she ends up sobbing in the rain. Ramsey finds her and takes her back to his suite to try and look after her. She ends up having sex with Ramsey and he discovers she's a virgin. It pretty much tosses any lingering presumptions he had about her out of the window.

Aware of the delicacy of the moment and *needing* to take care of her, Ramsey asks for her to promise to be there in the morning when she doesn't want to talk then. Only when he wakes up at dawn, KC is gone.

That, of course, brings us to Party Crashers.

Whew.

Triggers to be mindful of: There is some stalking, and I will give a warning for a severe health diagnosis concerning a side character. An assault occurs, but it is not an SA.

If you have read this far, thank you. Party Crashers is the third in a four book series following Kaitlin Crosse as she attends Blue Ivy Prep, an exclusive boarding, prep, and college school for the wealthy and the privileged.

The series is reverse harem/why choose. This means the female main character will not have to choose between the guys in her life. This series is also slow burn, and begins with bullying, secrets, lies, and complicated family ties.

While the first book was told exclusively from Kaitlin's viewpoint except for the prologue, all other books in this series contain multiple points of view.

Thank you again for taking a chance on this series, I can't wait to hear what you think of KC and the douchebags three. Be sure to join us in my reader group on Facebook where we talk books, book loving, some spoilers, teasers for the future, and bonus scenes. Don't forget to sign up for news and updates on my website to get all the latest news, releases and more emailed right to you.

xoxo

Heather

Part One

Prologue

LACHLAN

Sex had a smell. It was a little musky, a little sweet—depending on the girl, I supposed—and if you did it *right*, there was that stink of sweat from the effort. It added just the right touch of salt to the headiness of it all. If you did your job, you needed a shower after…There was no mistaking the scent of it.

None.

It was how I knew Ramsey had gotten laid while I was gone.

Good for him.

Ace's damp clothes in the bathroom, on the other hand, put a whole new spin on that revelation. Ace's clothes—Ace's *damp* clothes. Why were her clothes here? Why could I smell sex?

Why the fuck did Ramsey jerk so hard when he stalked out of his room upset? I curled my hands into fists and fought the urge to tear into him.

Fortunately, Jonas had no such compunction, particularly where Ace was concerned.

"Why are KC's clothes in your suite?" he demanded as he held them up. Maybe he hadn't added the presence of the clothes and the lingering perfume of sex in the air together.

Arms folded, I stared at our big brother. Jonas didn't need much to fly off the handle regarding Ace. Right now? I'd be okay with him breaking Ramsey's perfect nose.

If I didn't get there first.

Ramsey raked a hand through his disheveled hair and twisted to glance back into his room. That was when I spotted the red scrapes down his back.

"You son of a bitch..." Jonas hurtled at Ramsey, and as much as I wanted to let him—I slammed into my baby brother and hauled him backwards.

"Story first," I said, locking my arms. "Then we can kick his ass."

Because right now, I wanted to know what happened with Ace...

And I *needed* to know where she was right now. 'Cause if she wasn't *here*, that had to mean he'd fucked up.

One

RAMSEY

She was gone. From the moment I opened my eyes, then rolled out of bed to head out here in the desperate hope she was still present, I couldn't escape the fact that she'd left. She was supposed to be here. Siren *promised*.

Siren—goddammit.

She had not been in a good place, to begin with. And then —fuck me, all I wanted to do was talk to her, make her breakfast, have coffee, and *talk*. The way we *should* have before…

Instead of her, however, I had my brothers glaring at me. Jonas held up her jacket. It was crumpled, the wrinkles of the crushed and damp fabric utterly disheveled.

"Why are KC's clothes in your suite?" he demanded as he held them up. They'd been soaking wet when I peeled them off her. They would need to go to the cleaners regardless.

Hostility practically sizzled in the air around Jonas. His attachment to Kaitlin Crosse had waxed and waned from problematic to beneficial to dangerous. I'd be lying to myself if I said I didn't see all of those possibilities.

Lachlan was no help, his arms were folded and his gaze was practically ice. He'd taken Jonas out the night before, a distraction—I guess that hadn't worked, or maybe it had.

Honestly, the last thing I wanted was to discuss her with either of them. Especially before I spoke to *her*.

Raking a hand through my hair, I turned to head back to my room. If we were doing this, I needed to get dressed. Get dressed. Get coffee. Get KC.

"You son of a bitch..." Jonas shouted. I pivoted to meet his charge. It was hardly the first time Jonas' temper devolved into pure physical violence. It was always a struggle, though he'd been getting *better*, and now... Lachlan half-tackled our brother. He leveraged his height and strength to lift Jonas off his feet and drag him backwards.

"Story first," Lachlan snapped as he narrowly avoided Jonas slamming his head back into Lachlan's nose. "Then we can kick his ass."

"Fuck you, Lachlan," Jonas spit. Yeah, he was not a fan of it any more than I was.

"Enough," I said, holding up a hand. "We'll talk, but I need to get dressed and find her *first*." That actually had both of them going still.

Shock rippled across their expressions.

"Yes, Kaitlin was here, and now she's not..." It was just a little after six in the morning.

"When did she leave?" Jonas asked, well more like demanded, though it was slightly better than his spitting fury.

"Before you got back," I muttered, diverting into my room. I'd yanked the bedsheets up and the blankets. There was no mistaking the sweet scent of her in here, however.

Shuttling that aside, I yanked open a drawer and pulled

out a t-shirt. Once I had that on, I swapped the pajama bottoms for sweats, then grabbed shoes and socks. Carrying both out to the front room, I ignored my audience.

The air practically vibrated with all the questions they weren't asking. "Sit down," I told Jonas when he kept looming. "I'm not talking to you in this mood." To prove a point, I didn't say a word as I got my shoes on and then walked over to the little kitchenette and started a brew. I needed about four gallons.

Then I needed a plan that included a few more details than go knock on her door, or her friend's, and find her. Both of my brothers stared at me with such intensity that it was hard to ignore.

Fuck.

Did I come clean about the sex? As it was, they'd guessed. I hadn't confirmed it, but I doubted they'd believe me if I lied and denied it.

Pinching the bridge of my nose, I adjusted my glasses before I pulled out my phone and called her. I had her number in my contacts because of tutoring.

Yeah, that was why I'd kept it.

Whatever.

It rang twice then went to voicemail.

Right, she didn't want to talk. Only that wasn't really an option right now. I hit redial.

This time it went straight to voicemail.

Fuck.

I tried again.

Same result.

What was the definition of insanity?

She was supposed to be here. She *promised* to stay and to talk. I should have pushed it in the middle of the night, but she'd been so exhausted.

"Ramsey," Jonas snapped, everything in his voice a demand. "What did you do to KC?"

"Pretty sure he fucked her, baby brother," Lachlan drawled.

I closed my eyes. "That's not the important part right now."

"Excuse me?" Lachlan was across the room, and I spared him a look. "You fucking my girl is one hundred percent the important part."

"She's not yours," I said in the same breath as Jonas, and he scowled at me.

"Ace is *mine*," Lachlan argued. "I kissed her first. I've—"

"Stalking doesn't make her your girlfriend," I reminded him. "The last thing she needs is your temperamental ass— and I'm not having this argument with either of you. I need to find her and check on her. *That* is the important part." Give me five minutes to make sure she was all right.

Then we could deal with the rest of this shit.

"You had sex with her," Jonas said, and the disappointment in those five words sliced at me. "Even after..."

Dipping my chin, I got my own ego and feelings in a fist then pivoted to face them both. "It's not about you," I told him before I flicked a look at Lachlan. "*Or* you."

When Lachlan opened his mouth, I held up a finger.

"Don't."

"You—"

"*Don't*," I emphasized the command this time. "This is *not* about you. It's about her, and after the news she got, I need to know she's fine. You want to have a temper tantrum about the sex, have it later."

"News?" Jonas' demeanor shifted. "What news? Is it about her—"

He stopped abruptly as Lachlan wheeled around on him. "Her what?"

"She's not here," I said, not answering that as I filled a cup with black coffee. It was hot and bitter, much like my soul at the moment. I burned my tongue and throat on the first swallow, but I almost craved the pain.

I should have pushed her to talk the night before. Especially after figuring out she was a virgin.

Goddammit.

"You know, maybe she took off because you had sex," Lachlan said. "Maybe she didn't want to look at you today because you took advantage of a vulnerable situation and now she regrets it."

That—stung. If it was the case... "Fine, she can tell me that to my face *after* I know she's alright." The tears in her voice and the broken notes when she described Pen...the baby and how sick she was. I still couldn't wrap my mind around *who* the baby was to her. Not her daughter.

Did Jonas know?

A part of me wanted to ask, but right now I had no allies in this room and I highly doubted they saw each other as on the same side either. Brothers—kid brothers, had always been challenging.

This was bordering on impossible.

"Maybe she took off 'cause you sucked in bed," Jonas muttered.

Lachlan snorted, but there was no mirth in his faint smile. If anything, he looked angrier.

"Not discussing that either," I said. If she had complaints about my performance—fine, whatever. The feel of her wrapping around me seemed imprinted on my skin and, appropriate or not, my dick twitched.

I'd wanted her there when we woke up so we could talk. But I'd also wanted to kiss her awake. First times were not gentle—she was probably sore. I'd wanted—

I tried her number again.

Voicemail.

Smirk or not, Lachlan frowned. "We can just go upstairs."

"How about I go upstairs?" Jonas wasn't asking; he stalked out of my suite and slammed the door.

"Not going to follow?" Lachlan asked and I took another long drink of coffee before refilling it.

"Do you really care?"

"About her?" Lachlan said. "Yes. You, however, are debatable. What the fuck were you thinking?"

A torrent of retorts danced on the edge of my tongue, but I kept them to myself. "Look, if you care—call her? Maybe she'll answer you."

He glared but pulled out his phone. The door to my suite slammed open and Jonas stomped inside. "She's not in our suite."

Not in the suite. Not here.

I checked my watch. It was still early.

Super early.

Where—

Maybe her friend?

Lachlan scowled at his phone then redialed. "Just voicemail."

"She doesn't want to talk to you," Jonas said as he pulled out his own phone. From here, I could see the series of one-sided texts.

She hadn't answered him either.

Fuck.

"If she went to her friend—"

"Aubrey," Jonas supplied.

"She may not be answering us, period."

"She wouldn't go to her room," Lachlan countered. "She can't stand Payton."

"Who can blame her," Jonas grumbled as he stared at us, even though I didn't think he was seeing us.

"Fuck," Lachlan said before I could comment. "She called me."

"Payton?" Jonas' lip curled.

"No," Lachlan said. "Ace."

"When?" I straightened and narrowed the gap between us.

"Not even an hour ago, but the message just showed up. Goddamn voicemail." He pressed the message and then with a look at us, hit the speaker.

"Hey," KC said, her voice a little rough, but she sounded like she was moving. "Right, I thought you'd answer. Do I leave a message? Do I not leave a message?" She sounded like it was an internal debate with herself, however the length of time on the screen suggested she decided to leave the message.

"Fuck it," she muttered. "Look, I just placed an order for some coffees. I'm gonna call Jonas after I get them and then head back to Ramsey's suite..."

That snapped my head up and Jonas'. All three of us looked at the suite door.

"It's early, so he may not be up. Still, you're usually up for a run and I debated going for one, but—what I think we need to do is talk. All of us. You, me, Jonas, and Ramsey."

A fist closed on my heart. Yes, we needed to talk. Where the fuck did she go for coffee? She didn't drive as far as I knew.

"Maybe we should have talked last year. I don't know. There's a lot of—misinformation and shit between us, so maybe we clear the air. Jonas and I graduate soon? It doesn't matter. I have one set of finals left. I think. Look, that's not important; the thing is, we need to talk. So when you get this, I guess head to Ramsey's suite if I haven't already seen you before then—coffees are ready so I guess I'm heading back now."

I frowned.

"Anyway—I can't decide if—"

If? The voicemail cut out like it was done and then there

was a grunt. No it wasn't done or cut off. Something skidded —a sound like she'd dropped her phone.

"What the hell?" Lachlan said as he pumped up the volume on his phone.

"Get—off—" Then there was a grunt, and someone swearing, except I had no idea who that was. It didn't sound like her at all. Then a shriek—an actual shriek that was KC. I'd never heard her make that sound.

All the hair stood up on my body. There was a grunt, then someone swore—*who the fuck was that?* And KC wasn't talking anymore.

The call ended.

Just stopped.

"There are three coffee places on campus," Jonas said.

"Only two open this early," Lachlan said as he headed for the door.

She wanted to talk to us, and now... fuck, my heart sank. "I need to call campus security and admin..." There were procedures. KC was still a student here and—

"Fuck admin. I'm going to find Ace," Lachlan said. "She could be hurt. You heard her."

I had.

Fuck.

"The coffee shops are on opposite sides of the campus," I snapped.

"I'll take the Pit Stop," Lachlan said. "I'm faster than you two anyway. You head for the Goats."

Jonas spared me a look as I grabbed my keys. "We find KC, all of us talk—then we deal with this."

It was probably the most reasonable and mature reaction he'd had so far this morning. "Done."

Lachlan held up his phone. "If you find her, call."

"Yep," Jonas said and then we split up.

Did she twist her ankle? Fall? There were other voices, however.

Other voices and she screamed.

I started running, and Jonas was right with me.

Two

JONAS

Dancing Goats was the closest coffee shop. It was also the one KC favored. Ramsey didn't jog down the path past the damaged dorm toward the dining hall where the shop was. He ran.

I was right behind him as he yanked the door open. The sun was up, the air was cool, and it looked like the beginnings of a perfect day.

Not that it could be perfect.

Not with KC missing. She hadn't really spoken to me since the video of Gibs playing my song. She did, but it was always just perfect politeness and distance. We weren't friends or friendly.

Not anymore.

She couldn't be more distant if she'd moved out of the dorm and into another building. I didn't know where Gibs even got the song or why he thought I wrote it for him.

I'd left him several messages but hadn't heard back from

him. If he was in his studio and testing material in a few appearances, I might not.

I could call Mom...

I didn't want to.

Ramsey strode past the other people in line right up to the front. Some of the other students protested, but Ramsey ignored them. One idiot went to grab him and I glared. Bo wasn't a bad guy, but he was a jackass.

I'd also kicked his ass three times during Freshman year. He avoided fights with me now.

Chicken shit.

One look from me and Bo raised his hands, backing off immediately.

Good, I didn't have time for him.

"Fucking whackjob," Bo muttered.

I ignored him, focusing on Ramsey, who flattened his hands on the counter. "Tadeo, did Kaitlin Crosse come in and get coffee this morning?"

The kid working the register blinked at Ramsey from behind his glasses. His dad was some kind of diplomat, Guatemalan maybe? Tadeo had more or less grown up here at the school, like we did.

"Kaitlin—I don't know a Kaitlin." He probably didn't. Tadeo was a hardcore gamer and if it didn't happen in the MMPORG he was addicted to, he didn't really pay that much attention.

"KC," I supplied, then held up a hand to my cheekbone. "This high, blue hair."

"Oh, yeah, she was here," Tadeo said with a grin. "But the line was long so she went across campus."

Ramsey was already shoving away from the counter and I was right behind him, then hesitated a second and glanced back. "Thanks, Tadeo."

"Asshole," Bo muttered as I passed him. I could have

punched him. But KC was more important. I'd punch Bo later.

Ramsey was already racing ahead and I had to push it to catch up. He had his phone out—calling Lachlan. Who knew? I didn't care, unless Lachlan found her.

That—I hoped he found her. I didn't care if he would gloat. I was panting when Ramsey slowed abruptly and I saw why a split-second later.

Lachlan stood near the gravel end of the running path where it met the parking lot. We were still a good five-to-six-minute brisk walk from the dorms. I slid to a halt.

"That's the coffee?" Ramsey's question jerked me out of my reverie. I'd been searching for a sign of blue hair, but now I was looking at the ground near Lachlan's feet.

There were a couple of discarded coffee cups. Another one lay at the edge of the grass, crushed, and there were flies humming around the grass. Three cups—there should be four, right?

I wasn't the only one looking around. Lachlan glared at the grass, at the paths, and then at the building that housed the Pit Stop. The doors didn't *face* this way but—the campus had cameras, right?

"There should be four cups," Ramsey said, his tone flat. Like us, he was glancing around.

There was a small car park allowed for temporary parking only, no longer than thirty minutes, just for customers. You didn't need a school parking permit 'cause this coffee shop was actually closer to the administration buildings and the road.

Locals could come in to get coffee. They didn't, but they could. Or maybe they did, I didn't care.

No one was here *now*.

"Found it," Lachlan said, and I jogged over to where he stood. Another coffee cup, but this one was flattened—like someone ran over it. "That's four cups and there's no other trash out here. Going inside..."

Then he was striding away and I stared at the cup, then back to the other cups. Ramsey still had his phone out.

"What are you doing?" Who was he calling?

"Campus security has to be notified," he told me. "Administration too. If she's missing—"

"*If*," I stressed and then curled my hands into fists. "We don't know she's missing."

"She's missing," Ramsey said flatly. "She isn't answering her phone. She isn't where she said she would be. She left a message and we heard her scream."

Screamed.

I turned in a circle. "Why aren't there cameras here?"

Ramsey sighed, then shook his head. "I don't know, there are usually cameras on all the lots. They definitely beefed them up by the dorms."

Not that those stopped the fire.

"Someone broke into our suite."

"I know," Ramsey said, his knuckles white where he held the phone.

"They hurt her."

That got me a glare. "Why do you think I want to call campus security?"

"You haven't called them yet?" I didn't want to call them. Calling them meant something was seriously wrong with KC. We weren't here. She was going to call me, but she ended up calling Lachlan first.

And she had sex with Ramsey.

I glared at him as he dropped his chin and blew out a breath.

That was why he didn't want to call. The minute he admitted what happened, he was going to lose his job. A door slammed in the distance, and we both twisted to see a furious Lachlan stalking toward us.

"She *was* here."

My heart sank.

"She bought four coffees and left. They didn't see her after that." Anger radiated off of Lachlan like heat shimmered off a desert road.

Coffees from the building. Talking to Lachlan's voicemail. "Give me your phone," I said to Lachlan and he stared at me.

"Excuse me?"

"Phone. I want to hear her message again."

He and Ramsey both stared at me, making me roll my eyes.

"Just pull up the damn message and walk with me if you have to."

Lachlan didn't hand over his phone, the dick, but he did play the message *and* followed me as I headed toward the building.

"Hey..." She sounded raspy, and rough. Like she'd been singing all night—or maybe crying. I didn't like it. "Right, I thought you'd answer..." We were at the building now. The back had no windows. There was an enclosure around their garbage area, a door that accessed it, and a little gate. Otherwise, you couldn't see anything from in there.

They had a camera—pointed at their door.

Yeah, that didn't help.

I moved toward the side, closer to the front door as she talked about how maybe we should have spoken the previous year. Then the coffees were ready.

"—coffees are ready, so I guess I'm heading back now."

She walked out of the building and I started across the parking lot toward the cups. Those were only a few steps; I was there before she got to her next statement.

I frowned and Lachlan hit pause.

"She was over there," he said pointing to the cups. Those might be hers but she walks faster than that…it's the running."

Without waiting for us, he rewinded the message then started across the lot again.

"Anyway—I can't decide if—"

She grunted, and the phone skidded. I pivoted in a slow circle and so did the guys. If her phone went flying—had she tripped? Nothing here looked like that.

I didn't see her phone.

I didn't see her.

I saw the coffee cup.

"Get—off—"

The sounds that followed didn't make sense. Grunts. Scuffling. Swearing.

They didn't make sense unless someone was hurting her.

I looked at the crushed coffee cup then the other cups.

They were almost clear across the parking lot.

Which means someone threw them over there.

Her scream ripped through me.

She *screamed*.

Someone hurt her and threw them over there.

I reached the edge of the grass when I saw it. Blue and glittering.

Part of her phone case.

It was here. The coffee cups were here. But she wasn't…

The call ended.

No KC and no sign of her.

Ramsey put his phone to his ear. "This is RA Ramsey Malone, I need campus security to meet me by the Pit Stop and I need someone to call the Admin. We're going to want the dean down here too."

It was barely seven-thirty in the morning. And we were calling security. I dug my phone out of my pocket. No messages from KC. Nothing.

Still, I called her anyway.

Maybe her phone would ring.

"It's not here," Lachlan said as Ramsey moved away talking on the phone. "I've been calling her every five minutes...thought maybe..."

Yeah, maybe. "I was hoping she tripped."

Lachlan nodded once, before he glared at Ramsey. "You need to go."

What...?

It took a minute to register that Lachlan was talking to me. "Why?"

"Campus security is going to have questions," Lachlan said as he cut a look back at me. "Ramsey's about to get busted, and I'm on no one's favorite list, but Dad scares the fuck out of them. You have a history of violence..."

I glared at him.

"If we're tied up, you can continue looking for her." The reminder dunked ice water over me. "Besides, her friend likes you more."

"She might not anymore. Aubrey stopped talking to me around the same time KC did."

"At least she doesn't look like she's planning your murder when she stares at you," Lachlan said with a faint smile.

"Yeah, 'cause I'm not a dick," I commented. "You pissed her off."

"Apparently, baby brother, so did you. So, J, take your shit and get the fuck out of here before campus security shows up. We're already catching flack for sexual misconduct. Since Ramsey surely just committed that particular crime..."

"He's gonna lose his job." Guilt raked through me. He kind of deserved it, even though...

"Maybe, maybe not. Right now, not our problem. Finding Ace is our problem. Keep calling her and go find her friend. Don't flip the fuck out and don't beat up anyone."

I scowled, but Ramsey got off the phone and looked right at me. "Jonas..."

Yeah. I got the message. "I'm going. Although I'm not going to stop looking for her."

"Good," was all he said and then he lifted his chin like he was telling me to move it.

"Running trails," Lachlan said, pointing me away from the lot and toward the trees. "Go that way." I was surprised he was sticking around.

The running trails criss-crossed campus but they were also tucked into the trees so there was an element of privacy. I was already heading back to the dorms when I heard the first cars. They weren't racing in there, and there were no sirens.

I tried KC's number again as I jogged up the trail.

No answer.

I tried twice more before arriving at the dorm. I headed straight upstairs and across the hall to Aubrey's room.

Not even Payton's presence living there was enough to keep me from knocking.

Three

KC

EARLIER...

When I opened my sore eyes, I found myself staring at a slumbering Ramsey. We were both sleeping on our sides. His disheveled hair and stubbled face made him seem almost human.

More than almost. I unfolded my hand and half-reached over to brush his cheek. The urge to touch him was right there, but... If I touched him, he might wake up; if he woke up, we would have to talk.

Did I want to even *have* that talk?

I didn't have to dig too deep for that answer. Clearly, I didn't.

Closing my eyes, I debated all my options, including grabbing my clothes and just getting out of here. Running away wasn't the solution, no matter how appealing avoiding the confrontation might be. Before I made any decision about whether to run or to wake him up, I needed to pee.

Not quite sighing, I slid out of the bed and winced as I straightened. Okay, the ache was not entirely unexpected I supposed. At the same time, I glanced back to where Ramsey was sleeping. He seemed—softer somehow. Warmer.

Kinder.

The demand in his kisses and his touch seemed to linger and I suppressed a shiver before it made me pee myself. My bladder was not similarly distracted. I tiptoed into the bathroom and closed the door softly.

One look at myself in the mirror made me grimace. Wow —bedhead had *nothing* on me. My hair was completely flat on one side and standing up on the other.

Charming.

Shaking my head, I made use of the facilities. The relief was profound. Finished, I washed my hands, splashed my face, and used some toothpaste on my finger to clean my teeth.

Yes, I kissed Ramsey the night before—I kissed him a lot. I enjoyed the fuck out of that and having him shove his monster dick inside of me. At least it felt like a monster.

But I wasn't using his toothbrush, 'cause that was just gross. It took some effort to clean my teeth with a finger while the whole time staring at myself. Did I stay? Did I go?

None of my clothes were in here. Shit—where had I put them? All I remembered was stripping them off before the shower. Annoyed, I searched the bathroom, but they weren't anywhere. When I checked inside Ramsey's room, there was a laundry bag—and there were my clothes. Fuck. They were still damp and soaked in some places. So I went ahead and hung them in the bathroom since I couldn't wear them.

Great. No clothes. I had sex with my TA, who was also my stepbrother, and now I was stuck naked in his room. How the hell did I think this was going to go?

I used my fingers to try and comb through the tangled mess of my hair. It wasn't like he had product in here or hair ties. I looped it up and back, then tied it into a loose knot. Looking down, there were bite marks on my chest.

Little bruises on my neck. My pussy was aching a little, and I could definitely feel the burn in my muscles. It was like I'd done a long show, then collapsed without showering.

A quick sketchy wash cleaned up the mess. Enough hanging out in the bathroom, I told myself. I turned off the light before I reopened the door to his room. I ventured back into his room as quietly as I could. Maybe he had something I could borrow. No way I wanted to walk out of his suite in anything that looked like his. So that eliminated all the suits and dress shirts.

I checked his dresser drawers carefully, using my phone for a light. I found some boxers that work as shorts and—*yes!*—an actual t-shirt. Ramsey had a secret life as a normal guy. I squinted at the shirt I pulled out from the bottom. It was one of Dad's band shirts. Made sense. I grimaced but didn't want to keep rooting around in the drawers. So I just dragged it on.

It would do.

Time to go. I hesitated at the door. His suite was laid out a lot like mine was, the other door in here went to Lachlan's room.

Fuck, was Lachlan here?

The earlier flutter of nervousness turned into a full-blown storm of panic. Right—Lachlan opening that door right now was *not* how I wanted him to find out I had sex with Ramsey.

That would be *bad*.

While I didn't owe Lachlan any explanations, he didn't deserve to be ambushed with it either. No matter how much of a douchebag he'd been.

They'd all been really.

Until...they weren't.

Twisting around, I stared at Ramsey. He'd rolled onto his back, one arm stretched out to where I'd been and the sheets draped his waist...and his dick was definitely waking up because there was an obvious tent, even in the half-shadows of the room.

I needed to call and check on Pen. The pang in my heart was a visceral ache. If it was a matter of money or specialists, then we'd figure it out. I could—I could think about it today.

The news the day before had just gutted me and Ramsey had come through for me. The sex was more than a pick me up, it was a connection and I'd *needed* that.

Like I'd needed the company Lachlan gave me on those runs, when I just didn't want to talk or to fight.

Or when Jonas went out of his way to watch those shows with me. The song—the song thing hurt. It was hardly the first time Dad chose someone else over me, but...

No, no buts. I needed to understand this, to understand them. On the one hand, they were all caring and on the other —they were all strangers.

Coffee.

What I needed was coffee and then we needed to talk. Not just me and Ramsey, but Lachlan and Jonas too.

School was over soon, and Pen needed me back in California. Running away wasn't the answer, so, fuck it. I'd meet them head-on.

It took me a minute to find my phone and my wallet. Somehow, my damp shoes also made it in here. Fine, whatever, I stuffed my bare feet into them. I needed coffee before I talked to Ramsey. When I let myself out into the sitting room, I shot a look at the other bedroom. The door was open and the lights were off.

Had it been closed the night before?

I really didn't know. But it was—I checked my phone—

the time when I was usually running. Maybe Lachlan had gone out.

Right.

Get the coffee. Then call them and see if they could meet back here.

It was early but it would be better to get all the cards on the table.

There was a message from Jackie on the phone, she wanted me to let her know I was alright. If she didn't hear from me by noon, she'd be calling.

Another from Aubrey letting me know she was with Forrest, she was considering giving him a second chance. She'd also call me later.

Yvette sent a check-in and so did Trish—oh, that wasn't a check-in, she needed a check.

I rolled my eyes. Whatever, I'd deal with it later. About a dozen voicemails were waiting, most from the management team. They wanted us to cut another album. School was almost over, maybe we could start on studio time.

Flipping them off, I closed the messages and slid the phone into my pocket. Dancing Goats was closer, so I headed over there but there was already a line.

Yeah, no.

I didn't want to socialize and I needed to clear my head anyway, so I cut across campus toward the Pit Stop. It got traffic from off campus visitors too but it was early. I looked bedraggled enough for comment, so hopefully I didn't run into anyone I knew.

All the way to the Pit Stop I mentally rehearsed what I would say when I called. It all sounded bad or worse. I got the coffees ordered, then dialed Lachlan's number.

I wasn't sure whether to be relieved or thrilled that I went to voicemail. Still, the rambling message helped. Yes, we needed to talk. All of us.

Coffees in hand, I headed back toward the dorms. A car had pulled into the lot while I'd been inside, but I ignored it. Probably one of the locals coming for coffee.

I was still trying to frame words when the sound of running feet pulled me around. I didn't even get a word out before someone slammed into me—bodily.

My phone went one way, the coffee another, and all the air whooshed out of me as I hit the pavement. Oh, that hurt. I grunted even as pain kind of muddied everything.

"Get off," I said, when the weight didn't vanish. Pushing my hands against the pavement, I tried to get up but the person who'd tackled me shoved me back down.

My face banged off the cement. Pain. I grunted when they leaned their weight into my back and I couldn't get any air.

I tried to push out another word when an arm pressed against the back of my neck and shoved me down. Yeah, that hurt and it hurt a lot. I managed to grab the hand pressing me down and bent a finger. There was a hiss of pain as they let up and I went limp.

First rule of self-defense, escape, and between their pain and my ceasing fighting, I suddenly had wiggle room. I managed to get free, long enough to kick and scratch and then I was up on my feet.

I didn't make it far before they fisted my hair and dragged me backwards. My whole scalp lit up as they pulled hair *out*. I screamed but then a fist slammed into my face.

An actual fist, and the world tipped crazily sideways as pain exploded in my head. I tasted blood on my tongue and I would have fallen except for the hand in my hair.

"Goddammit," a familiar voice said. "You had one job."

"Fuck you," the other person replied and I tried to force my eyes open. I knew those voices but they sounded really far away and everything hurt.

My head.

My face.

The world cut off abruptly and my next blink was inside a trunk...pretty sure it was a trunk. It smelled like exhaust and oil. I tried to raise my hands but they wouldn't move, then we bounced and my head hit something and the world danced with spots.

The next blink and I wasn't in a trunk anymore. What the hell—? I wanted to be sick cause my head really hurt and there was a mask on my face.

I still couldn't lift my hands. I tried to twist them but they wouldn't budge. Every pull yanked at my legs. Oh, were they tied to them?

Something cold settled next to me, and I squinted against the sunlight backlighting the person looming over me. "Send the note," he said.

It was definitely a *him*. I knew him. I had to—the voice was so familiar, but I couldn't keep my eyes open, they were watering and the icepick burrowing into my brain was killing me. A hiss of air escaped and the cold rushed against my nose and mouth.

Air.

That was an air tank and a mask...

Then the man vanished and the door closed above me. It was definitely a door. I couldn't move, I was all curled up, my arms were tied to my legs or maybe my feet. I was having a hard time determining that and my head was swimming with pain.

But I had on an oxygen mask and I was in—a crate? A coffin?

Panic threaded through me and I tried to struggle but nothing worked and the pain flared more spots against my eyes, not that I could see shit inside the dark—whatever the fuck this was...

Tears burned in my eyes.

I should have just woken up Ramsey.

Four

LACHLAN

"Mr. Malone," the dean said in his stuck-up, holier than thou, dickish voice. "I'm unclear on why you've called campus security and myself out here for a student who hasn't missed any classes that we are aware of over—tossed coffee cups?"

The note of warning in his gaze wasn't lost on me. Campus security had asked a handful of questions. One of them had gone to check with the baristas at the coffee shop to confirm that Ace had been here.

After a cursory scan of the area, the other just wrote up a report. The dean had shown up five minutes earlier, incensed. He didn't quite slam out of his car, but he'd dismissed me with a look and glared at Ramsey.

"Dean..." Ramsey began, his shoulders squaring as he lifted his chin. He might be dressed in sweats and looking like he'd just rolled out of bed, but he didn't hesitate to meet the dean's gaze.

"Because I pissed her off again," I offered, sliding right in and yanking the full weight of the dean's irritation right at me. Frankly, I didn't give a fuck what he thought about me. He wasn't *my* dean. I was in the college division, so he could suck my dick. "We had a fight, nothing new. But she called me this morning, said that the three of us should talk."

"And why would Miss Crosse need to speak to the *three* of you, Mr. Nash?" Man could make your name sound like an insult. It was a skill. My father could make it sound a lot worse. If he wanted to throw his verbal dick around, I'd get Dad involved.

"Because we're her stepbrothers," Ramsey said, his irritation rifling every syllable as he shot me a look. Yeah, he wanted me to stay out of it. No can do. If he gave Mayfair a reason, he was going to fire Ramsey.

Not saying he didn't deserve it, but that was the least of our problems right now.

"I believe I asked Mr. Nash," Mayfair said, his expression granite. "Mr. Malone, you were warned about Miss Crosse."

"And cleared," Ramsey reminded him. "If you want to rake me over the coals for that again, fine. But right now KC is missing..."

"You haven't established *why* you believe this."

Oh, I was going to slug him. What a fucking dick. "Tell you what, you shut up, and I'll play the message for Mr. Creglin."

Murray Creglin, head of campus security, had just gotten out of his car. His guys straightened up as he approached, and Mayfair seemed even more annoyed. Maybe the stick up his ass left a splinter.

I liked that kind of karma for him. As it was Creglin looked at the dean, then us before he settled his attention on Ramsey. "Have you found Miss Crosse?"

"No," Ramsey said. "She's not answering her phone. It

goes straight to voicemail. Not even a ringing attempt. Guys inside said she was here and she bought coffee, then she headed this way."

Mayfair opened his mouth, but Creglin simply held up a hand. "You are here as a courtesy, they are witnesses. Please wait."

Well, at least he said please, but Mayfair looked like he sucked on a wasabi-infused lemon.

"How did you know to look here?" Creglin asked, his stern, no bullshit expression a reminder the guy actually used to be a real cop once upon a time.

"I had a voicemail from her," I said, lifting my phone. I hit play on the message and ignored Mayfair, whose dark expression promised retribution.

Yeah, I'd like to see him try.

The sound of her phone falling, the muffled struggle, and her scream had Creglin's expression tensing. Every time I heard it, I just wanted to punch something. Of all the days to have stayed out all night.

Jonas needed a pick me up, so I'd taken him into the city for a night out, some games, and a break from school. Ever since Ace cut him off, he'd been in a dark place. If I'd been *here...*

"Play it again," he ordered, so I started it over at full volume.

Both of the campus security officers who'd already been here closed in, and they shifted, their gazes moving over the area as if they were trying to place where she'd been too.

"No sign of her phone?" Creglin eyed his guys.

"No sir, just the coffee cups. There's spilled coffee and chocolate. Didn't see any signs of blood, but—it may be under the coffee."

My stomach sank at the very idea of *blood*. I really should have fucking been here. Been there when she came out, if nothing else, I could have walked over here *with* her.

"We found a piece of her phone," Ramsey volunteered the section, then motioned to where we'd found it.

"Check the CCTV," Creglin ordered, but he was already scanning the buildings.

"Nothing points right at this lot," one of his men said and Creglin scowled.

"Why not?"

Neither of his guys answered, but I had an idea. "Probably because someone paid to have them aimed elsewhere. This is a good spot to hook up."

Ramsey sighed as Creglin snapped his focus to me. "Are you implying you paid off one of my men?"

I snorted. "Nope, not even inferring it. It's an open secret. If you can't get lucky in your dorm and you have a car, this is a good spot at night. Hardly anyone patrols this area, cause the shop is closed and admin buildings are shut down. There are no cameras over here for the same reason."

Rubbing his jaw, Creglin studied the area. "Pull all the footage from an hour before to an hour after," he ordered his men. "From every camera between here and the dorms, and every single one over there. Maybe we get lucky..."

"That's a lot of footage," one of his men said and Creglin shot them a look that shut them up and they hurried away.

"Are you calling the police?" Ramsey asked.

"Of course not—" Mayfair began.

"Not yet," Creglin cut him off and then gave the dean a long look. "This is a security matter, not a political ass kissing one. Miss Crosse's safety is more important than your reputation."

Creglin was officially my favorite.

"That said," he continued almost like he had to grind his teeth before he could get the words out. "I need to investigate more before I involve local police. Technically, this is our jurisdiction—however if we do believe a crime has been committed or that she's been removed from the campus against her will... then we will do what is needed. I may have more questions for both of you, so don't leave campus and be where I can find you."

"We'll be at my dorm," Ramsey said. "I want to check with her friend and former roommate..."

"Aubrey Miller," Creglin said. "We'll be talking to her first." He fixed Ramsey with a look and I didn't roll my eyes. "Agreed..."

"Are you going to call her parents?" I asked more to tweak Mayfair than anything else, but the minute I asked—I *wanted* to know. We could call Gibs, but I wasn't sure about her mother.

"She's eighteen," Mayfair leapt in to announce. "Previously, she was a legally emancipated minor..."

Creglin did not roll his eyes, but he merely turned his back on Mayfair. "We'll notify her legal emergency contact. That will be on file. If we determine it necessary, we will notify her parents. For now, gentlemen, return to your dorm. Be available. Don't leave campus. If you hear from her, contact me immediately."

With that, he refocused his attention on Mayfair and Ramsey motioned to me to walk. I wanted to stay and ask more questions. They weren't *convinced* something had happened to her...

At Ramsey's impatient look, I rolled my eyes and stalked away. He was a half-step behind me.

"Mr. Malone," Mayfair called before we made it a half-dozen steps. I halted to twist back and look as Ramsey pivoted to face him. "I will expect you in my office, and dressed appropriately, within the next hour."

"No, you won't," Creglin said before Mayfair could

continue. "For now, this is a matter for campus security, Mr. Mayfair. You will not be tampering with my witnesses."

I damn near snorted, but managed to contain the reaction. Barely—but I managed it.

"On your way, gentlemen," Creglin said, not glancing at us. Mayfair looked apoplectic.

Maybe he'd drop dead from a heart attack.

Couldn't happen to a better jackass.

Still, I'd call Dad as soon as we were back.

Ramsey sighed and when he glanced at me, I jerked my head toward the running trail. It was the fastest way back. It wasn't until we were safely out of sight on the other side of the trees that big brother found his voice.

"Thanks," he said.

I could play dumb, but I just shrugged. "Mayfair's an asshole. You still need a punch in the dick, but this is about Ace and not you."

"Right, you can't just say, 'you're welcome'?"

"Nope," I informed him as I checked my phone. No messages from Ace or Jonas. I fired off a text to him. He'd headed straight back to the dorm and hopefully, he'd already tracked down Aubrey. If not, that was my next stop.

Instead of making conversation, Ramsey moved like my shadow. Inside the dorm, I checked his suite first. There was no note on the door from Ace. Pivoting, I headed for the stairs.

Ramsey had waited right next to them and he was already climbing them before I got there. On Jonas' floor, I stopped in the wide open door to their room. Jonas sat on the edge of the sofa, his gaze fixed on the door across the hall.

The door to Ace's room was open, but there was no sign of her.

"No one's in Aubrey's suite," he told me before I could ask. "What did security say?"

"Not much," Ramsey answered. "They are taking it seri-ously and investigating. But they don't know anything."

The silence around us elongated, stretching so tight it made my skin itch. Ramsey pulled out his phone and stared at the screen before he declined whatever call it was and then looked up a number.

"You have her friend's number?" Yeah, I moved closer to see who he was calling.

"Of course, I do. She's a resident in this dorm." He hit the contact then put the phone to his ear. This close, I couldn't miss the ringing. It went to voicemail.

Fuck.

"Miss Miller, this is Ramsey Malone, I need you to call me as soon as you get this. It's an emergency." He ended the call then stared at Jonas.

"She's dating a guy named Forrest."

We could go look for him...

"He isn't answering either." Jonas turned his phone around. "I checked with some other people, didn't say what was going on, just asked—they haven't seen KC either."

Fuck.

I flexed my hands.

"Maybe we call her boyfriend?" Jonas suggested and I pivoted to stare at him.

"She doesn't have one." I knew he wasn't talking about RJ.

"She might," Jonas said slowly, chewing at his lower lip. Whatever he was batting around in his head bugged him. "She's got a picture in her—"

I diverted right into her room. Privacy didn't count when she was missing and she'd called *me!* Called me and instead of ringing through, my damn phone went to voicemail.

Scanning her room, I looked around. What pho—oh. I

walked over to the dresser, tucked against the mirror was a photo of Ace, a guy, and a—

She had a kid?

"The little girl isn't her kid," Ramsey said from behind me. Both he and Jonas had followed me. "She told me…"

"She has Ace's eyes." It was hard to miss. Darker skin, curlier hair, but—I'd know those eyes anywhere.

"Still not her kid."

"Are you sure?" Jonas asked, the troubled look on his face giving way to confusion.

"Positive," Ramsey answered flatly and I narrowed my eyes. "She was a virgin and that's the end of this discussion."

She was a—

All at once, I wanted to crack my fist into his perfect face and I was halfway to him when Jonas slammed into me.

The fuck was he doing? I glared at him.

"Not yet," Jonas said. "If I have to wait, so do you."

Ramsey shook his head and then jerked his phone up. The buzzing was his phone. Was it Aubrey?

Please be Ace.

I could wait to punch him. Just be Ace.

"Mom," Ramsey said. "I can't—*what*?" He frowned and looked at us. "Wait—Mom—wait a sec." He lowered the phone and put it on speaker. "I've got Jonas and Lach right here…"

"Deal with that girl. Gibs does *not* need this kind of stress right now. If she wants to play pranks and get attention, she doesn't need to waste our time."

What the hell was she talking about?

"Mom, what prank?"

"This ridiculous ransom note." Honestly, Mom sounded almost unhinged with how she hissed that out. "Really, a ransom? Really? This is not some movie set. If she wants drama, she should go find her mother."

I wasn't the only one frowning.

"That doesn't sound like her, Mom," Ramsey said, his tone careful and her half-screech had me wincing.

"Are you just going to take her side? After all the hell she's put Gibs through?"

I opened my mouth but Ramsey held up a finger and warned me with a look. He was lucky I didn't *want* to talk to Mom or deal with her.

"I'm not taking anyone's side. Just take a photo of the note and send it to me."

"Oh," Mom let out a long sigh. "Thank you, baby. Maybe tell her that the adults do not have time for this, yeah?"

"Sure," Ramsey said, even as Jonas practically vibrated next to me. "Just send it over. How did you get it?"

"I didn't," Mom said, even as Ramsey's phone dinged. "It was in Gibs' email."

In his email—

"What does Gibs think?" Ramsey asked carefully.

"He doesn't know what to think. No word from her in forever then this ridiculous note from a trash email that just bounces back when he tried to answer it?" Her scoff said everything. "I need to go, just—deal with that girl for me. Thank you baby, talk to you soon. Love you all."

Then she was gone.

"What. The. Fuck." was about all I managed to say.

Ramsey changed screens and then he was staring at the note. We crowded around him to stare at it.

Pay five hundred thousand in Bitcoin to the following address in the next ten hours or you'll never see Kaitlin Crosse again. No one will.

There will be no further contact.

Ice spilled into my veins.

"They have to pay it," Jonas said. "She'd never do this."

"No," I said slowly, shaking my head. "Ace wouldn't."

But we were both staring at Ramsey. "This happened today—someone took her today..."

And they didn't think it was real.

Son of a bitch. Where the hell were we going to get five hundred thousand dollars?

Five

RAMSEY

Five hundred thousand dollars. That—that was not an insignificant amount of money. The message Mom sent us came from an email address that didn't exist. A spoofed one—maybe they could track it back.

To do that, though, we needed to get law enforcement involved. Mom thought it was prank, a cry for attention but—

"This isn't Ace," Lachlan reiterated like he needed to convince me. "I don't know who that kid is in that photo or who that guy is, or even why she has that picture with them. But that—" He pointed to my phone. "I know *that's* bullshit."

"You don't have to persuade me," I told him as I continued to stare at the note. "I just—we should report this."

"To who?" Jonas asked. "Law enforcement won't pay a ransom. And it clearly says there will be no further contact."

"Her mom?" I hazarded the guess. "She's wealthy too. If Gibs won't pay..." And I really couldn't wrap my mind around that. Why the hell would Gibs think this was a prank? She didn't need his money.

There was no way they knew about the call this morning. Or how fucking heartbroken she'd been the night before. This was...

"Maybe we should call Gibs," Jonas suggested, his expression troubled. "Mom—Mom doesn't like KC."

That was the *understatement* of the year. Mom was utterly irrational on the subject of KC.

"She might not be thinking clearly on this." The hesitance in his voice wasn't lost on me.

"No shit," Lachlan said, pacing a circle in the room. A slam from down the hall had all of us glancing at the door. "Mom has a serious hate-on for Ace...and I don't think it has to do with Ace not seeing Gibs."

I frowned. "I talked to Juliet about her." That yanked both of their gazes toward me. "Just wanted to know if she knew why...was it because we live there?"

"What'd she say?" Lachlan asked, though he resumed his pacing. I could hardly blame him. I was restless as hell.

"Just that she was a wonderful girl, but their touring schedules clashed—that was what she thought anyway." I shook my head. "This isn't getting us anywhere. I need to show this note to Creglin, he needs to get other law enforcement involved."

"Then what?" Lachlan asked. "We know they won't negotiate. That's up to the family...usually. And the terms are right there, send the payment and they send her location. Don't send the payment and we get nothing."

"Can your dad pay it?" Jonas turned to Lachlan. "He's loaded, right?"

"No way he'd pay it." Despite his words, he was already pulling out his phone. "We need to find Aubrey, Torched has to pay them a pretty penny. Maybe we can pay it that way."

I'd never felt so fucking helpless in my life. At least when I found her crying in the rain—I could *do* something about that. Scrubbing a hand over my face, I tried to think this all the way through.

Someone had kidnapped her. They kidnapped her right off campus. Not only that, they kidnapped her in a blindspot. We didn't know who, but we knew why.

The ransom was why.

Kidnapping KC for ransom, though, was not even a possibility on my radar. "Someone broke in here and took her guitar, trashed her room, and hit her..."

"Your point?" Lachlan asked his expression grim. He hadn't called his father, he'd texted him. My guess? The response was bad news.

"Just—when the fire happened, someone wedged something in the door to the upper floors. It wouldn't open from the other side. I had to yank it out."

"You didn't say that," Jonas accused. "When that happened, why didn't you tell someone?"

"I half-forgot at first, my focus was on getting them out, not what was there. But—looking back. She wouldn't have gotten out if I hadn't. None of them would."

"So you think her kidnapping is related to her stalker assault? And the arson?" Scowling, Lachlan shook his head. "None of those have similar outcomes—I mean, the fire could have killed her and a lot of other people." He looked sick at the idea.

Hell, it made me sick to think about it.

"The robber took her guitar," Jonas said. "But that guitar is important to her, and then they trashed her room." We all looked at that door. "Do you think they meant to hurt her or was the campus security guy right, it was just a crime of opportunity?"

I had no answers. None. "To get her this morning, they would have had to have been watching her. She doesn't go for coffee there usually, does she?"

This time, both Jonas and I looked at Lachlan.

"Right, cause I'm the stalker in this room."

"If the shoe fits," Jonas said.

"You also ran with her a lot," I pointed out. Right now, we did not have time to fight.

"She almost always went to Dancing Goats," Lachlan said. "The Pit Stop is hella outta the way for her and when we're running, we don't stop there, we wait until we're closer to the dorms."

"So, someone saw her come out of my suite this morning... and that someone could be on the cameras here." Cameras, I wasn't supposed to access without a damn good reason, and this was one.

"Aren't they monitored by campus security?" Lachlan asked as I stalked out of Jonas' suite to head downstairs.

"They are recorded and stored in the cloud," I told him. "But I can access recent recordings in the event of students behaving badly..."

And it was also in case of vandalism, usually. Though underage drinking had been a real problem a few years back. It still was, just the kids got better at hiding it.

"Creglin will be coming to look at those, won't he?"

"Probably," I said as we hit the bottom floor. The halls stirred as people woke up and headed out for the day. I ignored them, just nodding here and there as I let myself into my suite. I needed my laptop.

Jonas hadn't followed us but that didn't surprise me. He went back to staking out Aubrey's room.

"I'm checking the cameras, and then I'm calling Creglin to give him this note." I couldn't justify keeping this to ourselves. Everything we could do for her, we needed to be doing.

"Fine," Lachlan said. "Dad told me if this was serious that we should call the cops and let them handle it."

"You told him it wasn't?" I pulled out my laptop and

flipped it open. It took me less than five to login, go to the website, enter my credentials, then pull up the camera feeds. Lachlan shrugged as he folded his arms and watched my screen.

It was choppy, but I could see the angles. Panning through them, I looked for the best one of the front door. There was another of the circular drive, but I went to this one first and rewound it.

Absolutely not supposed to be doing this, but I'd tell Creglin when I gave him the note. I just—

"There," Lachlan said even as I fixed my eyes on her. She was coming out the front door and she looked tired and—rumpled. But she glanced at her phone then looked around before walking away.

Walking. Not running.

She went to Dancing Goats first. That was what it looked like from the angle. We stared at the door for another couple of minutes. No one else came out.

At the five minute mark, Jonas and Lachlan were coming inside.

"Are you fucking kidding me?" Lachlan swore. "Five minutes? We missed her by five goddamn minutes?"

"Apparently." I couldn't judge. I'd been in bed and asleep when she'd left. Then I'd been upset she walked without a word. Only...

Yeah, problem for another day. I tried another camera. This one wasn't the best angle but it let me look around the side toward Dancing Goats.

I scrolled to the time stamp we saw her leave and—there she was. The cameras were not in color, so black and white was going to have to do. But she didn't go that way long. She turned and headed back away from the building—and then she was gone.

"Nothing."

No one else popped up on the cameras and I wanted to shove my laptop off the table or throw it.

"We should call Gibs," Lachlan said. "Jonas is right. Mom isn't rational about Ace and we need to tell him this is real."

"You're right," I said, staring at the screen then glancing across the room. "We need to call him and Creglin."

"But?" Lachlan demanded. "You have 'but' face." He was so damn sober and serious, he didn't even laugh at his own joke.

"But he already thinks it's a prank and I thought—I thought she meant the world to him and now I've got a lot of questions." Not the least of which had to do with that baby, what was wrong with her, why she had my siren's eyes.

Gibs' eyes.

I pinched the bridge of my nose and then straightened. "Go get Jonas. We call him together."

Lachlan had his phone out. "Already texting him."

Jonas didn't keep us waiting. "I don't want to miss her if Aubrey comes back. I called Forrest but that dick isn't answering either. I have someone watching his room."

"We'll keep looking, we're calling Gibs."

"Good," Jonas said, then motioned to us. "We should have called him right away."

Sinking feeling in my gut, I pressed Gibs' contact. When he and Mom were on tour, we weren't supposed to call him directly. Mom had us call her phone and leave messages because she didn't want to get in the way of his muse.

Yeah, she was about to be pissed off again and I couldn't summon up the energy to give a shit. When we went to voicemail. I hung up and called again.

Voicemail.

Third call.

Jonas pulled out his phone and he was hitting another contact. So was Lachlan.

Yeah, we were all calling him.

"Hey there," Gibs said in a low, hoarse voice when he answered Jonas' call. "Was in the studio...must be something big if you guys are all calling. What's wrong?" He coughed once, then cleared his throat before we could respond. "Need to get a drink, hang on."

Lachlan's knuckles went white.

It took a good two minutes for Gibs to come back, he sounded less hoarse this time. "All right, talk to me before your mother gets back in here and yells at me for having the phone in the studio. Supposed to be working on this album—oh that reminds me, Jonas, I need to thank you—"

"Thank me later," Jonas said abruptly. "KC is in trouble and needs help."

There was a bit of prolonged silence on the other end of the phone followed by the distinctive click of a lighter. After a long exhale, Gibs said, "This about that note we got?"

"The ransom note?" Lachlan said, his tone incredulous *and* annoyed.

"Your mom said it was a prank."

Mom said...

"It's not a prank, Gibs," I said flatly. "Kaitlin was here this morning. She went out for coffee. She called Lachlan and left him a message about the four of us getting together for coffee. Then in the middle of the call she got attacked or taken—"

"Ramsey, her mother's a bit melodramatic and you know —KC does take after her some. She's got a good heart, but Jennifer never knew when to quit and—"

"It's *not* a *prank*," Jonas argued. "She's in trouble. She needs help—that note told you that."

"That note—it came through email, Jonas. It could be nothing. Maybe she's pranking you—"

"Holy shit, Gibs. Are you high?" Lachlan glared at the phone. "Ace is in trouble. She's been assaulted twice at this school, and her room ransacked. Now she's missing—and you want to talk about melodrama? What the hell?"

"Sweetheart, I thought you were working," Mom's voice carried. "You know you shouldn't bring your phone in the studio."

"It's the boys," Gibs said slowly. "They're telling me my Kaity is in trouble."

"You know how she is..."

"Linz," Gibs interrupted. "She's not cruel."

"But she is spoiled," Mom countered. "And she craves attention. She takes after that bitch Jennifer too much..."

"Mom," Jonas barked out. "Shut up. KC is *nothing* like her mother. She's in trouble. We need to help her."

Dead silence greeted that command. Of all of us, Jonas never raised his voice to Mom.

"Jonas—honey..."

"I'm not kidding. Shut up. Gibs—you told me KC was the most important person in the world to you." Jonas was almost shaking and I put a hand on his shoulder to steady him. "Put your money where your mouth is and help us save her."

Six

I couldn't believe Mom was saying these things. Not right now.

"Jonas," Gibs said, the patience in his voice a chastisement all its own. "You shouldn't talk to your mother that way."

"Maybe, maybe not," I said, waving off that concern. "I can apologize to Mom later, *after* KC is safe. But she's not right now."

"I think—"

"Linz," Gibs said. Just her name. Nothing else. And she fell quiet. I could almost picture her face. I was glad we weren't there to see that disappointment *or* recrimination in her eyes.

I'd care about that later.

"Gimme a minute to talk to the boys."

"I think—"

"A minute," he repeated in that slow, steady voice. Mom

huffed out a long breath then there was silence before a door closed. It didn't slam. But the click seemed to carry weight.

A message from Mom appeared at the top of my screen and I swept it upwards to ignore it for now.

"Talk to me, boys," Gibs said. "Why do you think this isn't a prank?"

"Cause we got a message from her," Lachlan answered before I could say anything. "Someone *took* her. We found the coffee cups and we got campus security involved…"

"I didn't realize she was actually going to school there with you boys."

Disbelief swept through me.

"I suppose I knew—then again maybe not. She doesn't call anymore." His long sigh scraped over me.

"Gibs," Ramsey said in the most reasonable of tones. The one he reserved for when he needed me to focus. "Kaitlin's in trouble. We need to help her. *You* need to help her."

"You talk to her mother?" The element of grumpiness gave way to discomfort. "Maybe she got the note too? We should call the cops. Not that I'm a fan of them."

"We've already talked to campus security here," Ramsey continued, keeping his focus on the present. "Murray Creglin heads it up. If you need to talk to him to get this paid, then let's talk to him. But whatever you do, we need to do it fast."

"How long has she been missing?" Was he coming around? Why was he being so damn difficult to convince? I thought he loved her.

"Almost four hours," Lachlan said, with a brief look at his phone. "Check that. It's been five."

Had it been that long? It seemed an eternity and no time at all. A part of me wanted to throw the phone and yell. Why were we even *having* this conversation? KC *needed* us.

"You guys have been getting to know her?"

I glanced up to find Lachlan and Ramsey staring at each

other. "Yeah," I answered for them. "We have. She's my room-mate this year."

"I want to ask why you didn't mention it, but I guess that's not important right now."

"No," Ramsey said, stressing the word firmly. "It's not. *Kaitlin* is the important one. Can you help? We can try to reach out to her mother, but I don't know her. We've been waiting for Aubrey to get the fuck back from wherever she went..."

"Those girls are inseparable," Gibs mused. There were some clicks and another message popped up on my screen. Another one from Mom. Then Lachlan glanced at his phone, rolled his eyes and shut off the screen. "Fine, I'll have to call my business manager. He pays all the bills. Not even sure I know how to get to my money these days..."

The empty laugh did nothing to make me feel better.

"How long?" Lachlan asked as he white-knuckled his phone.

"Sending him a message now," Gibs told us. "Your mother is going to be upset...and you should apologize to her later, Jonas."

"I'll get right on that." After I knew KC was all right and *after* we got a chance to talk to her. Right now, I'd be okay with her going back to the cold silences. At least I knew she was okay then.

"Good boy, your mother worries about you three, and I haven't forgotten your argument with her Lachlan."

"Me neither," Lachlan said in a flat tone. When Ramsey glared at him, Lachlan shrugged. I couldn't blame him.

"Okay, Bill's not a fan, but we're going to send the payment just as requested. Then what?"

"We wait," Ramsey said. "Are you looking at the email where you got the message?"

"Yeah," he said briefly, before the sound of a lighter clicked over the line and he sucked in a breath. Mom didn't like it when he smoked, but his studio at home was where he did his best thinking. "Just waiting for Bill to confirm the payment is done."

"We still need to tell the authorities," Ramsey said. Warning us? I didn't care what we told them as long as we got her back.

Gibs stayed on the phone, smoking. "Bill says it's been sent."

Relief spilled into my veins but it froze in place because we still didn't know where she was. I looked at the time on my phone. Five and a half hours.

Longest morning of my life.

Ramsey raked a hand through his hair as he paced a slow circle. The suite seemed almost claustrophobic. Should we be out somewhere ready to go find her?

"Nothing yet," Gibs said, blowing out a long breath. "I need to work on some music, just not really feeling it right now."

"No shit?" Lachlan said. "You just paid a ransom for your daughter and you're worried about not feeling the music right now?"

"Don't be so harsh, kid," Gibs' idea of scolding didn't truly chastise. "Music is the language I get. Used to be how Kaity and I could talk. Even when things were tough with her mom, the music...that was ours."

"So why don't you talk?" The question just fell out of me. Lachlan smirked, but I didn't see him trying to stop me asking the questions.

"Not really sure anymore. I knew she was taking a break, but I figured they were just working on a new album. Didn't know she was at the school." He grunted. "Suppose I could have seen her last summer when we came to pick you up."

I shook my head. The others may not have seen KC's face, but *I* had. "Not sure I get that," I admitted.

"What part?"

"How you can be so clueless about her." It wasn't a question. But the distance in his voice right now was so damn far away from the way he used to be about her. I used to envy the way he would talk about KC, the lavish pride and the caring.

I wanted him to feel that way about me.

Now?

"It's a long story, Jonas," Gibs answered finally. "Kaity and I don't have that relationship anymore. She walked away, never looked back. I tried—you know to respect her wishes, give her the freedom and the distance. But..."

But?

I opened my mouth except Ramsey gave a sharp shake of his head. I wanted more answers, but we were stuck waiting.

"Still no response," Gibs mused. "Maybe it was a prank?"

Lachlan scowled. "It's not a prank. They may need time to verify the money is there. Fuck if I know..."

Ramsey had Creglin's contact information up on his screen. Yeah, I got that. We were calling him as soon as we had something.

"Bill said it's pretty fast," Gibs answered. "So they should have it."

"Maybe they need time to get to a computer?" I was guessing now. I really didn't get Bitcoin or any of the so-called cryptocurrencies. Money in video games made more sense.

"Maybe. You got any more songs, Jonas?"

I frowned. "Why?"

"Really liked that one. Took me back—had lots of depth and emotion. Something I've been lacking lately." The chagrin made me think he was stubbing out his cigarette and shaking his head. "Thing is—felt that one all the way to my bones. I appreciated you leaving it for me."

The words "I didn't" danced on my tongue. I still wasn't sure how he'd gotten the whole thing. I showed him some of the music, parts of it...

"Your mom was really proud too."

I frowned. "Mom gave it to you?"

"She said you left it for me. I really appreciated it. The pick me up I really needed."

Mom was really doing a lot lately.

"Anyway, if you have more—I'd love to see them. Maybe we can do one together, yeah? Be like the old days?"

"Yeah," I said slowly. "Maybe."

An hour.

It took an hour of just standing there, making small talk while Ramsey paced and Lachlan glared. Mom was still texting but none of us were answering. I had to wonder, did she do the same thing to him?

"It's here," Gibs said abruptly, some of the tired leaving his voice. I wasn't the only one who stood up. "It's just coordinates."

"Send them," Lachlan said. "Hopefully it means she's close."

A few hours since she'd gone missing. The note had been sent almost right away. We were just lucky Gibs stayed up so damn late.

Lachlan's phone dinged.

"Sent," Gibs said. "You boys call me when you get to her? Let me know she really is okay."

It was the first time he sounded genuinely concerned.

"We'll take care of her," Ramsey said and I hung up without another word.

I really didn't know what to say to him.

Lachlan had his keys in hand and he was already cutting out of the door. Aubrey was walking in the front doors as we headed out.

She looked like she wanted to say something but I shook my head at her as I dove after Lachlan out the door. I didn't think he'd wait for us. Ramsey was right behind me. We could talk to Aubrey later.

"I'm calling Creglin," Ramsey said as he pulled up the passenger seat to let me slide into the back. It was a tight fit, but I could sit back here. He barely got his door closed before Lachlan was backing out. "Where is she?"

"Says an hour away," Lachlan motioned to the GPS. "Looks like on the other side of Old Mill River out past the Patch."

The Patch had been popular when we were in the lower grades. We got to go apple picking there. Pick apples. Eat applesauce. Have all kinds of apple products. Usually there was a petting zoo and other stuff.

A day of quaint fun as it had been described.

"So they sent the ransom before they got her somewhere?" Did that make sense?

I rubbed a hand against my face. If Lachlan hadn't taken me out for the night to just go fuck off and get some distance, we could have been here.

Maybe she wouldn't have been at Ramsey's or going out alone. Maybe this wouldn't have happened.

"I don't know," Lachlan said. "And I don't much care. I just want to get to her and know she's okay. Everything else can wait until then."

"Yes, Mr. Creglin," Ramsey said. "We have some news— Kaitlin's father got a ransom note..."

How he could keep his cool, I didn't get but right now it was fine. I leaned forward between the seats like I could make us get there faster.

"Put on your seatbelt," Lachlan said over his shoulder as he pulled out of the school grounds and onto the backroad that led to one of the interstates. He put his foot down and the jolt sent me back against the seat. "I'm probably gonna get my license suspended, but I don't give a fuck."

I slid the strap on and clicked it.

Be okay, KC. Just—be okay.

Seven

KC

My arms had gone to sleep. I couldn't feel my fingers. It was hard to stay awake. The air was at least cool, even though the rest of me was sweating. My eyes kept trying to drift shut. Sleep was a retreat from all of this, right?

I didn't even know what *this* was. Some distant part of my brain scoffed at me in Aubrey's voice. "It's a kidnapping, Kaitlin. You were *kidnapped.*"

Right.

Someone collided with me. The ground had been hard. Had I hit my head? It was all kind of foggy and getting foggier. I really wanted to go to sleep.

Sleeping was a bad idea though. In the crime shows, that was when the victim was gonna die soon. They would fade out. Really shitty thing to focus on. I'd rather think about *Love is Blind* or whatever that crazy-ass island show was.

Jonas and I were gonna watch it. That had been the plan, anyway, but then...

Then Dad played the song...and then Pen.

Was I not going to get out of—what was I even in? It was dark. Was it? Or were my eyes closed? I blinked.

Yeah, the light, or lack thereof, didn't change in the slightest. So they were open. I strained to see something—anything.

Frustration welled up in me cause nothing seemed to be working. I struggled against my bonds, but I wasn't able to even get it to budge. The walls were close though and I banged my feet off of them.

I hoped it was my feet. They were so heavy and didn't move. No feeling.

Taking a deep breath, I tried to flood my lungs with oxygen. One deep breath, then another, and on the third—I went for a scream.

Even that sound seemed muffled and it should be louder right? Louder to me.

Tears burned in my eyes as I twisted and banged. Nothing was coming loose, I couldn't free my hands and I was stuck. Stuck in this *box* or whatever.

Kidnapped.

By who? And what did they want?

They had to want something.

Or were they just—

What was that?

Did I make that big clanking sound?

I'd been struggling but none of my kicks had done anything to loosen my bonds. Or done much more than made a little hint of a thud.

Another clank seemed to echo around me. Then the space began to shake. Was it shaking? Or was that wishful thinking?

There was nothing for an excruciatingly long time. No clank. No shaking. No movement.

It had all been in my—

I fell against my back, and banged my head as I tumbled.

Definitely tumbling and rolling over and over. The shifts in gravity pulled at my face and at my head. Just because I couldn't feel anything didn't mean I wasn't moving.

Abruptly it stopped and I was on my side again. More clanking and then something hit the outside of my box prison so hard it vibrated through to my bones.

The clanking turned to a slamming noise and then the lid —not a lid—a door yanked open and light flooded in, blinding me.

Relief swarmed and fear made for a rave as my heart beat out a ruthless cadence. There were hands on my arms. I was being lifted, but I couldn't see who it was. My eyes were watering so bad.

Struggling, I tried to get away as the mask got yanked off me. "Ace," a voice I never imagined I would be so goddamn relieved to hear. "It's okay, Ace—it's us."

The sunlight seemed too damn bright and I squinted.

"Hang on, Ace," my douchebag ninja assured me. "We got you."

"Knife, we need a knife." Jonas. I wanted to cry. I think there were tears running down my face.

"Siren, it's okay, lean on me...they need to get a knife— what the fuck did they tie her up with?"

I couldn't unfold from the fetal position. Then there was a sudden lapse in pressure and I could lean my head back. "There," Lachlan said, pressing a hand to my cheek. "Stay with us, Ace. I need you to get all pissy with me in a minute."

Why would I get pissy with him? Then there was another sudden release and my arms were free. Someone was lifting them and almost instantly white hot pain lit them as a thousand pins and needles inserted themselves into my skin.

A sob tore from my throat and I tried to twist away from the contact but that just made it worse.

"I know," Lachlan said, making the two syllables sound

like a curse. "Gotta get the feeling back, Ace...Jonas, rub her legs."

"Don't—" I wanted to cry all over again as Jonas must have listened because he pulled my legs straight and this time it was white lightning shooting through me. The cramps were vying with the flood of sensation.

Just like being in the box, I couldn't get away. I was caged right up against—Ramsey. He frowned down at me, his expression furious and worried in equal measures.

"You with us, Siren?"

"You guys suck," I tried to argue but it came out a whimper.

"Yeah," Ramsey said. "We do...but I need to know if you can feel this?"

This was him holding my hand. The warm calluses on his fingers were almost soothing. Also the burning was gone. Or at least, it didn't feel like I was being stabbed a million angry hornets.

"Yes."

"Good...can you feel Jonas?"

Someone was squeezing my calves and moving down to my feet back up again. "What happened to my shoes?" I had on socks. Jonas was squeezing the pain out of them and I could flex my feet.

"No clue," Jonas said and when I looked toward him, he wavered in my vision. I had to blink back the tears at the very real concern shining in his eyes. "You can feel me?"

I nodded, not trusting my voice.

"Hey, Ace." Lachlan pulled my attention to him and he looked like hell. There were dark shadows under his eyes and his hair was disheveled. "Remember what I said about being pissed at me?"

"Ye—" I didn't even get to finish the whole thought before

he cupped my face and his lips fused to mine. The kiss tasted like coffee and bad breath—probably mine—and it was all tongue and teeth. I groaned under the sensuality of it all.

As swiftly as it started, it ended with Lachlan jerking back.

"—the fuck off her," Jonas ordered as he shoved him again. "What is wrong with you?"

"Both of you, stop," Ramsey ordered as he slid an arm beneath my legs and then he was lifting me. There were sirens in the distance and the obnoxious sound was getting closer.

"The cops are almost here," Lachlan said, but his expression held me prisoner. "And I'm not sorry I kissed you, Ace. I needed that kiss—you scared the hell out of us."

Scared them?

"What happened?" Oh that came out a brutal croak and Ramsey wasn't waiting for their responses, he was walking us away from the...

I twisted, trying to ignore the discomfort in my shoulders, arms—hell my whole body. The pins and needles had abated, but it definitely wasn't comfortable.

"Is that a refrigerator?"

"Yes," Ramsey answered in a clipped, furious voice. I tried to focus on him, and the dimple on his chin. "The cops are going to have questions for you Siren. If you don't want to answer them, tell me."

Tell him?

"But you need to go to the hospital and we need to call Aubrey—and when you're ready, we need to call Gibs."

"Woah," I said, pressing a hand to his chest. "Why do I need to call him?"

"Cause he paid your ransom."

My ransom—then the cops were there in blare of sirens and flashing lights. An ambulance wasn't far behind them.

I was trying to remember his name when he walked up to

me. "Murray Creglin, Miss Crosse, damn glad to see you're all right."

The guys hadn't budged, only letting me go to sit on the gurney, as the paramedics were taking my vitals. They were also checking the abrasions on my wrists and thighs. I had bruises on my face and on my feet.

"We're going to get you to the hospital here as soon as we can," Creglin said. "But the detective and I have a few quick questions..."

"Sure," I said. My head hurt, but I'd do my best to answer him. "Is there any chance I'll get coffee at some point? I haven't had a cup today."

Lachlan actually chuckled. "First stop as soon as we get you cleared."

"I'm holding you to that," I informed him and he grinned.

"If it's late, I can make you coffee too," Jonas volunteered and I gave him a little smile.

"Thank you."

Creglin cleared his throat. "Let's do the questions. Gentlemen, if you would excuse us—"

"I'd rather they stayed," I said. They found me. "Please."

"That's fine," the man Creglin identified as the detective said. "My name is Jay Harrington. We're going to keep this simple, then we're sending you to the hospital to get checked out. Okay?"

"Sure." I swallowed and one of the paramedics offered me a small cup with water. I managed to sip some with Jonas' help. My hand was shaking.

"Do you know who took you?"

"No," I said. "There was a guy and a girl—I think. He sounded familiar, but I hit my head and he sounded a million miles away. Then I was in that—fridge."

The idea nauseated me.

"Did they say anything to you? Were they talking to each other?"

"Both." I frowned. "I think...I don't know. I don't even know where I am right now."

"Old Mill River," Lachlan told me and I shook my head. That was a mistake, it made my stomach want to revolt. I didn't know where that was.

Creglin and Harrington only asked me three more questions. Did I remember how I got here? What was the last thing I remembered? Would I be willing to walk through the crime scene later? See if we could reconstruct what happened?

I had no idea to the first. The last thing I remembered was the door closing on me. Sure I could try to relive it but I didn't know how much help I would be.

"Go ahead, let's get her checked out. I need to make some calls." Creglin ushered the paramedics to load me in the ambulance. I didn't want to go but I really felt like crap. "Mr. Malone?"

"I'm not staying here if she's going to the hospital." The bite in his voice almost made me smile. Ramsey could be a douche on my side too...I liked it.

"Not asking for that, was going to say good job and thank you for calling us."

Jonas hopped up into the ambulance with me and Ramsey was a step behind him. "Following?" he was asking to —oh, Lachlan.

"Not losing me now," he said. "I'll be right behind you guys. You want me to call Aubrey, Ace?"

"We should—" She was gonna kill me. It wasn't until the doors were closed and the ambulance jolted into moving that I let myself close my eyes.

Tears burned in them. Kidnapping. Ransom.

Dad paid the ransom.

I couldn't even process that and then a hand slid over mine

and I dragged my eyes open to meet Jonas' gaze where he studied me.

I wasn't alone. Next to him, Ramsey stared at me with equal calm.

Not alone.

Eight

LACHLAN

Leaving the scene with the cops, I climbed back into the AMG One, and put it into reverse. I navigated around the cop cars, and the still arriving forensic teams. On the one hand, it would be interesting, on the other —I wanted to be where Ace was.

Resisting the urge to spin the vehicle around, barely, I made it a smooth turn. We arrived at the location without getting pulled over or a ticket. That might come in the mail later—but whatever. I wanted to be where she was. That meant I was following that ambulance.

A part of me envied Jonas and Ramsey for getting to be inside with her. The rest of me needed a minute. A minute to stuff my temper down.

The location had been a damn junkyard. Or at least an abandoned hoarder camp of some kind. She could have been *anywhere*. We'd spent thirty minutes yelling for her, hunting for her, and nothing.

The place didn't even have a dog.

Despite the sunshine, it was eerie—abandoned. Tucked behind trees, the old yard was a relic of the past. Hidden and forgotten.

Until today, when some asshole stuck her in a fucking *fridge*. I had to stop at the traffic light even as the ambulance raced through it. The hospital wasn't that far, I could get there.

Might even have my temper stuffed back into a box. The kiss helped. Fuck me, that kiss helped. The tension in her mouth, the soft inhale turned gasp, and the way she relaxed her mouth under the pressure of mine.

All of it *helped.*

I didn't even mind Jonas shoving me or the heated glare he shot my way. Ramsey's expression darkened, but he kept his mouth shut on offering up an opinion. The fight between us continued to simmer. It could wait right now.

Wait for a doctor to tell us she was fine.

Wait to make sure she was all right for real.

Wait to get her back to campus.

I'd say wait to catch the mother fuckers who hurt her, but that might take longer.

We'd get there.

As soon as the light changed, I floored it. She was already too far away and it made my skin itch.

Three more traffic lights before I could turn into the hospital parking lot. Plenty of time to replay the three of us ranging out to search the unending places she could be hidden.

Then that thumping.

I thought I'd imagined it but Ramsey and Jonas came racing over. When it happened again—we found her.

In a fridge, with the door face down. We had to get the other items off of it and then flip it over. The fact it was chained and bolted shut was another clue.

It took more time—too much damn time—to find bolt cutters and then we yanked the door open. She was inside, trussed up like a Christmas turkey, wearing an oxygen mask with a little tank.

The thing had probably saved her life.

But it was almost empty.

Nauseated, I put the car in a spot and gripped the steering wheel.

Almost empty.

They hadn't been kidding in their note, pay or don't pay, they weren't contacting anyone again and they weren't going back for her.

Someone had legitimately tried to kill her. This after the fire where Ramsey swore someone fucked with the door. Had that been an attempt on *her* or someone else? The assault in her room though, that had been on her and they'd definitely hurt her then.

I couldn't wrap my mind around this. Even when we thought she was a bitch, I hadn't wanted to cause her pain. The shit with RJ was to get her away from him, especially when she wasn't listening.

Course, then I threw her in a pond and cut off her bra, so maybe I wasn't much better.

But I didn't do anything with the idea of truly hurting her. I wouldn't then and I couldn't now.

Hurt the fuckers who touched her? Absolutely.

My phone buzzed.

It was a message from Ramsey. They were putting her in a private room and he sent me the number. Also said we had incoming so I better get the fuck up there.

It took me less than five to get inside and up to the floor where Ramsey said they were taking her. I managed to get to the room just as they moved her gurney inside.

"I can walk," Ace protested, but she sounded like hell.

"You can also ride," Jonas said. "You're still shaky."

"Fine, but I would like someone to run me around later while I throw my arms wide and yell 'I'm king of the world!'"

Ramsey pulled his glasses off to pinch the bridge of his nose. I wasn't sure if it was irritation or laughter he was trying to suppress, but I grinned.

Ashen-faced and hoarse-voiced, she *sounded* like herself. The fact her arms and legs hurt so much when we'd been trying to get feeling back into them made her fucking cry.

Officially, crying Ace was my kryptonite. I wanted to kill what made her cry.

"Soon as the docs clear you, Ace," I told her. "It's a date."

Jonas shot me a look but I ignored baby brother's recriminations for the moment. My attention was on Ace and the fact she smiled.

She fucking *smiled* and it was the best goddamn thing I'd seen in forever. Pretty sure I'd break laws for that smile.

"You'd do it, too," she murmured in that rough, whispery voice.

"And you like that I would," I countered.

The corners of her lips tilted and I leaned back against the wall and folded my arms. Or I'd cross over to that bed and kiss her senseless. I made her smile. We found her. I made her smile.

"Maybe we wait for what the doctor says," Ramsey said pointedly.

"Killjoy," I muttered and Ace laughed.

A real, honest-to-god laugh.

The scowl eased from baby brother's expression, and Jonas covered one of Ace's hands with his. More, she linked their fingers.

I rolled my head from side to side. Annoying?

Sure.

Did I hate it?

T.B.D.

A knock on the door pulled all of us around and Ramsey straightened. Despite the fact he wasn't any better dressed than I was in his sweats and t-shirt, he greeted the doctor with a handshake. "Dr. Wheeler? I'm Ramsey Malone. The patient is Kaitlin Crosse."

"Yes," the older man said, gripping Ramsey's hand briefly, as he and the nurse stepped inside. "I was briefed on the patient and we've taken all the proper precautions. If you gentlemen would step outside..."

I was all set to object when Ace said, "I don't mind if they stay."

She didn't? Then again, she hadn't wanted to go on the ambulance ride alone and she sure as hell hadn't wanted to talk to the cops by herself.

I got that on a lot of levels.

"You sure?" Ramsey said, his gaze dipping to where she white-knuckled her grip on Jonas' hand before he focused on her face.

"No," she said without an ounce of artifice and gave a little shrug. "Just—at the moment, you're on my side, right?"

"Yes," Jonas answered without an ounce of hesitation and I nodded once even as Ramsey's expression tightened.

"We are," he said, though the last word came out more like he had to push it through his teeth. Maybe it was the "we" he was clenching on. When he shot me a look, I rolled my eyes and focused on Ace.

"Whatever you need. You want me here? Not moving." Period. End of story.

"Right," the doctor said when Ace focused on him again. The nurse helped her change into a hospital gown behind a folding room separator while the doctor waited with us on the other side.

Security guards appeared at the door while I was watching,

a pair of them. Good. They weren't taking any chances with her. An administrator knocked on the door and said there was an attorney on the phone for the doctor.

"I'll speak to them after," Wheeler told her and she nodded. "Provided my patient agrees. I don't care who they are."

Oh, I liked him more and more. When the nurse said they were ready, the doctor moved the room divider out of the way and the three of us ranged out in a semicircle.

I didn't want to be in the way, but I also didn't want to miss anything. They checked her vitals. Then the bruises—holy shit the bruises—they were all over her arms from where the wire ties had gouged into her skin. It was like a wicked crosshatch pattern on her skin.

It matched a similar one on her legs. When she shifted and grimaced on the bed as the doctor moved to examine her back, I straightened.

And I wasn't alone.

There were *darker* bruises there and one looked distinctly like a shoe. Another one was on her ribs and she let out another hiss as he examined it.

"I'm going to order a round of X-rays, Miss Crosse," the doctor said, his voice clinical and detached, but also extremely serious. "Your vitals look good, but you are having some issues with breathing. Your ribs are definitely bruised, if not cracked. I want to check your lungs for function. Considering the fire a few months ago, we need to make sure there are no other underlying issues."

Her expression tensed. "If they're cracked what does that mean?"

"It will take some time to heal, you'll need to take it easy. Rest is good, light exercise, and we watch for any signs of fluid in your lungs."

"But if I had to have surgery?"

The whiplash of that question was like a record scratch. The doctor frowned, apparently, he hadn't been expecting it either. "I would tell you one thing at a time. It would also require a consult between myself and your surgeon, as well as a determination of whether or not the surgery could wait."

He seemed to be choosing his words carefully.

"What surgery do you need?" Jonas asked. Baby brother didn't bother. Some days, I fucking loved him for asking the questions I wanted answered.

"Why don't we wait on that," Ramsey suggested. "Your health first, Siren."

"That's not the point," she started but he held up his hand.

"It is the point, right *now*. Let's see what's wrong then go to the next step, okay?"

"I agree with your—friend," Doctor Wheeler said. "We should wait until we have all our results. I'm also concerned about the time in the fridge, the possible oxygen deprivation, and any head injuries. So let's eliminate all of those then discuss this surgery?"

Ace let out a long sigh. "I had on an oxygen mask, I think."

"You did," Ramsey said. "And an air tank but I have no idea how much air it had."

"Right, and I may have hit my head." She touched her fingers to the bruises on her face. "I know I hit the pavement." There were scrapes on her forearms too.

Every single mark just pissed me off.

"Okay, then let's do all of this one step at a time. X-rays and I think an IV, we want make sure you're hydrated. Then we'll take the next step. For right now, we're going to admit you." At her grimace, he smiled. "We'll use a Jane Doe name, don't worry. We've marked the VIP status and we'll make sure no one bothers you. My daughter is a huge fan and she will be furious that I'm not telling her about this, so I would say secrecy protects us all."

Ace laughed, another real one. "Tell you what, Doctor. Get me out of here tonight and I'll send your daughter tickets to our next tour..."

"Done, *if* you are well enough to be discharged."

"I'll be right back with the IV and I'm going to have radiology bring up the portable X-ray," the nurse told us.

"Thanks," Ace said before she sagged back against the bed with a wince. The moment the doctor was out of the room the forced brightness and easy smile vanished. "Fuck, that hurts."

"We can get you—"

"Who am I?" Aubrey Miller's voice carried from the hallway with all the power of being in concert. "I'm her family, now open that damn door."

I was closer so I yanked it open. "She's fine," I hurried to tell the security guards. The scathing look she shot me had me holding the door wider. "She's right in here."

Aubrey strode into the room and I closed the door behind her. Unlike all of us, she was in uniform and everything about her said, cool, controlled, and poised.

Everything except her eyes.

Those said she was about to gut us all.

Then she focused on Ace and the hostility in her expression suddenly turned to pure fury. "Which one of these douchebags am I killing first?"

Nine

KC

"Aubrey..." I scooted forward but she pointed a finger at me as she marched across the room. "I'm okay."

"You're in a fucking hospital, Kait, a *hospital.*" Yeah she didn't call me Kait unless she was pissed. "*Again.* I went out on a goddamn date, and I got back today to eight thousand messages from these pricks asking me about you without telling me anything about you and then they didn't answer their phones."

She shot them all a look but the only one who looked even mildly chagrined was Ramsey.

And I wasn't sure if that was chagrin or weariness. I wasn't going to try and guess right now.

"I know," I told her, tired swarmed me. Everything hurt. Not just my chest. My legs and arms were sore from how I'd been folded. Yay for flexibility, boo for the stiffness. "Can you hand me the water?," I asked Ramsey since he was closest.

They hadn't given me an IV yet, and yes, I needed one, at least for hydration. Didn't mean I wanted it.

"Also, I would kill for coffee."

Lachlan eyed me. "I'll get it."

"They didn't say she could have any," Ramsey argued even as he filled the plastic cup with water and held it over to me like he was going to hold it while I drank.

"They didn't say she couldn't either," Lachlan said with a dismissive look before he focused on me. "Same thing as usual, Ace?"

"I'll take roadie black at the moment if that's all they have."

Aubrey made a face. "Do not get her roadie black, get her the real thing or I will."

If Lachlan got snarky with her...

"Got it." Lachlan faced Aubrey. "Would you like anything?"

"Yeah, for you three to fuck off while I talk to my girl." Direct as fuck, that was my Aubrey.

I tried to take the water cup from Ramsey but he didn't move his hand and I was stuck holding his hand while we both held the plastic cup.

The intensity in his gaze struck me even as my fingers tingled where they rested against his warmer ones. All the air backed up in my lungs and I held my breath as he raised his eyebrows.

His eyes held so many unspoken comments and questions, apprehension trilled up my spine. "It's okay, Siren," he said almost softly. "Just have your drink and we'll figure this out."

The absolute confidence in that promise rocked me. At the same time, there was so much left unsaid. Unsaid and we needed to talk. But I wasn't sure Aubrey would go for it and to be fair—I kind of wanted privacy with him for part of it and I still needed to open that can of worms with all three of them.

Letting him keep the cup steady, I took a drink. The cool water on my throat was a gift. Locking gazes with Ramsey while I took a second deeper drink threw me all the way back to the night before, and desire blew through me like a hot desert wind.

With a mental shake, I dragged my gaze off of him to the room where Aubrey stared at me along with Jonas. Lachlan had vanished. Right.

Coffee.

"Do you want us to give you a moment?" Jonas asked, and the longing I'd been ruthlessly suppressing for our burgeoning friendship burst forth and I found a smile for him even as I kept hold of Ramsey's hand.

"Thank you," I told him, sparing a glance up at Ramsey then back to Jonas. "For finding me." For coming for me. For whatever the ransom thing was. They hadn't filled me all the way in. Yes, I needed to call Dad but... "I really didn't know what was happening."

I swallowed the sudden lump in my throat, but Jonas nodded and some emotion seemed to bleed back into his face. "Missed you."

Two words and fuck did I feel those. "Me too."

"Talk later?"

"Yes."

"Okay." He looked at Ramsey. "Let her go and let them talk."

Amusement softened Ramsey's expression as I made myself let go of him and he set the water down. "We'll be in the hall."

"Thank you," I managed before he nodded, then he wrapped a hand around my nape while I was still looking up at him. The desire collided with apprehension, and I curled my toes under the blankets when he dipped his head to press a kiss to my forehead.

It was the sweetest, hottest kiss, that offered comfort with the promise of intimacy. Even more because this close, I couldn't miss the warm, sunny scent of him or the fact he still smelled a little bit like me.

Fuck, I hadn't showered. Had he? And all at once, all I could think about was the way he looked in bed a few hours earlier.

Was that really only a few hours earlier?

"We'll be close," he murmured. Then he let me go and strode across the room to where Jonas had pulled the door open. The loaded quiet in the room seemed to practically pulsate until the door clicked shut.

"What the hell happened?" Aubrey asked, her fury giving way to fear and concern as she crossed the room to perch on the edge of my bed. "Talk to me."

"A lot happened," I admitted. So much. It hadn't even been a full twenty-four hours since we last talked, or maybe it had been. Honestly, I didn't know, it seemed like years. I missed the hell out of her and she was right there.

When Aubrey reached for me, I wrapped my arms around her in a hug. It hurt like hell and pulled on my ribs but she was so damn gentle. The tears I'd battled with earlier resurfaced.

"Easy," she whispered and when she would have let me go, I held on a little tighter.

"Just a bit longer," I pleaded, and it was a plea. Aubrey relaxed into me and smoothed her hand over my hair, in a petting motion.

"Long as you need, Kait," she promised. It steadied me as I sniffled once and tried to put the tears back into their bottle. I had to let her go sooner than I liked, my ribs really hurt and when I eased back to sit, she frowned.

"I had sex with Ramsey," I admitted and her eyebrows shot up.

"What..."

Raising a hand, I tried to ask her for patience. "Let me tell you all of it then you yell at me."

"I'm not planning on yelling at *you*," she muttered but I had a feeling that would change when I finished.

"You say that now."

"Uh huh, tell me the rest of it." She linked our fingers, scowling briefly at the bruises on my wrists before she reached for the water and held it for me.

I really needed that drink, after, the story just fell out of me. "I got bad news about Pen..." I told her what the doctors had said, the tests they needed to do. "I need to go back there, as soon as possible or have them do tests here."

"They want to see if you're a match."

I nodded. "I may not be," I sniffled. "Bronson is gonna get tested too. We can't ask the littles, they're too young—but I can send a message to Trace. I don't know if he'll answer..."

"But we need to know. I'll get tested too. Yvette will. We can put out a call on our fan club and the website. We will find her a match."

Neither of us mentioned Dad. "I have to call him too."

"Because he's shown so much interest up until now." That protectiveness—it was the same way I felt about her when dealing with her parents.

"I know but—he paid my ransom." That sounded so fucking weird.

"Back up," Aubrey said, the two syllables clipped as she studied me. "Ransom?"

"Oh, yeah—so—after I basically fell apart and cried like a damn baby, Ramsey found me. He couldn't get much out of me and he was trying. He carried me back to his place and he was being great, but I just—I couldn't see around how fucking unfair all of this is and I couldn't get it together."

"Uh huh." Head tilted, Aubrey studied me with a dead neutral expression. "And...?"

"Well, we had sex."

Anger flickered in her eyes. "He took—"

"He didn't take anything," I told her, squeezing her hand as I sat forward some. "He didn't," I repeated at her skeptical look. "I asked, he offered—it doesn't matter. I knew what I was doing and—it was—it was better than I imagined, but I don't think I want to talk about that part right now."

When I glanced at the door then back to her, she nodded. Lachlan would be back any minute with my coffee, as it was, I drank more water. When I finished the cup, she refilled it.

"Okay. So why are we here? What happened? And get to the part about the ransom." Concern radiated off her in waves and it made me want to cry all over again. Not because I was surprised, but—Aubrey was already there for me. No questions. If I said we needed to kill someone, she'd probably just ask me what I needed her to bring.

Sniffling, I shot her a watery smile. I wasn't usually this emotional, but it had been a long fucking day. When I tried to suck in a deep breath, I winced. Right...shallow breathing. Fuck, my ribs hurt.

"It's a long story..." Only it really wasn't. I told her everything from waking up at Ramsey's to going to get coffee to calling Lachlan and finally the assault itself. Weirdly, that part seemed like it happened to someone else, even the being squeezed into the fridge.

"I still can't believe it was a refrigerator," I admitted, as Aubrey scowled.

"Who—so these so-called kidnappers reached out to Huey, Dewey, and Louie?"

"Um, I don't know about that part," I admitted. "They just said that Dad paid whatever the ransom was."

The fury in Aubrey's eyes deepened. "That's why they were calling me though, but they didn't fucking *tell* me something was wrong."

"Maybe they didn't know..."

"Bullshit."

"Babe," I said, wincing when I tried to shift again. "They came and got me. They got me out of that fridge, they cut me loose and they took care of me." I didn't know much, but that I did know. "And you saw them just now..."

"Yeah, they seem like a bunch of champions after being raging fucking dickheads for nearly two years. But I can see why sex might change your mind." She rolled her eyes, then shook her head. "Be grateful, but don't let them off the hook. They fucked up."

"I'm not letting them off the hook..." Too much of what they'd said and done had *hurt*. "But I'm—I still need to clear this air and I need to focus on Pen...and whatever the hell this was."

Kidnapping.

"You also need to call Dix." When I opened my mouth, she shook her head once and her expression tightened. "You call him or I will. We agreed to do this your way and to have the freedom and the anonymity. But you just ended up in a fucking refrigerator, you need security and that's happening. So fight me on this all you want but I'm going to win, cause Yvette will be on my side too."

I swallowed around the lump in my throat. "I can't believe someone kidnapped me."

That was just—surreal.

"I can't believe we got you back," Aubrey whispered and real fear crept into her eyes. "If we hadn't..."

This time she was hugging me and trying not to squeeze.

"Stop it," I whispered, rapidly losing the battle against tears. "I'm right here...not going anywhere. But if you cry, I'm gonna cry and I already look terrible."

"Yeah," she admitted when she pulled back. "You do look rough—"

"Thanks."

"All the love, Kait, but that hair?" She grinned and pulled out her phone. Then she snapped a pic of me, the bitch. "Has to be seen to be believed." Then she showed me the picture and I really did look the very definition of bedraggled.

"You're sending that to Yvette, aren't you?"

"Yep and saving it for Christmas cards sometime when we're over all of this."

"Bitch."

"Hmm-hmm." But she was smiling even if there were tears in her eyes.

A knock on the door announced Lachlan's return and the guys spilled back inside. Aubrey still shot them dirty looks, but she'd notched down some of the hostility.

Some.

When Lachlan handed me the coffee, I wanted to orgasm right there. The smell was just fucking everything. Of course, I barely got a sip and the radiology people showed up.

Dammit.

"I got extra." Lachlan motioned to the bag next to the door. "In an insulated tumbler. It will be hot when you're done—kind of like you now."

I snorted and I wasn't the only one, but at the same time, I smiled. "Thank you."

"Anything, Ace," he said, fixing a firm look on me. "And I mean it."

That was an unsettling thought.

"Right, Romeo, get the fuck out so they can take pictures

of her ribs." Aubrey plucked my coffee cup from my hand and took a sip. "Not bad. I'll bring this right back for you."

A laugh escaped me and I hissed at the pain but Aubrey managed to defuse the moment and give all of us shit at the same time.

"I'll know if you take more than a sip," I retaliated and she grinned at me before she took a nice long drink.

"Well then, I won't try to hide it."

Fuck, it hurt to laugh. "You're a bitch."

"Love you too." She tossed the last over her shoulder as she herded the guys out. Hopefully the X-rays wouldn't take that long.

Ten

RAMSEY

Jonas kept his own council during our wait in the hallway while Aubrey and KC spoke. Aubrey's anger at us might be justified, she was a loyal and protective friend.

Might be?

Fuck.

I pinched the bridge of my nose before I rubbed at my eyes. Not going far from her room, I paced down the hallway. The image of her folded in on herself was going to haunt me. That and the broken sound of her tears when we cut her free.

It wasn't quite the sobbing from the prior night, nor did she appear to be nursing the same broken heart. If anything, she was more bewildered and confused.

"She was surprised about Gibs," Jonas said, his tone as mystified as hers had been. Only his held the echo of questions neither of us had asked.

None of us really.

"Yeah, I got that." Turning back to him, I said, "Leave it alone for now."

"What?"

"The Gibs thing—whatever is going on between the two of them. I don't think we've had it right. At all."

And didn't that make me the biggest fucking dick on the planet. I'd been blaming her for everything. Dammit.

"I don't want to wait," Jonas argued. "We haven't talked and that's the problem."

"It's not the only problem," I told him as I rubbed the back of my neck. I needed a shower, some ibuprofen, and a gallon of coffee. The headache wasn't going away any time soon.

"The people who kidnapped her."

"Yes," I said and tried not to snap. Clearly, the kidnappers were a problem. "But it's more than that. There's—" I hesitated. Bringing up the baby right now probably wasn't a good plan.

At the same time, she said something was wrong with the baby. That was the reason I found her sobbing in the damn rain. The reason I took her back to my suite.

"There's what?" Jonas asked as he narrowed the distance. The security guards were still on her room but neither of us felt like talking in front of them. We didn't *know* them.

"The life she's led—everything in a paper or a news story. All the gossip," I said. "How much of that was truth and how much speculative bullshit?"

Jonas shrugged. "She's not the girl in all those stories."

No, she wasn't. "At least not the ones we always heard about." The Tattler stories that got all the clicks and the social media garbage about her mom and their life in Hollywood.

"Have you ever looked up Gibs?" Jonas asked and I glanced at him.

"What?"

"I was thinking about it—after he played that song of mine and how she acted...have you ever looked him up?" Nothing in his tone gave away where this was going.

"No," I said. "He's just always been good to Mom, so I didn't much care about the rest of it." I didn't even like his music all that much, but nobody asked me. So...

"I think we should." He didn't explain it but then it didn't need explanation. "The only reason we know so much about KC is Mom."

That stopped me cold. "What?" I pivoted to face him and Jonas stood there with his hands in the pockets of his jeans looking like he didn't give a solid fuck about anything.

"You heard me."

"I'm back," Lachlan announced as he walked up with a tray of coffees. "Why are you two out here?"

Not that he'd waited for an answer. The next few hours dragged by as we waited on X-rays and the doctor ordered some blood work as well, just to be on the safe side.

Eventually, they gave her permission to leave, with a few caveats. No lifting, avoid straining her chest, particularly the bruised ribs. The concussion was minor but we needed to keep a look out for specific symptoms and it would probably be good for her to be seen by her own physician sooner rather than later.

"Why?" KC asked, not argumentative, but seemingly puzzled.

"Because, young lady, the records you allowed us to scan indicated you had a concussion just a few months ago..."

"Oh," she said with a wince. "Yeah, I kind of forgot about that."

She hadn't but there was far more on her mind would be my guess and that incident didn't register as much. Didn't mean I had to like it.

"Good. Now," the doctor said. "Take it easy, hydrate. If

you have any of the following symptoms, you come straight back into the ER. No waiting to see if it gets better. We err on the side of caution."

There was a gruffness to the doctor's kind words.

"Thank you, Dr. Wheeler," KC said as she went to climb off the bed. "I appreciate it. Don't worry about your daughter, I'll make sure she gets tickets the minute we have a tour planned." She shook his hand and then we were stepping out again so Aubrey could help her get dressed. The hospital provided her with a pair of scrub bottoms to wear.

Probably better than a stolen pair of my boxers. The shirt though, was mine, and I didn't say a word. Whether she noticed or not, she didn't bring it up either.

We didn't make it out of the hospital before the cops showed up with more questions. That took another ninety minutes and the problem was, she couldn't tell them any more than she already had.

Creglin said they were assigning someone from campus security to our dorm and he said he'd text me the three names, they'd be working in eight hour shifts. They were going to create a very real presence around her.

She was going to hate every minute of it. While I felt bad about that part, I didn't object to even one ounce of extra precaution where her safety was concerned.

Finally, with her release in hand and the police clearing her, it was time to get her back to the school. Aubrey had also brushed out KC's hair and though it lacked its usual bounce, it was smoother.

That came with a challenge all its own. While she might fit in the backseat of Lachlan's AMG, it would be tight and she needed to not be squeezed. Jonas barely fit back there by himself. It would be uncomfortable as hell for both of them.

"I ordered a car," Aubrey said before we could even really begin the debate. "We have a service, and they're here. So—"

"I'll ride back with you," Jonas offered, focusing on KC. "If that's okay? I just want to make sure you both get back there."

Aubrey didn't look thrilled, but she ignored us in favor of checking with KC. "It's up to you," she said. "Though—we know Jonas is useful in a fight."

Lachlan snorted. "We'll follow you. You're going right back to campus?"

"That's the plan," Aubrey said though she clearly didn't look thrilled by the idea. "Personally, I'd be fine with just dumping out and heading up to Boston. Even if they've postponed graduation."

"They what? It's this week—wait...I have another final... Fuck I don't even know what day it is. " KC frowned. "And I actually need to go to California. So...back to school then see what we can work out."

"Don't worry about dates or timing. We'll take care of it, and I messaged Dix." She raised a hand as if staving off an argument. "I know, you hate bodyguards. But I'm done."

For my part, I couldn't argue with that. The school was already making moves. Shifting final dates and graduation. Texts had been coming in constantly. Covering their ass was in full effect.

"I'm not arguing," KC said. "Thank you."

The whole moment was intensely private. I felt like some kind of voyeur standing there. At the same time, the interplay between them fascinated me. It was such an intense bond of loyalty, love, and friendship.

I envied their closeness. The trust.

I had a lot of ground to make up.

"Come on," I said as a nurse showed up with a wheelchair. "Let's get you out to the car. We can figure everything out later. Will you let Jonas go with you?"

"Yes," KC said, focusing on me with those brilliant eyes of

hers. "I still want to talk and I need to—wait, was my phone there?"

That got a look between all of us.

"I didn't see it." But then I hadn't really been looking. "We found a piece of the case—but no phone."

"We'll call Creglin," Lachlan said. "If it was there, the cops might have it."

"We need to get my phone turned off and bricked." She shot a look at Aubrey.

"I'm texting Teddy to take care of it, then get you a new phone setup and overnighted."

Well, that was one solution.

I supposed.

"We can get more coffee on the way back," Jonas volunteered. "Or I can make you some…"

The nurse wouldn't let any of us drive the wheelchair. As it was, all of us hovered as they got to the car. I didn't know the guy driving them, but he matched the picture and the credentials on Aubrey's phone. It included a certification.

The nurse and Jonas helped KC ease into the car and Aubrey shot me a look when she caught me studying her phone.

"The service always provides us with the full details of the driver and picture identification. It's useful for not getting into the wrong car."

They were barely eighteen and they had to think about shit like that.

"It's a good plan."

The look she gave me clearly said "no shit," but she didn't snap at me.

"Would you mind asking the driver to idle for a couple of minutes so we can go get Lachlan's car?"

She spared a look at the car then at me. "No more than

five. I really want to get her back, and she needs rest. She looks like crap."

"It could have been a lot worse," I cautioned and I had no idea why I did. "I'm just glad we found her in one piece." Even with the bruises, the oxygen had been enough to let her survive. Maybe not a lot longer, but I didn't want to focus on that part.

It—it disturbed me on a far different level, and that conversation I needed to have with KC before I had it with anyone else. I didn't care how close they were.

"Yeah," Aubrey said with a low sigh. "Thankfully it wasn't. You two should get moving. Five minutes." The last she directed at Lachlan, who'd been standing there listening but not actually participating in the conversation.

We waited for Aubrey to get in and then Lachlan set off with me right behind him. Jonas was with them and he wouldn't let anything happen. At the same time, I found myself agreeing with Aubrey, I wanted KC somewhere safe and sound.

Thankfully, the small area hospital didn't have an expansive parking lot. But just as we got to Lachlan's AMG, he pivoted and his fist slammed into my jaw.

Surprise and pain were a double blow and I staggered a couple of steps. It wasn't enough to knock me on my ass, but fuck it knocked my teeth together. I nearly bit my tongue.

"That's for putting your hands on Ace," Lachlan said when I met his furious gaze.

I rubbed my jaw and checked for blood on my lips before I gave him a grudging nod. "I deserved that."

"Yes, you fucking did," he snarled. The raw anger in eyes and the flat line of his mouth were dead giveaways. He was really pissed.

And jealous, a little voice in the back of my head whispered.

Fuck.

"But not because of you," I warned him.

"What?"

"What happened between Kaitlin and me had absolutely *nothing* to do with you, Lachlan." My jaw throbbed. "Let's be clear on that."

"She's *mine*," he argued and I shook my head.

"She's not a possession. She's a person. Get that through your skull. Now, are you driving or am I going back to get in the car with them?" Because they weren't going to wait past that five minute mark.

"This isn't done," Lachlan said before he stalked around to the driver's side.

No, it wasn't. "This isn't about us."

"The hell it isn't," Lachlan said as he slid into the driver's seat. I climbed into the passenger side before he decided to pull out and leave me behind. "Jonas wants her, you're breaking every damn rule for her, and I..."

"And you what?" I said as I leaned my head back. Lachlan didn't say a word as he slammed the car into reverse and then accelerated out of the lot. We pulled into the round just as their car began to pull out and we fell in right behind them.

After ten minutes of silence, I glanced over at him. "First time you admitted it to yourself?"

"Fuck off, Ramsey."

Yeah. First time he admitted it to himself.

I had no idea how we were going to deal with this.

Eleven

KC

The ride back to campus was quiet, exhaustion weighed down every muscle and as much as I tried to stay awake, I kept nodding off. Every application of the brakes or curve in the road had my head bobbing then snapping back up.

The back seat was large, but I was still sandwiched between Jonas and Aubrey. When he shifted to put his arm on the back of the seat, he gave me a questioning look.

"If we roll the jacket up, you can use it like a pillow."

It was Aubrey's jacket, she'd draped it over my shoulders but I wasn't cold. Aware of Aubrey's scrutiny, I debated the shift in Jonas' posture and position and then the jacket I had folded in my lap.

A yawn cracking my jaw decided me. Everything hurt, no matter which way I was sitting. So I rolled up the jacket, tucked it against Jonas then leaned against it and him. It wasn't the softest pillow but it did offer support.

My ribs protested until I adjusted a little. I couldn't stand the shoulder strap over my chest so it was behind me leaving only the lap belt.

No sooner did I begin to relax then a gentle touch on my arm roused me from sleep. "We're back at the school," Aubrey said, then she rubbed my arm lightly. "You with us?"

I blinked slowly. I hated to be groggy.

I really hated it.

"Yeah." I glanced up to find Jonas regarding me patiently. Oh, yeah, I was still laying on him. "Thank you."

"You're welcome." He didn't move until I tried to sit up and I didn't think I'd done more than blink but I was already stiff. "Need help?"

"Please..." Then he settled his hands on my shoulders and helped me into a sitting position. At once, he unlocked my seatbelt then passed the jacket over to Aubrey.

"Hang on," he urged before he opened his door then he held out his hand. "Ease this way and I'll help you out."

Aubrey closed the door on her side, making the decision even easier as I scooted over. Wow, I wasn't fragile or weak but I hurt worse than when I'd been in that hospital room. Jonas held out a hand for me and I clasped his.

Rock steady, he braced me so I could lean on him to pull myself out of the car. "Wow, bruised ribs *suck*."

He smiled, but the humor didn't reach his eyes. It was late in the afternoon. We'd missed the whole damn day. There were students milling around, more than one glanced in our direction.

Great, I was gonna end up on TikTok looking like death warmed over. I really needed to call Jackie and Bronson, as well as the rest of the sibs, before the news broke. Yvette knew. She was *fuming* and likely on her way here, but she knew.

Ramsey appeared with a rapidly darkening bruise on his jaw with Lachlan a half-step behind him.

"No cameras on campus, Miss Tolan," Ramsey snapped

to a girl I hadn't even noticed. The freshman let out a squeak as she lowered her phone. "Hand it over," he continued as he blocked her view. "Or delete it while I'm watching."

"I just—"

"Rules are rules," Ramsey said in a tone populated by such stern disappointment, my own stomach bottomed out at the idea of being in trouble. Lachlan dropped a jacket over my shoulders as soon as I was out of the car.

"I'm sorry," the freshman said to me with wide, tearful eyes. "I knew you went to school here but—I hadn't actually seen you where..."

"If you want," I said, needing to fix this for her. The embarrassment in her eyes reflected in the red flush on her cheeks. "Give us your address and we can send you a signed photo of all three of us."

"Oh my god," the girl said, her eyes rounding. "Really? I mean—that would be awesome. My sister will just die."

"Well, hopefully not," I said, trying to keep it light but the twinge vibrated inside of me and the chord of sadness just... yeah I couldn't follow that thought right now. "But we would be happy to."

"Yep," Aubrey said without missing a beat. "We would be —here, give me your details." She slid between us but not before she gave me a pointed look. "Go on, I'll be inside in a minute."

"Thanks," I mouthed and she lifted her chin.

"Oh, this is the best," the girl was squealing and frankly, the pitch reminded me of my headache. "Thank you...you know I love you guys so much, I can never pick a favorite between you..."

"Let's get you inside, Ace," Lachlan said as he moved to offer me an arm. I was still holding onto Jonas though and I hadn't even meant to keep leaning on him.

"Suddenly hating the fact we're on the fourth floor," I mumbled.

"We can go to Ramsey's," Lachlan offered and it was—sweet, but no.

"Actually, I would rather be in my own space." Now that we were here, I kind of wished we'd just gone to a hotel or straight back to California. Couldn't do that...*yet.*

We earned more than a few curious looks as I climbed the stairs *slowly.* Not that they lingered on us for long. Jonas would glare or Lachlan would. That shut a lot of people up.

I was panting pathetically by the fourth floor. And the shallow breathing wasn't as bad as trying to take deeper breaths, but it still *hurt.* Lingering for a moment, I tried to get it all under control.

The guys gave me a minute. It gave Aubrey and Ramsey time to catch up to us. I realized, rather belatedly, that Ramsey had stuck it out downstairs with her while she talked to our fan.

That...was really kind.

"Why are we still out here?" Ramsey asked with a frown, sweeping his gaze over me. The concern in his eyes—it was unsettling. I wasn't used to this but they were all trying to be kind.

"Cause Ace needed a minute." Lachlan's belligerence ramped up as he glared at Ramsey. Yeah, that wasn't good.

"C'mon," Aubrey said as she beckoned to me, but Lachlan refused to cede his spot. Nor Jonas. Blowing out a breath I really didn't have, I pushed on and began what seemed like a mile long walk down the hall.

Yep. The bruised ribs definitely *sucked.*

We all bypassed Aubrey's room. The last person I wanted to see was Payton. Fuck, I missed when Aubrey and I were roommates, when we could just shut the door on the world.

Jonas got our door opened and Lachlan ushered me

inside. They were all following. It was like having a personal entourage. I wasn't a fan.

Once in the suite, there was a long moment of hesitation. What to do next... I glanced down at my stolen shirt and borrowed scrubs.

"Coffee?" Jonas offered.

"Yes please," I said. Gratitude swelled in me. "A big one."

He nodded.

"I need a shower." I glanced at Aubrey and she held out a hand.

"C'mon, we'll keep it short." She spared a look past me. I glanced over my shoulder to where Lachlan and Ramsey stood like a pair of stone sentinels. "You two might think about showers and changing."

"We can wait," Lachlan said but Ramsey only frowned, his gaze tracking to me.

"Are you hungry?" The question surprised me. But now that he mentioned it...

"A little..."

"Fine, we'll get food and bring it back. Any preferences?"

"Nothing heavy, no carb load." That just sounded awful.

"She likes General Tso's," Jonas said. "Maybe a double order with the brown rice instead of the white?"

My stomach grumbled loudly at the idea. "Yes, please."

"I'll go get it. There's a good place in town. I'll be back in an hour." Lachlan covered the two steps I'd separated from him and dropped a kiss on my lips before he strode out the door.

I was left staring after him, a little slack-jawed. It had been a sweet, but firm kiss. While he hadn't lingered, it definitely registered.

Ramsey sighed. "I'll be back up in ten minutes." The first he said to me, but then he focused on Jonas. "Lock up and keep it bolted. Make sure you know who it is before you open the door." Then his gaze returned to me. "Take it easy, Siren. We'll make sure no one else gets close."

Right—not touching that. "Thank you." At least not right now. Aubrey was already coaxing me into my room. It felt like a hundred years since I left here.

My bag was downstairs in Ramsey's suite, along with my soaking wet uniform. Aubrey didn't say much as she got the shower going. I stripped carefully. At least the scrubs weren't hard to remove.

The boxers took a little more effort, but they landed with the scrubs and then I lifted the hem of the shirt and pulled it off. The dark gray sleeves paired with the lighter gray basic t-shirt held my attention.

It was a band t-shirt. Reminded me of the ones Dad had for his group when I was a kid. I always loved the guitar and base they'd used as a crossbones for their band logo. I thought Ramsey had one of his but...

"That's one of ours, isn't it?" Aubrey asked from the open doorway to the bathroom.

"Yeah. I haven't seen this style in a long time." We'd designed it on the net in about fifteen minutes. It had a guitar base—the guitar Dad had given me, then we added roses to it and fire. Eventually, we'd stripped out the guitar entirely.

But...

"This is from our first real tour..." We'd been twelve, almost thirteen, when we kicked it off. I hadn't even realized how much I modeled the design on Dad's.

I started to fold the shirt. I needed to give it back. It was old and worn, like Ramsey had put it on a lot, which was a weird thing to wrap my mind around. But I paused when I saw the inky smudge on the back.

Fuck, had I damaged his shirt?

I moved toward the bathroom and into the brighter light. Aubrey stared at it with me as I squinted.

"Shit," Aubrey murmured. "You signed it."

"You sure it was me?" Cause, I had no recollection of ever meeting Ramsey.

"Yeah, look..." She took the shirt carefully and spread it out. "Right here on the left shoulder, that's definitely a 'K.'"

I stared.

"There's a Y here..." Aubrey squinted a little closer. "Maybe. But the top one is definitely a K, I'd bet the rest of that blob is your name."

Back when we signed with regular Sharpies and not fabric markers. I traced my fingers over the K slowly. Five years he'd had this shirt, at least.

We changed so much after that first tour, things changed while we were *on* the tour. I went over the rest of the shirt. It was dirty and a little frayed, but there was a tear near the hem. From before? Or from the refrigerator?

"All right, enough of the melancholic brooding." Aubrey took the shirt from me gently. "Get in the shower, sit down if you have to, but wash your hair. You'll feel better."

"What are you going to do?"

"Stand guard and keep texting with Teddy." She showed me her phone. "We've already locked down yours. He said the new phone will be here by seven tomorrow, delivered by courier. He also wants a call with us immediately. I'm putting him off for a day or two."

"What about Yvette?" Cause we needed to call her.

"She knows you're here, and she's on the train. She's coming down to see you. She'll decide then whether she's stealing you back to Boston or not." The last came out on a relatively dry note and I smiled.

"Thanks Aubrey."

"You know I have your back," she said.

"I do."

"Then you know I'll have your back dealing with the douchebags."

I pressed a hand against the tile and leaned forward to let the water rush over my head. Everything ached, but the water felt good, washing away all the half-remembered kicks and the way my face hit the pavement. I checked for injuries—the scrapes were there. A bump near my hairline.

More bruises littered my arms—including one that looked very much like a handprint. Creglin and the other detective had photos taken of it. I tried to place my hand over it...the size wasn't terribly off.

One was definitely a girl. The other a guy.

"Aubrey..."

"I'm here," she promised.

"What the hell am I going to say to Dad?"

"I dunno," she admitted. "We'll figure it out. But you don't have to do anything right now."

That was the problem. I had too much that needed to be done. The shower sapped me but I did feel better. Thankfully, Aubrey didn't complain as she helped me towel off and then used another to squeeze the water out of my hair.

"You need an appointment with Anastasia," she mused and I smiled. "Mani pedis, too. Your feet are scary."

"Bitch," I muttered but it was hard not to laugh.

"You know I only tell you cause I love you." She winked. By the time I was back in my own clothes, and fuzzy socks, all I wanted to do was go to sleep.

Eyes closing for a minute, I sighed.

There was coffee waiting in the other room. Coffee. Food. Boys.

We needed to talk.

"They can wait," Aubrey assured me and I shook my head.

"We've all waited too long as it is...but will you stay? It may not be comfortable."

"Just try and throw me out," she said, her gaze firm. "C'mon, let's go run your douchebags over with the bus now. They deserve it."

A chuckle escaped and I groaned. "Stop making me laugh..."

Twelve

JONAS

As soon as I had her coffee ready, I checked the sofa and table to make sure there was no trash before I went to my room to change. I didn't close my door, so I could keep an eye and ear out. It didn't take me long to throw on clean clothes.

When KC emerged from her room, she was dressed in an oversized sweatshirt, leggings and fuzzy socks. Her hair was damp, and her face pink from the shower. She looked amazing...

She also looked tired.

"Coffee is ready," I offered, holding it out to her as she eased onto the sofa. "I made yours too, Aubrey."

It had taken some practice to get the coffees right. Now, I liked doing it. There was something soothing about the machine.

"Thanks," Aubrey said, detouring to grab it. She also came back with ice.

"Ugh." KC made a face, but she didn't argue with Aubrey as she settled it against her side. "Thanks."

"You're welcome." She sat on the table rather than perch on the sofa with KC. Maybe KC needed the distance. I hated how banged up she was. As soon as we found out who did it...

I blew out a breath as I moved to the chair. I wanted to sit next to her, but it was probably better if I didn't. At least until we talked.

"They should be back—" I started but no sooner did I say it than the door unlocked and the knob turned. I shot to my feet, but it was Ramsey.

"Sorry," he said. "Just used my key. Didn't want to bother anyone if they were asleep." His gaze tracked right to KC. Yeah, he didn't want to *bother* her. Sure.

Sitting back down, I cut a look to her. Ramsey had also showered and changed, but he'd skipped his dress shirt and slacks. He was in normal clothes. He looked like he did when we were at home, not here. Except, there was definitely a bruise on his jaw.

The silence rushed in to fill all the spaces, leaving me on edge and Ramsey frowning. He moved over to the sofa and took a seat slowly.

Right, of course he went straight there. "How are you doing, Kaitlin?"

"Tired," she admitted but seemed to find a smile. "I know I said we all needed to talk, but can we wait for Lachlan? I don't really want to have to say any of this twice."

"We can do anything you want," Ramsey said. "If you need rest—we can wait."

I did *not* want to wait, but I could see why he offered. "Just tell us what you need," I said. That seemed fair, right?

KC smiled at me, it wasn't strained. I really had missed her the past several weeks.

"I have a couple of questions that maybe you can answer..." The hesitation I got.

"Anything," I offered.

"If we can," Ramsey countered with a firm look at me. I ignored that bullshit. Anything she wanted to know, I planned to tell her. If we didn't know the answer, we would go looking for it ourselves. I was tired of *not* knowing and *not* understanding.

KC studied us for a beat then glanced at Aubrey. Her friend shifted on the coffee table, more so she could keep an eye on us and stay near KC. I should have taken the sofa and then Ramsey wouldn't be sitting there.

"You said ransom earlier," KC said slowly. "And I know you explained some of it at the hospital...but can I see it?"

Ramsey's expression turned grim. "You don't want to see that, Siren. It'll just..."

"Give me nightmares?" Her dry tone scraped over me. "Pretty sure that's covered." Not even her little cough before she took a drink of the coffee could cover her discomfort.

"Show her," I said when Ramsey still hesitated. "We wouldn't have known except...except Mom thought you were pulling a stunt."

"Jonas," Ramsey said but I shook my head.

"No, she needs to know. Mom doesn't trust her, but that was how we found out." I didn't care if Ramsey didn't like it. I didn't like any of this. "When we got back this morning we found your wet uniform..."

She flushed, dipping her chin a little but she kept her gaze on me.

"Ramsey complained that you left and we wanted to know what was going on. We all called you, no answer. I came up here to see if you were back, no answer. Then Mom called... she was mad 'cause she thought this was a stunt to get Gibs' attention."

Aubrey glared, not at me or Ramsey, she just looked mad.

"She sent me a copy of the ransom note—well message really," Ramsey said before he handed over his phone.

KC took his phone carefully and stared at it. I couldn't really read her expression. She seemed baffled. "This went straight to Dad?"

"That's what she said," Ramsey told her. "And Gibs confirmed it when we called him."

"You talked to him directly?" Aubrey asked, her eyes narrowed as she transferred that glare to Ramsey.

"Yes," he answered without further prompting.

"He didn't sound sure it was real," I told KC and I wanted to apologize for that. "I don't know why—even after we told them something was wrong. He didn't believe it."

"But he paid the ransom?" KC handed the phone back to Ramsey before she wrapped both of her hands around her coffee cup.

I hesitated, I didn't want to tell her we had to convince him. "If we'd had it, we would have paid it," I told her instead.

"Five hundred thousand is a lot of money," Ramsey told her. "I think he was—trying to be cautious. Maybe."

That wasn't what Ramsey thought. Maybe he thought the lie was better. I wasn't so sure.

"But he paid it, and then sent us the location as soon as he had it." I really wasn't sure what else to tell her. "We found you cause you were thumping."

"Cool," she said slowly. "I guess I should call him." The uncertainty there tugged at me.

When she looked at Aubrey, the other girl shook her head. "If they wanted ransom, why send it to *him* of all people?" There was no mistaking the dismissive skepticism there.

"Because she's his only child," Ramsey said slowly. "He adores her."

Aubrey wasn't alone in the scoff, they both snorted but

before I could say anything the door lock gave and I hit my feet along with Ramsey.

Lachlan arrived in a wave of spicy and savory scents while carrying two huge plastic bags of food. "Hey..." He paused, glancing at all of us before he shut the door. "It's just me."

"Oh, I hate feeling like this," KC admitted, and it got all of our attention. Aubrey was the closest so she just covered her hands.

"You're not alone. We're going to figure this out."

Maybe Lachlan could read the room, but he didn't ask any questions. When he started getting the food ready to pass out, I went to help. He had gotten something for everyone. KC brightened up a little at the General Tso's chicken.

We spread out, with Aubrey moving to sit on the sofa between Ramsey and KC. I kind of liked that she did that, it forced Ramsey to back off. We were all eating slowly, or at least some of us were. KC tore into her food, but she wasn't looking at all of us, she was just eating.

When she finished, she glanced at Aubrey. "Can I borrow your phone for a minute? I need to make a call."

"Yep." Aubrey passed it to her. "Going in your room?"

"Yeah, I need to stand up anyway. I'm getting stiff here." She was slow getting to her feet and I wasn't the only one leaning forward ready to offer her a hand. Then she half-limped to the bedroom. At the door, she glanced at us. "I still want to talk, but I need to make this call."

"Your dad?" Ramsey asked.

"No," she said. "I don't—I don't know what to say to him yet." Then she closed the door and I leaned back in the chair. Aubrey rose and started cleaning up KC's food.

"You know," Lachlan said without preamble and Aubrey barely glanced at him.

"I know a lot of things. You might need to be more specific."

"Why she doesn't want to call Gibs," Ramsey suggested.

"Yeah, but I was thinking who she did have to call and who they both think should have gotten that ransom note." Lachlan usually sounded smug, but that was more curiosity. Curiosity and confusion.

Aubrey carried the food containers in the kitchen. She didn't say a word as she cleaned out their coffee cups and then put the leftovers up.

"You know but you're not telling us." It wasn't a guess. It was loyalty.

She turned to look at me and touched a finger to her nose. "Got it in one."

"Can you throw us a bone, at least?" Lachlan asked, shoving to his feet. "She just went through hell. I mean—there has to be something we could be doing."

"Name me one reason I should answer you," Aubrey said flatly, folding her arms.

"Because you're her friend," Ramsey said, entering the argument. "Last night—I can't believe that was only last night —she was absolutely devastated and today... Tell us something we can do to help her."

"Well, see, normally, I'd suggest making nice with her best friend might get you an in, but since I'm her best friend and I already think you three suck—well two of you suck, one of you sucks a little less." She shot a look at me. "It's safe to say that I'm Team KC and you three are shit out of luck."

"Aubrey," I said before either of my brothers could jump back in. "I want to fix it...I don't know how."

"I know you don't," she said, her tone almost apologetic. "You guys have been treating her like you know her and you don't know shit about Kait. You never have."

That wasn't entirely true.

"You spend so much time thinking about the gossip

around her, have you ever bothered to look in your own house?"

"What exactly is that supposed to mean?" Lachlan asked.

"Well, maybe when you figure it out, you might actually develop a clue. Though right now, I don't think you'd know one if it walked up to you and offered to suck your dick." She was angry, angry as hell at all of us.

But I snorted at the last comment. "It would have to want to suck his dick."

"Fuck you, Jonas," Lachlan said and I shrugged as I flopped back in the seat.

"Look..." Ramsey blew out a breath. "I get it. We might have fucked up—"

"Might have?" Aubrey shook her head. "Tell you what genius, when you figure out what part of that is the definitive, let me know. Until then..."

The door to her room opened and Lachlan spun around to find a weary KC standing in the door. She glanced at each of us in turn and then said, "I don't want to call Dad because I haven't spoken to him in seven years."

Seven... what?

"Not that I didn't used to call him or that I didn't reach out. But right before I turned eleven, he said that he wasn't going to do the shared custody and exchanged visits anymore. If I wanted to see him, I could just come out—then he went on a tour for nine months."

I couldn't breathe.

"He didn't call me once."

Not... seven years ago had been the Righteous Tour. He and Mom had gone around the world, and both hemispheres. It was one of the few summers we didn't spend in Tahoe.

"Twelve may not be grown, but Mom had her movies and Dad had his tours. We formed Torched...and then we were the ones touring. He never came to a show...or called or even sent a note. He sent presents. Twice a year. Once on my birthday, and the other at Christmas. Nothing personal. Though he has sent three cars."

Lachlan frowned. "You don't know how to drive."

"Shocking present, isn't it?" Her tone didn't change in the slightest. "As for being his only child. Hardly. I might be the only one with the Crosse last name. But I have six half-brothers and sisters. All courtesy of Dad and his inability to use a condom."

"What?" I couldn't— "Gibs doesn't..."

"Have other kids? Yeah," KC said as she looked at me. For a moment, I swore there was sympathy or maybe pity in her gaze. "He has a few...including Pen, who is not even three years old and has cancer. Her mother is a drug addict and we have no idea where she is right now, but Jackie, my brother Bronson's mother, is fostering her. When we sent word to Dad about Pen's condition and where she was, the only thing we heard back was 'where did we want the checks?'"

He...

That...

I couldn't wrap my mind around it.

"Yesterday, I got a call about Pen. The treatments aren't working. So, I'm going to wrap up school and go home. See if there's anything else I can do." She let out a shuddering breath. "Yes, I had sex with Ramsey last night."

Suddenly, that didn't seem so shocking.

"Ace—"

"Don't," was all she said, holding up a hand. "I want to get through this once and then I need to lay down. I'm tired."

I didn't doubt it.

"Ramsey found me in the rain, we had sex—more my idea than his..."

"Siren—"

"I said don't," she repeated this time, focusing on him.

"You said you weren't sure it was a good idea and that what I was asking may just be because of how upset I was. Maybe that was true, maybe it wasn't. I don't know and I don't care. We had sex...and it helped for a little while. Then this morning..."

She shook her head.

"The thing is...I don't have people I can trust. I tried, with all of you...then you were douchebags. This morning—it hit me just how bad this could get and I wanted to clear the air. Find out why you all thought so damn little of me when you don't know me."

"To be fair, Ace—you never told us."

"Why the fuck should I *have* to tell you anything?" She stared at us. "Why do I have to confess all my life secrets? You three sure as shit didn't. It was *none* of your business, but you treated me like I was some kind of bitch who ruined your lives. You. Don't. Know. Me."

"But I want to..." It was my turn. "I was trying to get to know you. I thought—we were becoming friends."

"Me too," she admitted. "Then Dad played that song..."

"I don't know why he did that," I admitted. "I didn't *give* it to him. I tried to tell you, but I don't—I used to show him my music. Maybe he found it...maybe it was with something else." Something like Mom giving it to him, but I didn't want to bring her up right now. That—that was a whole other issue. "I swear I wasn't the one who gave it to him."

"I want to believe you, but I'm so tired. I thought we needed to air this out between us—to figure out what the hell we were doing and now..."

"Ace, c'mon," Lachlan took a step toward her. "Don't give up on us."

"There is no us," she said.

"Is the baby okay?" I had to ask. "I saw the picture before —I thought she was yours."

KC shook her head. "Just assumed that, huh?"

I frowned. "Yeah, I shouldn't have."

"It doesn't matter. Pen is sick and that—that is what I need to focus on and I need to sleep—Aubrey are you...?"

"Oh, yeah," she said, crossing to her. "I'm staying over."

"Look, I'm grateful you guys came today...I really didn't know what was going to happen," KC said. "But I have to worry about Pen and whether my mother is joining a cult and what we're doing next...I need to focus on that. Course, I now have to deal with security issues that I never wanted to but... thank you. Thank you for finding me today." She looked at Ramsey. "Thank you for finding me last night...but I need to sleep."

"Go," Ramsey said and I didn't disagree. Aubrey herded her into KC's room and the door closed, shutting all of us out.

"Shit," Lachlan swore as he pivoted to face us.

I raked a hand through my hair. Gibs had six other kids? And he cut KC off? It fucking hurt that she didn't trust us. Trust me.

But we kind of did that... didn't we? How the fuck did I fix this?

Thirteen

"I didn't ask for your permission," a very familiar, and *angry*, voice demanded. The sharpness of her French accent and exaggerated pronunciations promised she wasn't kidding. "Get out of my way before I tase you into the carpet."

"Oh shit," Aubrey mumbled as she rolled off the bed. I grunted cause the movement made me bounce and I wasn't even sure I could move, much less turn myself. Thankfully, she didn't wait for me as she jerked the door open to my room. "Yvette..."

"Where is she? And get this fool out of my way because I already hate them."

I'd almost made it to sitting up when Yvette appeared in the doorway to my room. The casual grace suggested by the sunglasses perched on the top of her head and the wisps of hair escaping her ponytail were completely undercut by the wild eyes and tense expression.

"Kait," she whispered and I made it to my feet just in time

to welcome her hug. She didn't quite slam into me, thankfully, but her grip was firm if gentle. The sweetness of the Dior fragrance she preferred surrounded me.

"I'm okay," I promised her. "I really am."

Then Aubrey was there and we were all in a group hug. Some distant part of my mind tracked the soft click of a closing door. The tears were sliding down my cheeks and I was sniffling almost as hard as Yvette was.

"I hate you bitches," Yvette muttered. "And this stupid school..." Pulling back, she stared at me with tears absolutely ruining her mascara. "Please tell me this experiment is over? No amount of so-called bullshit normal is worth this."

"It's almost over anyway," I admitted, then swiped at my own tears. "Graduation is soon. I don't need the ceremony—just the diploma, you know?"

"Fuck that." Aubrey scrubbed at her own face. "If we're staying for the degrees, you're gonna dance across that damn stage and break every fucking rule and we're gonna get pictures and video and everything..."

A laugh escaped and she scowled.

"You think I'm kidding?"

"No," I promised her. "I don't. That's why I'm laughing. I just thought about wearing one of our concert outfits under the cap and gown..."

"I approve," Yvette said. "But, I'm also telling you that as soon as Dix gets here, he's staying."

I didn't have it in me to argue. "Okay."

"Excuse me?" Aubrey said, blinking as she and Yvette both paused to look at each other before they stared at me. "Why are you suddenly agreeing?"

"I don't want to," I admitted, as I retreated a step to pick up the glass of water next to the bed. I was so goddamn stiff. I needed a shower. A very long, hot one. Clean out the cobwebs and ease the stiffness.

"Petite amie," Yvette said, her whole demeanor shifted. "You know we don't like the increased security any more than you do."

"I *do* know that," I said, catching her hand and squeezing it. "I do—and I absolutely understand why I need it here. Why we *all* do."

They shared another of those looks.

"Clearly, I need it more, my blue hair brings all the crazies to the door." It was the right thing to say, just enough flippancy to make them smile. "But...no more chances. I still can't believe yesterday happened."

It could have all ended so differently.

"I'm going to take a shower, then get dressed. Thankfully —it's the weekend..." I hesitated. "It is the weekend, right?"

"Almost," Aubrey said. "We missed classes yesterday, well you did...I hate myself that I was out all night and having fun, then going to classes while all of that was happening."

It was my turn to hug her. Yvette closed the circle and we clung to each other. "I'm okay," I repeated. And I'd say it again and again until we all believed it. "But I'm gonna shower, then caffeine...when does Dix get in? And when do I get my phone?"

Sniffling once, Aubrey went for her phone. "Dix was taking a red-eye, I'm surprised he's not already here."

"Bad weather in the midwest, the flight was delayed," Yvette informed us. "He was—not happy. But I think his last text said he would be here by noon. We were to not let you out of our sight."

I summoned a smile. "Good thing I don't have to go anywhere."

"And you have three watchdogs in the other room." Yvette gave me a pointed look. "Please say I can get rid of them..."

"One of them lives here," I pointed out.

"Then two of them. I can live with that option, at least the roommate seemed decent."

"Yeah," I pushed the hair out of my face. "I'm gonna shower." Cause all at once guilt raked through me for how sad Jonas had seemed when he brought up the fact we'd been becoming friends.

The problem was—we *had* been. Then Dad... well then again, they didn't know anything about Dad's other kids. Not like they were in the news. Most of the parents were more than happy to cash the checks and keep their kids out of the insanity.

Even Jackie—to a point. But me finding them, stitching us together... maybe we didn't need Dad, but I liked to think we needed each other.

"Hey," Aubrey said, sticking her head in the bathroom as I turned on the shower.

"Shouldn't you be out there keeping her from killing them?"

"She won't kill them. It's a taser. They might shit themselves and I'm fine with that."

I opened my mouth, then snapped it shut again. "Fair enough."

"You okay? And yes, I know you're not, but—are you okay? For real? With the security? With Dix? We know there's an investigation. With your dad?"

"It's going to hit the news sooner or later. The gossips are going to get it or the people who kidnapped me will leak it and I don't really want to think about that part."

"Kait." She never liked it when I deflected on the big stuff.

"Dix is great. I have no problems with him." He looked after me. He was also a friend. "He'll be protective and he'll watch my back and I *know* him. So that helps. I hate the idea of increasing security, but it's better than the alternative...as for Dad..." I lifted my hands. "I don't know. They said he paid the ransom, but they clearly don't know about the other kids and they don't know shit about me or my relationship with him."

"I accept that," Aubrey said. "But they want to know more and they are very invested right now."

"I can't do anything with that." When she raised her eyebrows, I spread my arms. "What do you want me to say, Aubrey? I don't know what to do with them or if I even want to—and I can't make them important. I just can't…"

The connections I'd made with them…

"Sweetie, it's okay to want more. I mean, I would prefer it if it were with less douchey douchebags, but—they did fight for you. They are fighting for you. They haven't left and Yvette is *not* as nice as we are."

The deadpan delivery damn near killed me. I put a hand to my side as I laughed. "Don't make me laugh."

"Think about it. You had sex with one of them. I know you've made out with him before and you definitely made out with the Ninja Dick."

I grimaced. "Ninja kisser."

"Yeah, I said what I said," she told me flatly. "Jonas isn't so bad though…"

"Are you advocating for him?"

"Maybe listening to *him* helps you both. Captain Inappropriate with his students and the Ninja Dick—they can work harder."

I would not laugh.

I would not laugh.

"I hate you."

"I know." She grinned. "Go ahead and shower, I'll be right out here if you need me. Then we'll do coffee and food. We can plan after…"

Some of my mirth fled. "Yeah…"

"Kait," she said when I kept standing there and I turned

away. She was already stepping out as I stripped off my night clothes. I moved slowly but I could do it.

Once in the shower, I braced a hand against the wall and let the hot water beat down on me. Fuck, that hurt. It was like it highlighted every bruise on my body.

Glancing down at my abdomen, I frowned at the clear footprint there. Had they fucking *stepped* on me?

The longer I stood there, the warmer my muscles became and the easier it was to move. Just letting the water wash over me, I tried to put together the pieces.

Waking up in Ramsey's bed.

Stealing his clothes.

Going for coffee.

Leaving a message for Lachlan.

I wanted—

Yeah, it didn't matter what I wanted. The sound of someone running up on me and then hitting me. Feeling my cheek bounce off the pavement. The ache in my jaw.

I lifted a hand to touch the scrape on my cheek. Being hit again... wait they were pressing down on me, not letting me get up.

Tears burned in my eyes—then the mask being put over my face. They said something.

I'd *heard* them. It was a *them*. But nothing brought the nebulous words or voices into relief. If anything, they seemed to be fading more and more.

Aggravated, I beat my hand against the wall then turned back into the water. As soon as I finished showering, I wrapped a towel around me. I tried to wrap one around my hair but that required bending...

Yeah, that sucked.

"Aubrey..."

"Right here, babe." And she was. Between us, we got my hair toweled down and combed. She offered to blow-dry it, but I left it damp for now. Since it wasn't a class day, I skipped the uniform and went for something comfy.

A sweatshirt to cover up the bruises, and leggings. Then she found me some fuzzy socks. I needed the armor. I studied the door to the other room and Aubrey raised a brow.

"Problem?"

"It's really quiet. Do you think Yvette killed them?"

"Nah," Aubrey said. "She's probably just glaring daggers at them and making them wish they were dead."

Another laugh worked out of me, and when I was ready, I glanced at Ramsey's t-shirt where I'd folded it and left it on the dresser. I still couldn't believe he had one of *our* first band shirts.

More, I didn't know what to do with that.

"Coffee?" Aubrey asked and I dragged my attention back to the present.

"Oh my god, yes," I said and she grinned. When she opened the door, I wasn't the only one leaning a little to see what the lay of the land was.

The guys were all still here.

That was impressive.

Yvette ignored them from the kitchenette where she stood guard over the coffee maker.

Jonas rose as soon as I came out, as did Lachlan. Ramsey was already on his feet, arms folded but the weight of his gaze settled on me like he'd wrapped an arm around my shoulders.

That was both unsettling and a little scary.

"I was going to make you coffee but Frenchy wouldn't let me," Jonas said.

Frenchy.

"Bitchy is more like it," Lachlan said.

Ramsey sighed. "Her name is Yvette." The patience in his tone suggested he'd said it a few times. Maybe he really did want a flag of peace.

"Coffee, KC?"

"Please," I said as I made my way across the room toward the kitchenette, with Aubrey moving in my wake. I was all too aware of the hands twitching as if they were resisting reaching out to steady me.

Only when I got to Yvette did I glance back and find all three of them staring.

Well, this was going to end well...

Fourteen

KC

The guys lingering while we had coffee wasn't uncomfortable at all. Yes, I was absolutely being sarcastic. My new phone arrived via courier. Ramsey descended the stairs with Aubrey to sign for it, leaving me with Yvette, Lachlan, and Jonas.

Tension practically vibrated in the air, but I focused on drinking the coffee and waiting for the pain relievers to kick in. The silence dragged over me as I took a long drink of coffee.

"KC?" Jonas broke first and I glanced at him. "Hungry?"

"No," I admitted. The coffee was nirvana. Yvette had added extra chocolate to it and whip cream. Too much sugar, but I kind of craved that at the moment. "I probably should eat," I admitted. "There's leftovers, I think."

"Aubrey put your food up last night," Lachlan confirmed. So many questions populated the haunted forests of his eyes. "I can go get you anything you want, too."

"You don't—have to, but thank you." I took another drink of the coffee.

"Think you're up for talking?" Lachlan's gaze was steady on me.

"Not really," I admitted, not fully turning the idea over in my head. "Not even sure what to talk about." I'd pretty much said all I had to on the subject.

Lachlan studied me where I leaned against the counter. "Well, let's start with how are you feeling today?"

"And maybe come sit down?" Jonas phrased it more as a question. "You still look rough."

"I still feel rough." I could admit that without giving anything away. Cutting a look at Yvette, I raised my brows. She'd said nothing since handing me coffee. Her attention wasn't on me. No, she saved that flat, narrow-eyed gaze for the pair across the room.

With a half-shrug, she gestured to the sofa and I made my way over there. Not giving into the need to limp or grimace, even if I was one long damn ache. If it had just been me and Yvette, I probably would have groaned and hammed it up. She would give me shit and then we'd both laugh.

It would hurt, but it would be so much better than this uncomfortable sticky tension polluting the air. The weight of Jonas and Lachlan's regard pressed down on me and I half-expected my ears to pop like we were on ascent.

As soon as I sank down on the sofa, Lachlan took a seat on the table right in front of me.

"You feel rough," he said, echoing my earlier sentiment. "I don't want to push..." The unspoken "but" dangled there at the end.

"Pushing is who you are," I told him before I took another drink. Fuck knew it was true. Lachlan was the pushiest of bastards, from dunking me in the pond to shoving himself into my company for runs, to all the ninja kisses.

A hint of a smile tipped his lips and his eyes flashed with humor. "It is kind of me, huh?"

"Probably not something to be proud of," Yvette commented. "Some of your behavior could be considered assault."

He jerked his gaze from me up to Yvette. "I never tried to hurt her."

"Well, good to know that wasn't your intention--but if that's how you treat someone you don't want to hurt...you might have more problems than you think you do."

"Yvette," I said softly. "I'm not making excuses for him, but this isn't helping."

"Fine, but he can keep his ninja dick, fingers, and lips away from you unless you request a visit."

A choked sound escaped Jonas. I canted my head to glance at him. He snickered. Even with his arms folded and one hand pressed against his mouth, he couldn't quite keep the chuckles contained.

"Laugh it up, asshole," Lachlan said, though his glare seemed neutered by his smirk and Jonas laughed harder.

The laughter shaking him was entertaining in its own right and I was having a hard time suppressing my smile in response. When Jonas met my gaze, his eyes lit up and his laughter increased.

"What's so funny?" Yvette demanded, irritation rifling every single syllable.

"The request a visit," Jonas admitted, a real grin on his face. "Lachlan doesn't know how to say please."

For his part, Lachlan snorted but he didn't deny it. "Sometimes it's easier to ask for forgiveness than it is permission."

"How is that working out for you?" It was my turn to challenge him and Lachlan sighed.

The door to the suite opened before he could respond and Aubrey strode inside with a package—my new phone. Relief swarmed through me. That phone was my lifeline to everyone and everything. Not knowing what happened to mine—even if we had *bricked* it, didn't make the lack any easier.

Instead of Ramsey following her inside though, Dix appeared. His scowl was ferocious as his gaze swept the room before he focused on me. I shoved to my feet, throwing my own balance when my sides twinged and I nearly lost my coffee.

Lachlan steadied me with one hand and he caught the coffee. Concern erased his smile and I grimaced. "Thank you," I managed to push the words out between my teeth before I pulled away. I didn't have to go far because Dix was just there.

"Goddammit, gorgeous," he muttered and I folded into his hug as he turned me away from everyone.

Silence blanketed the room as I leaned into Dix. He smelled like honey and coffee with a hint of syrup. There was a spot on his shirt. Probably from breakfast on the plane. When I straightened, he leaned back to give me a once over.

All at once, his expression turned furious. I braced for it. "I already informed the school you were going to have personal security on campus. They tried to diminish the reasons for it, but their head of security signed off immediately. He's got three men who will be in rotating shifts on the door downstairs."

Fuck. Yes, it was necessary. But what little normalcy I'd cobbled together had been utterly destroyed. We were back to my normal—the world I'd grown up in and probably shouldn't have bothered to try and escape.

He studied me a beat, his hands light on my biceps. Whatever he searched for, he must have found, because he nodded. "I'll be with you for all your classes and anywhere else. You don't walk out that door unless I'm with you. You want to go for a run, I'm with you. You want to go down to get coffee, I'm with you. You decide to shower somewhere that isn't that bathroom right there, I'm with you."

I wrinkled my nose but he wasn't kidding.

"It's not long, kid. This is how it is. You want to stay and finish your degree, we're doing it this way. I talked to the label and to your manager. They are paying for the security for any off-campus moves, we'll handle it on-campus. Your lawyers are already talking to the school…"

Shit. "My lawyers or Mom's?"

"Yours," he told me firmly. "I know what you wanted…I know *why* you wanted it. But this was the last straw. So agree and be a good girl about this or you and I are leaving for Los Angeles tonight. I'll carry you onto the plane if I have to."

"Excuse the fuck out of you," Lachlan all but snarled and I blew out a breath.

"It's fine, Lachlan…"

"It's not fine, Ace. I don't give a shit who he is, he doesn't get to talk to you that way."

"Who are you again?" Dix asked, moving so he was between me and the guys.

"Stop," I ordered. Lachlan took a step forward and to my shock, Jonas moved with him. Yvette looked moderately amused, but Aubrey seemed to be wearing a frown similar to the one tightening my own face.

Dix didn't back down, if anything, all he did was let his bag slide off his shoulder and to the floor. I'd never thought of him as the guy who embraced fights, but I'd seen both Lachlan and Jonas lose it.

"Stop," Ramsey echoed my command and he moved between his brothers and Dix. "This isn't open for debate—from us. If Siren decides she doesn't like it, *then* we can tackle the subject."

Jonas switched his gaze from Dix to Ramsey. The glare didn't lessen, if anything, his eyes seemed to go icier then finally he exhaled. "You're right."

"Wait—what?" Lachlan cut a look at Jonas.

"Ramsey is right. This is about KC. Not us. I want her safe."

The last four words steadied me. Not just because of what he said, but because he meant them. When he glanced at me, I sighed.

I missed him.

I missed the friendship we'd been forming.

"Thank you," I mouthed more than said the words.

He nodded. "Will Dix be staying in our suite?"

"I'd prefer that," Dix said without glancing at me. "But the school may not go for it. Space is at a premium. We'll figure it out."

"Agreed," Ramsey said. "If necessary, you can stay in my suite downstairs."

That offer surprised me and Lachlan jerked.

"What the actual fuck?"

"You're a student here," Ramsey told him. "You can stay on this floor. He isn't. We'll figure it out."

What a mess. I groaned and that pulled all of their attention.

"You know what," Aubrey said. "We can debate all of this later. For now, you need to rest." She glared at me. "I'll start your phone set up. You sit down. Have you eaten? Taken your pain meds?"

Just like that, the debates and the arguments were all shoved aside as they hovered. My headache seemed to increase but more because this was just making everyone's life difficult.

Eventually, Ramsey took Dix to meet with the school admin and with the head of security. Dix made me pinky swear to stay in my room. Not hard, I really didn't want to go anywhere.

Chinese didn't sound as appealing so *after* Lachlan went downstairs to shower, Aubrey and Yvette volunteered to go on a pizza run. I had a feeling they needed the break from the drama and probably time to discuss what to do with a problem named KC.

If Lachlan had been here still, I didn't think they would have both left. Jonas was different, so they just asked Jonas to promise he would also not leave until either Dix or they were back.

Not a hard promise for him to offer. The sudden evacuation made the quiet so much louder. Jonas made fresh coffee and brought it over to where I was seated.

When I glanced at him, he held out the fresh cup and I found myself smiling. Not much, but it was a smile. Even if it pulled at all of my bruises.

"Thank you," I said and he nodded. He cleaned up the other cup and straightened the room before he came back with a blanket.

Curious, I watched him as he settled it over my legs. My new phone was charging next to me as it finished downloading everything from the cloud. Once he draped the blanket over me, he sat on the other side of the sofa with his own coffee.

"KC?"

I glanced at him.

"I'm sorry," he said. Two such simple words yet so heavy in their meaning.

"Me too," I admitted. I didn't know exactly what he was sorry for, but I did miss our friendship. I missed the growing comfort between us. I missed—I missed what we had *before*. Before Dad performed that song. Before the attack and kidnapping.

Before the fridge.

"Think we can—fix it?" There was absolutely no pressure in that question. It was more a melancholic curiosity.

"I don't know," I admitted. "So much has happened."

"Yeah."

The silence elongated and then he picked up the remote

and turned on the television. When he went straight to the reunion for *Love is Blind*, I couldn't help the smile stretching my pained cheeks.

"We still have this," he said and I caught him glancing at me.

That we did.

He hit play and as the show started, I said, "Thank you, Hot Shot." Thank you for not making this any more strained than it was. Thank you for caring. Thank you—for just being there. I tried to pack it all in there, but I wasn't sure if it communicated.

He nodded once. "Thank you."

For being all right. For listening. For, if not opening the door, at least not locking it.

Okay, so maybe we didn't need all the words.

And maybe—just maybe—we could salvage our friendship.

<h1 style="text-align:center">Fifteen</h1>

RAMSEY

Two steps into my suite, I jerked my tie loose and worked to free the top two buttons on my shirt. I'd never been suffocated by the uniform before. On campus, at school, whether I was in a class to learn the material or to teach it, the dress clothes had always served as armor.

Right now, it felt more like a prison jumpsuit.

"Someone's in a bad mood," Lachlan drawled from where he sat on the sofa with a book open that he was ignoring in favor of his phone. There was a lot of that going around.

"Fuck off," I informed him as I stalked past and into my own room.

His low whistle followed me, but for once, my asshole brother didn't pursue me with his goddamn agenda. More than a week of arguing with him, *and* Jonas, while also avoiding Mom's calls *and* trying to keep tabs on Kaitlin had left me on edge.

I had to fight the urge to rip off the buttons on the dress shirt. My hands seemed to shake with the effort to keep them steady. It was ridiculous. It was like I'd done a triple shot of espresso.

As it was, I managed to strip, hang up my clothes, and get into the shower without ripping anything. I switched from hot shower to cold to try and shake the fog loose. Keeping my distance from her was killing me.

Ten minutes later, the smell of pizza, garlic bread, and—cinnamon rolls drifted in and my stomach lodged its immediate protest. I'd barely eaten today. If anything, all I'd done was shotgun coffee and stalk KC as she took her last final.

Jonas was with her, so was her *bodyguard*. He wasn't sleeping in the dorms, that was a small measure of mercy. Administration had given him a guest cottage that was usually reserved for visiting faculty and guest lecturers.

While Lachlan still occupied the second bedroom here, he went up every single night and slept on their sofa. I couldn't really fault him for it. If KC went running—bruised ribs be damned apparently—, Lachlan went with her along with Dix.

Yvette wasn't on campus at all, but she visited daily. She'd taken a room at one of the hotels near town. She also had a driver and security to bring her back and forth. Campus security wasn't being remotely surreptitious.

I hated seeing how much Kaitlin struggled under the constant observation. Was it the best thing for her physical safety? Absolutely. But what about her mental health? Her emotional?

I wanted to talk to her. Not just wanted—*needed* to speak to her. There never seemed to be a time when I could see her *alone*. Aubrey or Yvette was always with her or Dix. If Jonas got time with her, he wasn't sharing.

Dragging a t-shirt on, I stared at the bed in my room. *This* was why I hadn't wanted her to leave that morning. But I could hardly fault her for—

A rapid knock on my bedroom door had me pivoting to face it.

"Let's go, Big Brother," Lachlan called. "Family meeting. You, me, and Jonas."

"What?" I went for basketball shorts rather than sweats. I had zero intentions of going out tonight unless I had to. The school shifted final dates, delayed classes completing, and cited some bullshit reason. All of it was to cover for the massive breach in security. Finals for college level classes kicked off this week and I had my own to finish. And decisions to be made that I'd been putting off.

Yanking the door open, I stared out in the suite where Jonas stood opening a soda and Lachlan pointed to the food. "Family meeting," Lachlan repeated like I'd misheard him.

To be fair, I thought I had. "About what?"

"Ace."

One hand on my hip, I bowed my head. "Lach..."

"Don't even start that shit with me," Lachlan argued as he flipped open the pizza boxes. "This is not only me being obsessive."

"It's about you being obsessive, though," Jonas argued. He checked his phone.

"Like you're not."

Jonas definitely didn't deny it.

"We're all obsessed in our very different ways—I just happen to be blunt about it."

Lachlan sat down, then claimed a piece of pizza as Jonas and I stood there.

Twisting to look back at me, Lachlan stared. "Well? You going to sit there and brood like you have every other fucking night or get your ass over here and plan? I, for one, am fucking over letting her friends and her whatever the fuck Dix is make the decisions."

This had every single element of being a terrible idea. "I believe she made her feelings clear."

"Right, Mr. Robot, she was stressed, overwrought, and pretty pissed considering we'd just gotten her out of a *refrigerator*. I think she had every right to throw shade at us." He raised his slice of pizza as if it were a toast. "That was then..."

Rolling my eyes, I headed for the kitchenette. I grabbed plates, paper towels, and sodas before I headed back to where Jonas had taken a seat in one of the chairs, albeit reluctantly.

"She hasn't changed her mind," Jonas volunteered. "Whatever went down with Gibs—I don't think she was kidding about that."

"No, I don't think she was either." That had been another thought I wrestled with. Gibs had always boasted about her, his—you couldn't fake that kind of affection. So how the hell had it been seven years?

"Nothing we can do about him in the immediate," Lachlan said after he set his half-eaten slice on the plate I thrust at him. He made a face but I wasn't cleaning up after him. I pulled out a slice for myself.

"I think we owe it to KC to call him on it though," Jonas said.

"You did." Or had he already forgotten that he challenged Gibs on the call.

"I know, but he hasn't said a word to me since." Jonas' expression grew more troubled. "I texted him about her."

Lachlan paused, pizza halfway to his mouth. "And?"

"He didn't respond." Jonas shrugged. "He read it, but he didn't answer so maybe he's—I don't know."

That was a struggle. Jonas and Gibs were tight. They'd always been closer than Lachlan and I were to him. "Well, we can't make her reach out to him, and we can assume he isn't reaching out to her."

"Maybe," Lachlan said before he took another bite. He

washed that down and shook his head. "Nothing we do is going to change that for them. What I want to fix is *my* relationship with her."

Unsurprising. "Well, I guess we should be glad you decided to involve us." My dry comment earned a flash of a smile from Jonas.

"You should be," Lachlan said without an ounce of irony. "You're too damn much of a rule follower and he's too afraid of her..."

"I'm not afraid of her," Jonas snapped back. "Respecting her doesn't make me afraid."

"You share a suite with her."

"I also share *music* with her," Jonas countered. "And we were doing just fine until—"

I took a long drink while I waited and when Lachlan opened his mouth, I gave him a sharp head shake. Let Jonas work this out for himself. Granted, I didn't think "family meeting" was going to work here but it couldn't hurt.

"Until Gibs performed a song I scored and she added the lyrics to, and dedicated it to me." His sigh was so heavy it made *me* feel the weight of it. "The music thing—it was working. I could talk to her with the music, it—was a peace offering and then she gave it back with lyrics and I even helped her with another song."

He sounded so damn lost.

"Then Gibs just fucked that all up." That—that got me. The fact he was able to call out Gibs for being the one at fault.

Even Lachlan frowned. "How did he know about the song?"

"He knew I'd been writing music," Jonas admitted. "I used to show it to him sometimes. I've even given him some pieces before, nothing like this..."

So how did... "Mom." That was what he'd said on the

phone. Fuck, that part had barely registered when my main concern had been Kaitlin.

Jonas grimaced and Lachlan scowled.

"Makes sense, she was worried about him. If she found the music, she might have wanted to inspire him." Yeah, that was a stretch.

"Well, we know she didn't know Ace had anything to do with it," Lachlan said as he finished his drink and stood up. "I'm getting another one, you guys good?"

"Fine," I said and Jonas just waved him off.

"Maybe. I was going to ask, but then KC just stopped talking to me. We were friends, for real, and she just cut me off. So maybe when she says that Gibs hasn't spoken to her in seven years..." He sounded so damn hopeful.

"I think she's telling the truth," I said. "The night I found her in the rain, she was devastated. Absolutely broken-hearted. She'd gotten bad news about her sister."

Sister. Not her daughter. Her sister.

Lachlan walked back in. "So you thought you'd bring her back for a little comfort dick?"

I stared at him and he spread his hands.

"Sorry, I'm frustrated."

"And you're an asshole," I pointed out. "No, I didn't bring her back here intending to have sex with her. Have I kissed her before? Yes. Should I have? *No.* Did it stop me from kissing her again? Also no." I scrubbed a hand over my face. I needed to shave. "I wanted to calm her down, she wasn't *hysterical* per se, but she was the most non-verbal I've ever seen her, and she was devastated."

"So what happened?" Jonas asked after I went quiet. I stared at the slice of pizza I was holding then dropped it back on the plate.

"I wanted her to get out of the wet clothes and into a warm shower—*alone*—" I tacked that on to stall any of their idiot comments. "But she wasn't even moving and when she finally did, she just stood there crying and I was trying to help her. Then she kissed me or maybe I kissed her—"

This was not a conversation I wanted to have with either of them.

"She said she knew what she was asking me for and she managed to provoke me at the same time, but it was the most life I'd seen in her eyes since I'd found her."

Beautiful, tortured, and needy. She'd *needed* me.

"If I'm honest, I wanted her. It wasn't a hard argument for her to win me over. I was also convinced she'd already had a kid and was probably a lot more experienced..."

"Only she wasn't," Lachlan said and there was a tightness in his voice I recognized.

"Yeah." Blowing out a breath, I leaned back in the chair. "The rest of that night is a conversation between her and me. Not us. I asked her to stay, because I knew we needed to talk. She was still so broken and she didn't want to talk then, but I hoped after a few hours... and some sleep."

"She did call me," Lachlan said. "Called me and said she wanted to talk to all three of us."

"Then she didn't make it back here." That just brought that whole nightmare to life again. "When we did finally talk —I don't think she was interested in building bridges anymore. To be honest, I can't say I blame her."

"No," Jonas said. "We've—talked a little. But it's not like before, she's distracted and hurting. They're shielding her from us." He hated that part.

Not that I was a fan.

"So, we need a plan," Lachlan said. "Cause I'm not giving up on Ace. She needs us to prove that we're not the douchebags who can't be trusted, then we do that."

"We *are* the douchebags she didn't trust," I pointed out,

not that I was fond of that term. "We also made a lot of assumptions."

"We did," Lachlan agreed. "We fucked up. So we gotta fix it. Because I'm not giving Ace up."

I frowned. "You do hear yourself right now, don't you?"

"Yes," Lachlan said. "I came back to this school for her. I'll be here next year too—"

"If she comes back," Jonas said and I sighed. "She might not. I wasn't sure about college either. Los Angeles could be fun though."

Los Angeles. "You want to follow her?"

"You don't?" Lachlan challenged and I shoved up from the chair to pace. "Come on Ramsey, you just said you need to talk to her. That's not going to happen for us if we don't make it happen."

"Why are you including us?" Jonas asked and I couldn't really fault that question. So I joined him in staring at our brother.

"Because I can't do this alone. She trusts Jonas some and I think she wants to trust you," he continued, nodding to me. "I've got ground to make up. So you guys are going to soften the terrain up."

"While you what?" I couldn't believe we were actually having this conversation.

"Stalk her," was Jonas' response. "He's really good at it."

"Chase her," he countered. "I'm good at pursuing Ace, and I think she likes it more than she admits."

"You have a problem," I told him. "If she doesn't want you around, I'm not helping you torture her."

"It won't be torture," Lachlan said, reaching for another piece of pizza. "I have a plan."

Oh, kill me.

"Besides... it's going to be fun."

Not the word I would use and at the same time, I didn't

want to let her go either. We had a lot of ground to make up and a lot to prove.

"At least if we're close we can try to protect her," I offered up and that snared Jonas' attention.

"Now you're talking." Lachlan grinned. "Now, let's talk Los Angeles and how we're going to do this..."

END PART ONE

Part Two

Sixteen

Scrubs covered me from head to foot, my hair was tucked in securely, and I wore a mask. Pen hated the mask. Even sleepy-eyed and cranky, she tugged at it. As much as I wanted to give her everything she asked for, the risk of getting her sick was too great.

Capturing her hand gently, I fought my own sigh. "Song?" She didn't have to see my lips to understand the word.

"Sing-sing," she commanded and it eased one of the boulders off my heart. The doctors were all conferring on a plan. The chemo hadn't worked. It proved more of a stop-gap rather than a cure.

She'd lost most of her hair. Her bald head gleamed and I wanted to blow raspberries against it and tickle her. The sound of her laughter was a balm to my soul. But I wasn't here to make *me* feel better.

Three hours after graduation, Dix drove us to a local airport and we took a short flight to New York, where we boarded a longer flight back to Los Angeles. As soon as we were back, I'd headed straight for the hospital.

That was just a week earlier. I'd donated blood and everything else they needed to run their genetic tests. So had Bronson. We were both eighteen. Jackie, Aubrey, and Yvette had all done the same. We were going to cast as wide a pool as necessary.

I'd even called Dad.

Once.

He didn't answer.

So I left a message.

For Pen, I would do anything.

The ball was technically in his court, but if I had to drive up to Tahoe, I would.

Whatever it took.

"Sing-sing," Pen complained and I hummed.

"Sorry, sweet baby," I told her. Digging down deep, I looked for the words and the tunes. It was difficult to sing when all I wanted to do was cry.

We'd asked for all our siblings to get tested. It was tricky because kids under the age of eighteen couldn't be donors, but we were looking for even a glimmer of hope. The other moms in the equation weren't huge fans but they'd agreed. Everyone had, really, except Trace.

He still wasn't returning calls. Had he changed his cell? I'd asked Dix to see if we could get someone out near Trace to stop by. If I had to, I'd go there too. Whatever it took.

Whatever.

Blinking back the tears, I started with one of Pen's favorite lullabies. Today had been a challenging day for her, the fever earlier had made her restless. I'd spent half my day in meetings with the label and our attorneys. Another two hours meeting with Pen's medical team, Jackie, Bronson, and the girls came with me for that.

Dix had become my permanent shadow. Fortunately, it meant when I needed to cut loose, he was ready for it and kept a go bag in the car for me now. It was harder to slip out without Yvette or Aubrey noticing, but I could still do it. Then there was the issue with Mom…

I just didn't have the energy to cope with her so-called engagement, the rumors, her agent's absolute apoplectic tirade, Trish's demands, or Johnny's broken heart. Johnny, however, I would make time for and I'd invited him to come and stay at the house.

It wasn't like I didn't have the room there. He declined so far, but he did agree to dinner. I had a few days before that. I'd just keep working on him. One of the pediatric oncology nurses came in while I was singing. Dark eyes and skin tone told me it was Divya or Aditi. They were both on this shift and absolute magic with Pen when she was unhappy.

As she drew a little closer, I smiled behind my mask. Divya winked at me. I'd only met her once without the scrubs and mask, but she had the most playful eyes. Aditi was so much more sober. Pen squeezed a hand at her, waving.

"Hello, little darling," Divya murmured, miming a finger press to where her mouth was behind the mask. "Let your sister sing. Not often I get a private concert."

The lightness in her tone helped with another of the boulders on my heart, shifting it over and letting me breathe. I ran through all of Pen's favorite lullabies. Then just—segued right into the song I'd written for her—the one Jonas helped on.

Melancholy swamped me as Pen settled more and more. By the time the last note drifted off, she was sound asleep against my shoulder.

"That was beautiful," Divya told me. "I hadn't heard that one before."

"No one has," I admitted. I hadn't really sung it all the way through to anyone and had only practiced it minimally.

The song hurt and helped in equal measures. "I'm going to put her in her bed... please tell me we don't have to do bloodwork."

I hated when they had to stick her. She was such a trooper but her tears always wrenched me.

"No sticks for the little darling," Divya promised. "I just came in to run her vitals. I know you need to go soon, so I'll be with her. Miss Jackie is coming soon. She likes to spend the early evenings with her, and Ms. Davina has all but taken over the nights."

With care, I settled Pen back into her crib. Despite the fact the room was in a hospital, we'd added toys, a play area, and colorful blankets. Everything had to be sanitized before it could be brought in. Still, nothing we did made it *not* a hospital.

I feathered my fingers over her forehead, wishing I could press a kiss to it. "I changed her diaper an hour ago," I told Divya.

"Thank you. Now, you're going to go home and get some rest, aren't you?" The measured look reminded me that I'd been at the hospital daily since we got back to Los Angeles.

Bronson had dragged Jackie out to eat. He wanted me to go, but I just wasn't hungry. They'd be back soon and it would make them feel better if I at least *appeared* to be taking it easy.

"I'm going to head out." Rather than lie about the destination, I just left it off. "Are you sure you're fine to stay with her?"

"Absolutely, I have nowhere else I need to be and I'm on shift for the next twelve hours. So you can get some sleep." The last sounded like an order. Funny, everyone kept trying to mother me.

Everyone. Even Dix.

"Thank you, Divya." I mimed another kiss to Pen who snuffled in her sleep but seemed so damn peaceful. Leaving was always harder, because I had to leave Pen there. I just wanted to make all of this go away and take her home.

She should be toddling around and playing in a little kiddie pool, not hooked up with a port for medications and ravaged by the treatment that wasn't making her better. I had to wonder if her mother's drug abuse had contributed. The doctors couldn't confirm it, but they also didn't deny it.

Once through to the clean room, and into an antechamber, I stripped off the medical gown. Most of my stuff was secured in a locker, and it took almost no time to drag it on. I texted Dix as soon as I was in there. His acknowledgement vibrated a moment later, he was waiting to walk me down. The car was in the VIP lot.

Right, no more wandering on my own. The police, campus security, *and* FBI had nothing new to report. They'd lost the money on the web, hence the Bitcoin. The email address was obtained through a grab it and dump site to mask where it really came from.

Every lead had apparently vanished into the ether. They assured me they were continuing to look, but until there was some resolution in the case, I needed to take precautions.

Dix was one of those precautions.

Speaking of whom, he rose as I let myself out of the changing room and gave me a measured look. "Where are we going?"

"I need to move..."

He sighed, then nodded before offering his arm. I didn't need to hold onto him to walk but when I didn't take his arm, he had a tendency to just wrap it around me and tuck me close.

The kidnapping had amped up his protective instincts to a fifteen. Nothing I said or attempted to do would soothe him. At least Dix didn't want to lock me up in my room like it was a tower and dig a moat sixty feet deep around the house.

The same could *not* be said for Yvette and Aubrey. Jackie was also not a fan. I'd told her and Bronson but only because they did not deserve to be ambushed. At least when I told them, I was in one piece and had already begun to heal. My ribs were much better and the bruises were pretty much gone.

That didn't make *them* feel better, but it definitely helped. So far, the press had not gotten a hold of the story and whatever happened to my phone, I could only hope the security on it kept it locked and my info safe until we'd bricked it.

Hope was in short supply so I would take what I could get.

Once at the car, the summer heat swept over me and chased away some of the chill. Unfortunately, the scent of the hospital antiseptic lingered in my sinuses. I had a feeling I was never going to shake that smell or the apprehension.

"There's a silent disco on the beach tonight in Malibu." Dix offered as he slid behind the wheel. "A new club is having a soft opening down on the strip—Abaddon—multi-tiered and soon-to-be the hottest ticket in town."

The beach would be too open, even with a silent disco. Abaddon was on the cusp of burgeoning popularity, which meant it had a little more anonymity.

"And?" I pulled off my shoes before reaching for a bottle of water. Dix always offered up three possibilities.

He almost glared. Almost.

"The Dark Room."

Oh, I hadn't been there in a while. A converted warehouse that used to be popular with raves, now a dance and night club that offered privacy, sex rooms, strippers, and more, in addition to straight up dance rooms.

Sexy.

"Dark Room," I said, before checking my phone. It was after six. Later than I expected. "When do they open?"

"Two hours," Dix told me. "Time enough for you to eat before you go."

Right. There were a few messages, including one from Aubrey saying she was going out to dinner with Forrest. He was in town?

Frowning, I messaged her back. Had I missed his visit?

AUBREY

No, I didn't know he was coming. Texted this afternoon to say he was in LA for the rest of the week. You need me?

I shook my head.

ME

Always. But you need a break from babysitting. Take Yvette with you, she should check out Forrest too.

Delight curved through me at her immediate middle finger.

AUBREY

She already invited herself. You still at the hospital?

We hadn't left the parking lot yet.

ME

Yes and Dix is with me. Go, have fun. Get laid. Love you.

She sent back her own love and then she was gone. Well, that was those two dealt with. I glanced up to find Dix watching me.

"Yes, I'll eat. Go find us a food truck—I liked that Mediterranean we had when we got back. If not them— maybe tacos. Fish tacos."

"You got it," he said as he pulled out. "I brought the blonde and the redhead wigs."

I made a face but nodded. Never the same wig two nights running and never the same outfits. My tattoos stood out, but depending on what I wore, I could hide them. The hair though?

Yeah, nobody missed that. Anastasia was going to touch it up this weekend.

"Thanks Dix," I said, keeping my tone measured. "I know this is making you crazy."

"I like you safe, gorgeous. Not going to lie. But if you need to dance, then we'll dance. But no disappearing with the car this time."

I resisted the urge to flip him off. I went looking for him but he didn't let that go. Instead, I just went for mollifying him. "I won't."

I glanced at the bag on the other seat and unzipped it. Club clothes, cosmetics, and wigs. After I ate, I'd go be someone else for a little while.

"Good girl," Dix said with a nod. "Now, let's feed you."

I bit back a smile. At least he didn't call me scrawny or mock my tits. Just like that, all I could see was the three douchebags and I had to sigh.

How the hell was I supposed to get away from them if I couldn't stop thinking about them?

Seventeen

LACHLAN

Neither Gibs nor Mom showed up for Jonas' graduation—and Ace's for that matter. They didn't show up for Ramsey's college graduation either. Ramsey didn't bother with the walk, that surprised me. Then again, he didn't do what he did for the accolades. Ramsey's dad flew in to take him out to dinner.

Like mine had, Jonas' dad skipped the formalities but he sent a card and present. He'd also promised to see him over the summer. For now, we remained united in our plan. A first according to Ramsey. I didn't comment on his judginess. Not at the moment.

While Ace's friends and bodyguard—*bodyguard my ass, I see how he looks at her*—kept the circle tight around her, Jonas had been able to talk to her some. Other than letting us know she was exhausted and a little more receptive when she wasn't surrounded, he hadn't shared much more.

I half-expected the girls to do something for their graduation. Rumors, speculation, and jokes abounded. But I only half-paid attention to them.

The big day came and went rather unremarkably, except I'd managed to snap a photo of Ace as she accepted her diploma with my phone. While I'd hardly been the only one filming it, I didn't rush to share my photograph or the video. Rules be damned, there were students and family present that didn't seem to care.

The photo I'd taken arrested me. The quiet pride on her face rocked me. An almost shy smile on her lips and a definite glow in her eyes. The bruises had faded or were covered with cosmetics. From where I had to sit, I only had a limited view of her profile. Yet, when her friend was up on that stage she wore the exact same expression.

Genuine happiness.

I'd never resented someone else's friendships before. Yet, here I was. Particularly afterward when Yvette greeted them with hugs and the three of them wore the same smile. I resented their closeness because I envied it. I wanted to be the one smiling at her. I wanted to be the recipient of her smiles.

Really fucking annoying.

They left within hours though, only packing the minimum of their things, with movers coming for the rest. Jonas' regrets lingered in the air and mine were right there with them.

I headed for LA the following day. The drive took nearly four full days. Ramsey and Jonas arrived the day before I did because they flew, but I wanted my car out there. I spent the entirety of the drive listening to every single song in Torched's catalog, as well as a few they'd done with Bound Hearts—a group they were close with.

Whatever.

I was also working out my approach.

When I told Dad I planned to spend the summer in Los Angeles, he rented a place for me. It was large enough for all three of us, with some breathing room, and it had a pool. We weren't downtown or in Beverly Hills, but close.

Not that I spent much time there. No, I spent three days staking out her new schedule. They'd returned to her mother's house. According to Dad *and* gossip sites, her mother was currently at some retreat in upstate New York.

She was also engaged to some guru.

I'd never heard of him, but I wasn't sure what to do with the info but file it away. There had been no sign of them at the house in the three days I'd been watching it.

I saw Ace. I saw her friends.

I saw that fucker *Dix*.

If Ace left the property, it was *always* in his company. He drove, she sat in the back. I followed a couple of times. The destinations proved limited.

Hospital.

A place in Glendale. At least there, a guy had stepped out of the house to greet her and I recognized him from the photograph in her room.

Brother.

Yeah, that reminded me, I needed to talk to Dad about Gibs' "kids." Mom discouraged us from the gossip sites and she never mentioned any other children. She would know, right?

Or maybe she didn't care. Though her attitude about Ace suggested otherwise. That—that also annoyed me. Today, I'd followed Ace to the hospital. I kept watch on their car because getting inside proved difficult.

I tried.

You had to sign in to see the patient and I had no idea what the patient's full name was.

Fuck.

I'd bet even money that Ramsey or Jonas knew, but I was waiting to involve them in this part. I wanted them here because she might be more inclined to talk to them. Their relationships—as much as I hated to describe it that way—weren't as volatile as the one I had with Ace.

I liked that volatility. She never affected indifference with me. What I didn't like was being kept away from her.

What I hated was her *hurting*.

She *was* hurting.

Part of that was *my* fault, which meant it was on me to fix it. So, I needed to find my opening. Ace and I had built our relationship on—

"Stalking," Jonas' smart ass observation said from my memory, but I only spared him a mental flip-off. Conflict was our thing. She enjoyed it—some of the time.

I'd been a dick.

Most of the time.

Another sigh escaped me, but I was already starting the car when I caught sight of the BMW Dix drove leaving the VIP lot. Sunset was still an hour and a half off. I couldn't tell if she was alone in the car and I had to keep back a couple of car lengths.

It was easier when it was darker. I couldn't see if anyone else was in the car with them. They drove around for the better part of forty minutes before he diverted into a warehouse district, then to a converted warehouse.

A club.

Fuck yes, she was going to a club.

Good girl, Ace. Go somewhere I can find you.

I pulled over like I had to check something but used my phone to zoom in near the front where fucking Dix pulled up. He was handing his keys to a valet before he circled around to open the back door.

A redhead got out of the car.

She was so *not* a redhead.

Red hair to disguise her distinctive blue and a white outfit that looked painted on top and bottom. There was even a hint of fringe when she twisted to look up at Dix.

What got me was the jacket—what there was of it—covering her arms. She'd hidden everything distinctive about her. She better not be wearing fucking contacts. I gave them a beat to go inside before I found a spot.

It cost a little extra to grease the wheels and keep my car parked near the entrance and more to get inside. I'd heard about this club—The Dark Room. It was definitely not the kind of place she'd hit the previous summer.

Everything about this dance slash sex club was the kind of thing we thought about her before. So why was she here *now?*

No sooner did that thought take purchase than I was heading inside on the hunt for a redhead in a white skimpy outfit. I *needed* to see her more than my next breath of air. It had been too long since I'd seen her up close.

Since I'd touched her.

Since I'd fucking kissed her.

Music throbbed through the club. The Dark Room was definitely dark, with strobing lights and bass that beat in time with my pulse. The first floor was a straight up strip club. Dancers performed on the stage, tits flashed and ass was in abundance.

Male and female.

Equality on display. Nice.

I wasn't interested in them. Dance floors were upstairs. This was definitely a sex club because under the scents of sandalwood and incense, sex permeated the air along with the saltier scents of sweat. Clouds of perfume and cologne irritated my nose and my eyes but I scanned only as I headed for the stairs.

Dix was easier to find than Ace.

The fucker was parked at a bar on the second level. He had a glass in hand. The liquid sparkled around the ice as he swirled it. But he wasn't drinking. He was *alone*, however, so I tracked his gaze.

His focus was on the dance floor on the other side. There was a significant distance between him and that dance platform. Terrible spot for her bodyguard to hang out.

Good for me though.

I made my way around the balcony overlooking the strippers below. The cluster of writhing bodies was not a turnoff at all. I tracked the faux redhead as she moved deeper into the crowd. The lights played over her white outfit, shifting the colors of it as it danced over her skin.

Eagerness threaded me as I let the pulsating music guide me as I moved with it. She wasn't dancing with anyone specific. Her partners shifted to dance with her then away. The rock of her hips coupled with the sinuous movement of her torso and arms pulled me in like a provocative allure.

I was in a rapidly decaying orbit and falling quite happily toward her. When I slid in front of her, she moved with me, but she wasn't lifting her chin or looking at me. If anything, she just matched my steps and when she twisted away, I followed.

When another girl slid up to her, they writhed together, then split apart and then she was dancing back to me and when her body curved into mine, I dipped my head.

"Goddamn. Ace..."

She stiffened and then pivoted. The hair on her wig snapped against me, but then her eyes were focused on me and I wanted to drown in those blue pools.

"Lachlan..." Her lips formed my name. I saw it more than heard it. Hell, I didn't think I could hear anything over the sound. When the music shifted and everyone started bouncing, I threw my arms up with her and followed.

Her pink tongue appeared as she licked her lips and when she moved back into me, I dropped a hand on her hip. As much as I wanted to slide it over her ass, I kept it where it was.

She firmed her palm against my chest we moved together. Holy shit could she move and my dick was a stone just from the suggestion of her brushing up against me. Another twirl and her hair slapped at my face.

I hated the wig.

Fucking hated it.

When I looped an arm around her middle and dragged her back, she didn't fight me. If anything she ground her ass against me like temptation incarnate. The lights changed. The darkness deepened and the lights went blue. I fisted that wig and tugged it off as I pressed my lips against her ear.

"Missed you, Ace." I added a bite to her earlobe and she seemed to shudder. The wig fell from my hand and disappeared onto the dance floor and when she dropped her head against my shoulder, I spread my hand out over her abdomen.

Her skin was hot and soft. She leaned backwards, it pulled her ass away from me as she rolled with the music, but my view was incomparable. The ripples of her abdominals as she moved under my hand and the peek at her breasts tucked into what amounted to a fringed white-bikini top.

I was close to drooling, then she straightened and pulled away, until I tugged her again and then she was facing me. I dragged her all the way back until her body was pressed to mine. Sweat gleamed on her cheeks, the blue lights made her eyes glow and her hair spilled over my hands as I framed her face with my palms.

"Fuck me, Ace," I whispered and then I dipped my head. I half-expected her knee to slam into my nuts. It wouldn't be the first time. Didn't think it would be the last, but I needed to kiss her. I needed to fucking taste her.

Then her mouth opened beneath mine and I was drowning in the feel of her as I lifted her up so our heads were even. The lock of her legs against my hips had me grinding against her as her tongue dueled furiously with mine.

This was what I'd been missing.

My Ace.

Eighteen

"Ace..."

The weight of his lips on mine were a decadence I should soundly reject so why was I wrapping myself around him? Why was I determined to devour his mouth with the same ferociousness he applied to mine? His hands were on my ass and my arms were around his neck.

I thrust a hand into Lachlan's hair, the softness sliding between my fingers as I fisted it. My ninja kisser.

Fuck, I'd missed this. Even as his tongue teased and danced with mine, I drank in the heat of him. There was no mistaking the erection I ground against or the fact that I was fucking grinding on him.

Dragging my head up, I kept moving with him, hips rolling as he swayed. Everything about our connection mimed sex. He'd yanked my damn wig off and I couldn't find the willpower to care. He forever seemed to do what he wanted and the consequences be damned. I'd come out here to lose myself.

Lachlan—

I shoved all the other thoughts away. This wasn't about school or Pen or Dad or anything else. It was me and Lachlan and the music.

Yeah, consequences be damned right now. I needed the recklessness in his kiss, the hunger as he opened his mouth and sucked against my tongue. He stopped pretending to just hold my ass and began to massage it as he ground me more firmly against him.

We moved in a sea of people. The crowd surged around us as the music changed. A new hit started blasting out and I hadn't heard this one in a club before, but everyone went wild. The lights changed again, the darkness all but swallowing everyone except for the bioluminescent ink stamps on our hands and those wearing necklaces and bands. The floor had some light, it wasn't pitch black.

But no one was looking or seeing. We were just another couple making out in the crowd. His hand skated over the skin of my back and then he was kissing along my throat. "Fuck, Ace," he growled the words against my ear as he slid his hands under the skirt. My panties were hardly a barrier and the feel of his hot fingers sliding down the length of my crack should set off an alarm.

Somewhere in my head it did, I slapped the fucking snooze button as I twisted to catch his mouth with mine. Another kiss and then we bumped against someone. No—something, he twisted and then my back was to a wall as he yanked my panties to the side and a hot finger teased against my clit.

Oh, shit. The intimacy was almost too much and not enough. He drew out my lower lip, sucking on it as he pressed his thumb alongside my clit. With increasing pressure, he drew circles and I writhed, rolling my hips to ride his hand.

This close, I couldn't even see his eyes, though I could taste the heat in his kiss. Hints of chocolate. Coffee. Cayenne pepper. Sweet and spicy. My pussy was clenching against emptiness as he increased the speed and pressure of his rubbing. The orgasm storming over me crashed down and I let out an indecent cry as he swallowed it with his kiss.

Where I would have let go and floated on that sensation, he redoubled his efforts and it dragged another climax out of me that was damn near painful. I bit his lip and he slapped his free hand against my ass.

That just made me clench down more. When he raised his head, he finally eased his fingers off of me and wrapped his hand against my chin.

All I could smell was me on his fingers and it—holy shit that should not be so hot. "I want to fuck you right here," Lachlan said, his lips pressed against my ear. "I want you to hold that railing while I rail into you. We're going to dance, Ace—"

The railing was barely visible to our right. He had me thrust up against a column, one of the few that rose up from the floor to the ceiling. The lights were changing again and the crowd above and below were in a wild frenzy.

Out here, we weren't Lachlan and Ace...

"Do you hear me?" He nipped my earlobe as if to remind me that he was there and a shudder went through me. "I came here for a kiss and to see you—fuck I need you, Ace—but I want more."

"You always want more," I managed to pant out and forced myself to look at him. He traced his fingers still slick with my release against my lower lip and then his eyes seemed to bore into mine as he licked and sucked the taste right off of me.

The push of his hips into mine was a dangerous temptation.

"Yeah, Ace," he admitted before licking another kiss over my lips. "I just want you."

"This is a terrible idea," I told him, but I wasn't exactly pulling away. I wasn't even attempting to shove him away.

"Then tell me no," Lachlan invited before he deepened the kiss. It didn't last long. The combination of dizzying kiss where he was all tongue and teeth before he dropped his hand to tease my breast through the tiny top. "Tell me no, right now, Ace. I'll back off..."

"But only if I tell you no?" We weren't shouting, but we weren't exactly whispering either. The loud music and the thickening crowd around us just seemed to amp up every single one of my nerve endings.

I'd never been so vibrantly aware of someone. He growled against my throat, his arms tightening as he dug his fingers into my ass.

"You're right," he said. "I should back off...but—come with me?"

What?

I dragged my head up to stare at him.

"Come with me, Ace...run away from here with me. Let me—I don't know what you need, but let me do that for you."

I didn't want to run away from here. "I came here to escape," I said and when I slid my legs down, he eased his hand from my ass. We weren't even pretending to dance. The lights changed again, the blue spiking with purple in the darkness as a Torched song came on and I damn near laughed.

The insanity of it all...a song that ripped out my heart and reminded me why the only people I could trust were my girls, and here I was plastered against one of my stepbrothers.

"Then I'll stay with you," Lachlan offered and for a moment, the light illuminated his face and it wasn't a smirk or a sneer that he wore, but a sober intensity that stripped me more naked than I'd been when he teased my clit with his fingers.

Head tipping back, I fought the sudden surge of tears and

laughter. I didn't know whether to scream or to cry or to throw myself down...

I just didn't want to feel this. Dropping my chin, I stared up at him.

"Right here?" I dared him.

The strobe betrayed his surprise and then his very real hunger.

"Right here." He accepted.

I cupped my hand around the back of his neck and dragged his head down for another kiss. Then I bit his lower lip until it had to sting because he jerked back. "Don't ever rip my wig off again," I told him and this close, I could see his eyes. The haunted forests were lost in shadows, a lot like my heart.

But I saw them.

I saw him.

"I promise," he offered up the oath and my heart stuttered at the absolute lack of artlessness.

"I can't give you any promises," I told him, all too aware of how heavy the air around us had grown. I was too close to the edge. Too close to losing it.

"I don't care," he said then kissed me again. "Use me, Ace. Fucking use me."

Lachlan could be a real bastard—but he was also standing here offering me *everything*.

"I'm going to regret this," I whispered against his lips. I hadn't meant for him to hear it.

"Not if I can help it." He shaped his hands over my hips. "You using me, Ace?"

Head tipped back, I spared a single glance around us. This was insane. Anyone could see us. Fuck they probably had, but no one out here cared. We were all just a sea of writhing bodies and aching souls.

"Fuck me, Lachlan," I told him. "Fuck me right here."

Yeah, I was in.

His grin was wild, and ferocious. It had me curling my toes as he turned me around and moved up behind me. We were dancing again, only this grind held a lot more sensual promise.

A kiss behind my ear. Teeth on my throat. Then his hot whisper. "Hold that railing and don't let go."

Fuck...

Indecision held me captive for a split second. Then he bit down against my throat and sucked a kiss so hard against my skin it was going to leave a mark. Heat swept through me as the music changed.

This wasn't Torched anymore, it was a raunchier song with a hard beat and when I clenched the railing, he slid his hands down to flip up my skirt. His fingers slid between my legs and he tugged my panties to the side.

His lips never stopped moving against my throat as he traced biting kisses and then there was the hard push of his cock as he ground against me. It slid along my labia and I forgot how to breath because he was stroking my clit. Then he pushed in, one hard fierce thrust.

It hurt and felt so fucking good. A cry tore out of my throat and it was swept away on the roar of the crowd. One hand on my hip, with his other buried against my clit, he began to rock into me and fuck if he wasn't matching the beat.

I shook as I matched the pounding pace he set, the slap of his hips against my ass, and I bobbed my head as I moved. The only thing I wanted to do was let go of the railing, but he said to hold on and not let go.

The stroke of his cock matched the caress of his fingers and the twist of pain and pleasure provoked by his biting kisses kept me right on edge.

Then the club plunged into full blackness as the music cut off like a record scratch. Lachlan went still, buried to the hilt inside of me. I was violently aware of his panting breaths and my own.

Sweat and perfume flavored the air around us and we weren't the only ones gasping for air. When he began circling my clit in slow massaging motions, I almost let out a whimper but I held it.

"All right Dark Room—the sun is down and it's time for the wild ones to come out and play—who's ready to party?" The voice carried through the whole club and a roar surged upward.

My hips were bucking a little, but Lachlan kept me still, utterly impaled on his cock. Another goddamn monster, and it felt good.

The music exploded along with LED fireworks on the ceiling and the flashing strobes just added to the pulse. All at once he began thrusting again and the pressure on my clit split me in half.

I was sobbing as I came and he didn't relent, the wild pace ground me against the railing. My cry climbed. I couldn't hear it, but I could feel the keening notes. Lachlan gave three, last jerky pushes as he thrust his fingers into my mouth.

The hot flood of his cum rushed into me and he rolled our hips, keeping us moving as he filled me. All around us the party raged on and I clung to his arm where he kept me up.

The world slipped and slid around us as the dancers crowded closer. He was still in my pussy and there was a couple humping each other right next to us.

When I tilted my head back, I could barely make out his expression and then he was abruptly jostled and pulled out of me in a rush. I pivoted as my skirt fell down and Dix was just there.

Lachlan rushed forward, but Dix struck him and I could barely catch Dix's arm before he hit him again.

"Don't," I said, struggling to get between them. The

dancers around us didn't even seem to notice. Dix pulled me to him and then shoved me behind him.

"We're going now," he said, his tone absolutely firm and he glared at Lachlan again.

I didn't want to go—but Lachlan's raw fury as he glared Dix was too much.

We'd already played with fire tonight.

"Stop," I told Lachlan and he jerked his gaze to me. "I'm saying no—now."

I hoped he understood but then Dix all but picked me up and dragged me out of the club. It wasn't until he deposited me in the back of the car that I even realized how much of a mess was in my panties.

"I can't believe that little fucker was all over you like that," Dix complained as he started the car. "I didn't realize you'd lost your wig. Took me time to wade through that insanity. Then that fucker was just grinding against you, gorgeous."

"I'm fine," I told him distractedly, twisting in time to see Lachlan coming out of the club. He was disheveled and his belt was still undone and for a long moment, I swore his eyes locked on mine. No way he could see me and at the same time, all I could feel was the way he'd filled, railing me on that platform.

Slumping back against the seat, I closed my eyes. I couldn't forget the way Ramsey felt inside of me and now Lachlan?

What the fuck was I doing?

Nineteen

JONAS

"Fuck off," Lachlan snarled at Ramsey before he slammed the door to his room. The sound carried down the stairs to where I was working on a new composition on my keyboard. Lachlan had been gone more than present the last three days and all I could think was he was out stalking KC.

Literally stalking.

It was weird, like he couldn't help himself. For the most part, Ramsey and I had basically been stuck here *waiting* for something. The gentle thud of steps on the stairs had me glancing up to find Ramsey glaring at the front door.

"He found her."

I scowled. "And he's in a bad mood."

"So, either she rejected him or..." Ramsey spread his hands. "I don't like the sneaking around."

Leaning back against the sofa, I stared at him. "You going to call her?"

"Not sure she wants to hear from me." His lips twisted

"

into a grimace. "Not sure we should even be forcing ourselves on her."

I turned that over in my mind and then picked up my phone. There was a sheet of half-filled music on the table next to the keyboard. The song I'd been working on. I had about a third of it done.

"Do you mind if I try?"

With a jerk, Ramsey pivoted to face me. "Try what?"

Opening the message thread we'd started when she first settled in our suite, I added the photos of the song pages.

ME

Probably don't want to hear from me. But I can't stop thinking about you. I'm in LA. Can I come see you?

After a moment, I turned the phone to show Ramsey and he dropped into the chair on my right before he leaned back. With one finger, he rubbed against his lower lip as he studied the message than me.

"Bad?"

"No," Ramsey said slowly. "It's direct. I think direct might be the way to go."

"Then you should message her too. Lachlan's—"

"Impulsive. Reckless. Determined." He pulled off his glasses and rubbed at his eyes. "Jonas, do you want to date Kaitlin?"

"Yes." Shrugging, I glanced down at the message on my phone again. "I like her."

"I had sex with her." The reminder was not something I needed. "And yes, I agree bringing it up is probably tasteless and a little crass—but I know Lachlan wants a physical relationship with her, if not more."

"What do you want?" I didn't really care about what

Lachlan wanted. Not when he couldn't make up his mind if we were a team on this or not.

We were here cause he didn't think she was as pissed at us as she was him. A part of me did not agree with that sentiment, even if another part of me hoped it was true.

I didn't want her mad at me any longer.

Blowing out a breath, Ramsey said, "I want her."

That admission had me jerking my head up to meet his gaze.

"I did a lot of things wrong where she is concerned," he continued before I could comment. "A *lot* of things. I bumbled it. More when I didn't wake up before she left that morning…"

Before she was kidnapped.

Before the ransom.

Before that damn fridge.

Then her people swarmed around her and we were all cut off.

I glanced down at the message on my phone. The one I hadn't sent yet.

"Are we fighting over her?" Because…

"I don't want to fight you, Jonas." That wasn't a no.

"I don't mind the fight so much," I told him. "I *like* her." I'd gotten to kiss her once.

It had been a perfect kiss and then Gibs…

"I like her and I started Googling Gibs."

I don't know what I expected Ramsey's response to that to be but when he said, "I called my dad," I wasn't ready for that response. "He said Gibs has an attorney and a fund that handles his indiscretions. It's a well-known *secret* in the industry. But the women don't make noise and the trades stay away from it—Kaitlin is another story entirely."

That… "He cheats on Mom."

"That's one way to look at it," Ramsey said. "Dad

couldn't confirm how many kids he has—says all that is required is a proof of DNA, and Gibs' people set them up with child support and NDAs."

What the fuck? "He *cheats* on Mom." Anger threaded through me. Mom—she was not always a nice person, but she *loved* Gibs. She did everything for him. Went everywhere. She'd been devoted to him for all of our lives, or at least all of mine.

"Jonas," Ramsey said, yanking my attention to him. "That's just another piece of the puzzle. We're not going to leap to any more conclusions. We did that with Kaitlin because..."

"Mom."

She hated KC.

"Yeah, so we have some information. When Lachlan dislodges his head from his ass, I want him to ask his dad and I think you should ask yours."

"Why would Dad have anything on this?" He had nothing to do with the industry. He lived in Denver, did his art and his tattooing and ignored everything else.

"Because he had an affair with Mom that resulted in you. He likely knows something, and we can't discount it. Right now, we can't just use tabloids to get answers. That baby has Gibs' eyes—Kaitlin's eyes and she's what? Two? Maybe three?"

I had no idea how old babies were. She wasn't that old in that picture. I thought—we thought KC had her before she came to Blue Ivy.

Then it hit...

"He knocked someone up right before they got married."

"Got it in one. Mom's been with him for fourteen? Fifteen years? If he has that many kids, he's been knocking them up the whole time."

Which made *him* a piece of a *shit.* Anger and disappointment were a brutal cocktail. I stared at the music—how many days had I sat in Gibs' studio playing instruments, practicing different techniques and learning how to read the sheets because I wanted to write them?

"We blamed her..." For everything. We blamed KC for not being his kid... "What is going on?"

"I don't know, Jonas. The only thing I know for certain is, we don't know everything. We listened to Mom when she told us to not read the gossip sites, to respect their privacy..."

"And we listened to her every time she made a cutting remark about KC." It was so damn clear looking back. Mom never had a kind word about KC.

Never.

Little things, like calling her ungrateful.

Spoiled.

Dismissive.

Hollywood brat.

She hated KC's mom. That, she never pretended otherwise. Called her cruel, narcissistic, and vain.

My head hurt.

"I like her, Ramsey," I said abruptly. "I got to know her. More than you guys did. I got to know *KC* and I like what I learned about her. She's—she's funny and fun. She's smart. She's got a gift with words. She gets me."

The last part held me captive. She did seem to get me. Even when she wore that little smirk and called me *Hot Shot*.

"I like her too," Ramsey said. "It may not come down to what we like or what we want. She wanted to talk to us that day..."

"Before she was kidnapped." That just pissed me off all over again. We still didn't know who'd taken her. The cops said we might never know, and that wasn't acceptable. "She could have died."

That sobering reality sliced at me.

"And I think it changed her mind on what she had to say to us," Ramsey admitted and I took a good look at my big brother. At the tension in his expression and the worry on his face. "I think—or maybe it's just wishful thinking—maybe she wanted to figure this out between us the way we do. I can hope anyway...I want..."

"Her."

It was that simple and when Ramsey met my gaze there was a weariness there. "I do want her—I don't want to fight you two though."

"I don't mind the fight," I said with a shrug. "But we don't get to decide for her."

He frowned. "Excuse me?"

"We made that mistake. We decided we knew her. We decided who and what she was before we met her."

"And we were wrong..."

"Exactly. So you can chase her. Lachlan is. But I'm going to message her and see if I can see her."

Ramsey exhaled. "Then may the best of us win?"

I shrugged. "I don't know how it will work, but I think she's lonely and I know she was in danger. Maybe she wants all of us. Maybe none of us. But I have to try... no, I *want* to try."

"So we all date her," Ramsey said, squinting at me. "If we can persuade her, yes, I know."

"But you don't get to hurt her," I told him flatly. "I will fight you there."

"I don't want to hurt her, Jonas. I want to know her—I want to be real with her."

"Then we'll be okay."

When he glanced upstairs. "Lachlan may not be."

I shrugged. "Lachlan is greedy." KC could handle him. I was pretty sure she could handle all of us. I woke my phone up and hit send on the message.

Then I put it down. It was late.

"I'm going to order pizza," Ramsey said as he stood. "Then tomorrow, we will go shopping and discuss college."

"I don't care about college," I told him as I pulled my keyboard closer. I wasn't leaving LA until we solved this with KC. Maybe I wouldn't leave at all. That meant I needed to get a job.

"Jonas—you have to care." There was a lecture coming.

No, I didn't. But I'd let Ramsey tell me all the reasons why. It would make him feel better. I worked out the next couple of notes while he was on the phone in the kitchen. Then my phone buzzed.

KC

Come by the house tomorrow. Use the call box at the gate. I'll let you in.

My heart fisted and slammed against my ribs.

KC

But not too early—so like after ten or something, but before three.

Picking up the phone, I debated my next words.

ME

I'll be there. Thank you.

Was that too much?

KC

I'm crashing, it's late.

That seemed to be the end of it and then the phone buzzed again.

KC

Why?

Simple question.

ME

I miss you.

I offered a simple answer.

KC

You caught up on Love is Blind?

ME

Didn't we finish it?

KC

New season, Hot Shot. I'm on the second
episode. Catch up. We can watch it
together.

ME

Are they nuts like last season?

KC

Worse. See you tomorrow.

A little thrill went through me and I looked around for the
remote. It was under the keyboard. When Ramsey came out, I
was scrolling through the streaming service looking for the
show.

There was a new season.

I hit play.

"What the hell are we watching?"

I grinned. "It's terrible. She loves it."

I cut a look toward him when he sat down.

Yeah, first two episodes. So we could watch the next ones
together.

Fifteen minutes in and I grimaced. KC was right. It was
worse.

Holy shit what a mess. The pizza arrived halfway through
the episode and we invited Lachlan down but he didn't
answer. Fine. Let him sulk.

Ramsey actually looked pained when he settled back into his chair. "She loves this?"

I grinned again. "Yep."

His suffering made it even funnier. Cause the show really was awful.

I got to see KC the next day.

That made everything a little better.

I couldn't wait.

Twenty

KC

It wasn't even six when I rolled out of bed. It didn't matter how late I went to sleep, three, maybe four hours later, and I was awake again. My heart slammed against my ribs and I couldn't catch my breath.

For a split-second, when I opened my eyes all I could see was darkness. Darkness and I couldn't move. It was like my arms were lashed to my legs and nothing even twitched. Panic scrabbled against me until the light from my bathroom registered.

The light I left on when I went to bed.

That was when, all at once, I rolled to my feet and fought to get my breathing under control. The trembling was in my hands and my chest felt almost too tight, like I still couldn't get a deep breath.

That light kept me grounded, it let me see. I wasn't trapped in the dark. I had to leave the damn light on to keep the boogeyman away.

I hadn't been scared of the dark since—hell since I didn't

know when, and now I was jumping at shadows. The night before at the club, when all the lights had vanished had almost made me scream. Almost.

In that moment, I forgot how to breathe. The darkness closed in all around me, smothering. Then Lachlan had ground into me, reminding me he was there. The feel of his dick filling me, stretching me—

Annoyed with myself, I headed to the bathroom and that was when the aches from the club reasserted themselves.

Yeah, I was sore.

It was like I could still feel Lachlan. I'd barely managed to block the feeling of Ramsey out of my head and now I had Lachlan to compare it to.

Fuck.

I was losing my mind.

Aggravated didn't cover it so I dragged on shorts, a sports bra, tank top, and running shoes before I headed down to the kitchen. Davina always had everything stocked. I filled a reusable water bottle and diverted out of the house to the gym that was located on the other side of the pool house.

Mom was not a fan of the smell of sweat. She was less of a fan of losing her figure. The gym being out here was a compromise. The cool, fragrant air wrapped around me and there was a scent of lavender and rosemary on the breeze.

I loved Davina's added herbal garden. I needed to get over there and look at it soon. While I might prefer to go for a run on the beach or just take off to one of the running trails in the hills, I'd have to wake Dix for that.

Dix had been in a mood when we got back. A mood I didn't want to deal with, so I'd escaped to my room and a long hot shower to think about my choices. Then Jonas texted.

I should have known he would be close, since Lachlan was here. Did that mean Ramsey was here too?

After I threw the doors open to let the breeze race

through, I put my earbuds in and then climbed on the tread-mill. A run was what I needed.

Miles. A few of them at least.

Cranking up the music, I hit the button to turn the tread-mill on and I started the run. Maybe if I made everything else sore, the sensual ache would go away.

Maybe I'd forget about the dark—and being trapped in it.

Maybe.

I made just five miles in an hour and while not my best time, I definitely felt better if sore. Davina was in the kitchen when I headed back through. She gave me a firm look that held worry, but there were also shadows under her eyes.

"You're taking naps, right?" I checked with her. The hours she spent with Pen let me rest—okay it eased some of my worries. I couldn't be at the hospital all the time. When I was sick, Davina was the balm for my soul. I loved that she was sharing that with Pen.

"No fussing from you," she scolded. "You're still not sleeping enough and running a bit wild. I won't give you grief for it and you'll leave me be, yeah?"

I hugged her from the side, careful of how sweaty I was. "I just worry."

"I know you do and you stink. Go shower and I will make you coffee and crepes for breakfast."

My stomach gurgled. "With strawberries?"

The look she gave me had me laughing as I raised my hands. "I'm off to shower—oh, before I forget. Johnny will probably be coming in today. I told him he's welcome to stay, so can we set up a suite on Mom's side?" Since she wasn't here it might be easier for Johnny to stay closer to where she would.

"I'll take care of it. Anything else?" The knowing gleam in her eyes made me laugh.

"Yes, a—" I hesitated on what to label Jonas, so I settled for saying, "Jonas is coming today to hang out. Not sure what time, I think he'll text ahead of time but we need to add one for lunch."

"Sounds good, sweet girl. Off to shower so I can get your coffee going."

"I love you, Davina. I don't deserve you."

"Hush your mouth and off you go."

Laughing, I jogged up the stairs. Aubrey and Yvette were both still sound asleep. They didn't get up early at all. I was the weird one, but it was fine.

A few hours later, I was downstairs on a call with our manager when Jonas arrived. My phone had vibrated with his text that he was on his way. He'd be using a car service. Fair enough, I didn't really drive either. Something I needed to correct someday but that day was not today.

"So you'll think about a tour," Teddy said, leaning forward. It wasn't a question and it wasn't like him to push like this. "I know you just finished school, but I also know you've been working on some new material. The label would kill for another album and if I can dangle a flashback tour with some new songs sprinkled in..."

Yvette and Aubrey glanced at me. The question in their eyes likely mirrored my own. Did we want to do this? Write music? Put together a new album? Yes.

Tour?

I blew out a breath.

"Why don't we tell them that we're discussing it," Yvette suggested, her accent softening the words. "It's not a promise or even an offer." She raised her brows but Aubrey and I were already nodding.

"We'll discuss it." Maybe not today or tomorrow. But we would.

"Discussing is good," Teddy said as he settled back in his seat. Video calls on the big screen television made it seem like he was right there with us. "I can work with that. What about the album?"

"We're always working on music," I admitted. "And yes, I have written a couple of songs."

"Same," Aubrey agreed. "More worked out some feelings but haven't added lyrics to music yet. We need to put our heads together..."

"We do," Yvette said. "We've been busy with other stuff, but we'll make more time for music. Again, no commitments..."

"One new song?" Teddy pressed. "Maybe two? If we can do a surprise drop before the end of summer that might go a long way to boosting the brand and keeping you guys out there in the discussion."

I couldn't care less about being in the discussion, but there was another longer talk the three of us needed to have.

"One," I said firmly. I had one written. We could record it for Pen. "It'll be for childhood cancer research—all the profits."

"Yes," Aubrey said and Yvette nodded. "One song, we'll have it recorded before the end of July."

We could do that. Teddy blinked at us. "Charity recording —what if we pull other artists in? Ask for one song each—do it all for charity?"

Did the man ever stop trying to sell something? But if we had other artists, we could raise more money. More awareness.

"You want to do a charity concert," Yvette said and Teddy grinned.

"It's not a terrible idea. It would get you out there without the burden of a full tour *and* help raise money and awareness. Win-win." He spread his arms like please agree with me and I sighed.

"Tentative yes," I said after I shared a glance with the girls.

"Gonna depend on the when and the where—we have some other plans to make. But I like the idea. So, I say begin broaching it with other bands and performers. Take their temperature."

"Done. Thank you girls, I will let you get back to your summer vacation. Take care of yourselves and KC—you stay safe. I've added contingencies for extra security at any venue we choose."

I didn't make a face, but it was difficult. After that, Teddy signed off and left the three of us alone. I picked up my coffee and considered it, then them.

"Are we ready to have this conversation yet?" They'd touched on it when they decided to take the break. Touched on it and then tabled it.

I glanced at my phone, I didn't know where Jonas was coming from but he would be here soon.

"Soon," Aubrey said. "I mean, we do need to decide if we want to keep going, but I can't imagine a life where it isn't the three of us against the world."

"Agreed," Yvette said. "At the same time..."

"The independence is intoxicating and a little dangerous." Adding the last with a bit of a wry smile just earned me frowns. "I'm working on it and no, I still don't want to discuss what happened. I like the idea of working together and performing. I love singing with you guys, but I don't know if I want another world tour any time soon."

Yvette looked thoughtful. "Then this is a good way to dip our toes in and work toward something important to you and to us."

"I love you guys," I said easily. "I really couldn't do this without you."

"You absolutely could," Aubrey told me as she rose. "We just make you shine."

Laughter bubbled through me and then my phone buzzed again. This time it was the gate.

Jonas was here.

Yvette glanced at my phone then at me. "You sure about this?"

I hadn't mentioned the club or Lachlan to them. "I'm not sure about a lot of things, but—I can't keep running away."

"And you like him," Aubrey pointed out. When I cut a look at her, she raised her hands. "I like him too. Of the three of them, he's at least tolerable. I just—"

"We," Yvette cut in. "We're just worried about you. You have a lot on your plate right now and those three have messed with your head enough."

"True." It was hard to argue that. "But I know who they are now and I am getting an idea for who they want to be. Where it goes—I have no idea. Jonas is trying to be honest with me, I think. Words are hard for him and he didn't mince them. He said he missed me..."

"You miss him," Yvette said. It wasn't a question. "Then let him in, we have your back. But they fuck up again and we're going to do more than write a song eviscerating them."

I snickered as I sent a code to the gate to let Jonas come in. "You guys sticking around for this?"

"Eh, I need to call Forrest," Aubrey admitted. "I've been blowing him off and I really need to decide if we're a thing or not."

"I think you need the time," Yvette said. "I'll go harass Aubrey and threaten Forrest."

Rising, I met their hugs with one of my own. Then they headed upstairs and I left the media room with my coffee to head for the front door.

Time to play with fire, I supposed.

The flutter in my belly warned me I was looking forward to it.

Twenty-One

JONAS

The car pulled through the gates and followed the long drive up to the house. The angle of the drive and the slight incline meant the house wasn't really visible until we followed the circle around.

Weirdly, I'd seen pictures of the place before but it was different in person. More—open I guess would be the word I would use. Colorful and warm. Kind of like KC herself. For a moment, it hit me that her mother could be here.

I shook that off. My phone buzzed.

RAMSEY

Do me a favor?

ME

Depends.

He hadn't asked me for anything when I left. We'd both glanced up at Lachlan's closed door and Ramsey told me to go and enjoy. He'd deal with our brother, and I left. Not like I needed the permission from either of them. I had it from the one person who mattered.

RAMSEY

Tell her I said hi and that I would like to talk to her.

ME

Why can't you just text that to her?

RAMSEY

Because you're there and your foot is in the door.

We were almost to the portico and the car slowed further.

ME

No promises.

I wasn't risking my time with her bringing up Ramsey. If I thought I could and it wouldn't upset her, I'd see. Best I could do.

His simple thanks annoyed me. Why hadn't he said something *before* I left? A flash of blue chased away the irritation as the car came to a stop. The front doors were both pulled wide and KC stood there, hair in a pony tail, dressed in a t-shirt and shorts with bare feet.

She looked—great.

"Thanks," I said to the driver as I let myself out. I'd already paid his tip.

"You got it," the guy said and lifted his chin at KC. "Pretty girl."

I didn't respond but slammed the door. He could leave now. Thankfully, he took the hint and followed the circular turn back to the drive. I glared after him.

"Should I make sure he leaves through the gates?"

"Security will," KC said quietly, her voice washing over me

like a balm. Fuck, I really had missed her. "There's a gatehouse down there, it's not obvious, but they handle any deliveries that come in and they track all arriving and departing vehicles."

The sun was warm against my back as I turned to face her. In jeans and a black t-shirt, I felt overdressed. "You look great," I told her, refusing to keep the compliment back.

The corner of her mouth tilted up. "Who are you and what have you done with Jonas?"

"I'm still me," I said, shouldering my backpack. I'd brought music, and my lyric sheets with me. "Just—thought I should not keep things from you anymore."

Lips pursed, she studied me for a beat. "Catch up on the show?"

I grimaced and earned a fresh peel of her laughter. The sound was absolutely electric. "Yeah, you caught up. It's awful, right?"

Her grin was contagious. "I still don't get why you like it."

"You'll figure it out," she teased, then beckoned me to come inside. "Let's grab drinks and go sit by the pool."

"Okay."

I followed her as she led the way through the house. It was so open, and colorful. Except for the sofa, it was painfully white and offset by more vibrant cushions. It also didn't look like anyone ever sat there.

Art decorated the walls and there were gold-framed pictures following one curving staircase—there were two on opposite sides—that looked like movie posters.

So much to take in and KC seemed right at home. At the same time, it was almost too opulent. The kitchen was huge, bigger than ours at Tahoe, and it was like our whole suite at school would fit in here.

"Soda?" she asked as she popped open the fridge. "I can make coffee too."

"Soda is fine. Or coffee. Whatever. I don't want to put you out."

"You're not," she said as she pulled out two cans, then jerked her head toward the doors that were wide open to the back. The pool was visible, as was the grotto like landscaping.

"KC—this place is huge."

"You get used to it," she said as I followed her outside. The day was kind of perfect, warm, but not hot. There was a breeze. There was lots of shade around the pool. KC chose a table with chairs in a cabana. It offered privacy and at the same time, we could enjoy the day.

I liked it. She slid a soda over to me before she sat down and dragged a second chair over to stretch her legs out on.

Dropping the backpack down, I settled across from her and met her gaze. "Hi."

She grinned. "Hi, Jonas."

"Thanks for seeing me."

"Well, seeing you isn't the hard part."

I frowned.

"Talking to you is a little trickier."

I considered that as I popped open the soda. "You're still mad about the song?"

Her shoulders lifted in a careless shrug. "No, not so much. Dad doesn't owe me anything, he made that clear a long time ago. I was—I think I was just hurt." That admission seemed to cost her and it gutted me.

"I never wanted to hurt you."

"Never?" The challenge in her words looped around me.

I turned that over in my head. "Okay, I guess that would be stretching it. I wasn't a fan when we heard you were coming to the school."

The tilt of her head dared me to continue. I took a drink of the soda, debating how to press forward.

"You want me to be honest?" I winced, because probably not how I should have asked that question.

"I think that would be nice." She traced her finger around the rim of her soda. Her eyes seemed to glow even more with the reflection of the light dancing off the pool. "There have been enough lies and half-truths, yeah?"

Sighing, I tilted my head back. "Yes, and I want to be honest but I don't want to piss you off."

"Hot Shot, you pissed me off a lot when we first met and I got over it." Her careless shrug made me smile and at the same time it made me sad. "Look—I didn't like you and you didn't like me."

I frowned. "It wasn't that I didn't like you—you asked if I wanted to take your picture or something."

Laughter peeled out of her and I sighed. "You were staring..."

"I was waiting for you to recognize me."

"Then I didn't." There was almost an element of an apology in her voice. "And you left a note."

"I did leave a note," I said, then scrubbed a hand over my face. "The thing is—we've heard about you all our lives. I know that you said Gibs was being a dick to you and after..."

No, she didn't need to know that we had to bully Gibs into paying the ransom. She hurt enough.

"After?" The gentle prodding was hard enough to avoid. Then I looked at her and all I wanted to do was stare at her eyes.

"I don't want to tell you that part," I admitted. "Don't ask me?" It was a request and a statement.

She sighed, then dipped her lashes as she nodded. "If you say so, but I'm a big girl. I can take it."

The blasé comment pissed me right the fuck off, "Maybe you shouldn't have to fucking take it, you know? You've had to take a fucking lot."

The corners of her lips tilted up. "Life doesn't usually give a damn whether I can or not, so I've learned to adapt—"

"KC-babe," a male voice called and KC rose and held a finger up toward me.

"One sec…" Then she strode out of the cabana. I leaned forward to see her walking up to that porn star guy. He gave her a quick hug and they spoke for a few minutes. She gestured back toward me then pivoted to face the guy again.

I couldn't hear either of them. A part of me wanted to walk over and join the conversation, but she asked me to wait. Across the pool, movement pulled my attention and I met the harsh gaze of Dix. I hadn't seen him since he'd been at the school.

The flinty-eyed gaze he favored me with had me straightening. He didn't like me and he wasn't making nice. KC wasn't paying attention to us and the hostility rolled off him in waves. I had no problems with his dislike.

Shifting his stance, he reversed direction and circled the pool away from KC and toward me. Fine, if he wanted to throw down right here and right now, I'd take him on.

"You shouldn't be here," was exactly how he started his greeting.

"I was invited," I pointed out, not quite smirking. "Not that it's any of your business."

"I live here and KC is very much my business. You and your shit for brains brothers—"

"Hey Dix." KC's return shut him up abruptly. "Johnny needs to head to the Valley to pick up some of his things. Would you mind taking him? He's not doing well and I really don't want him driving with how little sleep he's had."

Dix didn't roll his eyes, but he did stiffen when she drifted up to stand next to me. Even better, she stayed right there. "You want me to drop this one off on my way?"

While I would love to turn my head and just study her, I

kept her in my periphery. Dix's hostility disappeared all too easily, but there was a tension around his eyes and in his jaw. I'd seen that look on plenty of other faces.

But even in my periphery, KC's smile was easy and seemed to soften everything about her. "No, Jonas is fine. He just got here and we have a lot to talk about." When she slid her arm through mine, I canted my head to glance at her. "Right, Jonas?"

"Yes." Then I focused on Dix and the absolute dislike in his eyes. "I'm fine right where I am."

He seemed to tremble with all the things he wasn't saying and he flexed his hands once. Blowing out a breath, he focused on KC again. "How long is Johnny staying?"

"Hopefully for a while. It's at least a week right now, but he's a mess over Mom and I'm worried about him. He hasn't been sleeping and I think he just needs friends."

"Right." Dix grimaced. "I'll take care of him, gorgeous." Then he leaned down and pressed a kiss to her cheek before he murmured something. His hand was on her biceps and I wanted to knock him right off and into the pool.

"Thank you, Dix," KC said. "I really do appreciate it."

"You promise to stay on the property until I'm back?" He didn't back off and his thumb was moving against her arm. I could break that hand really easily. In fact, I could break the whole damn arm.

KC glanced up at me with a grin. "Jonas and I have a lot to talk about so yeah, I'll be here. Promise."

He definitely wasn't happy to hear that we had a lot to talk about and I just grinned as I covered KC's hand on my arm. I was right where I wanted to be. Even if this bag of dicks was too damn crowded in next to us.

"I'll be back before dinner. Remember what I said, you stay on property." Then the bodyguard shook his head and gave her arm a squeeze before he strode away.

With a sigh, she watched him go and then glanced up at me. "Sorry, Dix is still in hyper protective mode."

He was a lot more than that. "Johnny?"

"He's my mother's boyfriend, or he was, but now she's engaged to some guru back in New York and it's breaking his heart. The whole thing is a mess, but he needs looking after so I invited him to stay here. We've got the room."

"And you're worried about him." I was more curious than annoyed. She patted my hand and then pulled away to walk back to the table.

"I am. Johnny's good people and there's so much going on. I don't want him to be forgotten."

Those words resonated.

"Anyway, you were going to tell me about your reaction to me coming to Blue Ivy?"

Dropping back into my chair, I said, "Before I forget, Ramsey wanted me to tell you that he said hi and he would like to talk to you if you're up for it."

"Well, give him my number," she suggested. "Though I'm pretty sure he has it. You manned up and texted me."

"And you answered."

"Yep."

"Right—I wasn't as pissed as Lachlan or Ramsey about you coming to the school. I wasn't a fan of that though."

"No?"

"No. All my life Gibs told me how perfect you were and how great and how proud he was. I always wanted him to sound that way about me, and now you were coming to the place that had been ours. It felt a little like an invasion and I resented it and you." I hated telling her this but instead of upset, all I saw was real curiosity in her eyes.

"Then you met me..." Her lips twitched. "You weren't that impressed."

I groaned. "Except—you were gorgeous and I had no idea how to talk to you."

"I'm really sorry about that note," she admitted in a sad voice. "Maybe if I had seen it..."

"Maybe," I said. "But I'm here now."

"Yes, you are," she murmured. "Yes you are."

Twenty-Two

KC

By the time late afternoon rolled around, Dix was back with Johnny and his things. Aubrey and Yvette emerged from their self-imposed exile, and they greeted Jonas—well, if not warmly, at least with a little more friendliness than had been present at school.

"Are you guys staying for dinner?" Aubrey asked as I slid my wallet into my back pocket. I'd changed from shorts into jeans and a cowl-necked blouse. Something a little warmer for being in the hospital.

"No," I said before Jonas could answer. "I'm due at the hospital in just under an hour." I got to spend two hours with Pen and I needed every single one. "I thought Jonas could go with me."

Surprise flickered across several faces, but I chose to ignore it for now. Yvette's concern translated as did Aubrey's. But Jonas and I were talking, or at least attempting this talking thing.

The fact was, the last few hours with him had relaxed me in a way I hadn't managed except for the sole, albeit brief, exception at the club, since the kidnapping. I wasn't in any hurry to send him away.

Dix reappeared as if summoned by the statement. "I don't know that you want to take him with you. We have enough trouble keeping it quiet that you're there."

"Well, you don't have to know," I told him as gently as possible. Dix, like the girls, was in hyper-protective mode. I appreciated that. "I do. We'll still keep it low-key. But with Jonas coming in, you don't have to worry about hovering in the hall."

Frown deepening, Dix stared at me. It almost felt like he was glaring, but more puzzled than mad. "I don't like it."

Blowing out a breath, I gave Jonas' arm a squeeze before I glanced at Aubrey and Yvette. "Can I leave Jonas with you two for a minute without any interrogation or intimidation techniques?"

Yvette's expression clearly said no but Aubrey shrugged. "We can try."

"I'll protect him," Johnny announced as he descended the stairs. "I haven't decided if I like or hate him yet, so I can be neutral."

Jonas looked more bemused than annoyed. "I'm fine."

"I know," I said as I hopped up. I paused to give Johnny a real hug and he pressed a kiss to the top of my head.

"Thank you for having me," he said in a low voice and I patted his chest.

"You're family. I know Mom's being—" I sighed as his expression crumpled. "Well, she's being selfish and a little off her rocker. So you can stay here for as long as you like. Davina said she got the suite all ready for you and you know where the gym and the pool are. Rest up, okay?"

"You're too sweet," he said with a sigh. "But I'll be fine.

Now, go let Dix scold you and I'll look after the boyfriend for you."

There was a bit of a jolt from behind me and I could correct Johnny, I could. But I wasn't even sure what label would apply, so boyfriend would have to do.

"Thank you." Giving myself the reward of it, I glanced over my shoulder to find three startled expressions before the girls could shake it off. The wonder in Jonas' eyes made me grin. "Hang tight, Hot Shot. I'll be back in a few."

Shoulders squaring, I headed out toward the pool so Dix could have some privacy for whatever lecture he was about to deliver. He didn't make me wait, following hot on my heels. The soft hush of conversation behind us cut off entirely when he closed the french doors.

I didn't go far but I also paced out toward one of the arbors with all the colorful foliage the gardeners looked after before I pivoted to face him.

"That boy shouldn't be here." Well, at least Dix got straight to the point.

"Maybe, but I invited him. He didn't just show up—"

"Or ambush you at a dance club to hump your leg?" Dislike kissed every single one of those words.

Folding my arms, I sighed. "Dix, I didn't plan on Lachlan showing up at the club. That said—I had fun dancing with him." The hell of it was, I had. The sex was—off the wall and it had felt so goddamn good. Even if it was a terrible idea, it was hard to regret.

The one regret I did was having to cut Lachlan off to keep him and Dix from fighting.

"As for Jonas, he's not his brother." Another solid truth. My issues with the douchebags three all started out very differently. That they *were* brothers was actually not the biggest problem we'd had. "He reached out, and I invited him here."

Dix scowled. "We don't know them. His being here could be a security risk for you, or at least a risk to your judgment."

"*Right*, because I'm incapable of making impulsive decisions on my own." At my flat stare, Dix threw his hands up.

"Gorgeous, I'm trying to protect your sweet ass and you're just hanging it out there like you don't care who gets to slap it."

Nose wrinkling, I shook my head. "That's a terrible analogy and description. You don't have to like them. Aubrey and Yvette don't, and I'm undecided a lot of the time. But Jonas *is* here and he is *trying*. For a little while, we were friends. If nothing else, I'd like to get that friendship back."

Maybe—whatever. For now the friendship could be enough.

"Part of being my friend though is he needs to understand me, and as hard as it's been for him, he is trying. So I can meet him halfway."

"That baby is a hell of a lot more than halfway."

I lifted my shoulders. "I've explained to you about as much of this as I plan on sharing. Now, I need to get to the hospital and Jonas is going with me. Are you going to drive us or do I need to get a car?"

Dix's nostrils flared and his eyes seemed to flash with real anger. "You aren't getting in *anyone* else's car. Is that clear?"

"Then I guess you better go grab yours." I met his flat glare with one of my own. I wasn't a child. Dix used to get that. But he was so damn overprotective that he was overreaching. I adored Dix. He was practically family, but it didn't give him the right to make decisions for me.

If this kept up, we were going to need to have a far more uncomfortable conversation.

"I'll pick you both up out front," Dix said in a stilted tone, then he was stalking away. Guilt pricked at me. Dix just wanted to protect me, but sometimes—sometimes it felt like he wanted the final say in what I did and that wasn't going to happen.

Mom didn't even tell me what to do and hadn't for a very long time. Hands on my hips, I tilted my head back and took a deep breath. I needed to dilute all the anxiety *before* we got to the hospital.

Pen was innocent in everything and I wanted everything nice and smooth for her. Maybe I shouldn't have invited Jonas...

"I could go back to our place," Jonas offered and it took everything I had not to leap out of my skin. He'd managed to step out and approach without me noticing.

Their place.

All three brothers had followed. Jonas admitted it. They were all here because of me. That was—a lot and I wasn't entirely certain what to do with that information, so I packed it away *for now*.

"I appreciate the offer," I said as I pivoted to meet his concerned gaze. Only it wasn't just concern, his attention was on the distance where Dix disappeared and the irritation in his eyes gave me pause. "Really," I continued when he finally returned his attention to me. "But I invited you for a reason."

And I had.

Hands in his pockets, Jonas looked thoughtful. "You want me to meet your sister?"

"I think you should," I said slowly. "Ramsey thought she was my kid."

For a moment, Jonas looked uncomfortable. "I saw the photo in your room—I thought so too." His sigh was so heavy and long.

"You didn't say anything." That surprised me. Jonas didn't pull his punches. If anything, he proved to be extremely

direct. Brutally so at times. It wasn't always fun, but I appreciated it.

"Not my business," Jonas admitted. "I didn't tell Ramsey or Lachlan. It wasn't their business either. But—it was before I knew you, and then I wondered if that was why you were taking the break and going to school."

"I guess that's fair, I just don't understand how you had no idea that Dad had other kids." I'd tried to turn that over and over in my head and it just didn't make a terrific amount of sense. "The man is the least celibate man ever, and I'm pretty sure he has zero clue that condoms exist."

For a split-second, Jonas looked like someone had hit him in the back of the head with a board. "Um..."

I grinned and pulled out my phone then showed him the family chat. "We could have been in a condom." His eyes almost seemed to bug out of his head.

"Here's the thing, we know about each other, took a while to find everyone, but we're out there."

His dazed expression sobered into one of deep concern. "We were always told not to look, not to follow the gossip, to just be *at home* with them. You know, treat him like people. My mom...she's crazy about him. We've lived with him for so long, I just—I just assumed they were always together if I thought about it—though, parents and sex are not topics I want to think about."

Laughter bubbled up through me at his absolute grimace. "Hot Shot, my mom dates a porn star and my dad can't keep it in his pants. To be fair, I've known way more about their sex lives than I wanted all my life—"

A whistle cut through the air and Aubrey motioned behind her. "Dix has the car up here."

"Thanks." When I held out my hand to him, Jonas clasped it easily enough. "We didn't get a chance to look at your backpack stuff yet, so do you want to bring it with us?

We probably won't at the hospital but I don't know how late you can stay."

"KC?" He firmed his grip on my hand and pulled me back around to look at him.

I raised my eyebrows.

"You were really pissed at us."

"I know."

"Are you still mad?"

I turned that over in my head. "Yes," I admitted. "I am—I don't want to be anymore, because the way I see it, there's a lot more important things to be angry about. But...you guys treated me like shit."

That—hurt.

"I wish I could take it back," Jonas said.

"Me too—but if wishes were horses, beggars would ride." Annoying sentiment, but still true. He made a face.

"So you're still mad, but you invited me here and now we're going to see your sister." It wasn't a question.

"Yep. Pretty much. You can hop off the merry-go-round if you want. Dix is dying to drop you off somewhere else. Maybe being around me won't be safe for your health or your reputation—"

"I don't care about Dix or any of that other stuff." He shook his head once. "I do care about you." For a moment, he seemed almost startled to have admitted it, and he wasn't alone. "I just—want to understand."

"Me too, Hot Shot. Me too." Blowing out a breath, I gave his hand a squeeze. "C'mon, I don't want to get stuck in traffic and not get to see Pen. She's always so happy when I get there..." Even when she was miserable.

And I needed to see her every bit as much.

"Will you tell me about her?" Jonas asked as we headed for the car. We bypassed Aubrey and Yvette, who both gave me looks that said I'd be fielding questions later.

But that was later.

"What do you want to know?" I asked as we headed out front to where Dix waited with the car.

"Everything…"

Twenty-Three

RAMSEY

Fifteen minutes after Jonas left for his date with Kaitlin, Lachlan finally emerged from his room. Despite his surly expression, he couldn't resist smirking at me.

"You planning to tell me you saw her?" I kept my tone neutral as I knocked back a long swig of water. I'd gotten changed for a workout. The property we were renting had a gym for the residents. Anything to get some of this edge off.

His smirk faded. "If you already know, why do I need to tell you?"

"Need?" I shrugged my shoulders. Was I irritated with him? Yes. "Clearly, I don't need anything *from* you. We're here because *you* wanted our help. But all you've done is take off on your own. I'm guessing our work together plan has ended?"

Raking a hand through his hair, Lachlan grimaced. "I saw her at a club."

I waited because Lachlan didn't do cagey. Brash. Loud. Cocky. Wild. Those fit. Cagey didn't. He also didn't play coy.

"In the interests of our agreements to work together..." He chewed over those words like they were overcooked and rubbery. "I had sex with her at the club."

Of all the things I could have imagined him saying. *That* didn't even make the short list. "You did what?"

Anger threaded into my veins. He did—

"With Kaitlin?"

"No, with Britney Spears dumbass." He rolled his eyes and then shoved past me to head to the kitchen. "Of course it was with Ace. I haven't fucking looked at another girl in over a year...hell, almost two years. Why would I tell you I *fucked* a different girl?"

My hand curled into a fist as I pivoted to track him into the kitchen. "Lachlan, she isn't a joke..."

He whirled, his eyes furious as he glared at me. "I have never treated her like a fucking joke."

"But you just said you had sex with her *in a club.*" What the actual fuck was he doing?

"You know, some of us aren't turned off by an audience or by crowds. You could say, that some of us get even more turned on by the energy. I should have known Ace would be one—our first real kiss was on a dance floor." His expression turned almost pensive, though it was the hint of wonder in his voice that neutered some of my irritation.

It didn't do a damn thing for my temper. "So what happened after? Because you were pretty pissed off when you got back here."

Lachlan grunted, but he didn't answer. Instead, he made coffee. I debated leaving it and just going to the gym. I was even more agitated now than before when Jonas left. Lachlan —had sex with her. It just...

"Now you know how it feels," Lachlan said in a voice I'd never heard him use before. His tone was cool, but not smug. "She's *my* girl, Rams. *Mine.* And you touched her first."

"She's not a possession," I reminded him. "If you keep bringing that up, we're going to end up fighting. For real."

"We're fighting now." The snappy comeback had me fisting my temper and I blew out a long breath.

"This isn't fighting. This is you having a tantrum over what you think you're owed from me, from Jonas, but most especially from Kaitlin."

"Don't tell me how I feel about her." The coffee hissed and spit behind him. "I—"

I gave him a beat before I prodded him. "You?"

"I don't know...I have a lot of feelings where she's concerned. More where that dick of a bodyguard is concerned."

"He was there?"

"Yes." A growl joined his snap.

"Good," I said with some satisfaction as I folded my arms.

"Good?" Fresh fury punched up that word. "He got in the way, dragged me away from her then hustled her out of there."

"Good that her bodyguard is watching her. If she's getting *molested*," I countered, giving him a pointed look, "on the dance floor, and he *didn't* show up, I'd have more of a problem with him. The reason her security tightened is someone kidnapped her, or have you forgotten that?"

Hands on his hips, Lachlan let out a frustrated sound. "I was right there. We were—having a moment and then she was just gone."

"Yeah, been there," I reminded him and ignored the hostile look he threw my way and paced over to the windows. The rental house was bigger than anything we needed for just the three of us. The gated neighborhood was expensive, but not filthy rich. It didn't feel like home, not that it was supposed to.

The relentless sunshine, green grass, and manicured lawns were just so—cookie cutter. I hated this place so much.

Southern California wasn't bad, but I was longing for trees, more rugged terrain, and...rain.

"Where's the baby brother?" Lachlan asked as the smell of fresh brewing coffee weaved around me.

I didn't glance away from the front of the house though I could see Lachlan moving via his reflection in the window. "He went to see Kaitlin."

"What?"

"He went to see—"

"I heard that," Lachlan cut me off, more or less joining me at the windows. "I just didn't know she contacted him."

Oh, someone was feeling the sting now. I could be a dick about it, but that wasn't why we were here. "She didn't, he reached out to her." Then she answered. I slid my hands into my pockets. My phone hadn't vibrated once since Jonas answered my earlier messages. "She messaged him back and invited him out to their estate today—so he left a little while ago in a ride share."

Lachlan said nothing.

He didn't say anything as he stood there. He said nothing when he turned away. He continued to say absolutely nothing all the way up the stairs.

Then the door to his room *slammed*.

That said everything for him.

I had no idea how any of this was going to work. But I may need to take a page out of my baby brother's book and reach out to her directly. When Lachlan wanted to work together, I did it as much to look after him and Jonas as to see Kaitlin.

Now...the desire to just *see* her and *talk* to her burned. Just following and waiting was not what we should be doing. Stalking her to clubs and fucking her wasn't what we should be doing either. I glared up the stairs.

Jealousy was a bitter pill to swallow. Especially when the

only conversations I managed to have with her after that single night had been completely monitored. That meant editing everything, unless I wanted to overshare, and I didn't.

Fuck it, I was going to the gym. A good workout, then back here to get some work done on my applications. I'd received an offer to return to Blue Ivy Prep full time as an instructor while I worked on my graduate degree.

A teacher, not a TA.

Before two months ago, I would have leapt at it.

Now?

I hadn't answered. I wasn't sure whether that was because I didn't want to do it or if it was because I didn't know what *she* was going to do.

Kaitlin's life choices weren't mine, but being at Blue Ivy if she were back off to touring meant I'd probably never see her.

That—that was an extremely uncomfortable thought. So, I'd asked for a little time. They'd given it to me, but the clock was ticking.

Despite his surliness earlier, Lachlan eventually showed up at the gym. While I was doing weights, he hit the treadmill and ran like the hounds of hell were after him. We didn't talk, which was fine.

I had no idea what to say to him anyway.

He was still running when I headed back to the house. Once I'd showered, I gathered up the dirty clothes—including theirs—and carried it all down to the laundry room. The rental came with a cleaning service, but I was capable of washing my own shorts.

Once the loads were going, I pulled out my laptop and spent some time reviewing degree options, then the offer letter again.

Blue Ivy Prep was a multi-layered school with a campus that could become some students' whole world. It had mine.

Teaching there? That would be like setting up shop in the one home that had been mine forever.

And right now, I couldn't think of something I wanted less.

Scrubbing a hand over my face, I stared at the screen. Like a compulsion I didn't want to escape, I tabbed open a new window and typed in Kaitlin's name then paused. Backspacing, I cleared that and then went to the Torched website.

News and gossip sites weren't going to offer much in the way of real insight. But if they were planning a tour or there were announcements, they'd be here...

No new tours. Just some updates. There were new Instagram posts, I checked those. Nothing that jumped out. They didn't feel—authentic.

At the same time, they were slice of life—the girls were "funning it up in the sun." At least according to the hashtag and close-ups on their manicures. There was a hint about music, maybe some nebulous plans, but nothing beyond "vague" references. The kind that let you fill in the blanks.

It was possible to be all true and at the same time, not be remotely close to all of the truth. The fan club took a hot second cause I couldn't remember my login or the email I'd attached it to. The guys would give me hell, but I signed up five years earlier because I'd been curious.

For a few months, I'd attempted Lachlan-levels of stalkerhood, then just stopped going there, even if I listened to the music. Right, the old email address was still accessible and holy shit, more than ten thousand messages and almost all of them junk.

Right.

Ignore that for the moment, once I had the password reset, I logged in and checked for notes there. Maybe I should have done this at the school when I was digging, but I'd half-forgotten this until I'd seen Kaitlin in my old concert t-shirt.

If it had been any other time, I might have been a little embarrassed to have been caught out. As it was, who cared about my past fascination and keepsakes when compared to her kidnapping and subsequent trauma? I could get the fuck over it, she needed the attention.

A new post was up on the fan pages. A request.

It was all about Penelope's cancer and the fact they were looking for a suitable bone marrow donor match. They were asking for people to be tested and there was even a website that let them submit results anonymously if you were interested in being considered.

The end of the message included a personal note from Kaitlin and a photo of all three girls showing they were gonna get tested as well.

That had me leaning back in my seat. Her devastation that night had been over Penelope—Pen's illness and her not getting better. Cancer was an ugly damn word.

They were searching for a donor...

How sick was she?

I checked the time and then the links to the form. Clicking them, I found a clinic not far that would do the tests and submit them. After I wrote it down, then made a call, I went upstairs.

Lachlan didn't have to like it, but the least we could do was try. We might not be a match, but I wanted the results because I had a question for Gibs. One that would probably piss Mom off, but considering she wasn't talking to me right now—well, how much worse could I really make it?

"What?" Lachlan demanded when he yanked open the door.

"Let's go—we're going to donate blood and get tested."

"Thanks, but I'm clean." When he would have shut the door, I put my palm against it and held it open.

"This is for Kaitlin. You coming?"

Twenty-Four

KC

Pen had been fascinated by Jonas. The nurses had given him a crash course in isolation protocols for the pediatric care unit she occupied. He'd listened intently, followed all instructions, then gone inside with me.

All the way to the hospital, I second-guessed, then triple and quadruple-guessed, but I wanted Jonas to *see*. Truthfully, I wanted them *all* to see. They'd all judged me, believing rumors and gossip, and deciding they knew who I was before they ever met me.

Maybe I was guilty of the same *now*, because I'd never made any attempt to even find out if Dad's latest had kids. But then, his latest was someone who'd been around forever. They all seemed to have relationships with him that I didn't. And they knew him when Dad still saw me so—how come I never met them either?

Those thoughts haunted me after Jonas got his own car at the hospital to take him back. I offered to give him a ride—

well, for Dix to drive us—but Jonas did something both strange and a little endearing.

"No," he said almost gently. The shift in tone snared me almost as much as his intent expression. "Not that I don't want to spend the time with you, I do. I liked meeting Pen. She's an adorable baby—I never really liked kids before."

Not something I had a hard time believing. "But?" I prompted.

"*But* Lachlan and Ramsey are both there." He didn't add any caveats or explanations. "Not sure you want to see them."

"Not sure you want me to see them either?" It was a guess and for a moment, a flush touched his face and then he shrugged.

"I don't know that it's okay for me to want anything where you're concerned."

Not an unfair answer.

"I don't know either," I admitted. Did I want him to want something? That answer was layered beneath landmines and barbed wire. Not a place I really wanted to venture, right? "I did miss you," I could tell him that much.

"I missed you too."

That left us staring at each other, and me, at least, violently aware of Dix's observation. "Text me when you get back?" It was an olive branch that I could offer.

"I'd like to," he said. "I'd like it more if you texted me back."

That made me laugh and the sobriety in his expression gave way to a smile.

"I'll think about it." Yes, I was teasing and his smile grew. "And if you're feeling generous...tell Ramsey to text me too. If he really wants to talk to me, he needs to talk to me."

"Do you want to talk to him?" Yah, Jonas wasn't letting anything slide.

"I saw Lachlan at the club yesterday." Should I tack on I

had sex with him there? Not something I wanted to share with Dix. Even if he was used to guarding me, this was still pretty private. "I didn't mind talking to him."

Yeah, understatement.

"And we should probably talk about that later." I didn't look at Dix. Jonas did. Okay, so I wasn't being subtle. "But thank you for coming to see Pen."

"Can I come see her again?" That—surprised me.

"Don't make an offer that you may have to take back someday." I folded my arms. "She already has too much sadness in her life. I don't want her to add missing you to that list."

Not like I'd had to.

"I'm not going anywhere," he said, cutting his gaze to Dix once before he narrowed the distance between us. Voice lowered, Jonas said, "I don't want to miss you any more. I want—"

He hesitated and I caught his glance at Dix who'd taken a step closer to us.

"Can you go get the car, Dix?" I asked. "Jonas is getting a car to pick him up, but he'll wait with me while you go."

The flat look on Dix's face promised me he was not happy with my request, but I kept my focus on him and my smile neutral.

"Pretty please?" The little jostle did what the earlier request hadn't, it got him to smile—a fraction.

"It's not far," he said, transferring his look to Jonas. "Don't get any ideas. Don't let her out of your sight—and keep your hands to yourself."

They stared at each other in a furious stand-off for a long moment and then Dix cut a look at me before he turned heel and stalked off. He wasn't quite stomping his feet, but he'd made his dislike plain.

"Sorry," I muttered. "He's really protective."

"He's really jealous too," Jonas said, tracking Dix's exodus and I sighed.

"He's just protective..."

Instead of agreeing, Jonas looked back at me. "And he's jealous, KC. He doesn't want us around you. He's made that clear..."

I shifted my stance. "I hope not...Dix has been around forever and he's almost family. I think the kidnapping has fucked all of us up." That I could even say "the kidnapping" aloud without an ounce of irony just freaked me out. Not that I wanted to discuss it. "What did you want to say?"

"I wanted to say I don't want to miss you at all. I want to see you again. I want to be friends again. And maybe...maybe more."

"Maybe?" As soon as the word slipped out, I had to laugh then shook my head. "Sorry, you were being serious. I'm still a little—messed up with everything." Blowing out a breath, I cut a look to the annex where Dix would bring the car in then looked back at Jonas. "I have missed you—I think I kind of miss them—maybe. But there's so much going on and you guys thought so little of me..."

"I know, I want to say I'm sorry, but words don't fix it."

"They don't...but they help." I could admit that. "And you should know I saw Lachlan last night. At a club...and we got a little freaky."

"Okay."

That was it. Just—okay? "And by freaky, I meant I had sex with him."

He frowned a little. "Why?"

"Honestly?" I spread my hands. "I don't know. It felt good...I needed the release—I wish I had better answers for me as well as for you."

"Did you want to have sex with him?" It wasn't an unfair question.

"I don't think it occurred to me at first—when he kisses me, I get all kinds of turned on and I needed to feel something and—I liked it." winced. "This sounds really bad."

"No," Jonas said. "I don't like it. But it's not bad."

"I've had sex with both of your brothers." It wasn't a question. "And—yes, I keep bringing it up because—" We did not have time for this conversation.

"Because no more secrets," Jonas filled in that blank. "And no more lies."

"That would be good." Cause I was pretty sure we both needed that.

"That morning at school—before they took you—you called Lachlan."

"Yeah..."

"It wasn't to tell us to fuck off."

My mouth twisted. "No," I said slowly. "It wasn't." My car was coming, and Dix did not look happy. I sighed. We were going to need to talk. Glancing back to Jonas, I said, "Text me when you're home and I'll do the same."

"Okay." Then Jonas held up his hands for a moment, the hesitation clear, but when I took a step toward him he settled them on my biceps before he pressed a kiss to the corner of my mouth. It wasn't a real passionate kiss, but it was a sweet one. Not backing off, he said, "Let me know if Pen needs anything? I can come see her again."

My heart did a little flip flop. "I'd like that."

He nodded before he let me go. Dix was there and out of the car. I pinned him with a look when he started toward us.

"I'm coming," I told him and he paused before he pivoted sharply to open the back door. Yeah, he was annoyed.

"KC?"

I glanced back when I got to the car and met Jonas' gaze.

"The song you were writing—that was for Pen?"

The corner of my mouth tipped upward and I nodded. "It was."

"It's a good song."

Pleasure unfurled inside of me. "Just wish it was for a better reason."

"It's because you love her," Jonas said, his shrug easy. "That's a good reason."

It was a good reason. "Talk to you soon."

He smiled. "Absolutely."

While he didn't flip off Dix, I swore the look he gave him basically said to fuck off, and I let that go.

Dix was definitely not being friendly to him. Jonas didn't move as Dix slid into the driver's seat and he didn't look away as we pulled out of the annex. No sooner did we turn toward the road than my phone buzzed.

JONAS

He's jealous. Be careful.

ME

I will. Talk to you soon.

I wanted to dismiss the warning, ignore it. Dix was my friend. He'd been a part of my life forever. But if nothing else, the last few weeks had taught me there was far too much going on for me to be cavalier about anything. Even if I didn't think it was a *real* problem.

"I don't like that they're around," Dix said flatly. "First his brother last night, now him today."

"You don't have to like it," I said. "You do have to be polite."

"Excuse me?" He frowned at me and flicked a look toward me via the rearview mirror. "They are not your friends..."

"Actually," I said slowly. "Jonas and I were becoming friends."

"Were—and then stopped when he screwed you over."

I sighed. "It wasn't like that. I know it looked bad..."

"You looked *miserable,*" Dix countered. "You trusted him and he betrayed you. Second chances are not a good plan."

Wow, how much had Yvette and Aubrey filled him in on? "Dix—thank you for wanting to protect me. Jonas didn't have to come out here. None of them did. I still kind of can't believe they did..."

"Yeah well, they clearly want something from you."

But did they? I didn't want to have this fight. Jonas had been direct and honest. He'd also listened to me say I had sex with his brother and didn't lose his shit. That had to mean something, right?

Fuck, I had a headache.

"Gorgeous, I'm sorry," Dix said, his tone easing as I leaned my head back. "I know you're going through a lot. I just don't trust those boys."

"Yeah well, I don't know if I trust them either." I glanced at my phone. There were no news alerts or crazy stories about Kaitlin Crosse getting fucked at a club so...that was something. "But for a little while, things were good and then..."

I shut it all down.

"You want to stop somewhere and get something to eat?" Dix asked while I stared out the window. "You haven't really eaten that much today."

No, I hadn't. "No, I'm good. Just—let's go home. I want to see the girls. We have things we need to do..."

A song to record. I needed to find out what the hell my test results were too.

"KC..."

"Just let it go, Dix," I said. "Please. I'm tired."

He nodded and my phone buzzed with a news alert. Had I made an assumption too soon—no, it wasn't about me.

It was about Mom.

And her engagement.

I groaned and rubbed a hand against my face.

Dix didn't ask, but then I'd just asked him to let stuff go. I didn't want to tab open the story, but I looked anyway. There was Mom with her guru. She looked—different. The picture was not flattering. No way she authorized that release.

Not a chance in hell.

I scanned the story. It wasn't more than a puff gossipy piece about their upcoming nuptials and her potential retirement.

Shit, I needed to go back to New York. This officially passed the point of stupid. A throwaway line mentioned Dad, and their so-called "rock fairytale wedding." It also had a picture of his current wife.

Jonas' mom. Well, Ramsey's and Lachlan's too.

I stared at the picture of her and Dad. He looked stoned and she looked like she was smiling way too hard.

Linzi.

Her name was Linzi Crosse, but it didn't list her maiden name. The more I looked at her, the more familiar she seemed. Had I met her before?

Twenty-Five

KC

"Your mother..." Trish's voice climbed with irritation before she blew out a breath. "Her accountants are no longer sending out payments for anything."

I rubbed the side of my nose and stared out the windows toward the gradually dawning day. I wanted to go for a run, but I made the mistake of answering my phone *before* my coffee was ready.

Davina gave me a look of rough sympathy as she set it in front of me. That she added a plate with toast and the jars of jam with the butter dish was a very unsubtle reminder to eat.

Ruthlessly suppressing a yawn, I took a long drink of the coffee. Eyes closed as I savored it, I let Trish vent for another three minutes. A second sip buffered the grogginess. Sleep had proven elusive. Bad news did that.

I'd returned home to more bad news. Aubrey and Yvette had gotten their test results and I'd gotten mine. While mine were closer, it made sense, she was my sister, it wasn't an ideal match. Aubrey and Yvette weren't at all.

Even though I'd half-expected that, it was still depressing. More depressing was Bronson's call that like me, he was close but not ideal. Half-siblings weren't the best. While they couldn't rule all of us out, we hadn't managed to get everyone tested.

Trace was still avoiding my calls, if he was even getting my messages.

Dammit.

Despite being exhausted when I went to bed, I couldn't evade the shadows waiting for me. If it wasn't the bound up feeling trapping my arms and legs together, or the pitch darkness yanking me awake, it was chasing something nebulous. Or worse, running from something.

The fear burned in my stomach. I'd tried to turn off the light in the bathroom and sleep without it. Didn't last long. The second time I jerked away to the endless dark, I rolled out of bed and turned it back on. Even leaving the door cracked with a slice of light bisecting the room was better than the pitch darkness.

Still, lights on and curled up in the bed, I couldn't quite go all the way back to sleep. Dread curdled in my veins at what awaited. A few more hours and I could go run. That was what I told myself over and over to stay in the bed.

If I knew how to drive a car, I could have just gone and found a club myself. As it was, they'd have all freaked if I did it. I'd barely stumbled out of the bed when Trish called.

The fact Trish finally shut the fuck up gave me a chance to say something. "Trish, her accountants stopped payments because she's stopped talking to them." I downed another mouthful of coffee. "Even my business managers require regular check-ins to verify that standard payments should go out. If Mom isn't talking to them then there's probably a real chance there's nothing they can do."

"Can *you* do something?"

Could I? Sure. Would I? "I don't know," I hedged, choosing to answer my internal question rather than hers. "Not sure what I can," or should, I tacked on mentally, "do."

"Kaitlin, darling..."

"Trish," I said, firming my voice. "I don't work for you. I didn't hire you. You're Mom's friend and cousin, but you and I are not close. Let's not pretend otherwise." Harsh? Absolutely. Sometimes Trish needed harsh. "I will see what I can do. But you might think about looking into a job of your own."

"I *have* a job. Looking after your mother *is* my job."

"Not sure I'd put that on my resume, since I can't say you're doing a stellar job there. You want a better answer, she's in New York. Go see her—oh and while you're there? Maybe look after her since she's about to jump into another bad decision."

The gasp from the other end of the phone wasn't manufactured. I'd shocked her. To be fair to Trish, I usually tried to be polite. But she *and* my mother were grown-ups, why was it supposed to be *my* problem to fix things?

"Good, we understand each other," I said before she could comment. "I'm afraid I have to go. Talk soon." Then I hung up before she could say anything else. Dropping my chin, I groaned.

Movement behind me had me opening my eyes as Davina set a fresh coffee in front of me. Oh, shit, I'd killed mine already. I should switch to water if I was going to run.

Instead of moving away, Davina stood there, hands folded on the back of the chair. When I met her gaze, my stomach dropped. "Am I in trouble?"

Her smile gentled. "Absolutely not."

That helped.

"While I don't usually talk out of turn," she continued before I could savor that minor victory. "I wanted to tell you that I'm proud of you. It's long past the time you told both of them to grow up."

Leaning back in the chair, I canted my head. "You mean Trish and Mom."

"Yes. I love your mother. But she is a mess without someone to chase after her. She wasn't always..." With that, she sighed and shook her head.

"Trish means well." And she had always been there for Mom.

"She does, but like your mother—" Davina didn't edit herself. If anything, she tended to be blunt and on the nose with a kind of roughness that promised no lies and softened no blows. She never meant harm though. Frankly, I preferred the honesty. "Jennifer wasn't always like this, Kaitlin. She affects the flighty starlet, she plays the role to perfection because it was what everyone expected—especially after how she and your father fell out."

I made a face.

"I know, I don't talk about them together. They were—a chemical reaction. Fire and gasoline. When they burned hot, they were incandescent. But they could never seem to not compete with each other—your father needed her and she needed him, and they were too blind to see what they were doing to each other—and to you—before it was too late."

I wrapped my hands around the new cup of coffee. "Mom hated competing with his touring schedule."

"No," Davina said, this time with a firm shake of her head. "She hated competing with his music. Music has been, and always will be, your father's first and primary mistress."

Right. I grimaced.

"It is the truth, Kaitlin," she chided me. "You love music the way he does—or at least how he did. He could get lost in it, and your mother...God bless Jennifer, but she needs someone to love on her and shower her with affection. She needs someone to prove to her over and over, she is worth it because she will never believe she is."

"She's gotten better," I said, wanting to defend her.

"With Johnny she is better, but even with Johnny, she could not handle competing with his needs. His wants. His desires. Trish caters to her ego and tells her everything she wants to hear—until even Trish is tired of it." Davina's smile was sad. "Your mother is not a bad person."

"No, she's just a selfish one." I knew that about her and I loved her anyway. "Is that why Dad didn't stay? I mean—I figured it was all the affairs and Mom never did like being second fiddle to another woman."

"No woman will ever be his first—fiddle as you put it." The corners of her lips quirked in humor as I grimaced. "But no, it wasn't the affairs. His relationship with Jackie was a fleeting thing, even she would tell you that."

Sometimes I forgot that Davina and Jackie had gotten to know each other over the last few years. "Yet Bronson's only a few months older than me...so he was having an affair with her while with Mom."

"I opened this door..." Davina glanced at the hallway and then at me before she pulled out the chair and took a seat. "Your mother threw him out. For one week. She got scared and a bit childish. Gibs is—not a perfect man and your mother is not a perfect woman. He'd been in his studio day and night, obsessing over some song. Jennifer wanted his attention, throwing him out—got her the attention."

Oh my god.

"She wanted him to prove it." I downed half the coffee and I didn't care how hot it was. "To grovel and do some rom com shit to get her back."

"Yes." Davina's grimace had to match my own. "And it worked. He had his affair with Jackie, yes, but his focus was getting Jennifer back. One week to the day she threw him out, he showed up and serenaded her for over an hour. A private concert just for her..." A little sigh escaped her. "It was beautiful, and as romantic gestures go? Well, they were married three days later. And it wasn't long before you were on the way..."

"But that honeymoon phase didn't last."

"No."

"The day he left...the last time..." I blew out a breath. "His decision or Mom's?"

"His." Davina confirmed. "They'd had another fight. She burned his music."

I shuddered.

"He couldn't stay after that, but I think he still loved her."

"Not enough to fight for her."

"Fighting for someone isn't always worth it if all you do is fight *with* them. They were just too intense together. He couldn't do for her what she needed and craved and she couldn't do for him what he wanted."

I knew most of this, not the finer details, but at least the big picture parts. Knowing the little stuff... that changed things. "Do you know why he decided he didn't need me around anymore?"

"Kaitlin," she admonished me. "Did he tell you that?"

"He said...they weren't going to rely on custody agreements and weekends with him or whatever anymore. If I wanted to see him, all I had to do was call." That conversation was permanently burned into my memory. Melancholy flooded me. He'd left me behind and all I'd had was his guitar. Now I didn't even have that. "Then he went on tour..."

"And you and the girls decided to form Torched." Davina had been there. "You chased your music...just like your daddy..."

"Music doesn't let you down," I admitted. "I tried to call him, you know... a few times. He sent presents, twice a year, but nothing personal. No notes. No calls."

"I know," she told me. "You made your peace with it. But I don't think that's the case anymore."

No, it wasn't. So I buttered my toast and put the jam on it and then I told her about the guys. I told her about Ramsey and his judginess, but also how he went out of his way to try and help me. How he *did* help me. I told her about Lachlan and his bullying—because it was definitely bullying from the moment he tossed me into the pond and cut my bra to the night he kissed me while we were in costume.

I told her everything. Including how Jonas started talking to me with music and how we might have been on the first leg of building a bridge. "Then I found out they were my stepbrothers."

It was hard to keep the tears at bay then but I lifted my shoulders. "They judged me because I was Gibson Crosse's arrogant bitch of a daughter who was too spoiled to appreciate her father, and it turns out they all have way better relationships with him than I ever did. That they've known him for years...he showed up for *their* parents' day."

All at once the hurt was just there, a gaping black hole. A sucking chest wound that made it hard to breathe.

"He doesn't give a damn about Pen fighting for her life, or Bronson who is going to change the world. He's never met Allie, or Cam, or Zeke." I swallowed around the lump in my throat. "But those three? They think he hung the fucking moon. It's not fair."

I swiped at the tears, then tried to shake it off.

"Every single time, I think I'm past it—I'm reminded that he chose to not be in our lives. And yet, he paid my ransom." That part baffled me. "He paid it and when I tried to call him? Voicemail."

"Did you leave him a message?" Davina's eyes were suspiciously damp.

"I left three," I admitted. "I don't want to call anymore." I coughed and cleared my throat, then finished my coffee. "Mom's locked herself away with that cult and I know I need to go and get her. But they creep me out. Dad's paying my ransom but he can't pick up the phone. Pen..."

"Penelope is going to be fine," Davina told me firmly as she stood up and put her hand on my shoulder. "You keep that a fixed point in your head. We will figure this out for Penelope. If I have to walk up to your father and belt him with a frying pan, I will. He should at least get tested...have you gotten through to Trace at all?"

Trace. My eldest brother. The only sibling I had that pre-dated Mom in Dad's life.

"Nope. Nothing. I don't know if he's ghosting me or if I did something."

"You leave that one with me. I'll find him. I met him once. He was a sweet boy. A little sensitive, but then all of you are." She stroked a hand over my hair then pressed a kiss to my crown. "As for your mother...let's talk to Johnny. If you're going there to get her, he can go with you."

I didn't want to drag him into that. "Just like that?"

"Yes. Just like that." She looked thoughtful for a moment. "Finish your toast, hydrate, then go run. After, you take a shower. We're going to make you an appointment with Anastasia to get your hair done."

She lifted up my hand.

"Your nails too. Then we'll invite those boys to dinner."

Wait... "Davina..."

"Nope," she said, facing me. "You are not running away from your problems and you do not ever ask for what you truly deserve. They want you, they are going to have to prove themselves. That means they will come to dinner here where I can get a good look at them. I have plenty of frying pans. They can all get smacked."

A wet laugh escaped me.

"Better," she said firmly. "Now, go run. You will feel better after. I'll have the appointments set up before you're back up here and after you shower, you will eat a proper meal. You are getting too skinny and not taking care of yourself."

Finished with the conversation, she swept away my dishes and then handed me a refilled water bottle. I headed out for the gym and pulled on my headset.

Cranking up the playlist, I climbed onto the treadmill. I'd kill to do this outside—in the air.

I looked at my phone and at the messages on it. Jonas and I had exchanged a few the night before. There was a single message from Ramsey that had come in after I went to sleep— well attempted to sleep.

Nothing from Lachlan.

RAMSEY

How are you?

I stared at the message for a long moment.

ME

Tired. Not sleeping well. Would the three of you like to come to dinner here at the house?

I hit send before I could rethink it then switched back to my playlist and put the phone down. I needed to run.

Run. Shower. Hair appointment. Manicure.

Then see the douchebags.

The day had a plan.

Twenty-Six

LACHLAN

"Dinner," I confirmed. "She invited all three of us to dinner?"

"My answer hasn't changed since the last three times you asked me," Ramsey said as he looped his tie. He'd changed into a dark navy shirt and gone with a lighter colored tie.

"You do realize we're not at school, right?" I wanted to make sure. We'd only been in LA for a few days, but it was more than long enough for Ramsey to dislodge the stick from his ass.

"It's not about school," Ramsey said, giving me an enigmatic look before he ran a comb through his hair. He finished getting ready and pocketed his wallet, then his keys before he headed out the bedroom.

"What is it about then?" Because he hadn't explained it. I followed him down the stairs to where Jonas waited. He wasn't in a tie or dress shirt, thank fuck. He wore a black t-shirt tucked into black jeans and the only spot of color of him not on his arms was the guitar pick he had on a tie around his neck.

"KC," Jonas said, giving me a look like I was an idiot. "And we're supposed to be there by seven."

It was just now six. I checked my watch. "We can take my car, but it's a tight fit."

"We'll take mine," Ramsey said as he headed for the doors. "The rental was delivered an hour ago. It's also got more space in case—"

"In case she decides to leave with us?" I'd pulled on a Henley, not as casual as Jonas but nowhere near as dressy as Ramsey. "You're not usually this optimistic."

"We don't usually get second, third, and quite possibly for some of us—" Ramsey favored me with a look, making it quite clear he meant me when he said, "a fourth chance. She has zero reason to want to see us. But she invited us. So we're going and we're going to be respectful and hopefully—hopefully we have a chance of repairing what we broke."

I didn't roll my eyes. Tempting, but I didn't. This was about Ace and I—I wanted the chance even if I didn't want to admit it. Letting that dick Dix drag her away at the club stung and she hadn't said a word to me since.

She'd seen Jonas and she'd messaged Ramsey, but me?

Not a word.

"Let's go," Ramsey said at the door. "Unless you're driving yourself."

Tempting... "The point is a united front." I managed to get the words out without grimacing.

"Wow," Jonas mused. "You almost sound like you mean it."

"Fuck off, Jonas. It was my idea to come here, remember?" Maybe they *should* acknowledge that. Ace was my girl. I'd had my eye on her from the beginning. Hard to look away, especially when she stood up to all of us. The dare in her eyes, and the sharpness of her tongue. They appealed to me almost as much as the sweetness of her lips.

"Guys," Ramsey said from where he stood by the door. "If you plan on fighting all evening, we're not going."

"That's not your call," I told him but before either could snap, I held up a hand. "But I concede the point." I wanted to see her more than I wanted to one up them.

Jonas wasn't the only one staring at me suspiciously. But I just spread my hands and Ramsey sighed. "Lach, don't make me regret going tonight. Please."

The last word killed me. "You haven't seen her since school."

"No, and I haven't really had a chance to talk to her since the day she was kidnapped."

The day they slept together Fuck... "Fine. I will do my best and that's going to have to be enough."

He studied me a moment then looked at Jonas. "She doesn't hate me," Jonas said with a shrug. "We're already talking."

"Asshole," I muttered, and I could have sworn Ramsey said the same thing but his lips never moved. Maybe I imagined it. Either way, Ramsey opened the door and motioned us to go out.

The drive took for fucking ever. Not really, but the traffic and the fact they stuck me in the backseat made it feel that way. Ramsey and Jonas backing each other up amused me. Half the time Jonas wanted nothing to do with either of us. Normally, he resented Ramsey more than me cause Ramsey was bossy as fuck.

But not anymore.

Still, it was exactly seven when Ramsey followed the drive to the security gate. The gatehouse was inside the gate by about a dozen feet. I couldn't tell if anyone was in there but Ramsey reached over to press the intercom button.

"Crosse residence," a woman's voice said—*not* Ace. "Ahh, you must be the boys."

I sat up a little straighter in the back seat as Ramsey smoothed down his tie. "Yes, ma'am. Kaitlin invited us for dinner. Ramsey Malone. Lachlan Nash. Jonas Dekkar."

The woman didn't answer immediately and Jonas leaned forward as if he could see a camera on the intercom. But there were two other cameras on the gates.

"Did we get the date wrong?" Ramsey asked as though testing to see if she was still there.

"No," Ace said and relief spilled through me at the sound of her voice. "You got the date right. Jonas knows where you should park. Come on up." Then there was a beep and the gates swung inward.

"Fuck," Ramsey said on an exhale as he accelerated slowly. I couldn't agree more. Jonas didn't say anything. The place hadn't changed since the last time I came here. At least I didn't think it had, but then she just had me drop her off and she'd vanished.

I didn't really care about seeing the place, but seeing—

And there she was. She stood under the *porte cochere*, arms folded. The covered area in front of her front door—and the only reason I knew it was called that was cause I looked the name up.

Her blue hair seemed to practically shimmer, the color so vibrant I could barely look away. Even more provocative were her long, bare legs on display beneath a pair of white shorts. For a split-second, all I could see was the way she moved at the club and how she felt there.

Then it had been a skirt.

The hard-on I seemed to always sport whenever she was around was almost painful. Ramsey slowed as he got there.

"It occurred to me that Jonas was here but he came by ride share," she said, with a hint of an apology in her voice.

"Hey, KC," Jonas said. The prick, when did he get smooth?

"Hey." She smiled as she stepped up to the car and put a hand on the door so she could duck down. I had to fight the urge to slide over and just let myself out.

Wait? Why the fuck was I even fighting that? I slid across the seat and opened the back door. She spared me a glance then looked across to Ramsey.

"Just pull through and turn to the right. There's three spots there for guests. I don't mind if you leave the car here, but Mom gets pissed at oil stains on the flagstones." She gave a little shrug.

"Sounds good," Ramsey said. "Do we walk back here? Or..."

"Back here," she offered as she stood and I climbed out. She flicked a look at me briefly before she backed up. "I'll wait."

"Me too," I said, ignoring Ramsey's glare and slammed the door. If I was only going to get five minutes with her—if that—then I planned to take the time.

Arms folded, Ace lifted her brows at me before Jonas said, "Do you want me to stay too?"

That offer pissed me right the hell off but she glanced at my brothers, neither of whom had moved and I bit off growl.

"Thank you," she told Jonas, her smile warming a fraction. "I can handle Lachlan."

"Damn straight she can, fuck off for a minute," I told them. Ramsey's sigh carried an eloquence of its own, but I wasn't kidding.

The car started to pull away and I let out my own breath. Finally...

"Hey, Ace."

She studied me for a long moment. "Hi."

A dozen different questions formed and died unspoken on

my tongue. I took a step closer to her, half-braced for the idea she'd retreat. Instead, she just canted her head and kept those stunning eyes focused on me. Car doors slammed in the distance.

"How are you?" I pitched it lower, cause—I had to know.

Surprise danced across her expression and she lifted her shoulders a little. "I'm okay...just a lot on my mind. How are you?"

"I'd say same, but I think your worries are a lot heavier than mine. I was—I want to say I'm sorry about the club." Movement behind her showed my brothers heading our way, but they weren't rushing.

That was something.

"I'm not," she told me and that jerked all of my attention back to her.

"No?"

"No. I mean, I guess I'm sorry that I let Dix just hustle me out but...I didn't really know what to say right then anyway."

Fair "I didn't want to use words." I could admit that.

Her smile grew and she laughed. "No, you were busy using other things." There was just the barest hint of a flush to her face.

"And you enjoyed it." It was and wasn't a question.

"I did," she admitted and I had to clench my fists to keep from grabbing her and kissing her right there and then.

"Does that mean we're okay?"

She bit her lower lip, her lashes dipping as she looked to mull it over. Then Jonas and Ramsey were there. She twisted a little to include them in the moment. It distanced her a little from me—but only a little.

"Hi," she told them and when Jonas held out a hand, he waited for her to nod and then he touched her arm before he brushed a kiss to her cheek.

The urge to punch him resurged.

Then she looked at Ramsey and jealousy flamed right through me. Those glances were so damn loaded. "Thanks for coming," she murmured, before she cleared her throat. "Before we go in, I should warn you that—Davina has made a huge meal and she's going to be giving you all the once over."

And we gave a shit why?

"Who's Davina?" Ramsey asked. Yeah okay, probably a better way to phrase that.

"She's the housekeeper here, but—a lot more. She half-raised me and she's the best."

"So, be on our best behavior," Ramsey confirmed and Ace laughed.

He got a laugh.

Fucker.

"That would be nice." She glanced at all of us. "Yvette and Aubrey are also here for dinner, they promised me they would give you a chance, but I don't know how long that will last."

Yeah, they hated us.

"And Johnny is here…"

"The porn star?" Now I said something. Why the fuck was he—

"Johnny is a lot more than that," Ace said, her tone firm and I scowled. "He's family. You don't have to like it—clearly, you are very good at not liking things."

The verbal strike landed.

"It'll be fine," Ramsey said before I could muster a single word.

The fuck it would.

I wanted to have dinner with *her*, not the whole damn *Addams Family*.

"He came for your parents' day," Jonas said, his tone more thoughtful than annoyed and I caught him staring at me, not Ace.

"He did," she said, her expression warming. "Who knows, you might even like him."

Yeah, I wasn't placing bets on that.

"Come on," she said, pivoting to head inside. Jonas was a half-step behind her and Ramsey grabbed my arm before I could follow.

I cut a look at him. "What?"

"Behave," he said. Before that patronizing tone could piss me off even further, he added, "I know you care and want more private time with her. So do I. But this is what we've been invited to. Try not to blow this."

Irritation dug bloody scores in side of me and I scowled. While he didn't add that we may not get any more chances, I heard it loud and clear.

Ace didn't regret having sex. We were invited.

"Fine," I said. "But if that dick Dix is here—"

"We'll do nothing," Ramsey said, cutting me off. "We'll be polite. Her friends. Her family. They belong here."

We didn't. The implication was there.

We didn't belong right *now*.

"Things change." Not an observation, but a promise.

"They can, if we don't burn any more bridges than we already have."

I hated when he was right.

His faint smile said he knew it too. When he strode inside to follow them, I turned to see Ace and Jonas waiting a dozen steps away.

I grinned at her and she rolled her eyes.

Jonas had gotten smooth and Ramsey was right.

Fuck it, she still said she didn't regret sex with me.

I could build on that.

Twenty-Seven

KC

From the moment Davina decided on the idea of meeting the douchebags, she'd been in full-scale plan mode.

A dinner party.

I didn't host dinner parties. Mom did—occasionally. More than once I'd had to attend one for the label, but that was all business. This—*wasn't*.

Still, she set the menu, the formal dining table and suggested we dress up. I said no. Shorts and t-shirts were fine. I should have known Ramsey would make an appearance in a dress shirt and tie.

He looked great. His appearance definitely scored points with Davina. Yvette and Aubrey were not so easily swayed. Though Aubrey had shifted the name placards around so the only one of the boys sitting near them was Jonas.

Fair.

They put Johnny in the middle, a buffer, between Aubrey and Lachlan. Yvette claimed the other end of the table opposite me. That left me with Lachlan on my right and Ramsey on my left.

My awareness of them was at an all time high, but it was Ramsey who kept pulling my attention. Not with conversation, because he wasn't saying much, but with his attention.

Each time I let my gaze trail to him, his focus was intense. A part of me kind of wished we were alone. There was so much left unsaid and—fuck, Davina was right. I didn't run away and I had been hiding.

Maybe not "full-throttle" fleeing, but definitely not facing up to the questions in his eyes or in my own head.

"So are you going back to school in the fall?" Johnny asked and it tugged my attention from Ramsey toward Johnny again. I paused, wrapping spaghetti around my fork. Davina had gone all out with my favorite three meat sauce, the different types of pasta, and hands down the best ever home-made garlic bread.

It took a moment to realize why the whole table went quiet. Johnny was staring at me. School?

Did I plan on going back for the autumn? I—the immediate "no" wouldn't unstick itself from my tongue.

"*Ta Gueule,*" Yvette swore, as she lowered her fork. The stricken look on her face damn near undid me. "Don't tell me you changed your mind... the experiment was not worth all those threats."

"In all fairness," Aubrey said before I could answer. "We hadn't made any firm decisions about college before we even went to Blue Ivy."

"You didn't?" Jonas picked up the thread easily. "It was all Ramsey ever wanted to do, and Lachlan had plans for Stanford, then came back to Blue Ivy."

"You didn't have plans?" I latched onto the lifeline he pitched out there whether he realized it or not.

"I want to do music," Jonas said, meeting my gaze without

an ounce of shadow or deflection in his eyes. "I wasn't really planning on college so much as trying to get the songs written."

"I know Dad sang one of yours." I kept my tone light. The sting of that was still there, but more and more, I didn't think Jonas was the one at fault. "Not bringing that up to be a problem—just—writing music can be a difficult field to break into. You can do it. A lot of artists don't write their own stuff."

"But you do," Ramsey said, pulling my attention from Jonas. "A lot of what you three have recorded was written by one or all of you."

"I'm okay at writing music—I see the words more than the melodies. Aubrey is good at melodies. Yvette is really good at tying it all together." I grinned at them.

"But you have written music," Lachlan said. "Maybe not a lot, but you were working on something on your guitar—I saw the sheets. Or was that you and Jonas working on something?"

The guitar. A pang went through me. They'd never found Dad's guitar. I guess that it, like my peace of mind, was gone for good.

"We have worked on some stuff," Jonas jumped back in. "KC was helping me, I like the melodies and the movement in the music. The poetry of interconnected notes and the motifs —lyrics are harder."

Johnny took a drink. "This is all pretty fascinating, but— what about college?" He focused on me. "Or are you three going to go on tour again?"

The temperature in the room shifted and there were three male gazes in addition to Johnny's pinned on me. "We haven't decided," I said, choosing my words carefully. "National tours are exhausting and world tours are—an exercise in patience and caution."

I locked eyes with Aubrey, then Yvette. Did they mind if I shared our discussion? Yvette considered it even as Aubrey shrugged. I gave it another beat then Yvette nodded.

"Our manager and our label want us to work on a new album," I said, snaring their attention again. "We're not quite ready to work on a full album." I swirled up some more spaghetti on my fork. "But we're going to record a single for cancer research fundraising and the label is going to work on a full album, maybe with other artists, to do a real fundraiser."

"For Pen," Jonas said softly and I smiled.

"For her and for others like her…"

"How is she doing?" Ramsey asked.

"Still sick, still looking for an answer. We're searching for donors and our fans are—amazing." I had to swallow back the tears that wanted to claw up my throat. "So many people are getting tested to see if they would be a good match."

I cleared my throat and then reached for my glass. The sympathy in the room was a warm hug. I did not want to start crying again. Instead, I focused on the glittering nail polish Anastasia's girl had done for me while Ana did my hair.

The tears were right there, the grief gouging deep into my chest. It was almost impossible to take a deep breath for how much it hurt. A hand feathered over my knee and I glanced to Ramsey briefly as he settled his hand more firmly on my leg.

The weight of it, the connection almost ephemeral until I blew out a breath. The light seemed to reflect off his glasses and add a sheen to his blue eyes. He gave my knee the gentlest of squeezes and I summoned a smile for him. Comfort.

He was offering me comfort. Just as he had when he found me shattered in the rain. Offering it without asking for anything.

Like the earlier pampering from Anastasia, Ramsey's contact grounded and buoyed me in the same breath. Nothing could make the pain go *away* but they helped to make it a little more bearable.

"As for um—college," I said, circling back to Johnny's question. "I don't know. The school—offered me two years of free tuition." I made a face. "And my pick of autumn classes."

"You didn't tell me that," Aubrey said, surprise dancing across her expression. Surprise, not reproach.

"Honestly, it all feels a little cover your ass for my taste..."

A leg brushed against mine, a foot sliding under my right leg even as Ramsey kept his hand on my left leg. The nudge came from Lachlan.

At my glance, he lifted his chin. "They should cover their ass where you're concerned. They didn't do enough for your security..."

"I don't know that anyone could have prevented that," I admitted and made a face. That being the kidnapping. "How many times did I go out running in the morning? Or go for coffee?" I got careless. Fuck, even when Lachlan had been a pain in the ass... I relied on *RJ* of all people. Clearly, my judgment was questionable. "Should have learned my lesson with you, huh?"

The minute the words were out, I regretted them. The evening had been going well but Aubrey glared at Lachlan and so did Jonas. Ramsey flexed his hands and when I shifted my gaze to Lachlan his expression flattened for a moment.

"I didn't want you running alone," Lachlan pointed out but before I could even get into how combative he sounded. "I didn't have to be such a dick about it."

"No, you definitely didn't need to be a dick about it. You seemed to enjoy it—"

"Define how you were a dick about it," Johnny interrupted, his whole attention on Lachlan.

Lachlan shrugged. "We had our wires crossed—"

"If by crossed you mean fucking whacked," Aubrey

stepped right in. "Then yes, you did. You made a lot of assumptions about our girl."

"We did," Jonas said swiftly. "Our mistakes."

"Agreed," Ramsey said. "Not only the assumptions, but not just confronting the assumption head on, particularly when nothing in your demeanor or behavior supported what we thought."

"Some of it did," Lachlan argued, and his leg jerked away from mine abruptly and I glanced at Ramsey who *glared* at Lachlan. "Okay, deny it all you want—I'm not saying every-thing was true, but Ace was arrogant."

He glanced at me like I should just agree with him.

"You were also not the friendliest..."

I rolled my eyes. "You were a fucking dick. Why would I be friendly? You and your *girlfriend* also went out of your way to make my life hell."

"She wasn't my girlfriend..."

"Anymore," Jonas supplied helpfully. "Not that he really liked dating her. She was more like a social disease."

I had to put my napkin to my lips to keep from spitting food when I laughed. Social disease.

"That's a very good description of her," Aubrey said.

"I'm still back on how you were a dick about it," Johnny said in a less than friendly tone. "What did you do to our KC?"

"I guess my worst crime was shoving you in the pond," Lachlan admitted with probably the least self-aware grimace ever. There was just enough snark in that comment and in his expression, that I didn't think he was being obtuse.

Not obtuse at all. He was just being a dick.

I pushed back from the table, and Ramsey had to let go of my leg as I stood. I was going to take the plates into the kitchen.

"Your worst crime was definitely not shoving me in the pond," I said as I glanced at Ramsey's plate. "Are you done?"

"Yes, but I can—"

I touched a hand to his shoulder. "It's fine. I'd rather move for a minute. I got it."

"Then what was my worst crime?" Lachlan asked as he stood. For a half-second, I thought he was going to step into my path when I circled him

"Really? You need me to tell you," I said, locking gazes with him. Johnny had risen with his plate and I rescued it from him. I could come back for the rest.

"Do your worst," Lachlan dared me. "I remember the parts you liked."

Right.

Okay.

Fuck you, Lachlan.

"That would be when you cut my bra off and then let me know there wasn't much to brag about where my tits were concerned." I didn't glare and I didn't raise my voice. But those words slammed down between us. "In case your memory needs a refresher, that would be right *after* you shoved me in a pond."

Pivoting on my heel, I headed for the kitchen with the dishes and left the dead silence in my wake. The door did a little whump after I passed through it and swung back and forth a little.

Davina frowned as I went to scrape off the plates, but before she could say anything a dish crashed in the other room. I made it back in time to see Lachlan picking himself up, nose and mouth bloody as Johnny loomed over him.

"You don't treat women like that, punk," Johnny informed him. "And you sure as shit don't get to treat our KC like that."

"Amen," Aubrey said, toasting Johnny with her water.

"Hit him again," Yvette suggested. "I don't think he understood the lesson."

I wasn't sure what shocked me more, Johnny punching Lachlan again when he got to his feet, or the fact that Jonas and Ramsey just watched. Hell, Jonas broke off a piece of garlic bread and motioned toward them.

"He's hard-headed, Yvette's probably right."

"Fuck you, Jonas." The teasing and the snark were gone.

I made it one step into the room and Ramsey rose. "Hey, Kaitlin... think we could talk for a minute?"

"Um—" I blinked at him then back to where Johnny was all but marching Lachlan out of the dining room. "Right now?"

"Now would be good. Lachlan's got to finish writing the check his mouth is trying to cash."

Jonas sighed. "I'll go watch... talk to Ramsey. I can talk to you after..."

"Oh, I wanna watch," Aubrey said with a laugh and then they were all gone and it was just me and Ramsey.

"Talk?" Ramsey asked, his smile almost gentle and I gave him a belated little nod.

What the hell just happened?

Twenty-Eight

RAMSEY

That Lachlan had to push it? That never shocked me. But a part of me *almost* understood why he was being such a raging dick right now. Didn't mean I supported it and I sure as shit had no problem if the guy my siren called *family* put Lachlan in his place.

He'd survive.

As if suspended by her hesitation, Kaitlin glanced to where the others had disappeared. There was no yelling or shouting. I'd prefer to relocate *before* they came back. Taking the risk, I brushed my fingers down the side of her hand.

When she turned, her palm brushed mind and she threaded our fingers. The jagged, uncomfortable bits inside of me began to settle. Something had snapped inside of me when I woke to her gone. The kidnapping, the bullshit with Gibs— and Mom—then my siren just pushing us all away seemed to break it further.

"Hi," she said in a softer voice. "You wanted to talk?"

"Please." I tried to infuse that single word with every

ounce of feeling I possessed. From the uncertainty of seeing her again, to the need to make right my own mistakes, to wanting to just *protect* her, I poured all that feeling into the word.

I had so much to make right with her and I just wanted the chance.

She searched my expression for a moment, then gave my hand a gentle squeeze. "Okay." But instead of heading out into the house, she turned to the kitchen and pushed the door inward. Thankfully, she never let go of my hand.

"Davina," she called. "Dinner was fantastic, but Ramsey and I are going to talk. If the others come looking for us, can you just have them wait?"

The woman approached the door, then gave me a measuring look. She'd worn the same when we were introduced to her shortly before dinner was served. "You will behave," she informed me. "I have a lot of frying pans."

Despite the lightness of her tone, there was no mistaking the absolute sobriety in her eyes. The woman pinned me with a look. It wasn't a threat.

It was a promise.

The fierce protectiveness in the people around Kaitlin made me happy. Maybe happy wasn't the right word, but I liked the implied security of it all. Especially after the past couple of years.

"You have my word," I said.

She nodded once. "Go on, I'll deal with the others."

Laughter escaped my siren and she leaned forward to brush a kiss to Davina's cheek. The affection was clearly shared, but what settled me more was that Kaitlin didn't let go of my hand.

Instead of heading in the direction of everyone else, she led me out of a different door of the dining room. It took us out onto a veranda. The breeze was cool, the sound of water lapping warned me of the pool before we continued around the house following the covered sandstone path to a different door.

Kaitlin opened that door and led me through to what looked like a sitting room, but we didn't stay in here. Instead, she guided me out into a hall and up a back set of stairs.

"Okay, I was going to wait until we got wherever, but how big is this house?"

Kaitlin laughed. "Pretty big, but we're in my wing—and yes, I know how arrogant that sounds."

"Not arrogant," I assured her. Especially after the crap Lachlan pulled. "This is your mom's house, right?"

"Yep," she told me, popping that "p." Upstairs was another longer, wider hall. It was cool and quiet. There was art along the walls—art and pictures.

I damn near stopped dead at the picture of Kaitlin and Gibs. She couldn't be more than five, but they were sitting side by side and she had the largest guitar in her lap.

It had to be one of his. Gibs had his own and he leaned toward her and she was grinning up at him. Artless, unaware of the world, and emotion was a sucker punch. That image encapsulated everything I'd ever believed about her relationship with Gibs.

"That was a long time ago," she said softly and I blinked. I hadn't meant to stop walking, but she studied the image. "I don't even remember who took that picture. Pretty sure Mom was doing a movie. I barely remember that week, just a lot of music and laughter. It was fun...then he had another tour."

She shrugged like it didn't matter, but that wasn't true. Pivoting, I faced her and raised a hand. "May I?"

Head tilted, she glanced up at me and then nodded. I cupped her cheek, giving into the urge I'd had to ruthlessly suppress for weeks.

The softness of her skin was a marvel as I skated my

thumb over the line of her cheekbone. "I am so damn glad that you're okay," I whispered. "All I've wanted to do since I woke up alone that morning was find you, kiss you, and tell you it would be all right."

Questions seemed to shimmer in her eyes, but she didn't ask any of them. If anything, she just stared up at me. Waiting.

I sighed. "I wish I'd known—that night—I wish I hadn't assumed anything."

"I don't regret it," she admitted, one corner of her mouth quirking upwards. "I don't regret you—I needed... I needed to not be alone. That's what I told myself, but what I really needed was someone to care. You cared."

"Yes, I did," I said on a long exhale. "I still care."

She licked her lips and the sight of her tongue gliding over her lower lip was provocative as hell. But I didn't come here to have sex with Kaitlin. I came here to repair what I'd damaged and to earn the right to have sex with her again.

One step at a time.

Cause I really wanted her.

If I had any doubts at all, they were erased the moment she welcomed us at the car.

"I don't know what to do with that yet," she admitted slowly. "But come on—the girls and Davina will make sure Jonas is fine."

I chuckled. Reluctant to let her go, I pressed a kiss to her forehead and then dipped my head a little closer. Not closing the distance until she pressed a hand to my chest and pushed up on her toes. Then I was kissing her. The softness of her lips parting against mine was almost an invitation.

But I didn't take control, giving it all to her even as I drank in that nearness. The first teasing brush of her tongue though and I slid my hand down to her nape and then wrapped another arm around her. Picking her up, I brought her level so I could devour the taste of her and soak up her nearness.

Heat licked through me as she scraped my tongue with her teeth and then she wrapped her arms around me. Reason went up in flames as she hitched her thighs to my hips. The light shirt in no way hid her breasts from me or the gentle weight of them where they rubbed against my chest.

Fuck, I wanted her. In between bites and almost kittenish licks, she whispered, "You wanted to talk."

"I do," I promised her. "We need to talk." I kissed a path to her ear. The scent of her shampoo held traces of coconut and something tropical. Latching onto her earlobe, I sucked against it gently even as I cupped her ass, "I need you to know something though..."

My good intentions were going up in flames. I found myself wanting to strip her bare again and take my time, where it had seemed too goddamned rushed before. I wanted to let her fall asleep after and then wake her up again.

And again.

I wanted to make her smile.

That was a punch in the gut. She fisted my hair, the tug sparked through me woke me the fuck back up. I focused on her as I pulled back.

"What?" The flush to her cheeks and the rapid, shallow breaths were an encouraging sign.

"Your breasts are amazing," I promised her. "Perfect to fit in my hand, and I love the way your nipples tighten up when I suck on them. I love even more how your skin flushes around them and the little sounds you make when I nip them."

Her eyes rounded and in the dim light of the hall, her pupils seemed huge. "The sound..." The half question was all the encouragement I needed.

Lifting her a little higher, I pinned her against the wall and then bit down on her nipple through the shirt. The swift in-drawn breath, the way her legs clamped to my hips and the first little gasp that gave way to a moan as I bit a little harder made me smile.

"Just like that," I whispered before I gave the other breast the same treatment. The bra she had on was thin and lacy. I could feel it through the shirt, and I spent some time on her other breast, laving attention to emphasize the point. The shirt probably muted some of the attention.

Sliding a hand up under her shirt, I caressed the skin and when I pulled back to meet her feverish eyes, I smiled.

"Your breasts are perfect. Lachlan's a fucking idiot."

Laughter bubbled out of her and when I nudged her shirt higher, she fisted my hair again. "Ramsey..."

I shuddered. There was just something about the way she said my name. "Siren, I'm trying very hard to not just throw you down on your bed and fuck you until we both scream. That—don't moan my name."

"What if I want you to?" The challenge there held me captive.

Running my tongue over my lips, I savored the promise of her kiss. "I can absolutely do that—*after* we talk." The declaration cost me, but it was important. "Don't mistake for a second that I want you. I've wanted you far more than I ever should have when you were still my student. Now? Now I want you over me, under me, in front of me, on your knees, on my face..."

Her face flushed a deeper pink.

"But I want us to be on the same page, Siren. I want to know what's in your head and you to know what's going on in mine..."

"And your brothers." Her soft pants encouraged me though, so did the fact that I was grinding my erection against the seam of her very thin fucking shorts.

"They're a factor," I admitted. "But this is about you and me."

Self-control, I reminded myself. I had it. She deserved it. She deserved everything.

Kaitlin closed her eyes and took several deep breaths. She tilted her head back, exposing her throat, and I pressed my lips against her pulse point. The frantic flutter of her heart steadied me.

"Do you want me, Siren?" I had to know. That was our first step. Her answer wasn't immediate, but I waited her out and when I lifted my head, she nodded.

"I probably shouldn't," she admitted.

"No probably about it," I agreed with her. "I'm—or I was — your teacher. One of them."

"And my step-brother," she supplied and I gave a faint smile.

"My brothers want you—" That was another twist. It wasn't just Lachlan and *his* arrogance, there was also Jonas and his devotion.

"Is it a problem that I like them too—even if I shouldn't?"

"Well," I said, nuzzling another kiss along her jaw. "Siren —I'm not telling you anything is wrong. I know Lachlan found you at a club."

"We—had sex." That admission didn't bother me as much as I thought it would. "It was different."

"Did you enjoy it?" That question lingered between us and she let out a little laugh. I leaned back to study her reactions.

"Yes," she whispered, then grimaced. "This is a weird conversation to have."

"Well, it's one we need to have. I don't want any other misunderstandings between us. Whatever happens with Jonas and Lachlan—whatever happens with me...understand I *want* more. I intend to pursue more—but we're doing this in a way that says we're both on the same page."

A shaky breath escaped her. She searched my face, then my

eyes. I had no idea what she was looking for, but I kept my gaze on hers. I kept it direct.

"I don't know how this works... and you were such an asshole."

"I was," I told her. "I can apologize and I want to make it up to you. But I *need* you to let me try...please."

Her pink tongue was so sweetly enticing as she licked her lips. "I don't know how to do this..."

"We'll figure it out," I promised her. "I'm pretty good at research and application."

Her expression went through some comical contortions before she started laughing and it was the sweetest sound.

"Is that a yes?" I asked and her grin gave me hope. So did her laughter.

Then her smile faded and her eyes sobered. "Please don't hurt me again."

"I didn't want to hurt you the first time." If that didn't fucking break my heart, I didn't know what would. "I never want to hurt you again."

I meant it.

"Then yes..." she said and I closed my eyes as I pressed my forehead to hers. "Yes...we can talk and figure this out."

We *could* do this...

We just had to make it happen for us.

Twenty-Nine

KC

Someday, I'd write a song about this. I could almost *feel* the lyrics tickling my brain. Some songs were a struggle to get out. Others sprang fully-formed like they were Athena leaping free from Zeus' forehead. The simile didn't quite work the same way, yet with my arms wrapped around Ramsey's neck and his intense stare seemingly holding mine hostage, I could feel the song unfurling.

I didn't want to hurt you the first time...

Probably not what I should be focused on right now and at the same time... I teased my fingers through his hair. It was a little longer than it had been before. Softer too. Or had I just not noticed? We stood there in the hallway, forehead to forehead, and I could probably stand like this forever. It was—oddly safe and that was so damn enticing.

Enticing enough I wasn't sure I *could* trust it.

"What are you thinking, right now?" Ramsey asked and I let out a long breath. It wasn't quite a sigh. His brow furrowed and the intensity in his blue eyes seemed to ramp up. All the moisture in my mouth fled and I pulled back a little, shaking my head.

"C'mon," I invited him, sliding my hands down his arms until our fingers linked. "You wanted a minute. We might be upstairs and in my wing, but the girls also have rooms here." I would never not have space for them.

Ramsey let me lead him down the hall. When I'd brought him up here, I'd intended to escape into the entertainment room. It was private without being intimate. Instead, I went farther down the hall to my room. When I let go of one of his hands to open the door, he crowded right into me, tugging me into his chest like I was going to escape.

"I'm not running away," I promised him.

His expression tightened briefly, then relaxed into a smile as he glanced from me to the room and then back to me. "You know I wasn't here to try and get you back into bed, right?"

There was something almost painfully sweet in the way he looked so fierce. "Does that mean if I invite you, the answer is n—"

His mouth fused to mine, not even letting me finish the question, and I didn't give a shit. The door closed and I reached past him as his tongue thrusts had me clenching up in excitement. There was a lock—there. Finding it, I twisted it once. The sound of the tumblers seemed really loud in the room as the deadbolt slid home.

Ramsey dragged out my lower lip as he lifted his head. His lips were wet and his formerly neat hair was disheveled. I swallowed hard because he looked—delicious. Even his tie was askew.

"I'm not telling you no," he said firmly. "I also don't expect anything either. The fact you're even talking to me is more than enough... *for now*." He traced his fingers down my cheek even as I loosened his tie. "Let's be one hundred percent clear on our communication."

"Let's," I invited him as I pulled his tie free. I folded it carefully and set it on the shelf nearest the door. "I wanted you that night...I know you were worried that I didn't. That I was too out of it from how badly I'd been crying." Even now, I could feel how sore and swollen my eyes had been. "But I did want you. I wanted you to kiss me and to touch me. I wanted you then." I emphasized the last sentence while holding his gaze. "And I want you now."

That admission took effort. I hated being this—needy. At the same time, every single word was true.

"I just don't want to get hurt again." I shuddered at that confession. I'd said it once, but repeating it just seemed to emphasize the hurt I'd already experienced.

When he opened his mouth, I pressed my finger to his lips.

"You didn't hurt me then—I mean yes, it hurt a little, but it also felt good. I'm talking about what happened next. You asked me to stay and to talk. I won't lie and say I didn't think about just taking off. I got a little scared and maybe a little shy and embarrassed."

Heat flushed my cheeks as I backed off a step and then I reached for the hem of my shirt. Up and off it went before I changed my mind.

"I really wanted to talk to all three of you and try to figure this out. Then the kidnapping and..." This time it was a shiver that traveled up my spine. The sound of feet slapping the pavement, the blow as someone slammed into me. Then my head hitting the ground. The shadowy images rifled through me like pages in a book being flipped. Then I was in the darkness, trapped, and alone... Ramsey covered my hands on my shirt where I was crushing it.

"Stay here with me," he murmured and those four words grounded me. I let go of the shirt and when he wrapped an arm around me, I was already pushing up on my toes.

"I'm here," I promised. The heat of him washing over me

was almost enough to chase away the chill. The stroke of his hands on my skin and then he was kissing me. Tongue tangling with mine, he walked me backward toward the bed. I knew every inch of this room, I remember to take the steps up to where the bed was—on a platform.

Everything in this house had a bit of a stage influence.

A laugh bubbled through me as he traced the line of my bra and then unhooked it. The scraps of lace were gone and I was still fumbling with the buttons of his shirt. Ramsey devoured my mouth or maybe that was me, trying to feed my suddenly voracious appetite. He'd tucked his damn shirt in—I swore against his lips and he chuckled. My shorts were already sliding down my legs.

"I win," he said and then he lifted me up and I landed on my bed. Staring up at him, I forgot how to breathe. He'd pulled off his glasses, and his shirt was open to his navel. His belt was open and he unzipped his pants slowly as he looked at me. "Ah," he said, when I started to sit up. "I got your clothes off first, which means I get to play with you first. Those are the rules."

Surprise filtered through me. "There are rules?"

"Hmm-hmm. Oh Siren, there are definitely rules where you are concerned. Right now, rule number one is you lay back and let me explore every inch of you. I've been wanting to taste you forever..."

Oh. Shit. My nipples tightened under his stare, but his words had my ass clenching even as he nudged my thighs apart. The way he studied my legs and my abdomen, and then my pussy had me shivering all over again. I was almost too exposed and not enough at the same time.

Did I like this? Fuck, I had no idea but I certainly didn't hate it. He licked two of his fingers and then traced around my clit. It was the lightest of contact and I lifted my hips up but he just chuckled.

"You waxed..." The comment teased me out the half delirious state between lust and panic. I blinked at him and then he was running his hand over my smooth skin.

"Bathing suit season," I said, scrambling for the first thing that came to mind. "Also—I—"

"Did you wax for me?" The soft timbre of his voice wasn't a tease and suddenly the weight of his gaze held me captive like he'd pinned me to the bed. "There was a stripe of blonde here before."

The heat flushing my cheeks turned absolutely scalding and I bit my lower lip. "I—I'd say swimsuit season but..."

"But?" He prompted, the gentle caress of his fingers almost too light to give me the friction I craved.

"But Aubrey and Yvette both told me guys like it bare..." I wasn't sure if it turned me on to admit that or if I wanted the bed to swallow me.

"Did they?" The half-mused aloud question didn't seem directed at me.

"Do you?"

"Do I what, Siren?" The faint tilt to his lips was definitely a tease.

"Do you like it bare?"

"Good question," he said and then went to his knees even as he slid his hands down my legs.

"Good—oh shit."

He hauled me to the edge of the bed and my legs were over his shoulders and he pressed the most carnal kiss to my pussy I could imagine. His lips and tongue were competing sensations between the thrusting tease and the sucking promises. The wave of embarrassment collapsed into pure hedonism as pleasure spiraled through me.

Fisting the comforter, I bucked up against his mouth as he nipped and licked. It was almost too much and not enough. I wanted to grind against him, but he had one hand on my hip and it kept me in place. In between lightning thrusts of his tongue against my channel, and the biting kiss of his lips to my clit, he would nip and suck kisses against where my thigh joined my body.

It was too much. The sting made it more and I was panting when I caught him staring up the length of my body as he tormented my clit all over again. "Play with your breasts, Siren," he ordered, the vibration of his words adding another layer of temptation.

It was kind of like my vibrator—only a lot sexier and completely *not* under my control. Licking my lips, I let go of the comforter and cupped my breasts. He bit down on my thigh again and there was a little more pain this time.

A soft gasp escaped me.

"I said play with them, Siren—massage them, pinch your nipples, roll them—make it feel good."

"I—"

"Do it," he murmured before he traced his tongue along my slit and warm gush seemed to escape me even as I clenched. "Hmm—I am enjoying my taste, but I want to see you help yourself to the pleasure."

"I want to touch you." Yes it was a complaint, but the fact his face was damp with *me* wasn't lost on me and I wanted to feel him under my hands and his cock inside of me again.

"You will," he promised, massaging my thighs. The gentle stroke of his palms eased some of the tension out of me. "C'mon, Siren. Play with yourself. I want to see you take the pleasure you deserve."

"I have a vibrator if I want to do it to myself," I retorted and his eyebrows edged upwards.

"Do you?" Then he glanced around my room. "Good to know. Stay right there." He pressed a kiss right to my clit, this time the scrape of his teeth sparked more pleasure than any pain and I clenched right up. "Keep it next to the bed, do you?"

The words died unspoken cause I wasn't sure I wanted to tell him, but he didn't wait. Instead he eased away and went to the drawer on the right hand side of the bed. How did he—my phone charger was right there. I rolled to my side to watch as he pulled the drawer open.

The sudden grin on his face killed any self-consciousness. "My siren likes variety." He glanced at me and I couldn't help but smile back. I wasn't sure if it was the pleasure in his voice or the fact he called me his that did it, but the delight in his eyes was hard to deny. "Good to know." When he picked up the small wand massager, I sucked in a breath.

"Ramsey..."

"If you don't want me to use this," he told me, his expression turning serious. "I won't."

"It's not that..." I licked my lips again.

"No?"

"No." I crossed my heart like he needed to see it. "I just want you more than I want it."

"Yeah?" He grinned as he walked back to where I was laying. I rolled onto my back to stare up at him. "You want me enough to play with your breasts like I told you to?"

"I'd rather touch you."

"I know, and you will. But I want to see you play with yourself."

"Then I can have you?" Hope swelled up within me and the fact I could see his erection straining against the front of his jeans told me that I wasn't alone in my desire.

"Then you can have both," he whispered, dropping over me and catching himself on one hand before he licked a kiss to my lips. I opened at the first brush to taste myself on him and it—wasn't unpleasant. If anything, it made me more curious and when I would have chased the kiss, he nipped my lower lip. "Breasts, Siren. *Now.*"

That whipcrack of command just—fuck it, I cupped my breasts even as he held my gaze and then I teased my nipples. Yes, I knew exactly what I liked, how much pressure to put there, to pinch and to tug.

"Good girl," he whispered before he kissed me again. "Keep it up."

It was so much more intense like this. And I was aching from wanting him to touch me but he wasn't, anywhere but where our mouths fused. When I let out a little gasp, 'cause the twisting pulls of my nipples just made them more tender, Ramsey smiled against my mouth.

"Such a good girl." He nudged my thighs up again, pulling me right to the edge as he watched me. "Keep it up, just like that…" Then his shirt was off and I drank in the sight of his chest and the ink there. I hadn't really gotten a good look before. Fuck, he was a pretty man. Then his jeans were off and his cock was thick, red, and angry looking.

Another shudder went through me and I arched at the teasing.

"That's it—a little more." He kept up the steady string of encouragement. "That's my siren, I want you to feel every inch of me and I want you to feel nothing but good this time—"

Oh. "It felt good last time," I promised him, but I was definitely revving my system. Though it was more to do with him than just my caresses.

"Good," he said, his smile growing as he stroked himself from root to tip. "Then you're really going to enjoy this."

He didn't give me a chance to ask, but I was much better with show versus tell, anyway. He lined himself up and then pushed into me and fuck it was so much better. No sharp pain. Yes there was a burn as I stretched, cause fuck, he and

Lachlan both had these monster cocks, and then he was all the way in before he eased out only to push into me again.

"You stopped playing with your breasts," he scolded.

"Sorry—"

"No worries," he said, his grin growing more decadent and I didn't know where to focus. "I have something else for you."

Then he touched that wand to my clit and he didn't start at the lower settings I usually did. He went full massage and vibration. My brain splintered and he thrust into me again.

My vision went white as I screamed.

At least I think it did, cause when I resurfaced, I was still impaled on his cock and he wore the best smile.

"Good girl, now we're doing *that* again." He wasn't kidding, cause he was still hard as a stone and he began to rock into me and this time, he played with the massager in and around biting kisses to my nipples.

I forgot how to think. I forgot everything except Ramsey. Ramsey and the way he moved in and out of me, how he teased orgasm after orgasm out of me. When I came again, I was crying from it, but he came with me and then we were kissing and clinging together.

Fuck, even shaking with the release and barely able to move, I wanted more.

I wanted him.

Thirty

JONAS

Dinner at KC's changed a lot of things. Not the least of which was Ramsey and KC's relationship. Nothing had been more obvious when they reappeared almost ninety minutes *after* Johnny took Lachlan out to give him a few lessons about *life*. As entertaining as that had been, I couldn't escape the niggle of envy at how relaxed KC seemed around Ramsey. Then she hugged me before we left.

Me, not Lachlan. She promised to text me. She had, every single day since that dinner. We didn't get to see her as much but I had gone to the hospital to visit Pen with her and the surprise on her face that I kept showing up reminded me of how much Gibs had not. It also made me more determined to be there for her.

Today was *family* meeting day for Ramsey, Lachlan and I. The last three weeks had blown past us and it was time to make some decisions. I could tell just from the amused expression on Ramsey's face that she was texting him. Only instead of on his phone, he was texting on his computer. She blunted the uptight edges around him, softened his scowls and gave him more reasons to smile. It was hard to resent that part.

My phone vibrated and I glanced down at it.

KC

I love the motif you're mixing in here. It's got a real Blues vibe. We don't usually incorporate that as much.

A grin tugged at my own lips.

ME

I wasn't sure where it was going when I started. But I was thinking about your guitar. How you looked when you held it— well the look in your eyes—but also the energy you had. It seemed to fit.

I debated hitting send on that message. The guitar was still a sore point for her. A place where grief and anger met. Everything surrounding her missing guitar made *me* angry. I couldn't imagine how it made her feel. What I hated more than anything was that *she* had been hurt and the loss of the guitar *kept* hurting her.

Despite the hesitation, I didn't want to pretend with her. I didn't want to pretend those things hadn't happened. I didn't want to pretend she wasn't seeing my brothers. I just didn't want to pretend.

I wanted *her*.

Firing off the message, I leaned back and glanced at the music sheets in my lap. KC and the girls had spent most of their time in the studio recording their single for the fundraiser when KC wasn't at the hospital with Pen. If they needed to work on this, then I was in. For the music. For Pen. For KC.

"Kaitlin said you're blowing her away with your latest stuff," Ramsey said and I met his gaze.

Pleasure suffused me at the compliment. "Really?" The word escaped me before I could swallow it, but instead of looking condescending or amused, Ramsey just nodded.

"She did. You ever think you'll play some of that for us to hear?"

I shrugged. "Never really thought about it."

"Okay," Ramsey said as he stood. "Think about it then. I'm grabbing a drink. Want one?"

"Please," I admitted, still turning his offer over in my head.

"Have you heard from—"

The front door locks gave, answering Ramsey's unfinished question, when Lachlan let himself in. He had three boxes of pizza with him and the smell set my stomach rumbling.

"Right, there you are," Ramsey said. "You want a drink?"

"I'd take a beer," Lachlan snarked but Ramsey just shook his head.

"You'll get water or a soda. I haven't bought any beer."

"Right." Lachlan dragged out the word as he dropped his keys in the dish. He was in a tank top and shorts with running shoes on. "I forgot you hadn't dislodged the stick in your ass."

He slid into the living room and put the pizza boxes down on the coffee table. The smell of sweat and sand hovered around him.

"Yes, I went running with Ace," Lachlan said. "She needed to get out of that house and away from that fucking creeper of hers. Not that he stayed *behind*."

I frowned. "Her security has been tight."

"I like tight security," Lachlan commented as he headed for the stairs. "I don't like this Dix asshole. There's something..."

"Off," Ramsey supplied.

"He's jealous," I informed them and they both twisted to

face me. "He likes her—too much. But he doesn't like us around her. I don't think he likes anyone except the girls." Maybe he had the right to, but I didn't like how he watched her.

Lachlan grunted. "Give me five minutes to shower and don't eat all the pizza."

Neither of us said anything as he vanished into his room. Ramsey walked back out into the living room and handed me a soda before he eyed me.

"Just ask," I said as I popped the top.

"How are you doing?"

I shrugged. "Better than I have in a while. Haven't missed an appointment or my meds. Spoke to Dad this morning since I never made it out to Denver. Once things are settled, I'll schedule a visit..."

"Those are good," Ramsey said slowly, and I could almost hear the words he didn't add. So I waited him out. "I want to ask you about Kaitlin."

"You're seeing her," I said. "There's nothing to ask."

"Yes there is," Ramsey said as his laptop dinged. He reached over to grab it and my phone vibrated.

KC

I miss that guitar and you nailed it with this. I want to work on the lyrics for it. We need to work out a contract if you're going to keep writing with us.

ME

I don't need a contract. I like writing the music.

She sent me back a crazy face emoji.

KC

> You deserve credit. You can like and love writing this, but credits builds up your reputation and your accolades. It means you can get more work as a songwriter.

I really didn't care about all that.

KC

> And I want your name on this. Own it, Hot Shot. You're a badass.

A grin pulled at my lips.

ME

> Does this mean I get to come to some of your studio sessions?

KC

> Yes.

No caveats. No hesitations. Just—yes. Warmth flooded my chest and I grinned.

"Kaitlin?" Ramsey asked and I glanced over to find him watching me with a hint of a smile.

"Yeah. She said I could go to the studio with them." I loved that. I loved creating with her. "She's been so busy getting this charity album done and prepping for that show. And all the stuff with the hospital." Some of my good humor dried up. "They still haven't found a donor for Pen."

None of us were matches. I'd gone to get tested too. KC didn't bring it up often, but I'd seen her face each time a nurse or a doctor told her that Pen was still on the list. The list.

"I know," Ramsey said with a sigh. A door opened above and the sound of Lachlan on the stairs came hot on its heels. "As for earlier, what I wanted to ask was how are you doing with me still seeing Kaitlin?"

"Hey," Lachlan commented. "Look at that. No more

beating around the bush. Are we putting our fucking cards on the table?"

"Pretty sure we already did that," I told them but then we all took a minute to get the pizza sorted out. I packed my music sheets off to the side and kept an eye on my phone.

"Have we?" Lachlan challenged as he eyed Ramsey. "Because your relationship has definitely changed."

"Yes it has," Ramsey said without an ounce of rancor or deflection. "Kaitlin's giving me another chance and I don't plan on fucking it up. That said—" He met my gaze for a long moment, then focused on Lachlan. "I know she is seeing both of you too."

Not quite throwing himself down, Lachlan said, "But she's having sex with you and not with us."

I didn't comment on that. The surly note in Lachlan's voice did make me smile. "Maybe you should consider not trying to feel her up the next time she's dancing."

His only response was a grunt, but it was Ramsey who sighed.

"Look guys—cards on the table. I'm not backing off on Kaitlin. I don't see either of you choosing to do that either. I'm also not asking you to back off."

Lachlan frowned. "You're not?"

"No, unlike you, brother, I do know how to share." That comment had me straightening.

"KC mentioned her friends..."

"Yeah, the couple that she's performed with that are not just a couple?" Ramsey checked.

"Frankie," Lachlan said. "Frankie with the four boyfriends." He grimaced. "Not sure how that even works."

"Don't have to worry how it works for her," Ramsey said. "If that's what Kaitlin wants to try, I'm not opposed. For the most part—"

He paused then took a drink of his soda before he liberated a piece of pizza from the box.

"Correction, no for the most part. I *do* trust you both with her. Even if I don't always agree with your choices." He didn't pretend to not stare at Lachlan. "Or worry about how you're handling it over all." The last he directed at me. "I reserve the right to worry. I'm your brother. I look after you guys."

Instead of issuing a smart-ass response, Lachlan just grunted. "Okay, so if the three of us are dating her, then no one else. Cause I don't want another fucking RJ even looking in her direction."

"Agreed," I said in one breath with Ramsey. "I don't want any guys thinking they have that right," I added. "I am worried about whoever kidnapped her before. The fact it hasn't been in the press and they've all kept it quiet doesn't mean the threat has gone away."

"No," Ramsey said slowly. "It doesn't. I've been talking to her about going back to Blue Ivy for school, not just for college classes, but because we would be there to keep an eye on her and we could—possibly figure out if this would work for all of us."

Possibly.

I turned that idea over in my head. "They don't want to go on tour again so soon," I admitted. It wasn't betraying a confidence. It had come up at dinner with her at her house. "I think they're more tired than they want to admit."

"I also think they aren't sure they want to stay as a group act," Lachlan added. "Though to be fair, I don't think they want to abandon each other either. There is some serious loyalty there." The last came out almost envious.

I got it.

"She doesn't have to make that decision. They are working on the charity album. She is really focused on her sister." Ramsey sighed. "And I want to be a part of the solution. I want to give her all the time she needs, but I have to go back to work soon or choose to leave my position."

There was the rub.

"Lachlan, you're still enrolled and you still have a chance to be," Ramsey continued, focusing on me.

"I don't care if I go to college," I said and at his swift frown, I lifted my shoulders. "Ramsey, the academic thing is yours. I went cause I had to. Now? Now I just want to work on music and be near KC. If she is going back to school, then I'll take classes with her and keep working on music. Cause one of us should always be with her at least until we're sure she—"

A knock hit the door, followed by the doorbell going off several times in a row. Ramsey frowned but he was up and on his way to the door before Lachlan and I were fully on our feet.

"Mom?" Ramsey actually sounded startled as he opened the door the rest of the way and I tensed.

"Don't you Mom me," she said in a tone that bordered on angry and sad. "I can't believe you." She pushed past Ramsey and into the room where she glared at all of us. What the hell was she even doing here? "Lachlan's thoughtlessness I'm used to," she said almost dismissively.

"Fuck you too, Mom," Lachlan didn't miss a beat.

"But you," she said, glaring at me. "How *could* you?"

I sighed.

Not that she waited for my response before she whirled on Ramsey. "And you? You know how hard I've worked and how long it's taken for Gibs and I to build our relationship and you're trying to sabotage it? You're telling him he has a child— one born *after* he and I were married. How could you do this to me? Don't you want me to be happy? What you spend five minutes with that little slut and it's all about her?"

"Don't call Kaitlin that," Ramsey said. "You haven't even bothered to get to know her."

"And Penelope *is* Gibs' kid," I interjected. "I've met her and I've looked into her eyes. She has his eyes. Just like KC does."

"Then it's probably that slut's kid and not his..."

"Mom," Lachlan snapped. "You might want to watch who you call a slut. You don't like her, fine. But fuck off with the names."

"Don't you dare talk to me like that," she snarled as she whirled on him.

"Or what?" Lachlan dared her. "You going to disown me? Throw my shit out? Tell Dad that he should cut me off? Oh, wait, maybe you'll lie to Gibs."

The deadpanning caught me off guard. Cause all of that sounded accurate. Way too accurate...

"Mom," Ramsey said with a sigh. "You're angry. Fine. We'll talk but this—none of this is about you."

Mom looked like she was ready to say something when she went absolutely still and the *rage* in her expression worried me as she glared out the still open door.

KC stood there, her hair pulled back into a ponytail and sunglasses hiding her eyes. "Am I interrupting?"

END PART TWO

Part Three

Thirty-One

KC

"So what happened?" Jackie asked after she passed the menu back to the waiter. Davina was at the hospital with Pen, so Bronson and I took Jackie out to dinner. I hadn't really had time in the last couple of weeks to catch up with them. The recording was taking longer than normal, probably because it was hard to get into the headspace for it.

Especially when each time I remembered why we were doing the new single, I just wanted to cry. My emotions were all over the place. I sighed. "I remembered where I'd seen her before…" I made a face.

"In Gibs' bed?" Jackie asked simply. There wasn't an ounce of judgment in her voice. Then why would there be. It wasn't like Dad had ever been a monk. It also wouldn't be the first time I caught him with a woman in or out of bed for that matter.

"Actually, yes but no," I said and took a drink of the lemon and lime infused water the waiter had delivered. I was so dried out that even my throat was a little sore. "I mean, I caught her later, but she was at my tenth birthday party."

Bronson made a face. "The big circus one?"

I shrugged. "Yeah. Mom and Dad were in the middle of that war of the presents. Anyway, she came with him for the party—" I was pretty sure she'd left alone cause I'd also found Dad up in my wing of Mom's house getting his knob shined by a couple of other women. Mothers—if I recalled correctly—of girls who'd been invited to the party.

So gross. Bronson made a gagging noise that cut off abruptly when Jackie fixed him with a look.

"Anyway..." I said. "She was there. Um—she and Mom got into it. Mom had been drinking though, but Linzi—yeah her name is Linzi, anyway, she ended up in the pool and it was a whole thing." I didn't laugh. At the time it hadn't been funny either, but a lot of people had laughed. I was pretty sure I'd laughed too. What else was I supposed to do?

"Huh." Jackie shook her head. "She's one of his backup singers." Not a question. "I keep trying to think if she was around when I was seeing him..."

"Mom, I beg you—do not bring up any women who may or may not have been with him when you were." Bronson threw me a pleading look and I laughed.

"Yeah, the less I think about that the better—anyway—I don't know what I was expecting. I'd gone to see them because I really did want to talk to them but her just flipping out at them and calling me names and Pen names—not what I was expecting at all."

"Please tell me you told her to shut her trash mouth." Jackie's demeanor shifted. "If not, don't worry. I will."

"I'm okay," I promised her and reached over to take the hand she was holding out. "I am. I didn't have to say much. Ramsey pretty much threw her out as soon as she started yelling at me."

Wasn't *that* an experience. I sighed.

"She really hates me."

"Bitch," Bronson said. "Sorry, Mom."

"No, that one is deserved. Anyone hating on a child because Gibs cannot keep it in his pants is absolutely a bitch." Jackie was so annoyed. "I have a feeling, I know why those boys were all so negative about you."

Yeah. Me too. But I left that alone. "They are trying to make it up to me now." It was so weird and at the same time... "Ramsey wants me to go back to Blue Ivy."

Bronson frowned. "Why?"

"College. The school offered me two years, open admission."

"Arrogant shits trying to cover their ass." If anything, Jackie's tone grew more disdainful. "The school needs to improve its security not its social image."

At first I wasn't sure if she'd meant the guys, but Jackie had seemed happier with them since Davina offered her tacit approval. Or maybe she was just trusting me since I said I liked them. I more than liked them but this was all so —freaky.

"He wants me to go back there so I can have some of the normalcy I wanted but also where we can see if this goes anywhere with us. I think he wants me to be where he can keep an eye on me too."

"What do you want to do?" Bronson asked as he covered my hand on Jackie's. That was the sticking point, right?

I wanted *them*, but did I want that school.

And frankly, should I want them at all?

* * *

Three days later...

"I can move out next week," Johnny said. "Just give me a

couple of days to find someone who doesn't mind if I crash on their sofa..."

"You do not have to move out," I told him. Yvette and Aubrey had gone to get massages while I had lunch with Johnny. "Even if I go—"

"What do you mean *if*?" Davina interrupted as she carried the platter of wraps out to the table. "Of course you're going. It's important and you *have* talked about college before."

"Davina's right," Johnny told me, his expression encouraging. "If those punks are getting their heads out of their asses, I *might* trust them to look after you there."

I sighed. "I haven't decided one hundred percent yet. I want to go—sort of."

"Explain," Davina said, putting a hand on the back of the chair.

"If you join us," I teased her and she narrowed her eyes.

"One moment." With a huff, she headed back to the kitchen and I made a face at Johnny.

"You're in trouble," he said with a grin and I laughed.

"My favorite kind of trouble—sort of."

Then Davina was back with another platter, this one with skewered potatoes and veggies that had been crisped perfectly. She set that next to the wraps before she pulled out a chair. "Eat, then tell us why you're undecided."

I tried not to laugh but then... "The reality—Pen. She's here. I don't want to be on the other side of the country if..."

"*When* we find a donor," Davina said sternly. "You can be on the first flight back. You also have to have a life, sweetheart. You can't live in that hospital. It's not good for either of you and you have songs recorded that we can play for her. I told you, I play all your albums when you're not there and she loves it."

My heart twisted.

"I can make sure I visit too," Johnny offered. "Davina's

there every day and so is Jackie. You have family, kiddo. We'll dive in."

I adored Johnny for the offer. "It's not just Pen—am I going back there for school or for the guys?" I groaned. "And should I do that? I mean...am I making the choice to do this because I want a relationship with them?" The one question I didn't voice was *why* did I want a relationship with them? I was in different places with all three of them but just thinking about any one of them and my body hummed.

Ramsey had invited me to stay the night but I wasn't there, not with all three of them in the same place. Then there was Lachlan, he was as much of a ninja kisser here as at school except—he wasn't. He showed up to run with me, even if it was just in the gym on property. He had helped sneak me out to go running on the beach.

Dix had been pissed and so had Aubrey and Yvette. Yeah, so no more ditching security. Lachlan wasn't pushing for more, either.

At least not yet. Would that change at Blue Ivy?

"Who cares?" Davina said, dragging my attention back to the present. "You want to know if you can have a relationship with those boys, that does actually require that you be in the same place. The only person whose opinion should matter on that is yours. Do you want to be there? Do you want to know?"

"And you can always leave," Johnny reminded me. "So you go for a semester but it's not working for you relationship wise —move to a different place on campus. Moving in with them might seem fast, but you have known them for a while, but you're not committing to marriage or even to next month."

I made a face. "What if I'm no good at relationships?"

Davina snorted, but it was Johnny who just shook his head. "Sorry, that's crap. You're one of the most compassionate and caring people I've ever met. You take into account everyone else's feelings. Mine. The girls. Davina's. Your mother's." His expression turned a little pained. "You want to know? You go for it. You want to try with them? Then try. If it doesn't work out, then it might hurt and I'll beat all three of them up instead of just the hardhead."

"Johnny..."

"I mean it," he told me firmly. "You have the right to build the life you want and to explore all of its options. Go nuts. Have sex. Have parties. Live your life for you and not for anyone else. If it doesn't work out—then you will know that you tried."

I blew out a breath.

"And we'll be here for you and for Pen," Davina stated. "I will send at least one frying pan with you."

The last made me laugh.

Because she was serious.

* * *

One week later...

"I hate it," Yvette said. "I want school to be over. That said, you should do it. You deserve to have the experience you wanted in the first place with people who may have actually learned to treat you well.

"I can be there," Aubrey offered. "I don't want you to be alone."

"I might be living with them." That was on the table. "They wanted me to have them around so I'd have more security. No more open dorms. Maybe a cottage on the campus. Ramsey's actually going to be teaching at the high school level, Jonas, me, and Lachlan would be attending the college. Ramsey isn't a student any more so no conflict of interest..."

"All three of them, huh?" Yvette's smile turned sly. "Turning into Frankie?"

I laughed. "Not sure about that yet."

"Did you talk to her?" Aubrey asked and I shook my head.

"Not yet. She's—she's closer to her guys, you know. Grew up with them and they didn't treat her like shit." At least not that I knew of. The guys were so damn good to her.

"Well, she has a relationship with four guys, so if you need advice there, she'd be the one to call." Aubrey flopped back on my bed. We'd piled in here to watch a movie. "That said, if you go, I go."

"Oh god, that means I should go." Yvette made such a pathetic face, we both laughed. "I'll do it, but I won't like you very much."

"You don't have to," I told her. "Neither of you do. Just—not ready to tour again. Not ready to lock down another album. This charity single has taken so much and all I keep thinking about is Pen. Then I worry about Mom... and the guys help with that. They just let me be me...even if I'm not sure who that is yet."

"We'll always have your back," Aubrey reminded me. "But you have to have security, especially after what happened last time. As for albums—fuck it, we work on it on our schedule. We write it when we want to. We sing it when we want to. We could even head off campus and do local clubs in New York for fun if we need the break."

"For fun," Yvette snorted, then flung a pillow at Aubrey. It bounced off her and her hair poofed. There was just a momentary downbeat, then I was grabbing a pillow as they went for theirs and we were chasing each other.

The pillows didn't survive and there ended up being stuffing and feathers everywhere. But I felt better...

Still, did I stay or did I go?

* * *

Two weeks later...

Dix sighed. "You're going back to that campus."

"That's the plan," I told him. "I can talk to Teddy about getting security there and the school..."

"No," Dix said. "Your security is my job. I'll take care of it."

Then I guess we were going...

Thirty-Two

LACHLAN

The vibration of my phone taunted me from the counter while I was in the shower. Chasing Ace had become something of a full-time obsession. In the past month since Mom showed up, though, Ace had kept her distance from all of us. Well, most of us anyway. She talked to Ramsey and Jonas, albeit on the phone. But they got calls *and* texts.

I got texts.

Was it a deterrent? No, I didn't think so. Not when she texted me regularly of her own volition and answered my texts. It was better than nothing. If she wanted me to work for it, then I was more than happy to do so.

The last few weeks had been as much about getting to know each other as it had been about her making me work for it. Fine. I'd work for *her*. I still couldn't get over Mom's atti-tude. Not once had Ace complained about her. Hell, she hadn't even brought her up. Mom treats her like dog shit and Ace was just a class act by far.

The phone vibrated again as I shut off the water. I'd shaved while I showered. With water still dripping out of my hair, I looped a towel around my hips and secured it before I picked up the phone.

Three messages from Ace.

A grin tugged at my lips.

ACE

I think we nailed the final track last night. Now we just have to lay down the vocals.

I got confirmation from the school. I'm officially enrolled. Yvette is going to Boston and Aubrey is coming back to campus. We're going to do the fall semester as a trial run.

I could work with a trial run.

So, I told Ramsey last night and Jonas a little while ago, yes, I'll share the cottage with you guys, but we have to have rules. I still feel like Aubrey and I should be roomies, but she said if I'm on campus, it would be safer to have you three around.

I could almost picture her face.

ME

We can apply for a bigger place, then Aubrey can move in too or put her in the place right next door. The cottages aren't as small as dorm rooms.

Did I want Aubrey right there? Fuck no. She hated me. So did Yvette. I was working on that, but Ace first.

ACE

I thought about that, but I don't think
Aubrey wants to live with you guys and I'm
not sure how that would work. Let me text
Ramsey and see if he has an idea about the
place next door.

While I'd presented the solution and I wanted to be the
one who resolved it, I had to bite my tongue and wait. This
was part of the "sharing" process. She dated all three of us. We
didn't sabotage each other and we supported her. The rules
were pretty simple, but they were also really fucking hard.

Especially when all I wanted to do was claim her for my
own and beat the shit out of anyone who touched her. She
liked Ramsey. She liked Jonas. She talked to them, sometimes
it seemed more than she talked to me. But—she was *talking*
to me.

Better my brothers to share her with than anyone else.
Even if I wasn't particularly good at sharing.

I stared at the phone as I dried off and then I picked it up
again.

ME

I'm leaving for campus on Friday. I'll be
driving. Why don't you come with me?

It took another ten minutes before she answered. Since I
could *hear* the sound of Ramsey's voice as he spoke but not
the content, I just assumed she was on the phone with him.
That was fine. I dragged on boxers and worked on figuring out
what clothes I needed to pack in my cases. I'd be shipping my
computer along with the guys.

ACE

You're driving?

ME

> Car doesn't get there by itself. She's too pretty to just let anyone touch her. I take care of what matters to me.

Cheesy? Maybe, but would she get the point? I fucking hoped so. The only problem with my car was it had been a gift from Gibs. That had begun to irritate me more and more. I was tempted to sell it and get a new one except I loved the fucking car. Selling it and using the cash for another wouldn't remove the fact Gibs gave it to me.

Not that I thought he'd care. We hadn't seen or spoken to either him or Mom in weeks. She'd frozen us totally out. I wanted to care, but I was too damn angry with her. For years, all we'd heard about was how insensitive and uncaring Ace was. A part of me wanted to believe Mom hadn't deliberately sabotaged the relationship between Ace and Gibs.

A part of me. The part that still believed in Santa and that Mom kissing my boo-boos would magically heal them. The rest of me? No, the rest of me actually saw all the deliberate, and conniving, choices Mom had made over the years. The way she'd reacted to Ace's presence? No, she *hated* her and I wasn't entirely sure why. What incensed me even more was the shock on Ace's face.

ACE

> So you drive? That's what three days?
> Four?

I finished getting dressed and then eyed my suitcases before I answered.

I debated the next comment but then just said fuck it and hit send.

Too much? Maybe. But I wasn't beating around the bush. I wanted her. She needed to know just how much.

I'd pulled on shorts and a tank top when my phone rang. Ace's beautiful face stared up at me from the screen. I'd snapped that shot a few weeks earlier when we'd gone for a run. The look on her face, a combination of amusement and disbelief captured the essence of her perfectly.

"Hey Ace," I said by way of greeting when I answered the phone. "You're not butt dialing me, are you?"

Her laughter was its own rich reward. Fuck, I'd missed the sound of it. Goddamn, she was tying me up in all the knots I wanted to keep her in.

"I am not butt dialing you. Promise."

"Damn, I like your ass so, I'd be okay talking to it." That earned me another laugh. I needed to play this cool. "What's up?"

"You're really driving all the way from California to Connecticut?"

"Yep," I said. "I've done it every year since I got the car. I was going to have it shipped the first time. Your—" I hesitated on that, then course corrected. "Gibs offered to pay for it but when they came to pick it up, all I could see were the possible scratches on it. So I said I'd rather drive it. Gas is pricey, but there's nothing like the open road to kind of clear your head and put everything in perspective. And my baby is a sweet ride."

"Is she now?" The notes of teasing warmth wrapped like a fist around my cock and I just wanted to strip her naked and pay some very special attention to every inch of her. "Should I be jealous?"

"Of my baby? No, she'd be good to you too. She can't compete with you anyway." Not a lie. Two totally different kinds of affection.

"I don't think I've ever done a road trip that didn't involve concert tours and stuff."

"Then we could make it a new experience for you," I offered.

"The problem is Dix is not going to go for me doing a road trip—"

Yeah well I didn't give a fuck what Dix liked or didn't like, but I bit my tongue cause she was at least talking to me.

"Whether I could get him to sign off or not is not the point as much as it would be for me to be that far out of reach if something happened with Pen."

Fuck. No argument against that. "I don't want to be the reason you add more stress."

"Really?" If not for the hint of teasing, I'd consider another apology.

"Look, the stress I want to add to your life is all about mutual pleasure and a damn good time." The faint hitch in her breath made me grin. "So, understand that while I will seek to complicate it for both of us in the very best ways—I will absolutely support you in anything you need to do for your sister."

"That's—really sweet."

"No," I promised her. "It's really not. You need to feel confident where she is concerned and you deserve to know what I will and won't do. I am one thousand percent looking forward to having you in our place this year. I can afford to be patient when I know we will be a lot closer regularly soon."

"Well the sleeping arrangements are still something we're working on..."

"There is plenty of room for us to each have our own bedroom." If it was just the two of us, one bed would be fine. But it wasn't... "I don't relish the idea of a chore chart to break up where you sleep each night, but I would like the opportunity to sleep with you as well."

"Just sleep?"

"Ace—believe me when I say that sleep would be had eventually or it would be all we had if you preferred it that way. That said, I reserve the right to attempt to change your mind. I have all kinds of ideas for you and I can't wait to play out those fantasies."

"I don't know whether to be flattered or amused," she said with a chuckle.

"Be both. Be anything you want." Be mine. "As long as you are still up for letting me try to repair the road between us..."

Her soft sigh worried me more than I wanted to admit. "There is so much between us Lachlan."

"I know, but I can't make it up to you if you won't at least open the door."

"Do you want to make it up to me?"

"I want to do everything with you and for you. We can go as glacially slow as you prefer, but it doesn't mean I have to like it."

Her silence seemed a poignant response all on its own.

"Intimacy is more than sex, Ace," I told her. "Maybe I get carried away and savor every single time I've gotten to kiss you. Maybe the torment of a hard-on every fucking time I lay eyes on you or my thoughts stray to you is the torture I deserve. You know what...no maybe about it. I deserve it. But here's the thing, I've never run from a fight and the best things in life have to be earned."

"You want to earn me," she murmured. It wasn't a question.

"Will you let me at least try?"

"You've been trying for a few weeks now—and maybe succeeding."

"I can take a maybe. What about a date? You and me. A real one. Not me staging a raid at the club or getting a dance with you because you think I'm someone else..."

"No more ninja kisses?" The surprise mingled amidst the hints of disappointment encouraged me.

"Do you like the ninja kisses?" Frankly, I loved that she called them that.

"I should probably tell you no," she admitted then laughed. "But I do like them, even when you made me crazy, those just made me crazier."

"Then I'll make sure you get one at least once a day. Maybe three times on the weekends. That still doesn't answer my question about a date."

"I'm not sure I know how to do this."

"Me neither," I said. "So let's fail together until we get it right."

She blew out a breath.

"Talk to me, Ace. What do you need?"

"I need you guys to not hurt me again," she said. "I asked Ramsey for that. I'm asking you. I don't want to hurt any of you, but I really—I really can't go through what we did before. I know your mom..."

"Our mom isn't us. Our mistakes are ours. I'm willing to do whatever it takes to fix this and to earn your trust. I want to promise you that I won't hurt you again, but I'm not that perfect. So I can only promise to do everything I can to avoid the hurt and if I fuck it up, then I promise to try and make that up to you too. I just—can you try to trust me? A little?"

Another long beat passed and if I couldn't hear her soft exhales, I'd have thought we lost the connection. Then finally, she said, "I can try."

Relief swamped me.

"And I'll go on a date with you—if you let me pick the date. At least the first one."

Intrigued, I raised my brows. "Tell me more—but before you do, the answer is yes, to whatever the conditions are."

All I needed was a shot.

Thirty-Three

KC

The drive onto Blue Ivy's campus had been surreal enough. Weirder, still? Using one of the round-abouts to access a different area of the campus, where tidy houses were tucked amongst the trees. It was almost a fairytale land of cottage retreats amidst the land of academia. Despite the fact the dorms were barely a half mile away on the other side of the trees, it was a whole new world.

As odd as those had been, Dix pulling up to the house where I would be living with Ramsey, Lachlan, and Jonas just amped up the Kafkaesque quality of it all. The guys had been thrilled to see us, swarming forward to get me and Aubrey out of the car and to meet the moving truck that had followed us in.

I tried to help offload, but got banished to check out my new room while Ramsey supervised the movers. The tension that amped up the minute Dix inspected the place gave me a headache. He didn't like the idea.

Not one bit.

There was no place for him in the house. Not unless he wanted to sleep on the sofa or, if I gave up my room to bunk with one of the guys. The fact he just smirked at Dix's irritation didn't help. Dix would be on campus, Ramsey had arranged for him to have a spot in one of the staff buildings. It wasn't perfect, but it would put him within reach of me if I needed him.

"So all is good with him?" Yvette asked as I finished unpacking the last of my cases. While the uniform code for the college classes wasn't as strict as it had been for high school, we did have to wear them.

"I think so," I said. My stomach was still doing summer-saults after Jonas and I walked with Aubrey over to her new place. It was a single. I kind of didn't like having her that far away and I worried about her being on her own.

"It's a locked building Kait, but I won't take any chances. I promise."

"What's wrong?" Yvette asked, affection gentling her accent. "Talk to me."

"I'm fucking scared," I admitted and the words kind of exploded out of me. I glanced at the closed door. While I couldn't *hear* them clearly, the rumble of their voices carried if they were out in the living room. The place was definitely bigger than our suites in the dorm, but also very cozy. The bedrooms were all upstairs, so that helped, but there was a landing that looked over into the living room...

"What are you scared of?" God, I missed her. I missed having her and Aubrey right there. I'd gotten used to it over senior year. The distance, stepping out on my own and now...

"Being back here," I admitted, sinking down on the bed. "Living with them. I mean I lived with Jonas last year, but that was different."

"Well, you have benefits this time, that helps." It was the barest edge of teasing that made me smile. Then that smile turned to a laugh. "Better," Yvette murmured. "Is Aubrey there?"

"No," I admitted. "She's in her new place and I came back here to get unpacked. Orientation is in three days and I'm supposed to have dinner with the guys."

"Okay. So, you're there, you have your things. Dix had the movers bring your television and stuff, yeah?"

They had. "And my barista machine."

"Then you have everything, but… and I am only saying this cause I can hear the stage fright in your voice. This isn't forever. You haven't turned your whole life upside down for three guys you are uncertain about."

My stomach bottomed out.

"You also wouldn't have done this if a part of you weren't excited to find out. You've never let the unknown stop you before. Don't let it do it now."

Eyes closed, I took a deep breath and then let it out. "I think I needed to hear that."

"I think you did too." Her smile practically wreathed the words. "Now, stop hiding in your room and go make those assholes earn your attention."

Chuckling, I stared up at the ceiling. "You do know if this works out, you can't keep calling them the assholes."

"I think if they can prove to you and to us that they are worth it, I'll consider giving them a new nickname. Until then the douchebags became the assholes and they are nowhere near good enough for you. So they are *lucky* that you like them. Even if I think you're cracked."

Real laughter bubbled out of me just as one of them knocked on the door. "I love you," I said to Yvette.

"I know, it's why I put up with your melodrama when you have these moments." She couldn't even keep a straight face.

"Bitch," I muttered.

"You love it. Now go. I am going to make a call because I

need to get laid. It's been months and Bob just isn't doing it for me anymore."

I was still laughing as we disconnected and I rose to open the door. Jonas' half-smile turned into a real grin. "Hey..."

Like me, he was also barefoot, but he had on sweatpants and a t-shirt while I was in shorts and a tank top. The nice thing was the cottage had central air and heat. We didn't have to rely on the building specs to adjust the internal temperatures. We had the windows open, but the guys didn't want them open if I was here alone so—air conditioning it was.

"Hi," I said, holding up my phone. "I was just talking to Yvette."

"That's cool," Jonas told me. "Ramsey has food ready and we wanted to invite you down to join us."

Now that he mentioned it, it was hard to miss the smell of grilled onions and what had to be steak. My stomach stopped doing the Macarena and growled. "It smells good."

"He's a good cook," Jonas agreed. "But don't tell him I told you that."

"I heard it myself," Ramsey called from downstairs and another laugh worked its way out of me. Jonas pivoted so I could step out of the room and Ramsey met my gaze from below.

"He made salad too," Lachlan called. "He went all out."

"I wouldn't call it all out," Ramsey countered and the fluttering nerves in my system vibrated like a hummingbird on speed. "But come on down."

"Jonas?" I said softly as Ramsey disappeared in the direction of the kitchen.

"Hmm?"

"Is this weird for you too?"

He looked like he was turning the idea over. Neither of us moved and I studied the tattoos on his arms while I waited. There were so many stories there. Just like I had on me.

"A little bit," Jonas admitted. "I don't always like living with them, but I did like living with you." His gaze dipped for a moment to my lips then back up again. A question lurked in his eyes and I narrowed the gap between us. Pressing a hand to his chest, I pushed up on my tip toes. He dipped his head and brushed his lips against mine. It was a there and gone again kiss.

The first one in a long time. The flutters increased but for an entirely different reason, while the thud of my heart seemed far too loud. "I liked living with you too."

He covered my hand with his then pressed another kiss to my lips. This one was softer at first, then I stepped into him and his mouth fused with mine. Like that very first kiss we'd shared, this one writhed with so much emotion, not the least of which was curiosity.

Tilting his head, he shifted the angle of the kiss and this time he added his tongue into the mix. Delicious shivers radiated out as I leaned into him. The tease and thrust of his tongue against mine, invited me to play with him. It was light and almost airy in the way we connected. Yet at the same time, the connection seemed to vibrate all the way to my bones.

My stomach growled, but the hunger invading me had less to do with food and everything to do with Jonas. Almost as soon as the kiss deepened, it ended and Jonas met my gaze. A flush touched his face and his eyes were almost too bright.

"Hi," I whispered again.

"Hey," he said in a voice that sounded almost as rough as mine. The sound of someone clearing their throat below intruded but neither of us looked away. "Dinner?"

Heat scalded my cheeks and I laughed. "I'm starving."

For more than food, but food was definitely something I needed. Bracing myself, I turned to see Lachlan watching us from downstairs. His expression held an element of curiosity but there was a hunger there that was hard to ignore.

Really hard.

Licking my lips, I followed Jonas down the stairs. Lachlan waited for me and I paused on the last step because it put my head nearer to Lachlan's. At his raised eyebrows, I nodded slowly.

He brushed his lips to mine. It was definitely a blink and you'll miss it kiss. Then he pressed another to my cheek before he murmured, "Down payment on your next ninja kiss. You saw me waiting so it's not really a sneak kiss here."

"True," I admitted and there was just a hint of disappointment curling in me. The anticipation chased it away though. When Lachlan offered his arm, I took it even as I slid my phone into my back pocket.

Ramsey and Jonas were already in the kitchen. The cottage had a dining nook. It wasn't a full sized dining room, but we didn't need it. Though being in here with all three of them suddenly seemed to shrink the space down incredibly.

"Hey," Ramsey said, motioning to the table. "Help yourself."

The table boasted a booth along the wall and then a couple of chairs to face it. Three of us could sit on the booth side pretty easily cause it shaped like an L, but whoever was stuck in the corner was stuck in the corner.

All at once, the uncertainty rose like some vicious backup singer who wanted to stomp all over the vocals. The simple fact I was nervous annoyed the hell out of me. Yvette was right, I'd come back here with them to go to school and to figure this relationship shit out.

To do that, I needed to be able to eat meals with them without freaking out. So I glanced at the table they'd actually set and then around the kitchen. "Should I help with anything?"

"Not tonight," Ramsey said, chin dipped a little as he watched me. Another shiver skated over my skin at the gentleness in his eyes. I was used to him provoking and pushing me. This sweetness was unsettling and at the same time... "Don't worry, we won't be doing formal dinners a lot but I thought tonight it would be good to sit down and talk over a good meal before we all get busy."

Oh. Talk. Right.

Lachlan laughed and tugged me over to the table. "Don't let the prof freak you out. Rams doesn't know how to do anything by half-measures. It's just a meal with all four of us."

"Just a meal," I muttered as I climbed into the booth, walking on my knees to settle in the corner. A minute later, Lachlan dropped onto the padded bench next to me while Jonas claimed the other side.

Ramsey stared at all of us and then rolled his eyes. Jonas snickered as he leaned back and Lachlan smirked. I slid down under the table and crawled out.

"Hey," Lachlan said and I stuck my tongue at him.

"Someone needs to help."

"You don't have to," Ramsey said but I bumped him with my hip to pick up the platter of veggie and the big bowl of salad. He'd already put tongs on each one.

"I know I don't have to, and you said you wanted to work out chores later. But it feels way too weird to just sit there and let you serve us." I didn't even let Davina do that unless I was feeling particularly shitty or she was in a mood.

Jonas bounced out of his seat and headed for the fridge. Then Lachlan let out an aggrieved sigh and rose to take the platter from me. "Ace is right, we should do this together." The tension splintered around me and I let out a slow breath.

Working *together* was better.

Ramsey stared at us as we hustled around adding the food to the table. There really wasn't enough room to set it all out, so grabbed the dinner plates and we went back for our steaks. When we were finally seated, I was back in the corner with Lachlan and Jonas on either side and Ramsey across from me.

The food was amazing. "How did you learn to cook?" I had to know. "Also, fair warning, I can cook in a pinch but I'm way better with takeout and a microwave."

Jonas grinned. "You make great coffee though."

"That I can do. Davina tried teaching me, but when you're on the road as much as I was, a lot of it didn't stick. We also lived out of hotels. I can tell you the best menus at about five hundred different hotels around the world, but I probably can't boil an egg."

"I can boil eggs," Lachlan volunteered. "Ramsey's the better cook of the three of us. Jonas makes great pizza though."

"You make pizza?" I twisted to stare at him and his ears went a little red.

"I can," he admitted. "My dad's grandmother used to make it and so my grandmother does and he does. He showed me how. He can't make much—he's better at art." He motioned to his arms. "But I can make pizza."

"Fine, you guys are gonna have to show me how." Then I looked back at Ramsey. "Who taught you to cook?"

"My aunt," he admitted. "She lives near my dad and whenever I spent breaks with him, he usually had to work during the day so I was with her. She believed in self-sufficiency and I kind of like it..."

"My dad pays a housekeeper to keep his fridge stocked," Lachlan admitted. "What I know how to do I learned from Ramsey or from Juliet."

Juliet—I knew that name... "Dad's housekeeper?"

Lachlan winced.

"It's fine," I told him. "I get that you guys lived there and spent time there. I haven't been back to Tahoe in years. It's okay to know these things even if I don't."

Did it hurt? Some. Did I like it? Not really.

Was it *their* fault? Hell no.

The last of the ice seemed to crack then and Ramsey told us stories about his aunt and cooking lessons that had us all in stitches while we ate. Dessert was chocolate ice cream with caramel sauce. I side-eyed Jonas but he just shrugged. I did like ice cream, I couldn't eat it all the time.

And if we ate like this a lot, I was gonna need to run more. Still, it was nice. We danced around the harder topics and kept it light. It was a great evening, really, we still had shit we needed to talk about but I didn't want to ruin the good mood we'd found.

Then my phone buzzed and I pulled it out.

AUBREY

Your guitar is up on an auction site…

My good mood plummeted.

Cause right below the text was a screenshot of my guitar.

Thirty-Four

RAMSEY

The appearance of her guitar on an auction site drained the evening's good cheer. Lachlan wanted to bid on it immediately, so did Jonas, but it was Kaitlin who said no. "We can't be us trying to buy it. Chances are if they realize it's me trying to get it they'll destroy it."

The roughness in her voice and in her eyes threatened to break my heart all over again. That guitar had been worth risking her life to carry out of the dorm when it had been on fire. When it had been stolen, it had genuinely seemed to rock her emotional stability more than anything except her sister.

Irritation scraped through me. The guitar was a connection to her father, a connection Gibs seemed to have tossed away. Yet, she still valued it. Her family meant everything to her and that couldn't be more clear to me now. I could hardly fault her for heading up to bed early. Maybe I could get my dad to put a bid in for the guitar. He wasn't directly tied to Gibs or Kaitlin.

Lachlan had suggested his dad and Jonas hadn't said a

word, but I had a feeling his dad would be on board to help out too. One way or another, we were getting that damn guitar back. Resentment surged up as I dragged on a pair of boxers. I'd showered after she went to her room. My room and Kaitlin's had en suites. Jonas and Lachlan had to share the hall shower.

Originally, the plan had been to kind of map out the semester. Figure out how we were going to make all of this work. Instead, we avoided all the heavy subjects until the information about the guitar showed up. Unlike my brothers, I didn't usually rely on violence.

Right now? I could go for a little violence. I wanted to get my hands on the person who took her guitar. Whether they did all that damage to her room or not, or if they were the ones who hit her in the head—taking that guitar had caused her so much pain. Pain she didn't—

A soft knock on the door pulled me around. I wasn't sure who I was expecting, but Kaitlin dressed in a sleep shorts and a baby doll t-shirt was nowhere on my list. All the moisture in my mouth fled.

"Can I come in?" Even though she was right in front of me, I could barely hear her. She pitched her voice low so it wouldn't carry. Also why she'd knocked so softly.

"Yes," I said, shaking off my stupor and pulling the door wider. She padded inside carrying only her phone and an extra charger cord. I pivoted to follow her progress as if tethered to her by an invisible cord. "Everything all right?"

I closed the door behind her and forgot how to breathe as she eyed the plugs on the side of the bed I usually favored.

"There's an extra USB port in the lamp—well in both of them." The bed barely qualified as a queen but it would be plenty of space for me. It didn't seem so large at the moment though. "If you need to charge your phone."

"Thank you." She plugged her phone in and then turned

to face me. The bed was in between us. "And I don't know if I'm all right or not but—"

Hesitation seemed to hold her captive. I picked up the book bag, I'd set on the bed and put it on the floor. I had files to go through and lesson plans to finalize. Classes started in less than ten days. While it was hardly my first time teaching, it was my first time to do it without a supervisory instructor.

It could wait.

Kaitlin came first.

"Siren, talk to me, what's wrong?"

"I was—I kind of just took back off to my room and I want to cry and at the same time I refuse to cry because some asshole took my guitar and is now listing it for sale like that. The fact they name dropped me *and* Dad? That's just insane. Right? That is insane?"

"It's something," I agreed. "There's nothing wrong if you need to cry."

"I don't want to cry," she said. "I want—"

I waited her out.

She put her hands on her hips and bowed her head for a moment. Every part of me ached to just go pick her up and cuddle her in my lap until she relaxed. But I could practically see the nervous energy rolling off of her. Kind of reminded me of a thrash metal concert where the bass was so deep it throbbed in the air.

Clearing her throat, she lifted her chin and met my gaze. Bare of any cosmetics with her hair falling in gentle waves, she was still so damn attractive it made me ache. As much as I hated the sadness smudging the stunning blue of her eyes, I couldn't look away from it either.

"I wanted to come in and see if I could sleep in here tonight," she said, her voice even. "Partially—because I don't want to be by myself, but also because I can't give us back that morning after we had sex the first time. That's gone, but maybe we could start over?"

For an answer, I pulled back the covers of the bed. "You can always sleep in here." That wasn't even a question for me. Sitting down and stretching out my legs, I patted the bed next to me. It had to be her call. She'd asked me to never hurt her again, not hurting also meant not pushing unless she asked for that too.

There was something so fluid about her as she climbed onto the bed using her knees and then scooted right over to me. I lifted my arm and then she was curling up against my side. The warm weight of her settled my own agitation and I wrapped her up tight.

"I don't know why this is all so hard," she whispered. With her head ducked down and her ear pressed against my chest, I couldn't see her face. It might be easier to talk without the open vulnerability so I reached over and snapped off the light. The room didn't plunge into full darkness. It was still dusk out and I hadn't closed the blackout curtains.

"Which part?" I asked, needing to figure this out for her so I could fix it—if that was even possible.

"Coming in here. Asking to spend the night. Moving into the house. Dinner was—" She exhaled, the rush of her breath over my chest teasing my skin. "Dinner was great and then the guitar and now I'm back to second-guessing everything."

"What part of dinner did you enjoy?"

"The stories," she answered immediately. "The food was good too." A smile kissed the last sentence. "But I loved listening to you guys talk about your families. I'm like that with Bronson and I used to be like that with Trace too. The younger sibs don't bring it up as much but they are still little."

"The different moms?" It was a guess, cause we had different dads so I could see the similarities.

"Yeah, and I like their moms, I mean I don't like all of

them equally, I guess. That's weird? It's weird right? I mean they aren't my mom and don't get me wrong, I love Mom, but she's a handful. I think Jackie's pretty damn perfect. Sandra is pretty cool too, but she's also only like a few years older than me. So that's kind of weird too. I feel like the next sibling is gonna end up being from someone younger than me and that will be really weird."

She went quiet and I could almost feel her wince.

"Sorry."

"Nothing to be sorry for," I assured her and began to rub my hand in a slow circle against her back. "I don't know exactly what's going on with Gibs, but it doesn't sound like he's been particularly loyal to anyone much less Mom." Might explain why Mom was on such a tear about everything, but it didn't excuse her behavior or choices in the slightest.

"But I am sorry about that," she said, rubbing her cheek against my chest. "You guys like him so much. Clearly you have good relationships with him. I feel like that's changing and it might be my fault."

"If he has feet of clay, that's on him and not you." I pressed a kiss to the top of her head. Inhaling a deep breath of her scent, I settled myself with having her right there. She had so much on her plate. I was used to managing stuff for Lachlan and Jonas. I could put some of my free time to work with her. I didn't have classes beyond the ones I was teaching this year. Next year I'd have other stuff to do but this year—this year I had time.

I could work on looking at the place where her mother had vanished off to, help find her guitar, and give her just a flat out safe space to be in.

"I called Creglin," she admitted and I nodded.

"Good. They should look into the site and see if they can track it down on their end, though he's just campus security..."

"I know, but the FBI got involved with questions because of the kidnapping and local law enforcement. He plans to kick it upstairs. Maybe they can get it back for me, I just—as much as I want the people who did all of this caught, I want my guitar more."

"Then we'll work on getting it back," I promised. "I have some ideas."

She went quiet, and the steadiness of her breathing made me think she'd gone to sleep so I contented myself with just holding her.

"Ramsey?"

"Hmm?"

"Can I ask you a question?"

I grinned. "You just did."

She pinched me and I chuckled.

"Oh, you meant you wanted to ask two questions."

When she pinched me again, I pressed another kiss to her head.

"Ask, Siren. You can ask me anything you want."

"The tattoo on your arm..." She traced her fingers over my right forearm. The pair of black bands. "I know those are for grief...for losing someone. Was it the girl that RJ hurt?"

"No," I said quietly. "It—it was a long time ago, but I had a friend here at the school when I first started coming. Jonas and Lachlan weren't old enough and Todd was my roommate. Fun kid. We kind of grew up together. He never treated me as weird cause I advanced so quickly. I skipped a lot of grades, but we were still housed by age."

Fuck, I hadn't really thought about this in a while.

"Anyway, you could say he was my best friend. I graduated when I was sixteen, from the high school segments. Then moved right into college. Todd was still in high school, and even with me in college, we still hung out. He went to one of the parties one night, got drunk, drove his car and well…" I shrugged.

"I'm sorry."

"Yeah, me too. I miss him. But it reminded me of why there were rules. He was always the guy who pushed things. Kind of like Lachlan. I got the tat for him, for our friendship. Friends like that are damn hard to find."

"It would kill me to lose Aubrey or Yvette," she admitted.

"Todd would have given me so much shit about you." I chuckled. "He would have been excited that I got the old man stick out of my ass, but then he'd wonder what the hell I was thinking chasing after my student."

"And your stepsister." The fact she could tease me about that helped, but still…

"Yeah, we were never really step siblings. It doesn't count if you had no idea."

"No offense," she told me, and I savored the way her breath danced over my skin. "I'm glad that we aren't step siblings. It's weird enough with everything else and all the crap that happened…" I could almost feel her wince. "Sorry, I keep bringing that up."

"You can always bring it up," I told her. "There are still raw pieces between us. Scrapes. Wounds. Insults. Assumptions. Little lies that we told ourselves…"

"Or were told," she amended for me.

"Yeah, so I know we had a rough start, and it's going to take some time to build up the trust. Luckily, we have that time."

"I want—" A yawn interrupted her and I shifted us on the bed so we could lay down. I half expected her to rollover onto her side like she had that first night. But she curled closer into me and tucked her thigh over mine. "I want to know everything. I like—talking to you."

"Good. I hope you like other things too."

She laughed and then bit my pec gently. "If I wake up first, I'll wake you up..."

"And if I do," I said slowly. "I will."

She let out another yawn and I cradled her closer.

"I like having a plan," she admitted.

"I like having you here." Then... "Promise me you'll be here in the morning? If you want to go get coffee, wake me up?"

"I promise." It came out more a sigh than a statement.

That quieted the niggling worry in the back of my head. I wanted to ask her more but her breathing had already evened out. She was exhausted.

She needed to sleep. I needed to plan.

My phone vibrated and I picked it up, careful to not disturb her.

LACHLAN

Dad said he's going to get bids going to get us the guitar. If necessary, he'll file an injunction to go after it legally too.

ME

Good. She's sleeping in here. So don't worry if you sneak into her room and she's gone.

LACHLAN

Just take care of her. That news knocked her hard.

Yeah, it had.

I hit the thumbs up and put the phone back, facedown. The news had done its damage. Definitely needed to revisit my philosophy regarding violence.

Thirty-Five

KC

Waking up in Ramsey's bed that first morning was a heady experience. Restlessness invaded me almost immediately. I woke him with a kiss and then admitted I wanted to go running. Maybe all this wild uncertainty that kept surfacing had more to do with me than them. So, running it was. Especially after Ramsey's story about Todd. His irritation with my so-called lifestyle made so much more sense.

Didn't make it better, especially considering some of the shit he'd said during the first few months of our acquaintance. At the same time, understanding it helped *me*. Helped me forgive him.

Thus, we fell into a routine. Every morning, I got up to run with Lachlan. Sometimes Jonas went with us. Sometimes Ramsey. Neither liked crack of ass, which, I supposed made sense. I wasn't a fan except when we weren't on tour. Lachlan, however, thrived on it. The two weeks leading up to classes kicking off officially flew by with orientations, schedules, and picking out what actual classes we were taking.

It also led to the four of us spending more time together. Making out was on the table, sex hadn't been. Not really. I had the feeling Lachlan would push it, but he didn't. Ramsey could have and definitely didn't. After that first night, I'd only crawled into Ramsey's bed one other time and it was after a nightmare when I couldn't go back to sleep.

He was so damn caring. He just wrapped me up and held me. I didn't realize how much I needed that until he offered the open affection. On the one hand, I kind of missed the sex. On the other, I wanted to get to know them all better. Like, really know them.

Part of our time involved picking out classes. Jonas and I took the same set of three, and Lachlan would be joining us for one of them. That was—weird. Aubrey was in one of my classes too. Not the same one with Lachlan. I loved that. After Ramsey's interference with my schedule, I hadn't had classes with her. The first week of classes had dawned finally and I was excited. Really excited.

"You're in a mood," Lachlan commented as we jogged back to the house. The five-mile run had left my legs pleasantly burning and helped sand the edges off my mood.

"Am I?" I asked, slowing to a walk. My breathing was already back under control, but the cool air on my sweat-soaked body felt good. I turned that idea over. "Maybe I am...I don't know, I'm excited for classes."

"You're worried," he said, matching his pace to mine. Since he had longer legs, it wouldn't be hard for him to leave me behind. "Dad is working on the guitar. Creglin said the authorities were looking into it, too, right?"

"Yeah." That irked me. I just wanted to buy my guitar and have it back, but everyone had a different plan. "I'm tempted to just make a large offer through an attorney."

"We're already doing that," Lachlan reminded me. "And I know you want it back, Ace…"

"Do you?" I challenged, pivoting to face him and forcing him to stop or run me down. "Do you get why that guitar is important to me? It's a part of me. Someone took that away. I want it back."

My eyes burned and I wanted to scream. Fuck it, I wanted to stomp my foot *and* scream.

"I think I do," Lachlan said slowly and the sobriety in his normally haunted green eyes held me riveted. "Maybe I can't get it totally, but it's important to you. That's really all I need to know." He sighed, dropping his chin as he stared at the ground for a moment. "I want to just get it back and have that fix everything, but I don't think it will. I think it would be another Band-Aid on a bullet hole."

I frowned. "Getting her back isn't about fixing anything. It's about reclaiming a piece of myself."

"A piece—" His lips compressed and he studied me for a long moment.

"Spit it out," I dared him. "Whatever the hell it is you're thinking, just—say it."

"Okay," he said slowly. "You're angry and you're hurt. You want to fix something in your life when so much of it seems out of control. I get that. I like control. So do you. Getting that guitar back doesn't fix anything because once you have it, the only thing you're going to think about was who was touching it and why they took it. It'll sit there like a taunt and it's going to make you angrier."

The record scratch in my brain was painful.

"Angrier might be better in some ways, but Ace, that guitar isn't what has you all tied up in knots."

"Maybe not," I said. "But it's *mine*—" The sound of shoes slapping the pavement at speed had me whirling. Hot and cold flash-fired through my system, leaving me shivering and sweating. The sun glare was right in my eyes and it took me a minute to process that the guy running right at us was Dix.

Even then, my heart rate shot up and my watch vibrated an alert that my pulse skyrocketed. I fell back a step and dropped my hands to my thighs as nausea swam up through me.

"I told you not to go out to run without letting me know where you were going," Dix half-snarled, concern and irritation radiating off him in waves. "You can't disappear on me, KC. This is not okay."

"Back the fuck off," Lachlan said, moving right in front of me. "She doesn't have to tell you shit."

"You back off, kid," Dix said. "Before I make you."

"I'd like to see you try," Lachlan dared him. "Remember you work *for* her. You aren't in charge of her."

"Lachlan..." I said, trying to get a hold of my scattered emotions.

"No, Ace, he doesn't get to talk to you like that." Lachlan didn't budge and when I straightened, there was no mistaking the very real anger in Dix's eyes. "I don't care how worried he is. You have your phone. You have your panic button. You have me."

Panic button. I hated that fucking thing, but it was looped around my neck like a locket. "You're a security threat," Dix countered. "Though you have the stalking part down..."

"Watch where you point that finger, asshole." Lachlan was spoiling for a fight. I finally got between them and put a hand on his chest.

"Lachlan, please," I murmured and his expression softened, briefly, before he glared at Dix again. Turning, I faced Dix. "I went for a run. I didn't go by myself and I do have my panic button. You don't like running as much and I'm fine."

"Yeah, for now you are," Dix said with a shake of his head. "Classes start today. I'll be going with you."

He was holding on so tight.

"You're not taking any more foolish risks on my watch. I don't like you living out here as it is. You should be closer to the center of campus. Better security…"

"We're hardly alone out here," Lachlan countered before I could. "And you don't get to make those decisions for her."

Pain pulsed behind my eye. The headache drained all the euphoria from the endorphins that the run had released. "You know what, I need a shower and food. Then we have classes." As tired as I was, I went for light. "So why don't we just do that and worry about the rest of this later."

"Sounds good," Lachlan said, holding out a hand to me. Bless him for not just taking my arm. As it was, Dix looked even more dour when I threaded my fingers with Lachlan's. "See you later—Dix."

"You shouldn't taunt him," I scolded when we got back to the house. I hadn't glanced back because guilt niggled at me. In all honesty, I probably should have at least sent Dix a text, but—I had Lachlan with me and I'd just wanted to run.

"You're right," Lachlan said. "I should just belt him."

The door opened as we walked up and Jonas frowned as he glanced past us. Twisting, I looked over my shoulder to find Dix still glaring after us. Fuck, I was going to need to fix that.

"Ignore him," Lachlan said, tugging me into the house as Jonas pulled the door wider. "Go shower. I can run over to the dining hall and grab food…"

"I already did," Jonas said. "Got a little bit of everything. First class in ninety minutes."

All of my butterflies returned with a vengeance. We'd picked up all the class materials in the last three days. "Musical theory." I grinned, because along with the nerves came the excitement. "First day of classes…"

"Why do you look so happy?" Lachlan asked, peering at me like I'd sprouted a second head.

My grin spread wider. "Because I get to be normal and I get a do-over of my first day at a 'normal' school. The last first day kind of sucked."

Both of them looked a little chagrined and I lifted my shoulders.

"So I'm happy that I get to do it again, only—we do it better?"

"Hell, yes," Lachlan said.

"Yes. Go shower," Jonas waved me off. "I'll make your coffee."

"What about mine?" Lachlan snarked as I jogged up the stairs.

"You can make your own," Jonas said and I didn't catch what he said after. Ramsey's bedroom door was open and he was fixing his tie as I walked past.

Pausing, I grinned at him. "Looking good, prof." Lachlan's nickname for him was kind of adorable.

"Don't you start," he said with a shake of his head. "Go shower. I want to have breakfast with you before the day begins..."

"Too late," I called as I sailed into my room. "Already did."

His laughter was my only response.

My mood buoyed all the way through my shower. It took me fifteen minutes to shower, wash my hair, put on some light cosmetics and get dressed. I left my hair damp to dry on its own. The color needed pampering and too much blow-drying would fade it out.

I pulled on the polo shirt and plain skirt before I slid my feet into a pair of flats. I skipped hose and thankfully, we didn't need to wear ties unless we were in dress shirts. I could also wear slacks but it was too nice a day out there. The jacket I snagged to carry downstairs. A concession to the tats on my arms, though that wasn't actually against the rules for college classes. Still, I'd take it with me in case the air conditioning was set too low.

Downstairs, Lachlan was in a dress shirt without a tie and Jonas wore a polo like me. Lachlan scowled at both of us and Ramsey snorted.

"I told you to pick up some polos before we came back."

"Bite me," Lachlan retorted as he moved so I could slide into the booth seat. There were breakfast burritos, fruit, and even some danishes. It looked like Jonas picked all my favorites. The coffee Jonas made for me was waiting and I took a happy sip of the caffeine. Eyes closed, I savored the perfect blend of bitter and sweet.

Coffee, it lubricated the world.

"I think I'm jealous of the cup," Lachlan said.

"Yep," Ramsey agreed.

Jonas just snorted. I bumped his shoulder and grinned as I opened my eyes. "Don't hate. Coffee and I have been deeply involved for years. You're just going to have to share me."

"We're all learning about sharing," Ramsey said and the heat in his eyes sent a delightful shiver through me. "I think we'll manage."

"Smooth." Even as Lachlan shook his head, he slid a hand to my thigh. He rested his fingers lightly against my bare skin right at the edge of the skirt's hem, but he didn't push it higher.

It was—nice.

Possessive, but nice.

"First day of classes," Ramsey said. "What's the plan?"

"To make sure Ace has the best fucking day possible," Lachlan answered easily.

A thrill went through me. "We need to swing by for Aubrey on the way to class."

"Already texted her," Jonas volunteered and I swore my

heart did a little fist bump. "Let her know when we'd get there and that you were good."

"Thank you."

He nodded once. "When does Jackie call with today's Pen update?"

Jackie called every day. Jackie or Davina. I flicked a look at the clock. "Right after our first class. I gave her the schedule and the doctors usually do the medical briefing after the first set of rounds."

"Want to send her my number to make sure she can get through?" Jonas offered. "Maybe all of us. Aubrey too. That way, no matter what, you get the updates."

"I can do that." I actually kind of liked that idea. "Thank you."

The silence from the other two became visceral so I glanced at Lachlan and Ramsey to find them both just staring at Jonas.

"You could have offered," Jonas told them before he picked up a breakfast burrito. "Do better."

I had to bite my lip to keep from laughing.

Yeah, today's first day was already getting off on a better foot.

Thirty-Six

JONAS

I checked my watch. It was just after six. By the time we walked to bonfire hill, they would be getting ready to light it.

"You got this?" Ramsey checked with me one more time from where he and Lachlan waited at the door to the cottage.

"We'll be fine," I told him. "You guys need to go, especially if you're taking the asshole with you."

Lachlan made a face. "I'd rather leave him here."

"No," Ramsey said. "We need someone, not us and not her, to run point. He wants to help, he can do it. We'll keep an eye on him."

They weren't going to be doing anything if they didn't leave. Especially because she'd be downstairs any minute. "So go..."

"Nervous about your date?" Lachlan said with a smirk.

I just stared at him. "Jealous it's not you getting the date?"

"Right," Ramsey said, opening the door and hustling

Lachlan out. I probably shouldn't enjoy needling Lachlan so much, but I did.

They couldn't have left soon enough because a minute later, the door to KC's room opened and she emerged. She wore leggings and a loose shirt that left one of her shoulders bare. She'd pulled all her hair up into a ponytail and there was—

"Why do you have glitter on your face?"

Her laughter drifted down the steps with her. "I thought it would be fun for the firelight—and really once you start with glitter, it just gets *everywhere*."

"You look good," I told her. She did. The smiles were coming more easily. There were still times when I caught her staring off, the sadness in her eyes would rake over me. It hurt to see her that sad.

Worse, it hurt to see her hurting.

"Thank you," she said, pausing in front of me. "You look pretty good yourself."

I glanced down at my t-shirt and jeans. Amusement seemed to fill her smile as she put a hand on my chest and then pushed upward. I dipped my head to meet her. These little kisses were becoming more natural. I liked them. We didn't kiss much outside of the house and I was okay with that.

KC was private. She was also too important to me to share these moments with anyone else. I barely liked sharing her with Ramsey and Lachlan, but they were the *only* ones I would.

"What was that for?" I had to ask. Her gloss was sweet, tasted a bit like cherry to me. Maybe.

"Do I need a reason to kiss you?" The dare in her eyes made me grin.

"No," I said slowly. "You may kiss me whenever you want."

"Good answer." Blowing out a breath, she glanced around. "I thought the guys would be back by now..."

I shrugged. "My date with you, they aren't invited." All true.

Her snort made my grin widen. "Fair point. Okay," she said, checking her pockets. "Phone. Panic button. Keys. Anything else I need?"

"Nope." I could wish she didn't *need* the panic button, but I liked that she had it. Not that I intended to let her out of my sight. "I haven't been to one of these in a while."

"The bonfires?"

"Nope."

"You don't want to go?" Curiosity inhabited her expression as I snagged our hoodies from the hook by the door. It was still the tail-end of summer, and while the fire would be warm—it might be chilly by the time we headed back.

"Didn't say that," I told her. "Just—I don't usually enjoy social occasions."

"If you don't want to go..." Worry filled her eyes.

"KC," I said, thrusting her hoodie out to her. "If I didn't want to go, I'd tell you. I'm going because you like them and you want 'normal.' Bonfires are normal. And it's a date. Maybe I'll even like it because I'm there with you."

When she took the jacket, I tugged and it pulled her right to me.

"I want to go with you," I stressed. "We could hang out here and make out, but I don't think that would be half as much fun as the bonfire."

Skeptical didn't begin to cover her expression.

"And my brothers would probably be back early and spoil all my fun." None of these were lies. I wasn't comfortable with lying to her. "The truth is, you don't have a reason to trust us fully yet. I want you to trust me. I need you to trust me again.

I lost that when—or maybe I lost that chance before and I just want another one.”

“I trust you,” she said slowly, not avoiding my gaze. “Maybe not as much as I should, but I *want* to trust you. I miss—us. That means I want you to enjoy what we do too.”

“Well, then let’s find out if I enjoy a bonfire *with* you.” It was as much a dare as it was an invitation. I really did want the time with her. Living together in the cottage was different from when we had the suite. Ramsey and Lachlan were around a lot more. Going to college classes together was also different. We were together, not just attending the same classes.

At the same time, the closeness seemed to have created another distance and I wasn’t sure how to close it. She didn’t sleep enough. She and Aubrey had been working late on their song. I’d also gotten us permission to use one of the practice rooms, so they could get everything locked in to record their tracks. Yvette was doing the same at a studio near her and they were going to mix it all.

Though, Aubrey mentioned Yvette might come down for a long weekend. KC could probably use that.

She tied her hoodie around her waist and I just kept mine over my arm. Hand in hand, we headed out. Dusk was still a bit away, but we had a hike. I liked the idea of getting a long walk together as much as the bonfire.

I liked it even better that Dix was off with Ramsey and Lachlan, which meant we had some privacy. The guy was *always* around now. She absolutely needed security, but that guy took it too far. He hated us. Fine by me. I didn’t like him either. But she didn’t see how jealous he was, and that worried me.

“Did you mean it when you said making out might not be as much fun as the bonfire?” Her quiet question pulled me out of my own thoughts.

"What?"

"You said that we could stay in and make out, but it might not be as fun..."

Rubbing the back of my neck, I grimaced. "I did say that, huh?"

She hummed, canting her head to glance at me. "You don't have to answer, I just—I like making out. I know we really haven't yet. Do you not—"

"No, I do," I rushed in and then winced. We were still on one of the far paths and not in the heart of the campus yet. We had another ten to fifteen minute walk to the bonfire. "I—I've never made out with a girl."

Embarrassment flashed through me. Was I really going to tell her this?

"I'm not Lachlan or Ramsey, I'm not good at this stuff." She tightened her grip on my hand as I faced her. "I haven't really dated. Girls didn't really look at me. It never seemed like a good idea. I don't like it when they get clingy or touchy—"

When she looked at our hands, I summoned a smile.

"You're different." I groaned. "I'm going to fuck this up."

"You're not," she assured me. "To be honest—I haven't really dated either. I mean RJ was kind of my first date."

I scowled and she lifted her shoulders.

"It never really went anywhere."

"Good," I said firmly. "He was a dick."

"I know," she reminded me. "After that—pretty much I have Lachlan's ninja kisses and constant..."

"Stalking?" I supplied and she laughed. The emotion lit her up and she nodded.

"More or less. When he would follow me on runs. Then Ramsey's tutoring sessions. None of that is really dating though..."

"And you didn't date before?"

She shook her head slowly. "Not really. I mean—we're

kind of dating now, with the family dinners and the hanging out...and the sex." The hesitation at the end had me studying her.

"Is the sex okay?" The minute I phrased it that way, I grimaced. "I mean—are you okay with it, not is it okay."

Her lips began to twitch and then we were both laughing.

"Yes," she said around her chuckles. "The sex is okay. We really haven't been having it since we got back on campus. I slept in Ramsey's room a couple of times, but not for sex. More for company and cause...sometimes I have bad dreams."

"You can come sleep with me if you need someone," I offered. "Or I can come in there." We were floundering on this awkward ground. "I know we're not having sex yet and I'm not opposed, but I don't think we're there. Not sure you were with Ramsey and well—Lachlan is Lachlan."

It was her turn to sigh and she did a quick scan of the area before she turned back to me. "I don't know if I was ready, but I also don't hate it."

"Good." If she hated it, we had a bigger problem. "Are you okay with me not..."

"Jonas," KC said, squeezing my hand. "I like *you* just the way you are. I call you Hot Shot cause you have a hot temper—"

"And you're a smartass."

"That too," she agreed with a grin. "But I'm no expert on relationships. We were friends or starting to be friends. We kissed. Then I felt betrayed and you were betrayed and now we're here—because you didn't give up on us."

"You didn't either." I had to point that out. "Maybe we were the ones who chased, but you didn't have to let us back in."

"I don't want to screw this up. Dating one of you seems like a lot and I'm dating all three of you."

"Sort of," I told her and the hint of surprise on her face as her eyes rounded made me grin. "Tonight is a date. We need to see the two of them step up. Make 'em work for it, especially Lachlan. He always gets what he wants...and sometimes I hate him for it."

"But not always?"

"No." Then I sighed, it was time. We hadn't talked about it, but I sure as shit wasn't keeping it a secret. "You know I take meds, right?"

"Yeah, I've seen them."

"But you don't know why?" Maybe Ramsey had told her.

"No, I don't and I'm not prying. That's personal."

"It is and it isn't," I told her and then I tugged her off the path to where one of the benches was under a tree. It wasn't the bonfire, but there was an air of intimacy here. I wanted that privacy. "The thing is...I have a problem with anger management. You might have noticed?"

Yes, I was making it a bit of a joke. Deflecting with self-deprecating humor as my therapist liked to say. The contortions her expression underwent as she fought not to laugh just made her even more adorable.

"It's okay to laugh," I assured her. "I know I have a problem. It's anxiety, or at least that was what I was diagnosed with. Severe anxiety and it manifests as anger. I'm more comfortable with anger than I am with other emotions." I'd never really understood why. "Except where music is concerned, then I'm good with all emotions."

"Okay," she said, twisting to sit sideways to face me. "So you take meds for that?"

"It helps me keep my reactions in check. Sometimes when I snap, I just—flip the fuck out."

"And beat up guys who are trying to hump me in the hall."

That son of a bitch... "Yes, I do. I also punch my brothers —and yes, they definitely deserve it. The point is, most of the time I have it under control. The meds help. The therapy helps. I'm honest with myself and with them. Lachlan—" Fuck me, I was really gonna say this. "Lachlan can be a real dick, but you know that. He can also be the best friend you'd ever want in a crisis. He's waited out my tempers with me, waded into the fights, and he's never walked away, even when I was the asshole."

"That was why Ramsey was so worried about you being around me."

I shrugged. "He worries that I can't temper my reactions. And yes, I know I beat the shit out of that guy. But he deserved it. No one gets to touch you like that without your permission and they were all being such assholes about it."

KC reached up to cup my cheek and I covered her hand with mine. "Thank you."

"For what?"

"For being you, and for telling me. You didn't have to."

"I want to make this work with you, I don't want to fight my brothers to do it. If we can make it work with all of us, fine but—I'm in."

She studied me for a long time. "Then tonight, we go to the bonfire for our first date—well kind of our second really."

I grinned.

"Next date? We make out."

I could support that.

"Think we could make out a little tonight? Or would that be pushing it?"

When she kissed me, I had to resist the urge to fist bump. Fifteen minutes later, we were still kissing and I didn't give a good goddamn about the bonfire except I promised to take her.

Five more minutes.

Then we'd go.

Thirty-Seven

KC

"**W**hat?" Surely I hadn't heard the lawyer correctly. "She wants you to do what?"

"She wants to transfer several assets into the account of..." He read off the name like he had to check it again. It had to be the creepy guy at the Sunshine Retreat. The so-called guru. Her *fiancé*. "A considerable amount, including her titles to her house in Beverly Hills, the penthouse in Manhattan, and the retreat in the Cotswolds."

"She can't—at least not on the property."

"No, it's also in your name," Arthur Hansen said in the most relieved of tones. "We can't draft a wire transfer or a full check without you signing off on it as well...she put your name on all of her accounts about five years ago."

Betty Ford.

That was when she'd put herself through a grueling rehab to reclaim her career. A headache pulsed behind my eyes. "And how much does she want to move?"

"Roughly six point seven million dollars, that's what's

available in liquid assets. If you include real estate and stocks, we're looking at considerably more. I would need more than just your verbal authorization. Her request came via messenger, so I would need you to physically come in to sign off on this."

Yeah. That wasn't happening. "How about we just say no then," I told him. "If you can't move anything without my authorization, then I absolutely do *not* give my authorization. In fact, can we prevent her from moving anything?"

"At the moment, yes. She has you as a second signatory. It was just how the accounts were all drafted. While you were underage, your attorney would act in your stead, but the fact you applied for emancipation and your mother agreed, gave you far more latitude at least where this is concerned."

"But I'm eighteen now." Almost nineteen. That was weird.

Really weird.

"Yes."

"So if I say no, what happens next?"

"We'll draft a response and notify her that the second signatory does not consent to the dissolution of properties. The house and the apartment are also in your name, the Cotswolds is not, but your aunt indicated she was not interested in allowing your mother to sell that one either. They have a different kind of contract, however..."

"Offer Trish whatever it takes to buy out her half," I told him. "She wants money and I'll bet that's why she was calling me. I want to lock up the Cotswolds too. I don't know what the hell Mom is thinking, but let's make sure she has a home to come back to."

"Thank you, Miss Crosse," Hansen said with a deep sigh of relief. "I will get this taken care of today. I will also have your personal business attorney vet the offer and the contract before we send it to you to sign. Do you have an attorney's office there?"

"I can find one," I told him. It was hardly the first time. "I could even go down to Manhattan if I have to. You have offices there and so does my attorney."

"Excellent. I'll be in touch, and Miss Crosse..."

"Yeah," I said with a sigh. "I'll check on Mom, thanks for calling me."

Exhaustion swarmed me and a light knock on the door reminded me I hadn't closed it when I came up here to change. The last thing I'd expected was Hansen to call. Lachlan stood in the doorway. "All good, Ace?"

"No," I said slowly. "Not really. I have a feeling I need to go to New York this weekend. But I don't have time. The concert is coming up."

We still had to finish laying the tracks so everything was ready. The benefit concert was going to be in Los Angeles, we'd need to take a few days off school to do everything, but Ramsey said he'd already put in for leave. Lachlan and Jonas didn't care, they'd just skip classes with me.

Lachlan studied me. "What can I—"

My phone rang again and I glanced at it and then did a double take. Holy shit. I held up a finger as I answered, "Trace?"

"Hey," he said, his voice sounding a little off—a little strained. "Sorry to have fallen off the face of the Earth."

"Are you okay?" I asked, fresh worry colliding with the old. "I want to yell at you for not calling or even texting, but—you're on the phone. Are you alright?"

He sighed. "Sorry, kid, I didn't mean to be an asshole. Just a lot of shit going on and—I'm calling you now. Tell me about Pen."

I closed my eyes as tears burned in them. Trace was the one sibling beyond Bronson that I actually relied on. We weren't as close as Bronson and I were. Half the time I thought Trace only put up with me cause I just wouldn't go away, but the last several months—he'd just been MIA.

The bed dipped and Lachlan covered my hand where it rested on my thigh. I sniffled once, then turned my hand over so I could thread my fingers with his. Then I filled Trace in on everything that had happened with Pen.

"Where the fuck is our sperm donor in all of this?"

"I don't know, we've called. Left messages. Nothing. But we're all getting tested to see if we're a match. She needs a bone marrow transplant. I'd give her every drop of mine—but I won't work. Neither will Bronson. The youngers are getting tested but the surgery is painful and—I just—"

"You need me to get tested," Trace said, blowing out a breath. "I'm heading to New York this weekend. I'm taking the train up. You want to come see me and we'll look into finding somewhere to do the test?"

"Yes," I said without an ounce of hesitation. "Where are you staying in the city?"

When he rattled off the name of the place, I grimaced. "That's all the way out in Washington Heights um..."

"It's fine if you can't."

"I can, I can make it work—"

Lachlan squeezed my hand and I glanced at him. He mouthed "I'll drive."

I stared at him for a long moment. "Are you sure?" I mouthed and he gave me a flat look.

Yeah, he was sure.

"No, we can definitely make it work," I told Trace. "I'm in Connecticut at school...long story. But I can drive down..."

"Wait, when did you learn to drive?" There was just a hint of teasing in his voice and it eased the strain.

"You'll see," I said. "Text me if anything changes? Otherwise, we'll be in the city Friday night."

"See you soon, sis," Trace said and then the call was over. I shuddered. My heart slammed almost too painfully against my ribs as I lowered the phone.

"Friday? Cool. We don't have classes." Lachlan squeezed my hand.

"If I go, I have to tell Dix..." And I was kind of tired of Dix looking so goddamn disapproving of everything. "And I'm going to see my brother, not some stranger..."

"Then we ditch him," Lachlan said. "I'll be with you every step of the way."

"We tell Aubrey, Ramsey, and Jonas. No one else."

"Done," Lachlan said, picking up my hand to kiss it. "We staying in the city?"

"We can. Mom has an apartment there if it runs too late."

Lachlan grinned.

"Don't get any ideas," I countered. "We still need to do our date."

"Too late, all I have about you are ideas, Ace." He winked then cupped my face before he brushed away a tear. He could have given me shit or pressed his luck. All he said though was, "Now, let's go eat..."

Two days later, I was curled up in the back of Lachlan's car under a light blanket. My panic button, that was also a tracker, was with Jonas in case. Ramsey wasn't thrilled with the idea but he also understood why I needed to see my brother. Lachlan swore he'd be with me every step of the way and Aubrey made me promise to call.

We left right after lunch. I'd taken the morning to talk to Dix and let him know Aubrey and I planned to hole up and work on music. Probably wouldn't even leave the house. He wasn't thrilled, but he bought it and then Lachlan and I were out of there.

He pulled over before the interstate so I could climb into the front. The drive down took way less time than I expected, then again, Lachlan drove like a maniac. It was kind of fun. The farther we got from the school, the more I could breathe.

"How you doing, Ace?" We were in crosstown traffic. I'd debated parking his car and just using the subway but he wasn't a fan of leaving the car anywhere.

"I don't know, nervous, relieved, worried, and hopeful?" I frowned. "I sound insane."

"The best people are," he said. "We'll be there in fifteen minutes and you can talk to your brother. Find out what's going on and maybe—"

"I know, he might be a match. None of the rest of us are. We can't test the littles because they're too young. That was why they didn't want to test me to begin with when it started but I'm eighteen..."

He put his hand on my thigh again and there was nothing overtly sexual about it. The comfort was enormous. My heart was racing. With everything that had happened, I didn't want to think what it might mean for Pen if he *wasn't* a match.

We were finally there and Lachlan pulled into a locked parking garage. I got my credit card out first and his glare didn't deter me.

"You're doing me the favor, let me cover this," I told him and he scowled. When he didn't back down, I sighed. "Lachlan.."

"Ace—you want to pay me back or something, then move up my date with you. But you don't need to pay for this or pay me back, I'm where I want to be."

"Okay, you lovebirds are cute, but you're holding up my line, so one of you pay or get this car out of here."

Lachlan handed him a credit card and I put mine away. Ten minutes later, we were heading to an apartment building not far from Colombia Medical Center. When we rang the bell, Trace answered on the intercom.

"You're early," he said and the strain was back in his voice.

That just amped up the worry. "Come on up." A buzzer sounded and then we were heading inside and up the stairs. Lachlan stuck with me. I'd worn a baseball cap to hide the hair and I kept it on all the way to the door.

It opened before I got there and Trace—Trace stared out at me and then past me to Lachlan before glancing at me again. At five-ten, he was taller than me but—

"Hey, little sis and stranger." The guarded tone was a warning.

"This is Lachlan," I introduced him and Lachlan stuck out his hand.

"Boyfriend." Lachlan shook his hand. "You're the brother."

Something was off, from Trace's uneasy posture to—had he lost weight? He just seemed different.

Trace shook his hand and then backed up a few steps to let us in. And then I got my first good look at him.

His dark hair was longer, but pulled back into a ponytail. Cosmetics decorated his face and softened his cheekbones. He wore a flowy kind of tunic top and leggings.

"Technically," Trace said as I stood there trying to process how different he looked. It had been almost three years since we were in the same place, but it wasn't until he folded his arms that the breasts registered. "I'd prefer to be referred to as your sister, and I'm going by Tracy now."

That—took a moment.

Sister.

Suddenly all the differences just clicked and I blinked.

"Cool," Lachlan said while I was still looking for words. "You mind if I get her a drink, Ace's had a really long week."

"No problem, I just checked in here this morning and got some things from the market delivered. There're water bottles in the fridge." Then Trace—wait, Tracy looked back at me.

"She and her then?" Oh, there was my voice. Tracy was

hardly the first transgender person I'd met, but maybe the first one to be so close to me.

"If you wouldn't mind," he—nope—she said. "I know there was probably a better way to spring this on you than inviting you up to be ambushed, Kaity."

The only other person who called me Kaity was Dad. "Not sure how you deliver this news."

"You okay?" The concern on her face couldn't quite disguise the worry, and my heart twisted. Of course she was scared.

"I think I should be asking you that—and you know, I don't have to be the big sister anymore. That's kind of cool."

A sudden smile softened her whole face and when she opened her arms, I flew at her and hugged her. "I'm sorry, Kaity," she whispered. "This has been a long time coming and when I started transitioning, I told myself I should tell you. But you were touring and then you wanted to go to school... and I'm a coward, cause I didn't want any of the attention on you to redirect to me."

All those damn stories. I blinked hard, then pulled back. "I get it. I wish I could escape the press too."

"I bet—course that blue hair is hard to hide."

I sniffled as I tugged the baseball cap off and ran a hand through it. "I'm rather fond of it. Otherwise, I look like Mom."

"Yeah, and I don't look like Dad so much now, you know."

The blue eyes gazing back at me were mirrors of my own. Mirrors of Pen's. "I get it. I wish—I wish I could have been there for you, you've had surgeries?"

"A few and I can fill you in, but I went ahead and had blood work done before I left to come up here. My surgeon is gonna look at it and then reach out to Pen's doctors—if I have to put off the female harmonization surgery, I will..."

Lachlan returned with three water bottles. "You want me to leave the two of you to talk?"

"I—I don't mind if you're here as long as Tracy is all right with it." Would getting used to saying Tracy take a minute? Maybe. But family was family.

She smiled at me and the tears in her eyes squeezed at my heart. "I don't mind, as long as you understand—Lachlan was it? I love my kid sister here and I will still kick your ass if you hurt her."

"Fair enough," Lachlan said, then Tracy led us over to the sofas and the chairs. All the distance suddenly made sense.

Sometimes, the truth could ruin a perception of that truth, but sometimes, we needed it to be disrupted so we could open up new doors. Tracy needed me to hear her and I needed to listen.

Whether she was a match for Pen or not, she was my sister too.

Thirty-Eight

LACHLAN

We ended up staying in New York until Sunday. Not that I got to enjoy the time "alone" with Ace. She was too focused on her sister—both of them really. I was—okay with that. Instead of going back to her mom's place in Manhattan, we just stayed in Washington Heights. Ace wanted to learn about the surgery Tracy was here for and they were still waiting on the type matching. Tracy and Pen were the same blood type.

That was a good first step.

So I crashed on the sofa while Ace took the second bedroom and I stayed close all weekend. So far, Dix hadn't picked up on our subterfuge. Jonas was taking particular glee in barring him from "bugging" Ace. On Sunday, though, we had to head back to campus. Her words, not mine. Frankly, I didn't give a damn. If she wanted to stay in Manhattan perma-nently, we'd figure it out.

"Good to meet you," Tracy told me before we left. "Look after her, okay?"

"Doing my best," I told her. "Look after you and don't be a stranger."

Ace poked me, but one good warning deserved another. Tracy hadn't seen the profound relief in Ace when she called or heard the layers of worry in her voice discussing her sibling who just fell out of touch. As irritating as Ramsey and Jonas were, I would kick their asses if they fucking disappeared on me.

"Soon as I hear anything," Tracy promised, "I'll call and my surgeons are waiting to finalize the surgical date. If I'm a match, I'll put this surgery off and do it later."

"Tell me when and where. I'll be there," Ace promised. "I'll keep it low-profile so no one bothers you. But—I want to be there for you if I can."

When we were finally back in the car, Ace was a million miles away. She'd messaged Ramsey and Jonas to let them know we were on the way back. Hard to miss the message where Ramsey invited her to bunk with him for the night. As unreasonable as it was, it pissed me off. I was trying to do this right, but I wasn't making any ground and Ramsey just slid right in there.

I fumed about it all the way up the interstate. If I complained, I sounded like a petulant child. If I didn't do anything at all, then I was just a bitch. The whole damn thing pissed me off.

"You okay?" Ace asked after we'd been on the road for a little over an hour and I glanced over to find her watching me intently. For the first time since we left her sister, she didn't feel a million miles away.

Comfort her? Or tell her the truth?

"Frustrated," I admitted, chewing the word over. "Frustrated, and I don't like that I'm frustrated."

"Okay," she said slowly. "Frustrated with me?"

"Yes." A little too on the nose? Maybe. "But also frustrated with me. With—I'm trying to do the right things here, Ace."

"And you want a cookie?"

I didn't slam my foot on the brakes, but I did clock the next rest area. Ten miles. Accelerating, I fisted my irritation. "No, I want to know that it's working. Ramsey seems to have already earned your forgiveness and a regular spot in your bed —or maybe you in his." Fuck that came out bitter. "Jonas seems to be doing just fine. The only one you're keeping at arm's length is me."

"Are you really gauging where we're at by whether we're having sex?" It wasn't quite outrage in her voice, but she wasn't happy with me.

"No, I'm gauging whether you even want to *be* in this relationship," I snapped back. "You've got one foot firmly pointed out the door. Ramsey is easier to take than me, he doesn't demand as much. Jonas—Jonas doesn't know what he wants. But he can take the friend-zone."

"But you can't," she challenged. I could have answered, but I waited until after I got to the exit. And after we got off the road. I scanned the area as I swung around the building. Security cameras were easier to avoid parking near and I followed the picnic area signs and pulled into the far side beyond some trees.

They offered us some semblance of privacy. Putting the car in park, I twisted in the seat to face her. "You don't trust us— actually, you know what. I'm going to let Jonas and Ramsey sort their own shit out. You don't trust *me.*"

"If I didn't trust you, I wouldn't have let you go with me to see Tracy."

"Let me?" I raised my brows. "You're the walking wounded right now, Ace. I fucking hate that you are. I hate it even more that I had anything to do with it. I hate even more that you're not letting me have a real chance. Maybe I don't deserve it. Fine, then fucking tell me that. Don't tell me you're willing and then keep yourself with one foot firmly out like you don't think any of this is going to work."

Anger flashed in her eyes. Real heat and for the first time in weeks, Ace was glaring back at me. My ace. "Who do you think you are?" She jerked her baseball cap off and let the spill of blue hair free. Fuck if that wasn't how I preferred her. I wanted *her*, not the face she put on for the rest of the world. The hair she hid because people might recognize her, but hair she clearly needed cause of her resemblance to her mother.

Yes, I listened.

"I think I'm the guy who has seen you from the beginning. I saw the wild child in there that desperately wants to come out to play, but is terrified of being judged for it." If anything, my words just pissed her off more. "You want 'normal,' you crave 'normal,' but that's not who you are, Ace. You are anything but...you're exceptional and you deserve exceptional things, and fuck knows you need to be pushed."

"Why are you being an asshole?"

"Cause you need an asshole." The minute I spat those words out, I realized how true it was. Wrapping my hand around her nape, I dragged her forward until my nose brushed hers. "This right here is what you need. You need someone who is going to fight with you and fight for you. You fight for everyone else, Ace...but I need you to fight for you too. I need you in this fight with me."

"I'm trying," she protested and I shook my head.

"No, you're not." When she would have argued, I kissed her, hard and swift. Fusing our lips together, all I tasted was her anger. She bit my lower lip and then her fingers were digging into my arms. She wasn't pulling away or shoving me back. She was fighting with me. That—fuck I craved that. "You're not trying," I told her on a hiss. "You're so ready for us to let you down and hurt you. Abandonment issues? Check.

Daddy issues? Holy shit, check. Lack of faith in yourself? Beyond all the checks."

"You don't get to judge me," she snarled back as she jerked her head away but I didn't let her go far.

"I don't have to fucking judge you," I snapped at her. "You do it already. You want your guitar back so just pay the money, why fight for it? Someone kidnaps you? You just want it to go away. You fuck my brother? You run. You fuck me—"

"I didn't just fuck you." Her nails were threatening to dig gouges into my arms and I wanted that pain. "As I recall, you were the one doing all the fucking—chasing me into the club, ripping off my wig and then just fucking me right against the bar."

Heat flushed her cheeks and her eyes sparkled.

"You wanted it," I reminded her. "You wanted me—and that scares the shit out of you. Then you ran," I gritted out the last two words. "You took off with that fucker Dix, and didn't even look back. You had my cum still dripping out of you and you just *left*."

"I hate you sometimes," she whispered and it was the sheen of tears that just added to the fire burning in her eyes. It sliced at me and then the distance between us just collapsed like the gravity on a dying star, imploding until her mouth opened to mine.

Chasing her tongue with mine, I poured every ounce of my frustration and need into that kiss. I wanted this to fucking work between us but we didn't have a chance in hell if she was always going to be ready to bolt.

I don't know who reached for whose clothes first, but her shorts were gone and I shoved the seat all the way back. When I lifted her over onto my lap, she wrapped her hand around my dick and I jerked her panties to the side.

"Hate me," I told her as she stared down at me. Her grip

on my cock was fucking everything right now. "Use me. Hate me. Fuck me, Ace. I'm right here…"

For a split second after she lined me up and all I could feel was the soaking wetness of her cunt teasing my cock, she froze up. "Right here?" The question was a gasp, anger and disbelief vied with the passion burning below her words.

Fixing my hands on her hips, I yanked her downward as I thrust up and then I was filling the hot glove of her cunt. Fuck that felt amazing. "Right here," I taunted her. "Fuck me, Ace. Fuck me right now."

Teeth gritted, she glared at me but she put her hands on my shoulders and then she rolled her hips. Yes, thank fuck. Right there. I helped her. My knuckles hit the fucking steering wheel each time I lifted and thrust her down against me. I wanted to be deeper.

"I want you naked," I informed her. "Do you know how often I've imagined fucking you on the running trail? The dance floor? The car? Bending you over in the goddamn living room or over the kitchen table—I want you wet and dripping my cum and I want you to feel me," I punctuated those last two words as I ground her down on my lap, "even when we're done."

She was soaking my pants and I didn't give a damn. We had on too many clothes. Her panties were tearing and I fought with the seam to tear out the bottom just so I could get my thumb on her clit.

Her mouth opened in a soundless cry.

"Yeah, that's what you want too—you want someone to fuck you who knows what they're doing and wants you to feel them. You want me—don't you, Ace?"

"I hate you," she whispered but she fisted my hair and then devoured my mouth as we kept slamming together. It was a fight to stay inside of her and keep teasing her as she waged war with my tongue. Desire and hunger twined as I feasted on her. My balls were so tight, I thought they would explode.

Her first.

Kissing a path from her mouth to her ear, I savored the scrape of her teeth against my skin. "I don't care," I whispered before I traced the shell of cartilage there then sucked against her lobe. "Hate me all you want, Ace. You're going to scream for me, cause this is what you want. You need me to fight for and with you. You got it...game on, cause this is a battle I have every intention of winning."

She arched her head back and her ass hit the horn. The blast of it didn't slow either of us down and then she was letting out a low, intense scream as she clamped down on me. There she was, the shattered expression as she let go was everything I wanted and I kept my eyes open to drink in the sight of her as my climax ripped through me.

I came in spurts, grounding her pelvis down as I filled her. The sound of our panting filled the humid air inside the car. The scent of sex wreathed all around us and she shuddered as she buried her face against my throat. Raising a hand, I ignored the faint tremble as I stroked her hair.

Barely aware of the world beyond the car, I spared it a look. We were still alone, still in the rest area, and she was still clinging to me. My softening cock was still safe inside of her even if the drip of my cum added to the rapidly spreading wet spot on my lap. I wouldn't trade it for anything.

"Lachlan," she said, her voice rough and ragged.

"I'm here," I promised her. Didn't matter how often I had to repeat it.

"Do you want me for real? Or just to possess me?" The question lacked some of the harsher elements of her earlier anger.

"Having you and keeping you are both on my agenda," I told her. "You've been mine since you came to the school—"

She lifted her head to stare at me. Lips kiss swollen and her cheeks red from my stubble was a really good fucking look on her. "You hated me..."

"I never hated you," I told her. "I was angry with you. I believed some lies about you. I was pretty fucking stupid, but I wanted you from day one and that want has only grown more intense. I do *not* want to share you with my brothers."

Shock rippled across her face.

"But I will—because you seem to need them too. Fine. Whatever. But you and me? We're endgame, Ace. I will fight you every step of the way to stay in this game. To stay in you..."

She licked her lips and I tracked the motion of her tongue, aching for me.

"Then—we do the date I want to do."

"Name the time and the place," I told her. "I'm in, and then you and me? We're taking a whole weekend, alone, no more obstacles, and you can set whatever rules you want or need—but understand, it's going to be *us*."

She rested her forehead on mine and I slid my fingers up to her hair.

"Okay," she whispered and I fisted the strands of blue, then dragged her closer for another kiss. My cock was already starting to get hard. "Lachlan," she exhaled against my mouth.

"Oh yeah," I whispered. "Keep groaning my name, Ace. That's just getting me harder faster...and we're staying here until we're both satisfied."

Maybe longer.

The fact she flexed around me and she began to rock her hips was all the answer I needed...

We'd get back to campus eventually.

Thirty-Nine

KC

Halloween was right around the corner. The concert was rapidly approaching too. Not only would we be performing live at the Hollywood Bowl, we were going to be airing it worldwide on Pay-Per-View and via special one time only theater events. Teddy had worked overtime to put on the concert of the century. The fundraising aspect of it all was a huge thing and it would mean a lot of press. Worth it though, for Pen.

A knock on my door had me groaning and I lifted my head, "Come in," I said, pushing up on my elbows. We'd been up until nearly two, but we'd laid down the final tracks and so had Yvette. We'd been working together over video call and now everything was with the engineers.

Ramsey stood in the open door, dressed in sweatpants and shirtless, he looked like he belonged in the bed with me and not out in the hall. "Don't look at me like that, Siren." Yeah, that order really didn't ratchet down the interest his arrival sparked.

"Why not?" I pushed up more to sit. The tank top was practically see-through but I didn't really have anything to hide. My hair though, that probably was a wreck.

The corner of his mouth kicked up. "Because I don't think Jonas and Lachlan would be thrilled with me locking us in here for the rest of the day."

"Nope," Lachlan called from downstairs. "Not to mention, equal time would be demanded."

I snorted and Ramsey just shook his head. "I know it's later than you normally go, but I was going to go for a run. Wanted to see if you wanted to go with."

"Did it snow?" Cause apparently, we were getting it early this year.

"A little, not enough to mean you can't use the trails." But Ramsey didn't usually use the running trail. He preferred the gym.

With a grunt, I shoved the covers off. It was definitely cooler than I liked it and my nipples beaded up hard. "Jonas and Lachlan coming with?" We hadn't really had much time just the four of us, school, recordings, and concert planning took a lot. So did trying to get my guitar back. They'd apparently made an offer, only the seller took everything down again.

Yeah, better not to focus on that.

"I want to," Jonas said, leaning in the door and the heat of his gaze and Ramsey's followed me as I stood there in just the tank top and panties. I really didn't mind their looking at all. Except, the level of interest it stirred had nothing to do with getting dressed to run.

"Cool," I said then yawned. "Let me—"

My phone vibrated and I snatched it off the nightstand.

"Sometimes," Ramsey muttered. "I hate that thing."

"Me too," Jonas agreed.

The words registered but I couldn't focus on them, not

when the message on the screen seemed to leap out at me. I read it four times just trying to make sure I was reading it correctly.

TRACY

I'm a match. Doctors are all conferring. But I'm going to have to go to California for the collection surgery. Just have to get Pen strong enough for it.

I'm a match.

A match.

She was a match. The words wavered as I kept re-reading it. Then everything seemed to tremble.

"Hey," Jonas said even as Ramsey threaded his arms around me. Then Jonas was there against my back.

"What's wrong?" Lachlan demanded from the doorway. I couldn't get the shaking to stop and I couldn't focus on him.

"We're right here, Siren," Ramsey said in a hushed voice.

"Tell me who we're killing," Lachlan demanded.

"Relax," Jonas ordered as he rubbed my back and then Lachlan was gripping my hand and I was surrounded by all three of them. The steady thump of Ramsey's heart seemed to dramatize just how harsh my breathing was and how much I was shaking. I flexed my hand on Lachlan's and then a laugh punched its way out of me on a sob.

"Shh," Ramsey murmured. "C'mon, Siren, talk to us..."

I would if I could find my voice but the sobs were shattering everything. After all this time...

Lachlan peeled my phone out of my other hand and then let out a sigh, "You just got this, Ace? Tracy's a match for Pen?" It was like he needed to confirm and even as he did I started to shake harder.

"She's a match."

Pen had a match.

One of us could help her.

Everything blurred as the tears poured out of me. Ramsey's arms tightened around me. Jonas pressed his forehead to the back of my head. Lachlan held on to my hands, but they were all there and none of them left while I cried. I hated the tears ripping out of me, but at the same time...

Pen had a match.

An hour later, I sat on the sofa downstairs with a cold cloth over my eyes. Jonas sat right next to me. We'd already juggled a half-dozen calls. Currently, Tracy was on the phone and the guys had it on speaker, but anytime I went to remove the cold cloth—I got scolded.

That was fine. My eyes hurt. My nose was stuffy. I probably looked like a blotchy, wretched mess. I didn't care. Pen had a match.

"You sure you're alright?" Tracy repeated. "You sound like you're getting sick."

"I was crying," I muttered. "Don't be a bitch."

Her laugh was everything and it pulled a grin from me. "Well, no more tears. As I recall it, you were never an artistic crier."

I flipped the phone off and somewhere in the kitchen, Ramsey gave a huff of laughter. I sniffled as gentle fingers brushed my face and then Jonas eased the cloth off as Lachlan pressed a cup of coffee into my hands. My whole face hurt. Ramsey's shirt still had a damp stain from where he'd used it to wipe at my face.

"When will they know if she's strong enough, did they tell you? I need to call Jackie and Bronson."

"Already did it, called them after your boyfriend messaged me that you needed a minute."

I glanced at Lachlan and he gave a little shrug. "You needed a minute." Any other time, I might be annoyed by the high-handed take, but fuck it. I really had needed a minute.

"Yeah," I admitted and Jonas shifted so I could lean against him and sip my coffee. "Anyway, what did they say?"

"Well, she's got a little way to go. But now that they know I can be a donor, they're gonna get her as strong as they can before they eradicate her bone marrow so we can give her mine."

That sounded so horrible. "They have to make her sicker." My stomach bottomed out.

"They do," Tracy said, she sounded so damn soothing. "They know what they're doing and word has it that you've hired the very best experts."

"What's the point of money if I can't use it to help? I'm pretty fucking useless to her otherwise." It came out way more belligerent than I intended.

"Hey," Ramsey scolded. "You are not useless."

"And no one is faulting you for hiring the best," Lachlan tacked on.

"You never gave up on me," Tracy joined in. "If I hadn't been freaking out about how you might react, I'd have called you all back sooner. So, you are not *remotely* useless."

"Sorry," I muttered.

"Don't have to be sorry," Jonas said, rubbing a slow pattern against my shoulder as I took a sip of the coffee. "You're upset. You're allowed. This is good news."

"I just—"

"It's a step," Tracy corrected. "I know you want instant answers and you've had to be patient for so long. You've stuck with her this long, let me do the heavy lifting now. You're a damn good sister. Now it's my turn."

I summoned a watery smile as I glanced at my audience. Ramsey had returned to the living room and now sat on the coffee table, facing me. They were all right there, I was in no danger of slipping or falling.

"Concert is coming up too," I said, swallowing around the hard lump. "You're coming?"

"I can watch, probably not a good idea for big crowds. Even my doctors here want me to focus on staying as healthy as possible."

"Right, colds and stuff."

"Exactly. I want to go to the hospital to see Pen, though. They're going to give us all notice because she's going to have to stay in the PICU while we get her through this."

"Okay." I took another breath. "Tracy, whatever you need before, during, after—I have it covered"

"I don't want your money, kid," she said, her tone gentling further. "But you need to do something, so I'll stay where you want me to stay, okay?"

Sniffling once, I nodded. "Thank you. This goes for when you have your surgery too—no more doing it on your own."

"God," she said with almost an element of a groan. "You're gonna be a real pain in the ass aren't you?"

"Yep," I said cheerfully. "I've been taking lessons." My gaze collided with Lachlan's and he smirked.

"Hmm...also, we're going to talk about multiple boyfriends at some point, but since I assume they can all hear me, understand the castration threat stands for all of you."

"Good to know," Jonas said. "KC has a good support group, so you guys could probably start with Lachlan. He likes to be the biggest dick."

There was just a momentary downbeat and laughter bubbled out of me. Ramsey dropped his chin and shook his head. Lachlan's smirk didn't fade and Tracy chuckled.

"I like that one," she said. "Jonas, right?"

"Yes, ma'am."

"Good to know. Look after my sister, and Kaity, don't make yourself sick. We got this."

All too soon, it was time to say goodbye and I leaned my

head back against Jonas' shoulder while I cradled my coffee. "If they clear them before the concert, I want to go out early."

"I'll put in for the emergency medical leave as soon as we know," Ramsey said. "Already talked to the dean about needing the time to help."

I blinked at him. "Can you take the time?"

"Doesn't matter. Pen's family. She's your family."

"And you're ours," Lachlan stressed. "We'll all go. Besides, I get to be backstage at your first on stage performance in years, not missing that for anything."

I grinned. "We're not having sex on the stage."

Ramsey groaned.

"On stage?" Lachlan said with a slow grin. "Nah, I was thinking backstage—or maybe up where they put all the lights —feel the music as we fuck."

"Really?" Ramsey said, giving Lachlan stinkeye.

"You could have offered," Lachlan countered, even as Jonas began to laugh. "You won't, but you could have. Besides, Ace is a bit of an exhibitionist, and I like to keep her very satisfied."

That just sent liquid heat spiraling through me.

"Are you?" Jonas asked, curiosity filled his voice and I tilted my head back to look up at him, then over at Ramsey.

"Maybe," I said. "I like privacy too."

"Good to know," Ramsey said slowly. "Maybe we need to have more talks about what you like..."

"I think I'm still figuring that part out." I snuck a glance at Lachlan and he chuckled.

"I'm all yours Ace, we can figure out whatever you want to know..."

Shivering, I bit my lower lip to try and contain the slightly hysterical laugh that wanted to escape. Before I could respond though, my phone buzzed and Jonas groaned.

Yvette's name was on the screen.

"Sorry guys," I murmured as I lifted the phone.

"This is your life," Jonas reminded me. "We'll get used to it."

I wasn't sure I wanted them to get used to it. At least not all the interruptions. At the same time, I was feeling particularly greedy because I wanted to get used to them.

"Thank you," I whispered, then brushed a kiss to his jaw before I answered. "Hey, bitch, guess what..."

Forty

KC

The next week flew by, concert prep was going almost twenty-four seven. Teddy had a dozen new ideas daily and kept blowing up our phones. It had been waking me up so much that Lachlan actually turned my phone off *after* he promised that Jonas messaged Tracy, Jackie, and Bronson to let them know to text the guys. I ended up sleeping right between Lachlan and Jonas when they piled into my room.

As weird as it was—I'd really only slept with Ramsey before then, but after that night, one of them crashed in my room, or I went to theirs, and my phone got shut off. Aubrey teased me about it but to be honest, I really liked it. The best sleep I'd had in weeks.

With the concert just four days away and the tracks ready to drop online, it was time to head west. Yvette would meet us at LaGuardia. Dix got a larger car so we could load all five of us in it. He was not a fan of the guys traveling with me. I offered to hire a different car and that got me a stony look and a slammed door as he left the cottage.

"Pissed him off, Ace," Lachlan commented. His dry tone didn't suggest he cared much. I felt bad, because Dix was practically family, but his mood had been growing steadily worse since we'd come back to school, and I actively spent more time avoiding him than anything else.

It might be time to invite him to go home to California and get someone different for security. Maybe after the concert I could talk to him. I packed a suitcase, keeping it light because we weren't staying long. Though if Pen was up for the surgery, I might extend a few days. Ramsey was limited to the days he'd taken off.

Lachlan, Jonas, me, and Aubrey let our instructors know we were taking a brief break and why. I'd also picked up home-work assignments. We could do them on the plane. Teddy made all the travel arrangements based on the list of names I gave him, so it didn't surprise me to find we were booked into first class with all the amenities—even Dix.

I was next to Jonas, with Ramsey and Lachlan in front of us, Aubrey and Yvette behind us, and Dix behind them. We could have slept, but I was practically vibrating. I should have gone for a run before we had to leave for the airport. As it was, Jonas had worked on some music and he slid the sheets over to me when we were about halfway there.

It helped.

Arriving at the airport and being greeted by the cars picking us up to head back to the house helped.

Getting home to find Davina waiting with a full meal and the house opened up helped.

Yvette and Aubrey had their own suites in my wing, but Davina opened up the guest suite right next to my room so the guys could use it. There were two bedrooms in my suite and two in that one. We just left the doors open in between.

Thirty minutes after we got to the house, I was in the gym and on the treadmill with Lachlan on the one next to me. Rehearsals were scheduled for the day after next. That meant I had time to go see Pen.

Ramsey went with me, and I got a different driver along with one of our security people. Introducing Ramsey to Pen was kind of surreal. Jackie and Bronson were waiting for us and Tracy was also there. The family reunion buoyed me.

"Two weeks," the doctor said. "We're happy with where her weight is, we want her to gain a little more then we'll begin the eradication procedures."

"That makes it Thanksgiving," I said slowly.

"That's the plan. We will have a full team. We've discussed it, we're doing labs and we'll keep monitoring. But we should have a firm date in a few days. Once we've booked it..." He continued on at length, walking us through the whole procedure.

Even knowing it was coming, I couldn't shake the agitation. I wanted to know what could go wrong. Tracy was staying in town for the duration. Jackie had all but packed her out of her hotel and over to her house until it was time for her to be admitted. After, I spent an hour with Pen. I had to be fully-gowned. Absolutely nothing could be exposed to her. We had to keep her as healthy as possible because we were about to nuke her immune system.

"Hey," Bronson said as he walked Ramsey and I out. My security guy kept a discreet distance and he didn't brood or glare. It was definitely an improvement. I needed to remember what his name was though.

"What's up?"

"Mom and I aren't coming to the concert," he said without preamble. "Too many people. Especially while Tracy is with us, no one wants to risk a cold. I will be watching it though, we'll play it for Pen too."

I grinned. "You hate how loud concerts are."

"I do," he admitted. "But I like supporting my kid sister." Bronson winked. Then we were near the car. "You mind getting in while I have a word with this boyfriend?"

I paused. "Excuse me?"

"Go be a good sister and get in the car so I can threaten him like all good brothers should. Besides, it's nothing he hasn't heard. Tracy already told me about the castration plan."

I snorted, but glanced at Ramsey. "Go on," he said, pressing a kiss to my forehead. "I can handle this threat. Better me than Lachlan."

Oh wasn't that the truth.

"Be nice," I said and Bronson smirked.

"Not gonna happen, but you go ahead and tell yourself that."

Fifteen minutes. It took Bronson fifteen minutes to give him hell. What was weird was watching them be really intense without a lot of gesticulating or angry expressions. Maybe that was what made it scarier. Bronson didn't yell.

He got even.

"I like him," Ramsey promised when he slid into the car next to me. Security had waited for him to get into the car before he slid in next to the driver. The privacy block was closed and I leaned my head on Ramsey's shoulder. "He's a good brother."

"He's the best." I grinned. When Ramsey clasped my hand, I rubbed my cheek to his shoulder.

"Talk to me, Siren," Ramsey said softly. "You doing okay?"

"No," I said with a slow shake of my head. "I'm a wreck. I can't be one right now though, I have to perform in two days and outside of some fun with Frankie and Ian, we haven't been on a full blown stage in almost three years."

"You ladies are going to be incredible." He seemed so utterly serious.

"You know...I never asked you about that concert shirt." The one I'd stolen from his room. I still had it. I hadn't told him that part either. It was tucked into a drawer at the cottage

"You want me to tell you about it?" The ease in the offer steadied more of my nerves.

Tilting my head back, I said, "Maybe after the concert? I want to know when I met you for the first time."

"You think we met then?" It was light, a tease, but the kiss he delivered at the end utterly gentled it.

"Yes, because that shirt has a partial of my signature on it."

He grinned. "After the concert then...maybe you can sign a new shirt for me."

Tucking my head back against his shoulder, I smiled. "I can do that."

The next thirty-six hours blew past us like we were sitting still. We had sound checks, meetings, and a quickie rehearsal. I'd gone for three different runs, and I was ready to vibrate my way to the stage. Aubrey and Yvette weren't much better.

Teddy had lined up more than three dozen acts, from soloists to bands to a *conductor* to join us. We would be doing original songs and covers. We'd also be mixing it up. The guys and Dix were with us as we headed to the Hollywood Bowl. It had sold out early, but they'd added some venues nearby with huge screens and sold tickets to those.

Theaters around the country, and in some other parts of the world, would be hosting it and so would a pay-per-view. Right now, after fees, Teddy crowed, we'd easily raised over fifteen million.

The album hadn't dropped yet.

Once we got to our dressing room, we had a roadie who would be handling our backstage notifications. "Just easier for you ladies to wait for us to get you, then we'll escort you right to where you'll head out on stage as the other act heads off the other side. We have your schedule here…" She passed it out and then left us to get ready.

"Hey, who told Teddy to break us up?" I asked as I checked it. I had a spotlight earlier than the one we would all be going out.

"Probably for the fundraising portion," Aubrey reminded me. "He mentioned something about doing a call to action as part of the opening acts. Then we'll do a series of performances, cycling through, then another one. Keep people opening their wallets…"

I didn't like it exactly but it made a certain amount of sense. When Dix showed up at the door, Lachlan leaned on it and didn't let him in. "What's up? The girls are getting changed."

"Let KC know that her mother is here…"

I snapped my head up. "What?"

"And her fiancé."

Kill me.

Yvette grimaced. "Dix, can you keep them away from the backstage area? They shouldn't have passes right?"

"Right," Aubrey said, but she already had her phone in hand. "Making sure Teddy doesn't give her any either."

My head hurt and my stomach cramped. Jonas held out a glass of water to me. I was mostly ready. We were performing in skin tight silver pants with shiny blue tops. I'd debated heels, but I was suddenly glad for boots.

"It's going to be okay," he said and I met his gaze in the mirror. "You're going to rock and I get to watch."

I wanted to lick my lips but the cosmetics didn't lend themselves to that. "You'll be just off stage, right?"

"We will," Lachlan promised. He'd closed the door and leaned against it. Maybe my nerves were communicating themselves but they were all looking fiercer and fiercer. "If you need us, we'll walk right out on that stage."

A laugh escaped me as I took the water from Jonas. "I haven't had a stage freakout in years."

"Avert," Yvette said, then pinched me. "You know better than to challenge karma."

I made a face, but got up and did a counter clockwise circle around the chair then grinned at her. "Good point."

"Better," Aubrey said as she double-checked her hair in the mirror. "Now... while the three of us look fucking fantastic. We need pictures."

I downed some water as the guys all whipped out their phones. The next twenty minutes devolved into laughter as Yvette, Aubrey, and I posed for a series of ridiculous pictures. Then I got pictures with the guys—including one where Lachlan dipped me in a kiss that left me breathless.

"Great," Yvette said in a dry tone. "Now she has to fix her lipstick."

At the comment, Jonas passed her his camera and then he gave me a very enthusiastic kiss that only amped up the temperature. Ramsey waited his turn and I was the one reaching for him.

"Worth it," I murmured as I passed them tissues to clean off the lipstick and then reapplied my own.

A knock came at the door and when it opened the dull roar of the crowd drifted in.

"Kaitlin Crosse, you're up. We had a slight change, your girls are coming on right after you, but you're up first."

I clenched my hands and took a deeper breath. Somewhere between this door and the stage lights, the nerves would fade away and the music would rise—and I'd find the magic space that I lived in during a performance.

Tonight was about Pen. About kids with cancer. About finding hope for them and their families.

About finding hope for us.

We set out as a group and while I'd begun holding hands

with Lachlan, I pulled away. They couldn't go out there with me. The strains of metal guitar, deeper base, and what had to be a baby grand piano trickled through the rising crescendo of applause from the crowd. I had no idea who was even on before us.

"We're running behind," our guide hurried us and I picked up the pace. She was handing me a microphone even as we hit the backstage area. "Go straight out—" Then she turned away. "Kaitlin Crosse on stage in five, four, three..."

I didn't slow down, the nerves began to fall away as every step brought me closer to the stage. I was as at home out there as I'd been anywhere.

The roar hit me like a tidal wave as the spotlights picked up my arrival and I focused to the side of the lights, smile firmly in place as I waved and the applause grew even more thunderous.

Movement had me turning to the man waiting out there in his own spotlight.

Gibson Crosse.

Dad.

"For the first time ever," a voice boomed over the loudspeaker. It vibrated through me as the speakers strained to deliver it to the crowd and they lost their goddamn minds. "Gibson Crosse and his daughter Kaitlin, from Torched, will be performing together right here for you tonight..."

I was going to throw up.

* * *

KC and the guys will return in Money Shot, the epic conclusion to Blue Ivy Prep.

Money Shot

Kaitlin Crosse wields an extraordinary power over me. She pushes, dares, and drives me to the brink of madness. Ever since our paths intertwined, my obsession with her has been absolute and unyielding.

Every aspect of her calls out to me, yet the very thing I yearn for the most might be forever beyond my grasp. She resists my attempts to possess and protect her. She refuses my claims, asserting her fiercely independent nature.

That same, unwavering self-reliance only intensifies my attraction to her, and ignites a fierce desire to eradicate the pain in her eyes. Pain we inflicted upon her. Pain her father has inflicted. Pain that the world relentlessly imposes upon her.

I don't want to share her with anyone. Not my brothers. Not her friends. Not the world.

But that's not what Ace needs...

And I need her.

So I have to become what she needs, and that means working with my brothers, her closest friends, and her family. It means fighting to keep her safe when the whole world seems to want to tear her apart.

I won't let that happen.
We won't.
Kaitlin Crosse, my ace, my fixation, and my future.

Afterword

You know, every book I write is a different experience. I often tell people that if it goes on the paper the way it happens in my head, it's going to be so cool.

Do you have any idea how often it doesn't go on paper the way it did in my head?

Le sigh.

Yes, I know, back to my corner!

See you soon!
xoxo
Heather

Reader group: facebook.com/groups/heatherspack
Spoiler group: facebook.com/groups/teammadatheather

About Heather Long

I *love* books. Not just a little bit, but a lot. Books were my best friends when I was growing up. Books didn't care if I was new to a town or to a class. They were always there, my trustiest of companions. Until they turned on me and said I had to write them.

I can tell you that my own personal happily ever after included writing books. I've always said that an HEA is a work in progress. It's true in my marriage, my friendships, and in my career. I am constantly nurturing my muse as we dive into new tales, new tropes, new characters and more.

After seventeen years in Texas, we relocated to the Pacific Northwest in search of seasons, new experiences, and new geography. I can't wait to discover what life (and my muse) have in store for me.

Maybe writing was always my destiny and romance my fate. After all, my grandmother wasn't a fan of picture books and used to read me her Harlequin Romance novels.

Friends to lovers, enemies to lovers, friends to enemies to lovers, you name it, I love them and love to write them. I started with Earth Witches Aren't Easy, the first in the Chance Monroe trilogy, but my characters and I have traveled a long way since I created that urban fantasy world.

One of the series I hear my readers recommend the most is the Untouchable series followed in quick succession by the Vandals, and that just delights me. No lie, whenever one of my readers brings up my wolves, I do a little a fist pump.

I'm active on social media, and I love hearing from readers.

Feel free to tag me with a question about any of my books, or just say hi!

Also by Heather Long

82nd Street Vandals

Savage Vandal

Vicious Rebel

Ruthless Traitor

Dirty Devil

Brutal Fighter

Dangerous Renegade

Merciless Spy

Reckless Thief

Fierce Dancer

Always a Marine Series

Once Her Man, Always Her Man

Retreat Hell! She Just Got Here

Tell It to the Marine

Proud to Serve Her

Her Marine

No Regrets, No Surrender

The Marine Cowboy

The Two and the Proud

A Marine and a Gentleman

Combat Barbie

Whiskey Tango Foxtrot

What Part of Marine Don't You Understand?

A Marine Affair

Marine Ever After

Marine in the Wind

Marine with Benefits

A Marine of Plenty

A Candle for a Marine

Marine under the Mistletoe

Have Yourself a Marine Christmas

Lest Old Marines Be Forgot

Her Marine Bodyguard

Smoke & Marines

Bravo Team Wolf

When Danger Bites

Bitten Under Fire

Cardinal Sins

Kill Song

First Chorus

High Note

Last Word

Chance Monroe

Earth Witches Aren't Easy

Plan Witch from Out of Town

Bad Witch Rising

Her Elite Assets

Featuring:
Pure Copper
Target: Tungsten
Asset: Arsenic

Fevered Hearts

Marshal of Hel Dorado
Brave are the Lonely
Micah & Mrs. Miller
A Fistful of Dreams
Raising Kane
Wanted: Fevered or Alive
Wild and Fevered
The Quick & The Fevered
A Man Called Wyatt

Going Royal

Some Like It Royal
Some Like It Scandalous
Some Like It Deadly
Some Like it Secret
Some Like it Easy
Her Marine Prince
Blocked

Heart of the Nebula

Queenmaker

Deal Breaker

Throne Taker

Lone Star Leathernecks

Semper Fi Cowboy

As You Were, Cowboy

Magic & Mayhem

The Witch Singer

Bridget's Witch's Diary

The Witched Away Bride

Mongrels

Mongrels, Mischief & Mayhem

Shackled Souls

Succubus Chained

Succubus Unchained

Succubus Blessed

Shackled Souls (Omnibus)

Space Cowboy

Space Cowboy Survival Guide

Untouchable

Rules and Roses

Changes and Chocolates

Keys and Kisses

Whispers and Wishes

Hangovers and Holidays

Brazen and Breathless

Trials and Tiaras

Graduation and Gifts

Defiance and Dedication

Songs and Sweethearts

Legacy and Lovers

Farewells and Forever

Wolves of Willow Bend

Wolf at Law

Wolf Bite

Caged Wolf

Wolf Claim

Wolf Next Door

Rogue Wolf

Bayou Wolf

Untamed Wolf

Wolf with Benefits

River Wolf

Single Wicked Wolf

Desert Wolf

Snow Wolf

Wolf on Board

Holly Jolly Wolf

Shadow Wolf

His Moonstruck Wolf

Thunder Wolf

Ghost Wolf

Outlaw Wolves

Wolf Unleashed